Aquamarine

Mel Keegan is an Australian whose previous books include *Ice, Wind and Fire* ("Rip-roaring" *Time Out*), *Equinox, Fortunes of War, Death's Head* ("Unputdownable" *Him*) and *Storm Tide* ("Gripping" *Scotsgay*).

AQUAMARINE
Mel Keegan

Aquamarine Mel Keegan

First published 2000 by Millivres Ltd, part of the
Millivres Prowler Group, Gay Men's Press, PO Box 3220,
Brighton BN2 5AU, East Sussex, England

World Copyright © 2000 Mel Keegan

Mel Keegan has asserted his right to be identified
as the author of this work in accordance with the
Copyright, Designs and Patents Act 1988

A CIP catalogue record for this book is available
from the British Library

ISBN 1 902852 14 1

Distributed in Europe by Central Books, 99 Wallis Rd,
London E9 5M telephone: 020 8986 4854 fax: 020 8533 5821

Distributed in North America by Consortium Book Sales and
Distribution, Inc. 145 West Gate Drive, Saint Paul, MN
55114-1065, USA   telephone: 651 221 9035 / 800 283 3572

Distributed in Australia by Bulldog Books,
PO Box 300, Beaconsfield, NSW 2014

Printed and bound in the EU by WS Bookwell, Juva, Finland

Chapter One

The heat of the midday sun was like a hand pressing heavily on Russell Grant's back, and sweat tickled his ribs. He lay on his belly on a rug, on the expanse of white sand above the tidal zone, listening to the hoarse cries of the gulls and the restless voice of the sea. A gaudy sunshade fluttered over his head, but at this hour the sun glared so ferociously off the sea that the shade afforded little protection. A coat of sunblock was still slick on his fair skin, and his eyes, shielded by polarized glass, scanned the endless columns of data that filed obediently through the screen of his laptop.

Hydrography was a consuming subject, though it was not Russell's own field. This project was Bill Murchison's, but as usual Bill had found a reason to be over on *Pacifica* when there was work to be done, data to be gathered and processed. He was, Russell decided, a pain in the butt. The next time Bill made application for a continuation of his funding, he would very likely find himself kicked out on a tender portion of his anatomy. Gerald Duquesne did not take kindly to passengers and parasites, and Murchison knew that too, but he seemed to attach little importance to the looming spectre of unemployment.

As he idled through the data collection and ran the preliminary analysis, Russell wondered if Bill were telling the truth, and that he *had* been offered a job elsewhere ... if the position could be dignified by calling it a job. Working as a hustler in a beachside crotch-shop would be just about Murchison's speed. And that particular sex shop, The Beach Bum, would suit him right down to the ground. He probably wouldn't get a pair of pants on for weeks on end. Just Bill Murchison's style.

Meanwhile, his project was going to wrack and ruin, and when several days' worth of data had mysteriously failed to appear in the main computers over at the master lab, memos began to arrive on the terminal Murchison shared with Russell. Russell could scarcely turn on the machine without seeing a message, flagged for his attention, asking what had become of either Bill or the data, or both. The back room boys were starting to get as restless as Murchison was bored

In the interests of peace and mental health, Russell let Bill go his own way. He loaded his laptop aboard the *Tiger Shark*, packed a lunch hamper, rubbed his arms and legs with enough sunblock to shut out the killer ultraviolet, and determinedly, repeatedly, paged his partner.

He was almost ready to shove off when Eric Devlin answered. He was calling from the reception desk of the Acropora Hotel, and he sounded more than a little annoyed. Perhaps his morning had been as big a bitch as Russell's.

"Yeah, Rusty, what is it?" he said quietly into the phone, as if he were also in the midst of unwelcome company, and overheard.

"Lunch," Russell suggested. "You hungry?"

"It's only ten," Eric said reasonably.

"And in two hours it'll be noon," Russell added. "I've packed the frij. I have to cruise over to Headland and Breakwater. I just thought you might like to get away from it all, come with me, if you've got the chance."

A pause, and then Eric's voice asked shrewdly, "Which means Bill Murchison's done another vanishing act, and Gerry Duquesne is bellowing for his data?"

"Something like that. You interested? Lobster, prawns, crab and shrimps, a little green salad, and I think I can manage a bottle of something white and dry." He paused. "If you can get away."

"Of course I can get away!" Eric chuckled. "This is the quiet time of the year, quiet time of the week. I'll be over in fifteen minutes, Russell. Don't you dare shove off without me!"

Not that Russell would have dreamed of leaving without him, and

Eric was perfectly well aware of that. Russell would have waited half an hour for him, if need be. Or an hour. So Duquesne would get his data an hour late, what difference did it make? None, to the Boss. But to Russell, the opportunity of a whole afternoon in Eric's company was too precious to be missed. They did not see enough of each other in these last few years, since their work had taken them in different directions.

The *Tiger Shark* was tied up at the lab's own private boatramp, between the fish farm on one side and the water purification system on the other. Atop the concrete boatramp, the lab sprawled along the artificial waterfront, looking into the southwest, where the Pacific Ocean was an almost unbroken frontier as far as Antarctica.

Few land masses remained above water in this part of the sea now, and even those were slowly being submerged. Duquesne was impatient for every morsel of data pertaining to the *rate* of the water's rise: was it still as rapid as it had been a century ago, when the continents were inundated and the whole face of the earth changed forever?

To a man of Duquesne's generation the picture was so much more clear than it would ever be to Russell, much less to Devlin. Gerald Duquesne was one hundred and two years old. His memory stretched back to a time when cities such as London and Paris and Los Angeles were still thriving megalopolises, and when humans went about their business, contentedly blind to the repeated warnings about simple, routine global warming, much less the risk of a cometary impact. People a century ago scarcely gave a thought to the planet's delicate climatic mechanisms. Only a handful of scientists and environmentalists were aware, or cared, that the machinery of the world's atmosphere was already in the process of breakdown even before the Event, the arrival of the comet called Chen-Goldstein 4.

At first it was slow. Russell had studied the data in his third grade school rooms, as did every child, and it was easy to see how people had overlooked the truth. But it was nonetheless accurate that massive typhoons often announced themselves with a single, stinging drop of rain.

First came the storms. Each winter brought worse storms than the one before, and locals and yokels were constantly reporting that the flooding was the worst they had ever seen in their long lives. Salt water was recorded fifteen kilometres further inland than ever before ... a bridge that had never been known to flood went under ... a ULCC oil tanker was overturned and broken it half by thirty-metre waves. Every year brought its one hundred year storm. And then came Chen-Goldstein 4, and her tidal wave changed the face of the globe. December 22 2049, she plunged in like a lightning bolt from Zeus - an early Christmas gift, and satellites photographed her awesome beauty as she crashed into Antarctica, just inland of the Ross Ice Shelf.

The tidal waves of massive typhoons were nothing new or surprising. In the early 1990s, after one specific event, such monsters were given a name. The Bangladesh Effect was a researcher's dream come true.

Scientists were morbid creatures, Russell had always thought. They were never happier than when they discovered some new fatal illness, some new plague, a comet about to impact like a battering ram with the earth, or a quirk in the planetary weather mechanism that spelled disaster. Grants galore would be allocated for the study of these catastrophes. Wives could be supported, kids educated, mortgages paid off, on the proceeds of study into the current media buzz.

This time, however, those scientists who were intent on settling their mortgages by studying the Bangladesh Effect found themselves victims of it. After the storms came endless floods, over every part of the world. Religious groups huddled together in a show of moral solidarity, likened the situation to the Deluge and blamed the state of affairs on Immorality. Several hundred individual Arks were actually built during the two decades, 2030 to 2050, but only one of them was effective.

The *Requiem Mundi* was launched in Kure, Japan, where she had been built by the same company that constructed such supertankers as the *Tokyo Maru*. She was built by a consortium of self-styled, not-soeccentric millionaires from Europe and the States, and with an extraordinary fanfare she launched in 2052, when the sea broke over the rooftops of the houses of the labourers who had finished her.

Chen-Golstein-4 was blamed for the catastrophe, but in fact she just put the finishing touches to a long, slow decline that had been in progress for a century. Global warming was a term Russell had always admitted he found difficult to grasp. He was born in 2074, and to him the world had never been any other than it was right now. Warm, balmy, serene, more or less peaceful ... more or less wet. To him, the world map was a thing not of wonder but of tedium. An unbroken sheet of blue punctuated here and there by a few co-ordinates which pointed out an island chain or a small nation.

The greatest surviving nations were Himalaya, Alpina and Andea, but in childhood he had learned - to his astonishment - that these rich, coveted lands had once been in the heart of impoverished nations. Not long before, they had been no more than spires of rock thrusting so far above sea level that their crowns were capped with ice.

The only major land masses in Russell's world were those which had been the mountainous regions of the old earth; the rest had gone the way of a place called Atlantis.

Gerald Duquesne was more or less sure that the water had stopped rising, but he wanted to be certain to the tenth decimal place before he closed the hydrographical surveys once and for all. Each year over a minimum of a decade, laborious, painstaking readings would be taken, collated, analysed. It was by no means a full time job, yet it paid reasonably well and it was a prestige position.

Damn it, Russell thought as he watched the data file through the screen in orderly ranks, Bill Murchison should be damned glad to have this work, not looking for a job, moonlighting at The Beach Bum! But Murchison had always been a waste of time. Back in college, where was he? A safe bet ... propping up the bar, screwing half the swimming team or dead asleep and probably stoned, in the back seat of his father's jetskiff.

Why Russell should be surprised when Murchison abandoned his work and found any, every, excuse to be far away from the lab, he did not know. He sighed, and his fingers tapped keys as he cycled through a set series of analyses. Once he got involved with the work it was interesting enough, but that was hardly the point. Russell had plenty of his own work to do, without pulling double duty.

Not, he admitted moments later, that the occupation was totally without its perks. Breakwater was a kay, a sand island deliberately created by the dumping of an enormous cargo of rocks, gravel and sand, and then the systematic, deliberate introduction of vegetation which would help to stabilise the tiny land mass. It was only a science platform, and Duquesne had funded the construction of Breakwater only because it was far cheaper to build an island than to leave a hydrographic research ship here, station-keeping, for a decade.

The sand was eye-blisteringly white. The coconut palms were five years old and well grown; the ferns and fronds, secondary growth, were well established. Even when Duquesne was satisfied and closed the project, Breakwater would remain on the map until another freak storm broke it up and swept it away, just as so many of the inhabited islands of the Pacific had been scattered on the four tides.

The satellite imaging report for the day's weather, sent down from the *Atlantis* at five that morning, promised light winds and a small chop, intermittent cloud, before heavy weather came in, in the mid-afternoon. Right now it was just before noon. Russell was hungry, hot, drowsy, exasperated by Bill Murchison ... and just beginning to wonder where Eric could have got to. Breakwater was exactly two hundred metres long by sixty metres wide, and the highest point on the sand-island was twelve metres above the tidal zone. How in the world could you get lost?

Not, he admitted, that the dimensions of the island would in any way limit Eric. In fact, Aquarians tended to look upon the dry land as the impediment. Often as not, it just got in their way. Russell lifted his head and looked up and down the beach, but of his partner there was no sign. The *Tiger Shark* was bobbing at her mooring line, twenty metres offshore. The blue and white hull was so highly polished and reflected the sea so perfectly that she almost seemed camouflaged. Russell feasted his eyes on her for some time. She was his. Lock, stock and barrel - whatever the old saying meant. Every nut and bolt of her, from the sharp-nosed prow to the transom, from the keel, with its fish-finder sonar to the single mast and its thorny crown of microwave communications antennae, belonged to him.

Yet the pride of ownership was not without a thrill of pain. Becoming the owner of an item through inheritance was a double-edged sword, and Russell had said a hundred times, he would rather have had his father back, alive and well, rather have been Junior Russell, as Duquesne called him, and still muddling along in the lab for his own amusement, than be *Doctor* Russell in his own right, lord of the lab, master of the *Tiger Shark*, coordinator of Project Aquarian.

A cloud passed over the sun but he did not notice. His mood darkened to match, and for a time he did not even see the data displayed within the confines of the screen. There were times when responsibility weighed so heavily on Russell's young shoulders that it threatened to overcome him.

And then, times, also, when youth and vitality were his best allies, and when he chose to forego his father's science in favour of what his mother had called "blood sense." Instinct. The sixth sense with which the healthy young animal knows what it needs. Russell's memories of his mother were few and faint, but that much of her wisdom, he never forgot.

The first he knew of Eric's presence was the soft rasp of a footfall in sand behind him, a shadow cast across his bare back and the drip of water, shockingly cold on his sun-hot skin. He yelped, rolled over and shielded his eyes against the glare of the sky. Above him, Eric was bronze, bare and ... Eric. Aquarians were mostly the same. They were proud of themselves, with good reason, and as the old aphorism went, "if you got it, flaunt it."

"I brought you something," Eric teased, and before Russell could move he dropped a very large, very live crab onto Russell's middle. With a yelp, Russell squirmed away and knocked the creature onto the sand. Eric snickered and picked it up by one claw. "Do you want it for lunch?"

"I packed the frij for lunch!" Russell protested. "Lobster, prawns, greed salad and white wine."

"I know." Eric looked into the crab's face. "I guess you get a reprieve, kid," he told it, before he looked down at Russell, eyes dancing. "I'll put him back. And I'll fetch the frij."

"Do that," Russell groaned as he sat up, propped his elbows on his knees and brushed damp sand from his torso.

Eric's eyes were very light in his deep, bronze face. His hair was a shaggy, uncut mane of rich brown which could be soft, silky, but was at this moment slick and shining with water, glued to his skull. The rest of him was almost hairless, as was so typical of the Aquarian sub-species. His legs, his chest, even his underarms and groin wore only the slightest suggestion of body hair. Apparently, it was the trade-off for the specialised nature of his skin.

As Russell watched, Eric strode into the surf and without even pausing to take a breath, dived under. But unlike Russell, or any normal human being, Eric did not resurface. If Russell was any judge, he would be down there, looking for exactly the right burrow for the crab, a nook in the rocks where he could place the creature and safely leave it. He could be down for ten or fifteen minutes. To Eric it was all the same. As soon as he went under, the rest was automatic. He did not even have to think about what he was doing.

The third eyelid, that nictitating membrane, would close over his eyes to protect them from the water. The muscles of his chest, so much stronger than Russell's, would begin to work, forcing the water into his lungs at ten regular breaths per minute ... and in those lungs, the magic itself took place.

Somewhere inside Eric Devlin, and inside the other fifty Aquarians who lived and worked in and around *Pacifica*, was something very like the eric pattern of a salamander. Something that modified the tissue of their lungs, made it so receptive to oxygen that even when that oxygen was suspended in water, it was possible for them to breathe it.

In air, Eric breathed only three or four times per minute. He could derive all the oxygen he needed to walk and work, run and make love, without breathing much at all. Only in water did he breathe as often as Russell breathed. Only in water did the profound differences between his physiognomy and Russell's become really apparent.

Sometimes the differences fascinated Russell; sometimes he hardly noticed them. Today, he could not have cared less how Eric had been bred, who his parents were, who had carried and birthed him. The sight of Eric's smooth, bronze skin, his wide back and the perfect globes of his bare buttocks as he walked into the surf to put back the crab - all this conspired to banish work from Russell's mind.

He waited, unconsciously marking time, until Eric surfaced. He had been down twelve minutes when his head appeared, far from shore, beyond the boat. He skulled lazily toward the *Tiger Shark* and hoisted himself over the transom, seemingly without effort. Aquarians were like that. They were born in the water, they took their first breath underwater, learned to swim long before they could walk. Even their thought processes were different.

They thought not in two dimensions, but in three ... they approached problems of logic from angles which a normal human would never have anticipated ... they were so strong, pound for pound of body weight, that they were disconcerting. They could run so fast, so hard, and for so long, not even an Olympic athlete of previous decades could keep up. It was all about oxygen-transfer, Russell knew, and yet none of the science made any difference when his glands began to play their own games.

He was two years younger than Eric, and he had no memory of a world without Eric in it. Once, he had stretched his memory back to its furthest reaches, trying to pinpoint his earliest recollection. He thought he glimpsed the sunlight dancing on the surface of the water, thought he felt the warm caress of the afternoon heat on his skin as he lay on his back and kicked. Someone picked him up, turned him over and held him, buoyant, in the water, until he learned to float and keep his nose up out of the liquid, and dog paddle in the pool. A shape was moving beneath him, fluid and supple, and quick as an otter. It surfaced then, and childish laugher gurgled into Russell's face for a moment before the older boy was gone again, down into the depths of the pool, where the lobsters and crabs nested. Russell tried desperately to follow his new friend, and was snatched back just as his lungs began to burn and his mind began to reel ... it was the first time he realised, he must never, *never* take a breath beneath the surface. He was not like Eric. He would never be like Eric. The knowledge infuriated him.

Twenty-seven years later, what had changed? Russell brushed the drying sand from his limbs and shaded his eyes as he looked out toward his boat. The *Tiger* bobbed, moving under Eric's weight as he found the refrigerated hamper and checked it. The engines started with a growl and he nudged the boat back inshore, into the shallows just off the white sand, where she had begun. In another hour the tide would carry her off again, but her mooring line would hold her steady. The current would not make off with her completely.

As her bow touched the beach Eric shut down the motors, and Russell watched him hop over the side. His skin was gleaming, the colour of burnished copper after a lifetime's exposure to the sun and elements. But that skin did not age the way normal human skin must. It would be plump, smooth and supple until Eric was in advanced old age.

The magic was just beneath the surface: fat. A layer of special fatty tissue, oddly similar to that worn by dolphins and orcas. To the touch, Russell was never aware of it, but it insulated Eric from the cold of the surface layers of the sea, and much more importantly, it prevented his skin from taking up very much water. If Russell remained in the sea for longer than an hour he would look down to find his fingers, toes (and various other extremities) reduced to prune-like wrinkles. Eric never pruned. His skin was smooth, plump as a child's, brown as a ripe hazelnut, hairless and perfect. Aquarian.

All this, Russell knew on an academic level. He could quote the eric syntheses that had been used to build his partner; he could quote the poly-chromosomic structure of the language of his biochemistry. Countless times, he had seen a videotape of the actual moment of Eric's conception, when John Grant's hands took the genetic material from a donor egg and implanted the vastly modified DNA of Eric's father. Russell had pored over the screen a hundred times, watching his own father's hands, the instruments, a glass dish and a wisp of living tissue that was invisible without a powerful microscope.

In that instant, under those lights and lenses, Eric Devlin *began*. Was Man playing God? And if he were, should he not? Where lay the future? Gerald Duquesne believed he knew.

The thoughts were inspiring, and disturbing. Russell thrust away the haunting images as he watched Eric hop back over the side of the boat and splash ashore through water no more than knee-deep, with the lunch hamper tucked under his arm. He was everything John Grant and Gerald Duquesne had hoped for. He was the first of the Aquarians, the great experiment, and for three decades they had called him "Russell's project."

Technically, if he was anyone's project, he was John Grant's. But since John's death old Duquesne had tacitly agreed to let Eric almost escape. Almost. The more rope he gave the young man, at this crucial age and time, the better the grip on Eric he would maintain. And Eric still had to fulfil one very specific duty before his involvement in the project could ever be properly concluded.

He must breed, and breed *true*. And that, Russell knew, was what worried Eric more than anything. He closed down the screen on the computer and shuffled sideways to make space on the rug as Eric fetched the hamper. It was past time that Eric tried to make a baby. He was thirty years old, and he could have been called upon to further the experiment as long as ten years ago, if Duquesne had chosen to insist.

If he had, Russell guessed, Eric would have quit *Pacifica.* Russell sprawled out on the rug and looked up at his companion against the sky. The nictitating membrane had closed over his eyes, protecting them from the brilliance of the sun, so he was not squinting. His hair was beginning to dry, falling in glistening ringlets about his neck and shoulders. His chest rarely ever moved when he was in the air, and his skin was so smooth, Russell felt his fingers seduced once more.

He ran them up Eric's smooth thigh, cupped his buttock, and when Eric turned toward him, Russell held the bony pelvis between his hands. Eric looked amusedly at him, and Russell deliberately kissed his belly, between his navel and the root of his cock. Eric gave a throaty, husky chuckle, and his own hands cradled Russell's head.

"I thought you said you were hungry," he protested.

"A man does not live by food alone," Russell remonstrated.

Eric fell to his knees, and his hands clasped at Russell's nape. His eyes were as blue-green as the sea, very light against his tan. "Something's bothering you, Rusty. It's been bothering you for days. When are you going to tell me about it?"

"Aquarians are not natural telepaths," Russell said drily, though he shivered. Sometimes it did seem that Eric could read his mind.

"You and I have been together our whole lives," Eric scoffed, "I don't need to be a mind reader to know when something's got you twitchy."

"The only thing that's twitching," Russell said gruffly, "is my cock, and that's because you're here, and close, and gorgeous, and I want ..."

"To be fucked?" Eric leaned closer and kissed him.

His mouth tasted of the sea, which was only fitting. When Eric came, the seed of his loins tasted of the sea too, and his musk smelt like the tide at slack water. Russell loved it, every scent and taste of him. He could not remember a day when he had not been in love with Eric, though he conceded that there must have been a few years in child-hood, before he had any knowledge of sex and physical love, when his feelings must have been better tagged as friendship.

The friendship was still there, as strong as ever. That would never change, but since Russell had been twelve years old and Eric had been fourteen, they had been much closer than friends and brothers. Russell celebrated the anniversary of the day when they become lovers more fervently than birthdays or holidays or graduation from school.

"So, what's wrong?" Eric asked as his tongue traced Russell's lips, outlined them and delved within. "Is Murchison bothering you? Why don't you kick him out of the lab? He's screwing up his project in any case. Two words to Duquesne, and he'd cancel the lunatic's grant right here and now."

"And what about his measurements, the survey?" Russell made a vague gesture at the sea.

"You can finish out the project." Eric threw open the hamper. "Lord knows, you're doing most of it now. If it comes down to the wire, Russell, I can take it over. When it comes to water, I'm qualified." His eyes sparkled.

"*Over*-qualified," Russell said ruefully.

"Have a prawn." Devlin waved one under his nose. "Is it Bill Murchison?"

"No." Russell sprawled on the rug in the shade and watched as Eric twisted in a corkscrew and then tugged the cork out of a bottle of *Pacifica* Moselle.

He sniffed at the neck of the bottle and made a face. "Phew. They're not improving the wine, are they? Still smells like it's been brewed from seaweed and old socks." Eric set it aside to breathe in the hopes it would improve, and returned to the hamper for the lobster. "So if it's not Murchison that's worrying you ..."

"It's you," Russell said quietly.

Eric hesitated, looking down at him with arched brows. "What have I done?"

"Nothing," Russell said drily. "Yet." He waited, watching as Devlin's forehead creased a little more, and nodded. "Yeah. That. The *big* that."

"You've had a memo," Eric guessed.

"On the system this morning," Russell affirmed. "From Duquesne. He's getting impatient."

The lobster went back into the hamper and Eric parked his buttocks on the rug. He cupped his chin in his hands and glared at the sea. "I don't have to take part in this."

"But you should." Russell rubbed his back soothingly. How soft and gorgeous was an Aquarian's skin. The little layer of fat that insulated him against the cold and the water gave him an almost childlike feel, and yet underneath this were the steel-hard muscles of a man. The combination made Russell shiver again, as it had made him quiver almost every day for twenty years. "Eric, will you just give it a try? It's only to please the old man."

"I know." Eric turned toward him, kissed his neck, tongued deliberately inside his ear, which he knew drove Russell wild. "Let's not talk about it now."

Russell sighed, even then surrendering. He let Eric move him down on the rug, flat on his back. Argument and logic fled from his mind and he grasped after the last tendrils of rational thought. "Got to talk about it some time," he warned as Eric straddled him, knelt astride his thighs and lifted him out of the scrap of white lycra he wore.

"Some time," Eric said huskily. "But not now. I'm hungry, I'm thirsty, I'm drowsy. I want my lunch, I want to fuck you and I want to take a nap before I have to go back to work."

"That's my boy," Russell said fondly as he stroked Eric's chest. "Never backwards about coming forwards."

"Why, should I be?" Eric kissed him soundly, while his hand did wondrous things between Russell's legs, fetched him up as hard as a harpoon. Eric's tongue traced down and down across his chest, circled his navel and explored territory that was long, long familiar.

The first time they had done this, they had been in Eric's jetskiff, four or five kilometres to windward of the *Atlantis*. The two young boys had gone out to collect fish samples, which meant that Russell could handle the holding nets, the Polaroid, the rule and scales, and Eric would dive down and fetch both the best and worst looking specimens. After an hour of this they were bored. Eric climbed back onto the skiff and stretched out to warm up, and Russell noticed that he had cut himself on the lines or nets. A little wound was bleeding sluggishly on his shoulder. Before he realised what he was doing, he was sucking it clean; and Eric was holding him; they were kissing and rubbing. Becoming lovers was so natural, they hardly noticed they had done it at first, but Russell's heart was suddenly so large it seemed to fill his whole chest, and even as a young boy he knew what love ought to feel like.

Today, the sky was fleecy blue, but the satellite pictures promised heavy weather. Flat on his back with Murchison's work and the cold lunch basket completely forgotten, Russell smiled and squirmed and sighed as Eric worked a lot of lotion into him and lifted up his legs. He wriggled his shoulders on the rug and cautioned, "Careful of that sand."

"You mean, careful I don't get any of it up you?" Eric leaned down and kissed the corner of his mouth. "Now, would I be so careless? What's this feel like?" Very slowly, he slipped his fingers around Russell's soft, well-accustomed anus. "That ought to feel like silk and velvet!

"Silk and velvet," Russell admitted. "I won't say another word."

"Yes, you will!" Eric was suddenly between his legs, taking them up over his shoulders.

"Will I?" Russell's voice was a little breathy, since his knees were pressed into his chest and his balls were churning with glorious excitement, like an exquisite fire. "What will I say?"

"You'll tell me how much you love me," Eric challenged. He laid the snub, hot tip of his cock against Russell's anus, stroked it there but did not even begin to enter. "Tell me before I do one more thing!"

"Or ...?" Russell would have chuckled if he'd had enough breath. "That sounds like it ought to be delivered complete with an ultimatum."

"Tell me, or ... I'll change my mind and have lunch instead," Eric said teasingly.

Mel Keegan

Not for an instant did Russell believe that, but he knew how much Eric loved to hear those words. In the dark at night, cocooned in their bed above the lab, it was Eric's pleasure to speak of love, and it was a language he spoke so fluently, Russell wondered if it was yet another characteristic of Aquarians. He caught Eric's forearms in a firm grip and held him tightly as he said,

"I love you. I *adore* you. I don't know what I'd do without you. Succinct enough?" His tone was light, bantering, teasing, but the words were absolutely honest, and their truth was not lost on Eric, though he appreciated the banter.

"Mmm," he rumbled, as if pretending to consider. "I think so." And, as if to prove it he thrust swiftly through the clench of Russell's sphincter and was suddenly inside him.

Thought fled from Russell's mind like clouds before a gale, and what became of the next half hour, he would never know.

Chapter Two

The clouds massed up while Russell was dozing, and when he stirred awake it was to find the whole sky grey, the sea some colour between gunmetal and green, and the wind uneasy. Out toward the horizon he saw whitecaps, and the *Tiger Shark* was shifting restlessly.

He looked around for Eric and saw him at once, perched on a boulder, a little way down the beach. The laptop was on his knees and if Russell was any judge, he was finishing Murchison's work. He seemed to relish it. Perhaps he did. Little academic was asked of Eric, and yet he had a fine mind. No one was more aware of that than Russell. As boys they had taken their schooling together, first in *Pacifica* and later on the *Atlantis* under Duquesne's eagle eye. Eric had never been behind Russell in the work, yet when they were eighteen it seemed natural for their academic ways to divide.

Russell went on, working alongside his father and slowly, deliberately building his degree. Eric was often called into the lab, but always "on the far side of the microscope," as he put it. The Aquarian wasn't *on* the project. He *was* the project. Eric bore it all with a resigned sigh and a smile. When he was not in the lab, enduring tests and scans, exams and exercises, he was in his natural environment. The sea.

He earned his living as a shallow-water diver, and around *Pacifica* he was never going to be short of work, though not all of it was well paid. Still, he earned better wages than Russell, who was muddling along on the last of his father's research grant while he waited for the approval of his own. This week Eric would be tagging fish or counting lobsters, examining shark nets and checking tidal charts; next week he would be conducting guided tours of the underwater wonderland beneath *Pacifica*, though that was the work he liked least.

Tourists from Himalaya and Alpina arrived in *Pacifica* by the plane load, almost every day. The big wing-in-ground-effect jets roared in from the north, docked on the North Quay and disgorged their enormous human cargoes. In an hour, after Customs were done scanning for illegal substances, the vacationers were installed in their closet-sized rooms at hotels like the Acropora, and began to look for amusement. The whole reason they came to *Pacifica* was to get into the warm, blue-green water and see the marvels of Gerald Duquesne's industry.

Their guide ensured that they put their breathing gear on the right way and did not actually drown one another, and Eric Devlin was very good in the part of chaperone. On the West Quay, his party would get into the dive skins, put on the rebreathers, and just before they hit the water Eric told them the truth. He was a living example of the very marvel they had come here to see.

Then, they gawped at him. They stared as he went under and began to breathe, they wanted to touch him to see if he was warm, as if they believed he was half fish, cold and scaly. Before they were told that he was an Aquarian, they treated him as they would treat any other human being, but as soon as they learned that he was different, Eric swore that he was treated like a freak. Not that it as anything he was unaccustomed to. Fifty more like himself lived and worked in *Pacifica*, and all of them, though they were unofficially called Duquesne's Children, suffered the same unthinking discrimination. It was never easy to be the outsider, the one who was ostracised for his differences.

In other centuries, Russell had read, men were given similar treatment because their skins were dark, their eyes were slanted, they called God or gods by a different name or names; or because they were sexually attracted to their own gender. None of this made any sense to Russell. Sometimes he wondered if he would have survived at all in the world of the past ... or if he would have wanted to. To a man of his age, it seemed so cruel.

He stretched, reached for his shorts and wriggled into them. He had been asleep for an hour after thorough sex and a large lunch, and every cell in his body felt renewed. When Eric fucked him, for hours afterwards he was aware of a delicious shivering inside himself. There was no other feeling like it, and he almost preferred it to the heart-racing excitement of being the aggressor in their lovemaking. Almost. Then again, there was no other feeling like being inside Eric.

The Aquarian was engrossed in the work and did not notice as Russell stood. Perched on his boulder, he was bronze-skinned and still bare. He had tied on a sweat band to keep his hair out of his eyes as the wind rose and he began to concentrate on the screen, but otherwise he was gloriously naked. The juxtaposition of the animal and the academic - the computer and the long, glistening bare limbs - never failed to woo and excite Russell, but for the moment he was sated. He only feasted his eyes for several minutes before he began to repack the frij and drop the sunshade.

"Are you anywhere near finished, Eric?" he called up the beach. "Going to have to leave soon ... see the sky!"

"I've been watching that come up for the last hour," Eric shouted over the tossing wind. "I thought you could use a little sleep, but if we don't get this done in the next half hour, Alice is going to be coming down on top of us like an express ferry."

"Alice?" Russell was rolling the yellow sunshade around its tubular steel legs.

"Tropical Cyclone Alice, first of the season." Eric gestured at the northwest sky, though he was still intent on the laptop. "It was on the radio while I was showing those tourist jerks around the fish farms this morning. The weather monitors been watching her for the past couple of days. *Pacifica* will go onto station-keeping in a few hours. The mechanics were rushing to fix a couple of the lateral thrusters while I was down there."

"Hmm. That means we ought to secure the lab," Russell guessed. "I wasn't aware it was going to be a full storm."

Eric looked at him over the top of the laptop's screen. "You scientists are all alike."

"What?" Russell was labouring toward him with the hamper under one arm and the bundled-up shade beneath the other.

"You can see about as far as your project, and anything else that happens is on another planet!" Devlin gave him a cheeky grin, knowing full well that he had invited a joke at his own expense.

Always quick to respond, Russell looked him over with hot blue eyes. "Well, I can certainly see as far as my project," he growled, and licked his lips salaciously. "I've still got a lot of research to do. A lot of study."

With a chuckle, Eric hit a key and closed down the computer. "What kind of study?"

"Responses and reactions," Russell purred. "I'd like to know how the Aquarian glands respond to various ... stimuli."

"Oh, yes?" Eric's brows rose. "Want to run a wire up me and see what comes up on the computer?"

"Nope." Russell leaned over and kissed him. "Want to run my cock up you, and see what comes up right below your belly."

"That," Eric decided, eyes sparkling, "sounds like a plan. Home?"

"Home." Russell nodded at the *Tiger*, which had drifted out on the tide again and was tugging hard on her mooring line. "You'd better get her in, I don't want to get this gear wet."

Leaving the laptop on the boulder, Eric was up and moving in one lithe bound. Russell envied him those genes. He didn't burn in the sun, never needed sunglasses, and he rarely seemed to feel either heat or the cold. He plunged into the hip-deep water and did not resurface until he had gone past the boat. The next Russell saw of him, he was hoisting himself onto the transom, water streaming from him in bright cascades.

The powerful V8 engines gargled into life and he brought the boat inshore with a few gentle nudges of the throttle. She grounded with a rasp of her keel on the white coral sand, and Eric perched on the bow, hands outstretched to take the hamper and shade. As he stowed them in the well, under a fluttering blue tarpaulin, the wind began to gust strongly, and Russell was not surprised to see his companion fiddling with the radio.

The mooring line coiled up on the bow, and as Eric tuned the big shortwave Russell reversed the engines, opened the throttle and let the *Tiger* pull herself off the beach. The sky was steely grey now, and the sea had that certain smell. He looked back, saw the palms along the whole length of Breakwater beginning to toss and thrash. Tropical Cyclone Alice would do the kay a lot of damage, and perhaps a repair crew would have to come out from *Pacifica* next week. Artificial islands were so delicate ... and natural islands were almost unknown now.

The bow came around as Eric found the channel, and Russell cocked an ear to the radio before he opened up the engines for the ride home. The weather forecast for the next twelve hours was repeating continually on Channel 44 in five languages, and many warnings were out. All of *Pacifica* would be determinedly battening down, and the pilots would soon be moving the *Atlantis* into a position where she could provide shelter, as a windbreak, between *Pacifica* and the incoming cyclone.

"Move it, sunshine," Eric advised as he turned off the shortwave, "or you're going to get your feet wet! And you," he added with a little self-mockery, "don't have webbing between the toes."

"Neither do you," Russell quipped.

"Only because your Dad didn't write frog code into the recipe that cooked me up," Eric sighed. He lowered himself into the seat beside Russell's and rummaged in the foot well for the jeans and tee shirt he had left there as soon as they had put *Pacifica* behind them. Eric was indifferent to being wet so long as he was naked. He detested clothes because they felt disgusting when they were damp, and yet the water was as natural to him as dry land was to Russell. If it had been socially acceptable for him to be naked in *Pacifica*, he would have been grateful, but even here, even now, the only men and women who went about in the state the gods created them were the hustlers, the star attractions from sex shops like The Beach Bum, and nothing annoyed Eric Devlin more than being treated like a hustler.

One afternoon when he was seventeen, his usual state of undress had got him into a lot of trouble and only his quick wits and quicker fists had fetched him out again. A crew was in from the Flinders Islands, the land masses that had once been the tops of a range of mountains in Australia. The vibrant, raucous, violent crew considered everyone in *Pacifica* fair game. Someone had told them that a beautiful bare backside on the waterfront was ripe for the plucking, because it invariably belonged to a hustler. No one had bothered to tell Eric that he was in any danger as he tied up his skiff, lugged his gear ashore and packed his bag for the walk home from South Quay.

The next he knew, he was caught between three enormous Australian tuna farmers, draped over a barrel between The Barnacle Inn and a bait shop. Kicking and screaming did not fetch anyone to his aid, nor did it deter the men. Not until he caught one of his admirers by the balls and the other by the ear, and wrenched both hard enough to draw blood, could he struggle to his feet. He was strong and quick, and a flurry of good, economical blows put the men down while they were still too astonished to protest.

Then he ran, and didn't stop until he was home. Outraged and indignant, he told the story, and John Grant snorted with laugher as he handed the young Eric a pair of cutoff jeans. Let that be a lesson to him not to flaunt his butt like a hustler, or he would be identified as one!

It was apparently the first time Eric had fully realised, other people saw him as a *man*, no longer a child. At seventeen he was almost fully grown, and his body was already superbly muscled since he had worked it all his life. He had taken no harm from the encounter on the Quay, and it changed the way he regarded himself. All at once, he began to think of himself as a man, an adult, and a sensualist.

Today, he wriggled into jeans and tee shirt as Russell jockeyed the boat through the rising chop. The ride was very rough and they were thoroughly shaken by the time they had put Breakwater on the horizon, but Russell had already seen the flash of colour, the masts and towers of *Pacifica*, and he throttled forward to get them home fast as the sky darkened another shade and a few enormous spots of rain began to fall.

Already the *Atlantis* was maneuvering, and Russell gave it all the sea-room he could manage. The prop-wash from the ship was so powerful, it could actually sink a small craft, and when she got up any kind of speed she was literally unstoppable. It took five or six kilometres to slow her, and tugs to stop her completely, so today she was maneuvering at dead-slow, just a few metres per minute, with her tugs, the ocean salvage vessels *Alexandra* and *Zenobia*, coupled port and starboard for safety. And still she was an awe inspiring sight. Russell could never see her without being overwhelmed, breathless, though he had grown to manhood in her shadow.

She was Gerald Duquesne's dream: three times the dimensions and mass of a supertanker, with six engines, six screws, powered by the reactors salvaged from two American nuclear submarines. She stood so tall above the water that clouds seemed to form around her radio masts, and from a position on her stern, one could not even see the bow. She was the life's blood of *Pacifica*.

Aboard that ship was the factory that processed seawater, producing every drop *Pacifica* drank; the generators that provided the city with its power; the schools and universities that educated its children; the hospitals that cared for its sick; the hydroponic greenhouses where *Pacifica's* fruit and vegetables were cultivated; the tanks where the city's sewage was turned into fuel and plant food. Aboard that ship were the machine shops that serviced and repaired every mechanism on *Pacifica*; the factories where clothing and furniture were made; laboratories where drugs were produced and tested; and the offices from which the entire city was controlled. On the massive stern was a landing field; on the bow was an earth-station dish twenty metres in diameter; amidships, multiple docks opened in the side, where smaller vessels, freighters and trawlers, could be drydocked to refit.

She was so massive, she even seemed to create her own weather patterns, and when a storm like Alice threatened, her enormous engines were started, to manoeuvre her into position where, like an immense wall, a mountain range, she would deflect the wind and calm the water in her lee.

In her shadow, *Pacifica* rested uneasily, but at least it did rest. The city was fragile, even flimsy, but for the past forty years the *Atlantis* had taken care of it like a hen with a single chick, and it was stronger now than ever. Five thousand vessels, ranging in size from Russell's powerboat to small freighters, were moored along the straggling quays that radiated like the arms of a star from a central body which had been known as he Waterfront since before Russell was born. Most of the boats were people's homes, but many more people lived on the Waterfront itself.

Businesses of all kinds throve ashore, from the bordellos where Bill Murchison liked to spend his time to the more conventional taverns, markets, and the arcades where traders jostled for space. Waterfront was the hub of *Pacifica*, and most of the city's people thought of it as dry land. In fact, it floated on a buoyancy tank the size of the dome of a cathedral, but it was so large - five hundred metres across - that it hardly seemed to move with the tide. When one was accustomed to the roll and yaw of a deck, Waterfront seemed completely stable.

When they crossed into the lee of the *Atlantis*, the wind fell away and the sea calmed. Russell had cut back his speed as he crossed the wake of the enormous ship, and threaded through the log-jammed inshore traffic with an expression of impatience. He had one eye on the threatening sky as he turned into his parking space and killed the engine, and Eric was already moving.

From West Quay they had only a short walk home, but the laptop was not exactly waterproof. Eric hopped over onto the concrete and reached back over to take the machine out of Russell's hands. "Go on, you get home and send the data," he said as Russell joined him on the sun-warmed ground. The impression was that one had actually come ashore, for white walls and gaudy banners, shingle roofs and communications masts at the far, inshore end of West Quay welcomed the traveller home. "I'll secure the boat and meet you," Eric promised. "I want to do some shopping."

"If you're sure," Russell said doubtfully. He twisted his neck to see the sky, up above the towering shape of the *Atlantis*. "You're going to get drowned."

"Me?" Eric tousled his companion's hair playfully. "Not possible, Russell!"

"Figure of speech," Russell said primly. "Even *you* can get a stinking cold, and you know how miserable that makes you. Six months ago, your nose was ..." he searched for a word. "Incandescent. You could read in the dark by it."

"I'm Aquarian, not immortal," Eric said tartly. "And I want to get some eggs and sausages and tomatoes, and beer." He straightened and helped Russell off the boat with the computer and hamper. "Ten minutes. Twenty, max, I'll be home."

"Tea or coffee?" Russell asked sweetly.

Eric gave him a grin. "Coffee. Black, with honey and a drop of the Irish."

"Your wish is my command," Russell said resignedly as he began to toil toward home and Eric jogged away from him down the wharf.

In fact, it was no imposition. Another day it would be Eric struggling home with a load of heavy gear, dive tanks or ripped nets, while Russell rushed off to market. *Pacifica* sprawled away along the line of Waterfront, a maze of humanity, a labyrinth of industry and activity, while to seaward a hundred boats were jostling into and out of parking spaces, reminiscent of the road traffic Russell had heard about, and seen on the videos that depicted a world which was gone.

Home was a building on the south side, on Aurealis Wharf. It could have used a lick of paint, Russell thought as he picked up his pace, hurrying through the steadily gathering rain. The sea wind quickly stripped the paint of any surface, and the only thing one could do was constant running repairs.

The lab was downstairs with the apartment overhead; long windows overlooked the wharf and the fish farm, and on the gentle slope of the roof sat their communications dish. In the alley between the building and the shed belonging to the fish farm was a rainwater tank that gathered the run-off from the roof.

Just as the rain began to pelt, Russell ducked inside. Harvey squawked loudly from the shelf in the window, among the potted plants, and Russell gave the big scarlet macaw a glare. "It's all right for you, tucked up warm and cozy," he grumbled to the bird as he kicked shut the door. "*Some* of us have to work for a living!"

The doorway opened into his tiny, cluttered office. The lab was to his right, the stairs directly before him. Harvey had the freedom of the whole building, but for some reason he preferred the office to the apartment. Perhaps because he could screech at the passersby more effectively from the window there. He hopped onto Russell's arm and pecked his ear. Russell scolded him, and headed for the stairs.

The apartment was warm, dim, a little airless. He flicked on the lights and the air conditioning, plugged in the kettle with one hand, and with the other put down both the laptop and Harvey. The screen in the corner was flickering for his attention with a welter of e-mail, and as he spooned coffee into matching mugs he scanned the list of messages that had arrived during the afternoon.

Two were from Duquesne's office on the *Atlantis*. Of course. Where the hell was that data? One was from Bill Murchison, and at that, Russell swore. Murchison was asking for "a small loan," which meant he had been gambling, or had been rolled by a hustler off a ship that had recently pulled out and left. The man was a fool, and if Russell could help it, he would not be separated from his money on Murchison's behalf.

The other messages were unimportant. An account from the gas-shop across Waterfront that filled his argon tanks, and yet another e-mail from an Aquarian girl on South Quay who had been trying to woo Russell into choosing her to be Eric's partner in the next phase of the Aquarian project. She was a nice kid, and Russell was seriously considering agreeing, so long as he could talk Eric around. That was the doubtful part.

The water was boiling, and he made his coffee while he transferred Duquesne's data to the master computer for transmission. As he sent it, an alarm in the corner of the screen gave him fair early warning of trouble, and he grunted as he read off the news. Harvey squawked for attention and Russell petted him absently. "Damn, we've lost a linker."

"Lost a linker, lost a linker," Harvey echoed in his hoarse little voice.

Russell looked into the macaw's dark eyes, and not for the first time wondered how much he understood. Not enough to answer the phone coherently, more was the pity. "Lost," he repeated, "a linker! And that means Duquesne's office will have to send someone over here for a hard copy of the data, because we're not going to be back on the air till it's been fixed, and it'll not be getting fixed in this weather!" He shooed the bird off the desk, picked up his coffee and the phone, in that order.

He was punching numbers when he heard the door and Eric's voice called, "It's only me! Do you know the wiring conduit is busted between the eaves and our aerials?"

"Might explain why we seem to have lost a linker," Russell said drily as feet thundered up the stairs. "I'm calling the *Atlantis*, they'll have to send someone over for a disk. I'm not climbing about on the roof in a gale." As Eric appeared, Russell made a face. "You're soaked!"

"I know." Eric lobbed a plastic-wrapped parcel at him.

Russell fielded it deftly as the phone began to ring and a voice said in his ear, "Hydrographic office."

"Hello love, is that Cynthia? It's Russell here. I know you've been waiting for your data, but we're off the air, sweetheart. Can you send a courier over for the disk? We can't send a thing till we make some repairs ..."

Mel Keegan

He listened politely as she rambled about her work, the office, her family, old Mr Duquesne, and promised to send someone, first chance she got. Russell was only listening with half an ear. Lightning flickered brightly, mauve and white, the lights momentarily dimmed and Harvey squawked in alarm. Russell shushed him and watched with appreciative eyes as Eric stripped out of his cold, sodden clothes and wrapped himself in an enormous blue and white towel. He stood by the heater, hands around a coffee mug, rubbing one foot on his other shin for warmth. Beautiful. The line of his back and hip and leg was sheer poetry, Russell thought, and he had lost the thread of Cynthia's ramble when she said loudly,

"You still there, Russell?"

"Still here," he assured her. "Say the last bit again."

"I said, it might be morning before I can get someone out to you for the data," she repeated. "This storm is just about right on top of us. We've got an incredible view of it from this side of the *Atlantis*. You're not going to see much from where you are, but if you turn on your tv, we're going to broadcast the whole time."

"Oh, great, I'll do that. Ciao, honey," Russell said swiftly, and took the opportunity to hang up. "My God, that woman can talk!"

"Because she fancies you," Eric said glibly.

"She what?" Russell scoffed. "She's old enough to be my mother!" He unwrapped the parcel and murmured in appreciation as he saw the fruits of Eric's shopping. Four thick sausages made of chicken, rabbit and herbs, two plump tomatoes and four big, brown eggs. "Nice! We having these for dinner?"

"Mmm." Eric stretched luxuriously. "My treat."

"Expensive," Russell said doubtfully.

"I can afford it." Eric dropped his towel and turned his chilly back and rump to the heater. "Dinner in bed?"

Russell chuckled. "You're a hedonist."

"I know. I like it." Eric gave him a wink and poised, hands on hips. "You shove the food in the wok, I'll fix the bed and tidy up some of this mess. It looks like a typhoon hit this place!"

They had been busy for days and the apartment betrayed their neglect. Books, tapes, disks, Russell's discarded clothes, used crockery, beer cans, littered every surface. While the food sizzled in the deep electric wok Eric made swift work of the mess, and by the time the sausages were crisp, the eggs were firm and the tomatoes soft, the "disaster zone" had been turned back into a comfortable apartment. The bed was made with the pale turquoise sheets, Harvey had been fed, the tv was on, and the mattress was still bouncing under Eric's weight as Russell fetched a tray and plunked down beside him.

"This is the life," Russell groaned as he punched his pillow, skewered a sausage on his fork, caught Eric in the crook of his arm and began to eat.

Thunder rolled and the sky whited out with lightning. Rain sluiced over the window glass, shutting out the whole world and making the apartment feel like a closed cocoon. Cosy, Russell decided. It was warm and humid, the food was good and the company was exquisite. Eric was warm and smooth, plastered down his right side as they curled in the middle of the bed. Drowsy and content, Russell nuzzled his shoulder and gave his attention to the tv.

As usual when a spectacular storm hit, the *Atlantis* broadcast a whole show. They were taping the storm, and every spectacular lightning flash was displayed. The film crew saved them over the space of ten or fifteen minutes, and then rolled their amazing footage. Between light shows they ran file footage of the great storms of years gone by, interviews with *Pacifica* personalities who told first-hand accounts of hair-raising experiences, educational segments which explained to children how storms were generated, what made them go, and sometimes curious music videos drawn from the last century, depicting storms breaking over the land.

Land fascinated Russell, because he had never seen it. His whole life had been spent in *Pacifica*, on the *Atlantis*, and on the tiny artificial islands, sand kays like Breakwater and Headland. One day, he promised himself drowsily as he finished eating and curled up with his head on Eric's chest, one day he would travel, go and see the world. He would get down to the Australian islands, take a look at trees that grew in dirt, see animals in a field ...but not soon. Not when there was trouble brewing again.

"You heard there's war again in Rhutan?" Eric whispered, as the video crew took a break and the *Atlantis* broadcast the day's news. "God damn them, they're at it again! Fighting over ten square metres of dry land. I mean, what's the point?"

"The point," Russell told him, "is that it's the only ten square metres they've got left and they don't want to get wet!" He reached over and turned down the sound as the pictures of atrocity, violence and despair in the tiny island freestate of Rhutan became too depressing. It had been a lovely little archipelago, and the idiots were ruining it. Russell could abide almost anything but stupidity. He turned his back on the tv and buried his face in Eric's chest. "I don't waste my time with that."

Eric's arms closed around him. "What do you want to do?"

Russell snuffled against the Aquarian's sweet, soft skin. "Guess," he invited as his teeth nuzzled toward Eric's left nipple and gently bit.

"Oh," Eric crooned as he wriggled down in the bed. "Now, *guessing* is one thing I just don't have to do!"

Chapter Three

Bill Murchison arrived an hour after dawn, hung over and limping, when repairs on the linker were an hour underway. Russell's hands were dirty and full of tools as Murchison appeared from the direction of Waterfront. He took one look at the prodigal, threw back his head and and guffawed with ribald, unsympathetic laughter. Murchison attempted a glare but failed miserably as he staggered toward the door.

Footsteps on the roof announced Eric, and Russell looked up as his partner's face appeared there. "Look what the cat dragged in," Eric quipped. "Where the hell's he been?"

"Took his glands for a night out," Russell taunted as he watched Murchison's struggled to make it up the stairs.

This morning the sky was burnished blue and the sea was almost calm. The *Atlantis* had moved back to her usual position, on the north side of the floating city, and as soon as there was enough daylight to work by, most of the population of *Pacifica* was out, making repairs.

The damage was surprisingly slight. A few roofs had been ripped away, aerials had been twisted, windows broken by flying debris. The fish farm had suffered only a little, and Russell had already been down to the Quay to check the *Tiger Shark*. She was safe, and for that he offered up a prayer of thanks.

Housed in the shed next door to the office-cum-lab - which actually belonged to the fish farm, though it had been leased by Russell's father and still remained on hire - the submersible was completely untouched by Tropical Cyclone Alice. The *Poseidon* was moored in her shed, coupled to the ramps at port and starboard by hawsers as thick as

Russell's arm. It would take a lot more than a high wind to dislodge her, and even if she did break her moorings, the robot pilot would simple take her down, under the city's vast buoyancy tank, and wait for the recall signal.

The shed was open, and Geoff and Jenny Wilson were busy with their stock. Bluefin and yellowfin, the herring and mackerel that fed them, and also Coho salmon on which delicate genetic work was being performed. The theory went, if you surgically removed the salmon's pituitary gland, it would spend its whole life happily at sea rather than committing ritual suicide in a brainless attempt to batter its way up a river in order to breed. All the salmon in the giant farm nets had under-gone surgery, and during the next two years the theory was about to be tested.

Strange, Russell thought, the lengths some animal species would go to, in order to breed. Stranger yet the lengths some humans would go to, in order to *avoid* breeding. The thought made him glance back up at the roof, where Eric was hammering sporadically, installing a few metres of fibreoptic cable and a new junction box.

Now, Eric was the exact opposite of the salmon. He would do almost anything to avoid the very thing which the fish desired most. The whole subject of sex with women was taboo, in or out of the lab. Russell had not even tried to broach the subject in six months, and for the last three of those months he had been quietly fielding Duquesne's increasingly impatient memos so that Eric never saw them. Of all the Aquarians, Eric Devlin was the one in whom Gerald Duquesne took the most interest, and yet of them all, Eric was probably going to be the most headstrong and make the most trouble.

Perhaps Duquesne's personal interest in this particular Aquarian stemmed from the fact that he was a personal friend of both Eric's parents. Steve Devlin had died before Russell was born, but if his photos were anything to judge from, he was a handsome and intelligent man with a lot of sensitivity and a great sense of humour. A lot like Eric, Russell mused as he swept the litter and broken glass into a heap and looked around for the bin. Then there were Eric's mothers - of whom there were, legally and morally, two.

Claire Stewart provided the ovum which was impregnated by Steve Devlin's sperm, following the weeks of meticulous reprogramming. But the tiny fragment of life that had begun under a microscope in the very lab where Russell now lived and worked, was implanted in Moira Ingram. Claire was a scientist, an engineer, she had no interest in being a mother. Moira had been pregnant four times already and seemed to relish the experience, so it was mutually beneficial if she carried the child and gave birth to him naturally.

One day in January, just a little over thirty years before, Eric Devlin was born in the warm maternity pool aboard the *Atlantis*, and a new sub-species of Mankind was born with him. It was dubbed scientifically *homo aquaticus*, but as John Grant had always said, that tag was a little premature. Before any such name could be awarded, the sub-species had to prove itself. The Aquarian babies had to grow up into strong, healthy adults; and then they had to prove that they could not only breed, but "breed true," pass on their characteristics to their own children, who in turn must grow up into normal, healthy and fertile Aquarians.

One mistake, and the product would be healthy mules. In itself this was no problem, but half the population of *Pacifica* had expressed an interest in having Aquarian children, and an entire sterile generation was potentially disastrous in a time and place where Mankind was having a struggle to keep up their numbers.

In his teens Eric's fertility had been clinically tested - there had been no need to test his potency. Russell could vouch for that! But his semen was collected and microscopically examined, his DNA printed. He was not merely a very virile young man, but his sperm count was uncommonly high and his DNA seemed faultless. Matched with an Aquarian female, he would be almost certain to produce a fine, healthy child who was as Aquarian as himself.

And therein lay the problem. Eric was technically a virgin. He had

Mel Keegan

never touched a woman, never desired to touch a woman. He had no interest in even watching women, though he was as sexy an individual as any Russell knew. In the old world, the word they used to describe him was "gay," and when this became obvious Russell did his homework thoroughly on the subject.

For himself, he liked women well enough. He knew he could go to bed with them and acquit himself quite well, if he had to ... not that women bothered to ask him, since every female on *Pacifica* was well aware that he was in love with Eric. The difference was that Russell sometimes noticed women and often watched them for the pleasure of it, while Eric never did.

Years before, Russell had run some subtle tests, which backfired and resulted in a scene which almost ruined their relationship. He ransacked the library over on the *Atlantis* and came home with several movies in a genre which had once been called "pornography." The films were digitised and stored on DVD, and were kept largely as curiosities these days. The three features he had borrowed had several points in common. They focused on the charms of women; the women were all *very* female, with large breasts and hard, pink nipples; and the sex was depicted graphically, especially the penetration shots, which were all filmed in close-up. These movies, Russell showed one evening when he and Eric were home for the night and settled.

But he watched Eric more than the tv, and mentally made notes. At first Eric blushed crimson and looked away from the screen. Then he grew restless and bored. He went out for a beer, fed the macaw, remembered a message he had to send. During the third film, he went to sleep in an abyss of boredom, and when Russell woke him, he curled up on the couch with his head in Russell's lap and deliberately initiated a seduction scene which Russell did not have the heart or the forbearance - or any real reason - to resist.

To be totally sure of Eric's inclinations, Russell bought a picture and hung it over his desk; and that was his biggest mistake. It was a calendar from the boat shop over on East Quay. Just a topless girl, her massive chest bursting out of a swimsuit two sizes too small. If that sort of thing was to your taste, it was a great photo. But when Eric saw it over Russell's desk he was white to the lips with fury, bright eyed with hurt, and without a word he stormed upstairs and began to pack.

He was leaving. If Russell had had enough of him and wanted to shack up with some woman, he said, he could take a hint. He knew when he wasn't wanted. Those films the other night - he should have seen what all this was pointing to.

The tirade went on for a quarter of an hour, and at last the only way Russell could stop him was to physically seize him, throw him onto the bed and pin him down. Eric kicked and fought, and Russell wore the bruises for a week, but somewhere in the course of the wrestling bout he managed to make Eric understand that he was sorry, it had been a prank, just a joke, and a bad joke which had gone wrong. Eric was wary, not sure that he was hearing the truth until Russell made love to him for over an hour. When they limped downstairs, later, the calendar came down off the wall and Russell ceremoniously cut it up with a pair of scissors, before Eric's eyes.

Where Eric's heart lay was obvious after that, and Russell was not in the slightest bothered until the memos began to arrive from Duquesne's office, each one more insistent than the last. Eric was thirty; he had his choice of six gorgeous Aquarian women who were all between twenty and twenty-five. When was he going to make his choice and get down to some good, old fashioned, baby-making sex?

The broken glass rattled into the bin and Russell straightened his aching back with a groan. Up on the roof, Eric was whistling as he worked, and Russell heard the lid slam on the junction box. His head appeared over the edge of the roof again and he gave Russell a wave.

"Go give transmitters a kick, I think we're back on the air!"

"Come down, I'll make a coffee," Russell invited. "You got any work on today?"

"Nope. My busy schedule isn't want it used to be," Eric said drily as he transferred his weight to the ladder and clambered carefully down.

He was in skimpy red shorts which pulled up into his cleft and disguised nothing at all.

Something in his tone of voice alerted Russell, and he snaked an arm about Eric's waist as he hit the concrete. "Hey, are you short of money?"

Green-gold eyes regarded Russell piercingly. "Not yet. But you know what *Pacifica* is like. It's a bloody expensive place to live, and I can spend it as soon as I get it. Stop worrying, Russell. Something'll turn up. There's just no more work this week. And I can't say I'm sorry ... I'm up to my eyeballs with guiding tourists. I get sick of the way they look at me and prod me, soon as they know what I am. Do you know, one of the buggers actually wanted to fuck me underwater!"

"Well, you're gorgeous," Russell said reasonably. "The truth is, they probably *all* wanted to do you, but the guy who actually came out and told you was the only one who had the guts to say it out loud. And besides, fucking underwater is fantastic."

A faint blush coloured Eric's bronze cheeks. "You got a point there. Ah, what the hell." He rubbed his face and stretched his shoulders. "Do you know how long it is since we had a night out?"

"Months," Russell guessed.

"Three months," Eric said succinctly. His arms circled Russell. "All work and no play makes anybody a dull little organism. Want to come into town tonight?"

"I ... well, maybe," Russell said guardedly, and for a moment would not meet Eric's watchful eyes.

For some time they were silent, and at last Eric kissed him to break the self-conscious quiet. "Love, it doesn't matter. It doesn't mean as much to me as it does to you."

"Then, it should!" Russell snapped. "Of all the things I hate, prejudice is the one I hate most. It's just so stupid, hating people for what they can't help being. Like, hating a man because of his race or his sexuality."

"You mean, being called a nig or a fag, or whatever it was?" Eric asked dubiously. "That's what they used to call it, isn't it? Not that I have the slightest idea what they meant by the words. They sound like exotic cigarettes."

"Lingual drift." Russell sighed. "A man can't help being born black or gay any more than..."

"Than I can help the way I was born," Eric whispered. "Russell, look at me. I said, look at me!" He caught Russell's head in both gentle hands and turned it toward him. "Why do you blame yourself?"

"I don't," Russell protested.

But Eric's head shook slowly. "Yes, you do. It's written all over your face when people taunt me."

The old anger surged up and escaped before Russell could stop it. "They have no right to taunt you!"

"Yet they do, and they're always going to," Eric said drily. "Oh, Russell, I wish you wouldn't punish yourself. Even if I was about to start apportioning blame - which I'm not - you'd be the last person in the world I'd stick with culpability for what I am."

Russell took a deep breath to calm his quick anger. Very rarely did his temper get away from him, but where Eric was concerned it was difficult to be indifferent to the bigotry of stupid, ignorant people. "If it's anyone's fault, it's my father's," he said stiffly.

"Rubbish," Eric retorted as he shepherded Russell into the office. He flicked on the computer and waited for it to run its boot-up diagnostics, check out both itself and its peripheral systems. "Your father was just the geneticist who did the work. The project was undertaken at Gerald Duquesne's request and behest. He put up the money and he's still hanging on every line of the feedback as if his pet Aquarians are characters in a half-assed serial on tv." Eric looked up with an expression of pure mischief. "And I don't even blame Duquesne. He's not responsible for the prejudice. Bigotry only happens when you run the gauntlet of visitors in *Pacifica*. The locals leave us alone."

The screen flickered and cleared, and Russell's practiced eye read down the column of text. "Hmph. Looks like we're back in business. You want to upload yesterday's data? Save the courier a trip over."

"Bright idea. What did you do with the disk?" Eric cast about for it, but did not see it on the desk.

"Damn, it's still in the portable. Sit tight," Russell told him, and swatted his mate's rump in the skimpy shorts on his way out of the office.

He took the stairs two at a time, and then paused at the top as he heard the sounds of gargling and groaning from the bathroom. Murchison's clothes were strewn like a papertrail from the stair well to the living room, and the man himself was naked, bent over the toilet with a bottle of mouth wash in one hand and a glass of dissolving seltzer in the other. He straightened as Russell appeared, and cast a bleary glance at his reflection in the mirror.

"You're an idiot," Russell said mildly. "Where the hell did you get to?"

"You know damned well," Murchison grumbled.

"Your favourite crotch-shop," Russell swiped the disk out of his portable. "I did your work for you. Where *were* you?"

"Earning some money." Murchison groped blindly for his pants, which he had dropped at the bathroom door. He thrust his hand into a pocket and withdrew a thick wad of notes. "I owe you. You got the data? Great. Here, help yourself to fifty."

"Fifty bucks, for collecting some data on Breakwater?" Russell demanded as Murchison lobbed the roll of notes into his hands. The wad of paper was heavy, and he whistled as he turned it over and over in his hand. "You've got a couple of grand here. It's Australian money."

"I was entertaining some Australian guests," Murchison moaned as he reeled into the kitchen and searched for the coffee.

"Entertaining?" Russell shoved the money back into Bill's pants and leaned on the door post. "Now, what the hell could you do in an evening that'd earn you a couple of grand, Aussie? Those are real dollars, not Rhutan Monopoly-money."

Murchison chuckled wickedly. "You know your trouble, Rusty, old mate? You never get out of the lab."

"Now, what's that supposed to mean?" Russell demanded.

"You're an innocent," Bill observed.

"You think so?" Russell looked him up and down, missing nothing from the telltale bruises on Murchison's limbs to the scarlet rawness between his buttocks. "You ought to see a medic. You might need a bum full of needles. You could have picked up anything from those turkeys."

"Oh, get out of here, Grant," Murchison groaned. "Let me have my coffee and get some sleep."

Russell's lips thinned in annoyance. "You've still got work to do, *mate*. So have I, and I am *not* doing your job as well as my own two days in a row! I've got a mountain of my own data to collate."

"So what's stopping you?" Murchison spilled coffee and sugar onto the floor, and did not even seem to notice what he was doing.

"That's enough!" Russell snatched the jars out of his hands. "Get your gear and get out, Bill. This is *our* apartment, you're supposed to have a home of your own. You're supposed to have a woman lurking in the background somewhere. You share my lab and my computers, and you're welcome to, but from now on you stay the hell out of our home!"

The warning seemed to rouse Murchison where being stuck with a sharp object might have failed. Hands on hips, he regarded Russell belligerently. "I don't need this aggravation, Russell. And I don't need your damned lab." He snatched up his pants and produced the wad of money like a conjuring trick. "I can do better than some pittance of a research grant. You'd be living on fish'n-fritters if it wasn't for the money Devlin brings home." He brandished last night's earnings under Russell's nose. "When you get sick of pratting around here, I can put you onto some real customers. Think about it."

Intrigued, repelled, annoyed, amused, all at once, Russell stood aside a jerked a thumb at the stairs. "Keep your hustle-money. Keep your Australian customers. Neither of us is a whore."

"Too bad," Murchison growled as he snatched up his clothes. "You'd be rich by now if you were. I can tell you, Russell, an Aquarian hustler fetches twice the price on the Waterfront. That skin, and the fact you can't drown 'em. You'd be surprised what customers'd pay for the privilege of doing it all to an Aquarian." He shoved his legs into his pants and glared at Russell. "I'll see you around, *mate*."

"Not," Russell breathed furiously, "if I see you first!"

The sound of retreating footsteps marked Murchison's exit, and with a sigh Russell swept up the man's mess and plugged in the kettle. "Eric! Coffee!"

Eric's voice drifted up from the office. "What about that disk? Did you find it?"

"Yeah, I've got it." Russell swung open the refrigerator, and was lifting out a jug of milk when Eric jogged up the stairs. "On the table." He gestured behind him.

Without a comment, Eric activated the slaved terminal in the corner of the living room and slipped the disk into it. The data would transmit from here as easily as from the office. Russell had stirred the mugs and handed one over when he said carefully,

"Bill left in a hell of a hurry."

"In a snit," Russell added. "I gave him his marching orders. I'm up to here with that man."

"And the whole project," Eric added as he sank into a chair and propped his bare feet on the corner of the table. "I heard some of what he said, and he has a point. You should get out more. You work too hard and you don't play enough."

"I don't what?" Russell gestured at the bed.

"Sex doesn't count," Eric said brashly. "We've been having sex almost every day for the last sixteen years. It's like working in a candy store. After a while you don't even notice it." He held out his hand and demanded that Russell take it. "We're going out tonight. On the tiles. Just you and me."

With a sigh, Russell slithered into the chair opposite and surrendered. "I hope you know what you're doing. Remember last time."

"Trust me," Eric invited with a green eyed wink. "Do you know there's a busting-full cache of messages waiting for you? We've been off the air all night and they're backed up."

"Shit," Russell hissed. He juggled his coffee cup into his other hand, reached over and swiveled the monitor to face him, and started reading. "Hmph. Unpaid bill. Letter from my sister. I'm being invited to lecture on the *Atlantis*, on the subject of Aquarian genetics. What a surprise. They invite me to bring over a couple of exhibits." He looked darkly at Eric. "By which, they probably mean you."

"They can think again," Eric said in barbed tones.

"Mmm. A pizza shop trying to scare up some business on the circuit ... and a bordello inviting all and sundry to a special night tonight."

Eric's brows arched. "Oh, yeah? Which one?"

"Bottoms Up, on East Quay." Russell took a swig of coffee. "They're doing a "one off special offer." Anyone who gets up and does a routine on the stage can have the hustler of his or her choice." He looked at Eric over the rim of his cup. "Strip routine, that is."

"You don't say." Eric chuckled richly. "Could be fun."

"You're kidding," Russell protested. "I hope."

"I don't mean it'd be fun to perform," Eric groaned, "but it'd be a laugh to watch. Oh, come on, Russell! Lighten up."

"You want to go," Russell concluded dubiously.

"Be the first time we've had a night out in three months." Eric wriggled down in the chair. "A couple of beers, watch the locals strut their stuff. Why not?"

"Well ... I suppose." Russell turned his eyes back to the screen and frowned. "Hmm. This'll douse your good spirits. A memo from Duquesne, marked "urgent," and tagged for you."

"For me?" Eric sat up and put his cup aside. At the touch of a key the memo began to run, and as he saw it his face set into mask-line lines.

Russell watched him closely. "Eric -"

"I don't have to," Eric said in an icy whisper. "I *do not have to*. I can leave."

Leave? In all his musings on the subject, Russell had never quite considered that Eric could just walk out of *Pacifica*, but in fact he was right. No law kept him a prisoner here, and though he was the first and favourite subject of the Aquarian project, the lab did not own him.

"Leave?" Russell murmured. "Where would you go?"

"Anywhere," Eric said tartly, "where the authorities stay out of my bed and away from my body!"

"But ..." Russell gestured vaguely at the lab. "You'd be alone. I mean, outside of *Pacifica* there's no one else like you."

"I know." Eric finished his coffee in one swallow and looked away. "But I just can't do what Duquesne wants, Russell."

"Can't make love with a girl?" Russell guessed.

Eric's shoulders scrunched. "I just don't feel like it. Why can't they leave me alone?"

"You know why." Russell hoisted himself to his feet, came around the table and laid his hands on Eric's shoulders. He dealt his lover a soothing back rub. "I've been telling Duquesne for a long time, you're what they used to call gay, and he'll have to stop asking you to do something you just can't do. But he wants a breeding programme, he wants to see that his Aquarians can make healthy children. An you're his favourite, you were his first born, and you're the best and brightest of the bunch. See it from his perspective."

But Eric buried his face in Russell's middle and said, muffled, while Russell stroked his hair, "I can't perform on command. I don't have those feelings for women. And besides, I love you. I don't ... I can't go with a woman just to please Gerald Duquesne and his damned breeding programme." He gestured blindly at the screen. "Tell him."

"I have told him." Russell studied the screen over Eric's head. On it were displayed a short list of names, a couple of biographies and some lovely photos. The girls were gorgeous. Most men would be pleased to get into bed with them. But Eric was not most men. Eric was Eric, and a law unto himself.

For a moment Russell chewed his lip and then said carefully, "Tell me the truth, now. Is it just that you don't think you could perform with a girl?"

The question was odd enough to make Eric lift his head. "Huh?"

"I mean, it's not some moral objection to the project?" Russell said more specifically. "Or, a moral objection you hold to having children."

"No. I don't mind kids ... so long as they're someone else's," Eric admitted. "And how could I mind the project? If it wasn't for Duquesne's dream of a species of human to whom the sea is as natural as the land, I wouldn't even exist."

Russell traced his features with a smile. "All right, then suppose we give Duquesne a flat-out refusal of what he wants. You're not leaving me and going over to the *Atlantis* to live for the next six months, and you're not hopping from lady's bed to lady's bed! They can send over some donor ova, the same way your mother's were sent, and I can do the rest." He gestured at the computer. "All I need is your semen, and God knows, you give me enough of that!"

Eric's eyes narrowed. "That's not what Duquesne wants. He needs to know that his pet Aquarians can make love like normal, ordinary people, in a family environment."

A faint blush tinged Russell's cheeks pink. "Then I can file a report. About us."

"About our love life?" Eric's voice scaled several octaves.

Russell thrust out his chin. "Then, you suggest another way to get around the problem!"

For almost a full minute Eric's mouth flapped mutely as he tried to make some coherent reply, and at last gave up in disgust. Russell snorted with laughter and gave his shoulder a mock punch.

"You know your problem? You're shy," he accused. "You're actually bashful!"

The Aquarian's green eyes widened in a mix of outrage and reluctant mischief. "You come to Bottoms Up with me tonight, and I'll show you how bashful I am!"

Head cocked at him, Russell mirrored his impish expression. "You going to get up on the stage and do a routine?"

"What," Eric demanded, "makes you think I couldn't?"

"This." Russell leaned down, both hands on his shoulders, and kissed him deeply. "I love you, and I'm asking you not to embarrass me."

"You're the one who's bashful," Eric whispered against Russell's soft lips.

"You could say. A little bit." Russell kissed him again and was gratified when Eric's arms slid around him. "No routine?"

"Just a couple of beers and a laugh at the antics of the yobs and slobs," Eric promised, and then he hesitated. "You'll send Duquesne a message?"

"About you?" Russell's brow quirked. "And me ... and us?"

"Yes." Eric seemed to steel himself and studied the screen. "There's some pretty girls."

Russell perched on the arm of his chair and stroked his cheek, soothing and teasing at once. "Pick one."

"Do what?" Eric demanded suspiciously.

"I said -" Russell nuzzled his ear. "Pick the one you want to share chromosomes with. I'll send your selection over to the *Atlantis* and the next time she ovulates we'll ... well, I'll go over and get one. I'll also arrange for a surrogate to carry the child."

Eric's face shuttered. "Like they did for me."

"Hey." Russell tugged him up to his feet and embraced him. "You've only got so many choices, honey. If you don't want to do it Duquesne's way, and start a family unit -"

"Russell! You know I can't. Won't," Eric corrected as he invited himself into Russell's big arms.

"Then, do you it my way or you're out of options," Russell coaxed. "You won't even have to know who the surrogate mother is, if you don't want to. But I think you should pick the girl who donates the ovum. Now, screw up your damn courage and take a look at the screen. Which one do you fancy?"

"I don't *fancy* any one of them," Eric grumbled, "but I take your meaning. He frowned over the sketched biographies and the snapshots, and indicated the lower left corner. "That one. She'll do."

"Blue eyes, black hair, pale skin, tall and well built," Russell said drily. The girl was so much like himself, she could have been Russell's sister. His *twin* sister. "You, my darling Eric, are predictable."

"At least I'm consistent," Eric sighed. He kissed Russell's neck vampire fashion and slid out of his arms. "I'm also hungry. Go on, I know you've got work to do. Go make a start, I'll whip up some breakfast and bring it down to the lab."

"You're a treasure," Russell teased, and fondled Eric's backside affectionately as he released him. "I'll owe you one."

"Pay me back tonight," Eric suggested banteringly.

"In bed?" Russell laughed, delighted that the potentially explosive situation was defused.

"Nope." Eric swung open the fridge and fetched out the muffins and peaches. "I want to see you let your hair down and have a good time. I'm going to get you mildly squiffy, and then I'm going to have you fuck me on the *Tiger*, in the moonlight, on the bay. A little wild living will do you the world of good."

In fact, the huskily-whispered promise had ignited Russell's blood, and his heart hammered at his chest as he wisely withdrew from the scene and swung down the stairs to the office, and the lab. His glands notwithstanding, he had an everest of work to do that had been piling up for three days. Bill Murchison's erratic performance did not help matters ... and Eric Devlin's constant, delicious source of distraction would have driven any rational man wild, Russell was sure. For himself, he was happily, deliciously insane.

Chapter Four

At ten minutes after seven the Waterfront club was not even in second gear, let alone high gear. Later, around midnight, the crowd would get the bit between its teeth and the police would probably be nearby, but for the moment it was quite wild enough for Russell's taste.

Two ships had docked in the afternoon, and their crews had come ashore - if *Pacifica* could be called "ashore." Russell was almost sure it could not. What seemed to be the entire compliment of the Australian freighter *Aurora* was getting very merry in the club lounge, even before the entertainment began, and the Chinese tanker *Fei Hung* had disgorged its much more modest crew. All of them were mildly plastered, as if they had been drinking somewhere else before they arrived here.

Bottoms Up was the shop-front connecting the Waterfront passing trade with the brothel behind the scenes. Out back and up a couple of flights of stairs were the bedrooms, blackrooms, playrooms, anything the customer might desire. From the front shop, one could buy a beer and hold a boy or girl by the hand for an hour, or clients could solicit the services of a thoroughbred hustler and then start any scene they desired.

Russell had not been in this place for several years, and he regarded it critically over the rim of a glass of beer. They had changed the decor, and he was not sure he liked it. In years gone by the walls had been blue, the floor had been piled with tinted-yellow sand and the walls were adorned with nets and beachballs and stuffed seagulls, all intended to give the impression that the clientele were at the beach. Now, the mood was something called "turbo raunch." The walls were a red so dark, they might as well have been black, the lighting was purple, fluorescent, and in the floor, which had the effect of making even con-servative people look grotesque, and the tables were amber plastic, cast in the shapes of contorted bodies. The table in front of Russell, where he tucked his legs and put his glass down, was formed like a young per-son of indeterminate gender, crouched over in a position that suggest-ed a brazen invitation to sexual intercourse.

The dance floor was still almost empty, though the music had begun to blare fifteen minutes before. A threesome of hustlers were chatting up the Australians, and as Russell watched Eric sauntered back across the club with a couple more drinks. For himself, a double Green Goddess on ice; for Russell, Hennessy in a cheap plastic beaker pre-tending to be a brandy balloon.

He was in fine fettle tonight, Russell decided. Eric had never looked better. He was in a pair of black denims, barefoot and bare chested, with a touch of green on his eyelids and nipples, which was the height of fashion lately. Russell had touched his own eyelids in blue; he wore tight white denims, his black silk shirt, and a scarlet headband - also right in the height of *Pacifica* fashion. They looked like a couple of playboys, but nothing could be further from the truth.

After a day's work in the lab Russell's mind was a jumble of infor-mation. His brain would not stop data processing until the middle of the night, and sometimes even his sleep would be a muddle of half-familiar statistics that slowly ravelled themselves into the fantasy of dreams. He may look like a young buck out for a wild night, but he felt more or less like a research geneticist in his best gladrags, dying to get out of the noise and go home for some quiet sex and eight hours' sleep.

"There you are, kid, get that into you," Eric invited as he slapped down the glasses. He swung his bare feet up onto the absurd table and surveyed the ragtag rabble of the club's clientele. "They told me the show starts in ten minutes."

"You mean, the clients taking turns to strip and strut?" Russell buried his nose in his glass and inhaled the vapours of the Hennessy. "Hey, this smells like the real thing!"

"That's because it's the real thing," Eric said mildly as he sampled his own emerald green liquor.

"You can't afford original, genuine Hennessy," Russell protested.

"My treat." The Aquarian wrinkled his nose affectionately. "Drink up before someone jiggles your arm."

The stuff was like liquid gold and Russell savoured it on his tongue. The beer, wines and spirits drunk in *Pacifica* were almost always the product of the "vats" over on the *Atlantis*. They grew grapes and hops by the acre, hydroponically, but the process of wine making, much less brandy making, was difficult and abstract. The liquor churned out locally was drinkable, if one stretched a point, but nothing remotely like this. The fine old brandy must have dated from a time before Chen-Goldstein-4, the inundation, and Russell relished it. It was tremendously rare now, since the areas of Europe where these grapes had been grown were long underwater. There would be no more like it until someone managed to coax vines to thrive under UV lights in a lab, and then evolved a method by which the juice could be distilled *in vitro*. A biochemistry lab, miles of glass tubes and computer monitoring were no fit substitute for the warmth of a summer sun, the fecundity of old, rich soil, the church-like quiet of the cellars or caverns, and the ancient craft of the wine maker who was the midwife of this extraordinary substance.

The pleasant heat began in Russell's middle and spread out to his extremities, painting a smile on his face as it went. Eric was watching him, taking a vicarious delight in his pleasure, and Russell gave him a self-satisfied smile.

"Your reward will be in heaven, my son," he promised. "I'm going to send you there, on a flying carpet, in about two hours' time when we get sick of this dive, and go home."

"Sick of it?" Eric gestured over his shoulder at the stage. "They haven't even started yet!"

"They're about to," Russell said darkly. "The Aussies are getting ready to cut loose. And you know what it's like when Flinders Islanders open the throttle."

"Awesome," Eric agreed as he twisted about in his seat and cast a glance at the stage.

The music was blasting now, creating a deep, heavy vibration through the floor, and a knot of crewmen from the *Aurora* were pushing and shoving each other, trying to get up their courage. The "prizes" were on display, posing in golden lobster pots, suspended from the ceiling. Three girls and three boys, almost naked, moving in time to what passed for music.

As the music soared into an inspired rendition of the Beach Girls' ten year old chart-topper, *California Boys*, one of the Australians was convinced to try his luck. The crowd surged in to watch, and Russell, despite his better judgment, was fascinated. The kid had a good body and some sense of rhythm and style, and as soon as he let go of his inhibitions the routine wasn't half bad. The hips swivelled, bumped and ground, the shirt inched off over his shoulders and he massaged his chest, twisted his nipples, before he got busy with his pants. The crowd stamped and clapped and he gave them more than their money's worth. Russell caught a glimpse of a round bare backside, a jutting cock, and then the boy's admirers were all around him, and it was over. He took his choice of the prizes - the Korean girl with the golden combs in her hair - and vanished through the fronded curtain behind the stage.

To stage right, the management was gleeful. The stout little man with the ridiculously ill-fitting wig was the house's boss. These shows were cheap to stage and dragged custom in off Waterfront better than a cabaret for which he might have paid a fortune. The beer was flowing like water -when did it not, when an Australian crew was in town? - and the entertainment was guaranteed to get the onlookers so worked up, the bordello would do business as rich as the bar.

For himself, Russell could take it or leave it, but Eric was right. The chance to get out of the lab, forget about work, mingle with real, live human beings, have a drink and remember that he was human too ... all this was worth much more than the evening out was actually going to cost, even if Eric *did* insist on spending his hard-earned cash on unbelievable luxury such as genuine Hennessy. He knew Russell loved it, and it gave Eric as much pleasure to see Russell enjoying something he loved as to relish a treat himself.

The music was loud enough to perforate the ear drums, and in self defense Russell slid out from the table, took Eric by the elbow and deliberately steered him into a less crowded, less noisy area of the club. A private nook afforded a good view of the stage, and also of the big video screens where all kinds of delicious perversion were being exhibited. On the stage, an Aussie crewgirl was stripping with lascivious gusto; on the screen two boys were getting it together with equal enthusiasm. Typically, Eric had turned his back on the stage and was intent on the screen. Russell divided his attention between the two until a voice, close by his shoulder said, "Sorry to interrupt your entertainment, gentlemen, but I'm looking for a Doctor Russell Grant. The manager said that might be you." The accent was Australian, the voice male, deep and just loud enough to get over the continual din from the transducers.

Russell turned slowly, looked up and back, and saw a face just behind him. Middle-aged, deeply creased, tanned as dark as pickled walnuts by sun, wind and weather. Brown eyes, so dark they were almost black, looked him over, and in an instant Russell was aware of a creeping sensation of suspicion in the pit of his belly.

"I'm Grant," he said cautiously. "What's your business?"

The man's clothes were well cut, his dark blond hair was swept back from his face and roped in a single pony tail, and his neck and wrists glittered with too much gold. Either he was determined to make an impression tonight, or he was as wealthy as he looked, and either case made Russell even more suspicious. People who went out of their way to impress were generally looking for something, and it might be something one did want to give ... then again, wealthy men were batting in a league of their own, not one in which Russell chose to play. Since the inundation, so few ways remained in which to amass wealth that prosperity automatically looked shady.

The Australian offered his hand. "My name is Calder. Graham Calder."

Russell shook the man's hand briefly, and gestured across the table. "This is Eric Devlin."

At the mention of Eric's name, Calder's eyes flickered. "Well, well, I'm in luck tonight after all. I'd thought I'd have to search half of *Pacifica* before I located you."

"Located me?" Eric offered his hand, and Calder shook it. "Now, why would you be looking for me?"

"Do you mind if I sit down?" Calder gestured at the empty chair at Russell's elbow.

In fact, Russell resented the man's presence, but good manners forbade him from telling Calder to vanish. He glanced over at Eric as the Australian sat, and Eric's brows arched into an expression of interest.

"What are you drinking?" Calder asked solicitously. "The next are on me. Boy! Another pink gin, and whatever these gentlemen are having ... and if Mr Royce gets here, tell him where I am, will you, kid?"

The waiter was just barely over the age of consent, and dressed in an apology for a jockstrap, into which were tucked various wads of money, Australian, Chinese, Japanese, Rhutan, and *Pacifica*'s own lurid scrip. He accepted another handful of paper from Calder and minced away toward the bar, which was beyond the stage and the loudspeakers. Satisfied, Calder sat back and watched the video screens, though he said to Russell,

"Relax, it's strictly business and I'll be out of your hair soon."

"What kind of business?" Eric leaned over the table, the better to hear the man. "You didn't come in on the *Aurora*, did you?"

The query made Calder roar with laughter. "No, son, that I did not. I have my own transport. I flew in late this afternoon. Just got my crew through your customs entanglements. You're a paranoid lot here, aren't you?"

"We're careful," Russell allowed. "We have to be." He paused as the crowd erupted in applause. An article of underwear drifted out over the club and was plucked out of the air. If that was a G-string, it wouldn't cover so much as a freckle. "Look, Mr Calder, we came here to relax, not to talk business. If you've got something to say, say it and we'll get back to you in the morning, all right?"

"All right." Calder swung toward him. "I like a man who punches straight from the shoulder. Cards on the table, Doctor Grant. I want to hire your submersible and your partner."

Russell had asked for bluntness, but he had not been ready to be hit by a brick. He cleared his throat, leaned back in his chair and looked across at Eric. "What do you want with the *Poseidon*? And if you don't mind me asking, what could you possibly want with Eric? Surely you have your own submersible."

"I do," Calder admitted, "but it's three thousand kilometres away, in the Flinders Islands. And the cargo I want to salvage is another six hundred k's from here, northeast of your charming community. Now, I want to get the job done while I have half a chance of getting a good price for the merchandise, and to do that I need a sub, and I need it fast."

The plain talking impressed Russell, and he looked across the table to see Eric's minute nod of agreement. A flat-out commercial proposition was never out of the question. Russell chewed his lip thoughtfully as the waiter returned with a tray of drinks. Another Hennessy, a Green Goddess for Eric and a very large pink gin for Calder. The boy took his money, a hefty tip and a playful pinch for his admittedly cute little backside, and as he withdrew into the crowd Russell inhaled brandy vapours.

"Are we talking business, son?" Calder asked.

"Maybe," Russell allowed. "Why are you interested in my sub? It's not the only one in the area."

"But it is the only one that's available," Calder said reasonably. "I made some calls. There's the *Neptune*, over on *Hayman Marina*. Dives deeper than your bucket, but they're asking a king's ransom and they can't get her out here for a week. She's drydocked for repairs, There's the *Stingray*, belongs to the Mao Kerr Hsu Oceanographic Institute, but she's not available for private charter. There's the *Deep Star*, over in Bali Highlands, but she's already chartered out and won't be available till next month." He spread his hands. "You're it, kid, so long as the price is right."

"Fair enough - you do your homework," Russell said with grudging approval. "So, if you've got the submersible on contract, what do you want with Eric as well?"

Calder's sun-worn face creased deeply. "I've read a lot about the Aquarians, and I need one. Someone who can work outside the submersible and not have to worry about depressurisation stopovers."

"That means your salvage is deep, and it's delicate work," Eric mused, "too delicate for the submersible's handling arms. And it also means you don't have a crew of professional divers with you, or the million buck's worth of helium or argon breathing gear they need to put them in very deep water and keep them working. You want an Aquarian to get out there and do the fiddly stuff while the submersible provides the lights and the salvage sled to bring up the cargo, once it's been loaded aboard. Am I right?"

"Dead right." Calder's dark eyes flicked to Russell. "The boy's good. Then again, it's his job to be. He was born for it. Do we have a deal?"

"Not so fast." Russell held up his hands to stall Calder. "I need more information. Just what the hell is it you're trying to salvage in such a hurry?"

He might have wrung an answer out of Calder, but before the Australian could speak a small commotion erupted among the crowd and Calder turned to looked over his shoulder. Another man was approaching, and Russell's eyes narrowed as he looked him over. Tall, broad shouldered, dressed in black, head to foot; no jewellery. He sported wrangler heeled boots rather than sandals or bare feet, and. his red hair was cut short and worn like a brush, standing on end, which gave him an aspect of menace. His features were heavy, with a long jaw, full, pouting lips, and eyes sharp as scalpels. He was twenty-five, no older than that, probably young enough to be Calder's son. Of the two men, this one was by far the more dangerous, and Russell registered the quickening of his heart as the newcomer pushed through the crowd and paced to their table. He moved like a big cat, lithe, graceful, and every bone in his body said one word to Russell: *mercenary.*

"You're late," Calder said by way of greeting. "I found them, we're talking it through right now." He turned back to the table. "Russell Grant, Eric Devlin, this is my partner, Brady Royce."

The introduction was pleasantly made, but Royce did not offer his hand, nor did he pull up a chair. He thrust both hands into the pockets of his trousers and stood, feet braced, looking from Russell to Eric and back again. When he was a kid he might have been called good looking, but the ravages of time were already showing up on his face, not as lines or creases but as a hard expression of such cynicism that his good looks were obscured.

"You'll take the charter?" he asked in a Flinders Islands accent even thicker than Calder's.

"That depends." Russell inhaled Hennessy vapours deeply. "As I just said to Mr Calder, it depends on the cargo you're attempting to raise."

"That's no concern of yours, Russell," Royce said over the din from the stage as a boy dropped his pants and began to prance about with a girl from the audience.

"It is, if you're going to hire my partner as well as my sub," Russell said flatly. "The submersible is replaceable. Eric is not. And that's another thing, Calder. If there's any danger involved in this salvage of yours, it's going to cost you extra."

"Danger money?" Calder chuckled. "Any reasonable fee, of course. But Brady has a point. We'll give you every guarantee we can that the risk is minimal, and that the work undertaken by your Aquarian is not hazardous. Beyond that, there's no more information you need."

Russell felt his hackles rising and took a sip of brandy to smother his temper. Across the table, Eric's face had shuttered the instant Calder referred to him that way. "Your Aquarian." As if Eric was a thing, an object which belonged to Russell since Russell was technically the head

Mel Keegan

of the project. Eric's face was a shade paler and seemed to be carved from wood. Russell, who knew him better even than he knew himself, was well aware that Eric was concealing a surge of anger and hurt that could never be properly expressed. The only expression for those feelings was violence, and if Eric started something the person who would be blamed for it was himself. Russell felt an upsurgence of the old anger, and negative energy rushed through him like a gale.

Pulling his face straight with an effort, he cleared his throat and stood up. "In the first place, Mr Calder, Mr Royce, I don't own Eric Devlin. He's not a prisoner, he doesn't belong to anyone, much less to me. He's not my employee, he's my partner. In the second place, I wouldn't let either my property of my friend walk blindly into any hazardous situation - and *any* situation which involves a deep dive and heavy machinery is hazardous. I regret that on thinking it over, the *Poseidon* is not for charter." He drained his glass, shoved the chair back in under the table and stepped away, toward the crowd. "Thanks for the drink, but it's no deal. Not under these conditions. Eric?"

They were on the street seconds later. Eric walked a dozen paces from the gaudy neon sign beside the door and stopped in a deep well of blue shadow. He leaned his bare shoulders against the wall and the heels of both clenched fists pounded into the paint-work, an expression of exasperation or anger. Or was it despair?

"Eric?" Russell hovered beside him, feeling like hell.

"It's nothing," Eric said quietly, looking out over the water, across the bay, toward the distant, ghost-grey shape of the *Atlantis*.

"Rubbish," Russell snorted. "That man insulted you, and short of starting a fight, punching his nose and getting yourself arrested, there's nothing you can do about it. You could try dragging him into court, but he'd deny what he said; and even if you could get an admission out of him, what *did* he say? He "referred to you in a prejudiced manner." That's the way the legal eagles phrase it, isn't it? And then there's a fine to pay. A small fine. And he pays it and walks out of the court laughing. Laughing at us."

"At me," Eric said hoarsely. "Oh, shit, Rusty."

"Christ, mate, I'm sorry." Russell seized him bodily, tugged him into an embrace and squeezed the breath from his lungs. "You know, you may be right. It might be time we got out of here."

"Out of *Pacifica*?" Eric said moistly against the side of his face.

"Yeah. Right out." Russell's hands covered his back, stroked him soothingly, restlessly. "The first time I watched you insulted that way and understood what was happening, I was ten years old. I couldn't do anything about it then, I can't do anything about it now."

"You're wrong," Eric whispered. "You're doing it."

"What, this?" Russell's lips brushed Eric's ear. "It's not enough. I wanted to break their legs."

"Russell." Eric silenced him with his mouth before the language of violence could spoil the tenderness with which Russell had overset the hurt. "They're just bigots. A century ago people were attacked in the street for being black, or Asian, or gay. Centuries before that, people were attacked for being lame, or witches, or even foreign, though they were the same colour and religion, and a socially acceptable gender. Nothing changes. It's just the way people are."

"I know. But I don't have to like it." Russell released him with a sigh. "At least we had the satisfaction of thoroughly screwing up the last hope they had of making a commercial salvage." He grinned, teeth very white in the glare of the neon from the club's entrance. "Probably cost those good old boys about ten million bucks. That's not a bad revenge."

A reluctant smile quirked one corner of Eric's mouth. "Not bad at all," he agreed, and slipped an arm around Russell's waist. "Ah, what the hell. Forget it. It's not worth getting into a mood about."

"If you can forget it," Russell said quietly.

"Me? I've had to learn how to." Eric ran his hands over his chest. "I am what I am. The first breath I ever took was water. Not *in* the water, but *of* the water."

"Oh, I know," Russell said ruefully. "They had to stop me from drowning myself when I was about a year old. You and I were swimming together and when you dived and stayed under I tried to follow you and took a breath, just the way you were breathing. You know, I had temper tantrums until I was ten years old."

"Temper tantrums?" Eric was thoroughly diverted.

"I wanted to be like you. I demanded that my father get me into that lab and make me like you, because I wanted to do all the things you do, and I screamed myself blue in the face when they told me, it wasn't possible."

"You're a hopeless case, Russell," Eric accused, and gave him a swift hug, an even swifter kiss. "Do you want to go on to another club? Or ... what we said before?"

Warmth flushed Russell's face and he was grateful for the comparative darkness. Eric was known to tease, when he was in the right mood. "If you want the truth," he confessed, "I have had it up to *here* with people. You know me, sunshine. I don't like people in the mass. Never have, never will. They're thoughtless, they're cruel, they're stupid."

"What about me," Eric protested, "I'm people too!"

"No you're not," Russell began.

"No. I keep forgetting." Eric cast a glance back toward the club's brash, noisy entrance. "I'm not even human."

Russell caught his arms tightly. "More than human. You were designed by Gerald Duquesne and John Grant, as more than human. Christ, Eric! Don't you know that you're very probably the future of the human race?"

"Aquarian," Eric whispered. "When I was a child, they used to say, "Why doesn't the kid have webbed feet?" Once, a whole bunch of the little bastards held me down and examined my fingers and toes. They hurt me, and your father grabbed one or two of the ringleaders by the scruffs of their necks and, right then and there, draped them over his knee and spanked them till they yelled blue murder."

"Like I said," Russell repeated, holding him, "it's just the nature of people. Doesn't matter how old they are, or how young, they can be cruel. And I've never liked them much."

"Misanthropist," Eric accused affectionately.

"Call it what you will." Russell kissed his neck and let him go. "And I love you. We'll go on to another club if you like, but I'd rather not." He paused and tugged Eric away, along Waterfront. "Come out on the *Tiger* with me? In fact, *come* with me? And I do mean, come!"

"Oh, yeah," Eric purred. "I promised you something. You can have that, if you want it."

Russell pantomimed a double-take. "If I want...? Devlin, you're a tease! I've wanted *that* since I was twelve years old."

"Been getting it since you were twelve, too!" Eric laughed, a harsh, brittle sound, and grabbed Russell by the arm. "Oh, the hell with those bastards. I don't know why I let them get under my skin. I ought to have more maturity than to let them worry me." He was tugging Russell along the wharf, back toward the space where they had parked. "And I want you."

Those three words, "I want you," electrified Russell. The old anger still hung on, making him long to return to Bottoms Up and crack heads together, but Eric knew how to seduce him. That gentle skill, he had mastered when they were little more than children, and Russell had never strayed from Eric's bed more than once.

He had slept with a girl when he was nineteen, but the experience was not what he had expected it to be. The girl was nice enough, but she wanted orgasm after orgasm, and Russell was good mannered enough to humour her. She came eleven times before she gave him permission to mount her, and by then Russell was so urgent that he climaxed in seconds after he entered, which made him feel inadequate. He crept back home in the wan light of pre-dawn, and found Eric asleep, curled in the middle of the bed which for years they had thought of as their own. The sheets were cold, but Eric was warm. Aquarians were always warm - they wore their own natural thermal insulation, that fine layer of dense fat just beneath the skin. Russell undressed, crawled into his arms, and with all the remorse of which only a very young man is capable, he confessed and wept in his shame until Eric forgave him for the betrayal. Eric had been resigned to Russell's experiment, because he knew Russell liked girls too and it had to come sooner or later. But he had also been badly frightened, worried that Russell would not come home. That he would like girls better.

There was no chance of that, but perhaps only Russell was fully aware of it. The night when he had slept with Josie Kemp was eight years in the past, and though he had looked at many, many women since then he had never felt the desire to go with one. Not when he had Eric at home.

The powerful V8 motors started with a bass gargle, and as Eric cast off their bow line Russell threw the engines into reverse and the *Tiger Shark* pulled herself out of the parking place. The inshore and mid-lanes traffic was light but still Russell kept the speed down as he arced out across the bay, down the immense length of Gerald Duquesne's dream ship. The lights of the *Atlantis* shone like yellow-white beacons, but as soon as they fell away astern of the jetskiff the night was blue and calm and quiet.

This was more to Russell's taste. Eric tripped the tape deck and the sound of Haydn filtered into the balmy air. He had set down a rug, and as Russell turned off the engines and let the boat drift. The moonlight blued his skin, sharpened his features. A shooting star arced high over-head, leaving a glowing, sparkling trail, and the sea itself seemed to shimmer. Traces if bio-luminescence lent the ocean something like the aurora effect, uncanny and beautiful.

With a quiet sound of longing, almost a sound of pain, Russell went down into his lover's arms and caught Eric against him. Ridiculously, he wanted to make amends for the things other

men said and thought, as if Eric was right, and at the bottom of him he did blame himself for the fact of Eric's differences. Eric would never blame him, no matter what went wrong, but none of that made Russell feel any easier. Intimacy was the only balm Russell knew that soothed and healed. When they were together and alone, he could convince himself that nothing in the world was wrong, or if it was, then it was fixable. Remedies, and would always be found.

For what must be the thousandth time, Russell celebrated Eric's love-ly, Aquarian body, and banished the rest of the world from his mind.

Chapter Five

As much as Russell would have liked to turn his back on the tv, the time had come when he must pay attention. A news crew was in Rhutan, the pictures were smuggled out, tight-beam broadcast, via the Comstar-14 satellite. Anyone in the world who possessed a ground station could receive them. The *Atlantis* collected every signal out of the air and processed them before networking them to *Pacifica*.

Rhutan lay eight hundred kilometres from *Pacifica*, and all at once that seemed uncomfortably close. On the old world map, the long-submerged continent of Australia lay to the west, and Duquesne's "island citystate" occupied a just few square kilometres of what had once been wide open ocean. Distance and time were a state of mind, Russell decided. When the world situation was peaceful, eight hundred kilometres seemed a long way. When a war began to thrash like a monstrous beast, it didn't seem nearly far enough.

The pictures were in a way breathtaking, since they brought the war directly into the lives and homes of ordinary people who could scarcely imagine what a battlefield looked and sounded like. A lush tropical forest filled the background; the sky was overcast and stormy; helijets beat in toward a village of thatched houses and dropped a load of explosives. The eruption was like a scene from hell, and when the fireball cleared nothing remained. Blackened people limped down the middle of a roadway; children struggled to carry water to parents who had become crippled, distorted travesties of human beings.

"This war," said the soundtrack as Russell and Eric paused to listen and for the moment were diverted from both their work and meal, "has been impending for twenty years. The hereditary ruler of Rhutan is the Emir Potan Kap, former royalty of Cambodian/Laotian extraction. After thirty years of his regime the people of Rhutan are impoverished and desperate for change. When their neighbours in the Bal Islands moved a force of missile carriers into the nearby lagoons, the people of Rhutan believed they were about to realise their dream of freedom. If they amalgamated their tiny island with the much larger Bal Archipelago, Potan Kap would be deposed, a new commonwealth would be formed and the socialist order of the Bal Islands would be welcomed into Rhutan, all of which would remedy the poverty and sickness in Potan Kap's suffering nation.

"Their dreams were not to be. The Emir committed his enormous fortune to his struggle to retain power and fetched in a force of the Ronin, the mercenary armies that terrorise the west Pacific. Under their control, this tiny nation has learned a new kind of captivity, and privation has been replaced by simple fear."

There, the broadcast ended and Russell thumbed the remote to turn down the sound. Across the table, Eric was hushed, still intent on the screen though he was not really seeing it. He had paused with a salad roll half way to his lips, as if hypnotised by the scenes of devastation. Once, long before he and Russell were born, such sights were common, but not lately.

"They ought to get the people out," he said quietly.

"But what would you do with them?" Russell was stirring honey into his coffee. "If you're going to evacuate a huge population - God knows, there must be twenty-five thousand of them! - you've got to think about where you're going to put them, how you're going to feed them. They can't come to *Pacifica*. We're already a touch overpopulated, and we're at flat-chat with the food and power situation. Add twenty-five thousand more mouths, and we'll all starve."

"I know." Eric regarded his food critically. "We live well here. So well, we're inclined to forget that it isn't like this everywhere. Have you seen the videos from the Flinders Islands?"

"Who hasn't?" Russell demanded. "Looked like hell on earth to me, but the Aussies don't seem to notice."

"It's what you're born to." Eric patted his lips.

The Flinders Islands were fairly large, supporting a population of almost a hundred thousand, but the people were crammed into a number of towering buildings on one islet while the other islands were given over to food production. Their big problem was simple: garbage. They made a lot of it, and they never knew what to do with it. Lately, they had taken to towing it out over the deeper parts of the ocean, ballasting and sinking it. The wisdom of this was dubious, and already there were dangerous rumblings from the Zealand Archipelago, where random rubbish was beginning to wash up.

Unless the Flinders Islanders wanted a small war on their own hands, they would stop sinking their debris, and yet that was the only option they had. The Islands themselves were overworked and overpopulated; food was strictly rationed, procreation was by license only, and homosexuality was actively encouraged.

The word "homosexuality" led Russell back to Eric in a direct line of reasoning, and he regarded his companion over the bench, where they were eating lunch in a corner of the lab. No such word existed in the modern vocabulary. Strictly heterosexual values had vanished along with the old world, and Russell would have said, good riddance. Yet Eric was certainly what would once have been termed a homosexual, and it did not gladden Russell's heart to realise that in the last century, when Gerald Duquesne himself was a lad, Eric would have been fighting for equal rights in some countries, and fighting for his very life in others.

He shook off the mood and turned his attention to his food. He was eating a mix of rice, eggs and shrimps on green lettuce, washed down with nectarine juice. At his left elbow the monitor was still busy with the data of Eric's last tests, and both of them were listening intently for the sounds of an incoming jetskiff.

The lab was a comfortable clutter, just the way John Grant had always liked it. Russell had changed nothing. Just to be in here at all reminded him of his father, as if at any moment John might suddenly walk in, pull a tall stool up to the bench and return to work. His presence was everywhere, on everything, and Russell felt pleasantly haunted.

He plucked up a napkin, finished his fruit juice and pushed away his plate. Eric's eyes widened and he wore a skittish look as he licked his fingers. "You, uh, want to do it?"

"There's not much point in delaying and delaying," Russell said reasonably. "They promised us delivery some time this morning, if Charlotte Farleigh ovulates bang on time."

Eric winced visibly. "I wish you wouldn't..."

"Be so blunt? Keep talking about it? Eric!" Russell gave him a brash grin. "All we're going to get is a nitrogen flask. Charlotte's not going to waltz into the lab in person and seduce you! I promise you, hand on my heart, all that'll happen is that the courier will arrive from the *Atlantis* with something that looks a lot like a thermos flask, and there'll be a super-cooled tissue sample inside, that you won't even be able to see without the microscope."

"I know," Eric said dolefully, "I know, I know. So, you want me to ...?"

"We might as well get it done," Russell agreed. "Might as well be ready to proceed, when the delivery gets here."

"You make it sound like a delivery of milk or ice-cream!"

"Do I?" Russell laughed, shoved back his stool, circuited the bench and caught Eric's shoulders. "Chin up and be brave. You've done this about a dozen times in any case."

"But never for this reason," Eric grumbled. "Always before, it was just your Dad doing a sperm count or something." But he stood, kicked the stool out of the way, and gave Russell that familiar old pugnacious look. "Oh, all right, get it over with."

"It's not exactly as if I'm going to pull teeth," Russell said exasperatedly. He stepped into the tiny exam room off one side of the lab and held open the door.

When it had decently closed, Eric dropped his shorts and perched on the side of the bench. The tray had been waiting for him for over an hour, and Russell had begun to think he would have to bribe him somehow, like bribing a kid to eat his vegetables or take his vitamins. A cold flask, a sterile glass phial, a surgical glove, an antiseptic wipe.

Russell opened the flask, put on the glove, handed Eric the wipe and stood by, holding the phial. Both of them looked at the plaintive organ between Eric's lean, brown thighs. It had not offered to twitch yet, much less get excited enough to produce the necessary sample.

"Go on then," Russell invited.

"Go on, and do what?" Eric demanded darkly.

"Get it up," Russell said with what seriousness he could muster, while his sense of humour threatened to overtake him.

"I can't," Eric grumbled.

"First time in twenty years you've failed," Russell teased, which won him a murderous glare. He sighed, wiped the grin off his face and stepped closer. "Spread 'em, loverboy."

The command produced a suspicious look, and Eric clamped his thighs together. "Not till you tell me what for."

"Eric!" Russell protested, and since his hands were full he shoved at Eric's tight-clamped legs with his own knee. "How do you expect me to help you if you don't open up a bit?"

I ... oh." Eric relaxed, allowing Russell so move in between his legs, and a moment later he groaned low in his chest as Russell ducked his head, popped the disobedient cock into his mouth and began to suck.

"Get ready with the wipe and the phial," he suggested around his delicious mouthful. "Tell me when you're ready."

"Mmm," Eric groaned. "Not yet. Not yet. Not by a long way. Just keep going. Keep ... on ... doing what you're doing.

Russell had never been reluctant, and he was too skilled for it to take long, no matter Eric's protests. A quick but thorough swab with the antiseptic, a swift but careful placing of the phial, and Russell chuckled. "Got you!" he snorted as he removed the neck of the phial, capped it, dropped it into the flask and secured the cold seal. "There, wasn't too painful, now was it?"

"Sometimes I worry about you," Eric accused, but his eyes were glittering with reluctant good humour, as if he longed to be annoyed but could not. He caught Russell's head between his hands and gave him a gentle shake. "I just hope this isn't going to change anything."

Puzzlement knitted Russell's brow in a frown. "Again, in English, please?"

"I mean," the Aquarian elaborated, "I just hope that *this* -" he gestured at the flask "- won't change anything between us."

"A quick wank into a glass jar?" Russell said blankly.

"A baby that some poor woman's going to get impregnated with," Eric sighed. "And afterwards I'll be a father and you'll be left about two steps behind."

"Rubbish," Russell scoffed. "First, it's all for the project. Second, it's to please old Duquesne, because we owe him that much. Third, I'll be puffed up with pride to see your son or your daughter running around, the living image of you. Fourth, I don't want to have kids of my own, and even if I did there's plenty to adopt on *Pacifica* already without increasing the population, and if I was going to adopt one -"

"Russell."

"- it'd be your kid I chose to adopt," Russell finished hotly, and then stopped for breath. "What?"

"I love you," Eric said with an absurdly shy look and tone, all his former pugnacity dwindled and gone.

"Well, now." Russell looked him up and down, from his long, bony feet to his tousled hair. "The feeling's mutual." There, he paused again, and tilted an ear to the window. "Timely."

Eric gave a start, as if Russell had jabbed him with something sharp. "It's here. My gods, Russell, it's here!"

They had been waiting for the courier since dawn. A swift cross-reference with the doctors handling Charlotte Farleigh proved that the dark haired, blue eyed Aquarian girl was due to ovulate within thirty hours of Eric making his choice. All Russell had to do was be as prepared as any boy scout, which meant keeping Eric in the lab until a sample had been collected, and then haunting the lab himself until he had done the work.

He rubbed his hands together, an expression of no little glee. "Here we go at last," he told Eric. "Put your shorts on and go and get it."

"Me?" Eric froze in the act of pulling on his shocking scarlet swim trunks. "I can't go out and ... and ..."

And pick up he cold flask containing Charlotte's half of the arrangement. Because the courier would know him, and would know what was in the flask, and what it was for. The shyness was at once absurd and endearing, and Russell was both amused and charmed.

"All right, I'll go," he said soothingly. "But what will you do when Libby Weatherall gets here?"

At that, Eric cringed visibly. Libby Weatherall was the woman who was scheduled to be impregnated as the surrogate mother. Here, in this very lab, deliberately, by Russell, as soon as the delicate genetic work had been completed. She was on call, waiting for the invitation to come down from East Quay, where she lived and worked, operating an electronics repair workshop.

While Eric was still gaping like a stranded fish, Russell stepped out of the lab and waved to the courier, whose jetboat had just cruised down to a stop in the calm bay off the water purification plant.

Mike Travers was a tall, rangy man, an American with a shock of silver hair and the weather beaten face of one who had lived his whole life in the open. He had been with Duquesne since he left school, fifty years before, and he had worked with John Grant until the accident John did not survive, just fourteen months ago. The crash report had actually been logged by Travers, and even through the dense veil of his grief, Russell had been compelled to recognise the professionalism with which Travers approached the difficult problem of a fatal accident.

The cause of death was officially listed as pilot error, and although he hated to admit it, Russell knew Travers was right. John was sixty years old, he was as fit and alert as a man half that age, but he was also deeply preoccupied with his work. The autopsy revealed no alcohol or drugs in his blood, nothing amiss with his heart, yet he had made a fatal error as if his mind had wandered at a crucial phase of his landing approach. The light plane simply missed the pad and ditched in the sea, and John's neck was cleanly broken. For what it was worth, he died so quickly, he could have known nothing, and certainly he did not suffer. Mike Travers was with the recovery team that pulled the body out of the sea.

"Hey, Russell, got a special delivery for you!" Travers yelled as he brought the jetboat in on momentum, with its engines turned off. "Seems the lady obliged, right on time! Got your boy ready?"

"Done and done, Mike," Russell assured him, wondering if Eric could hear their conversation. He would be pink as a hydroponic carnation. Travers attached no importance to the work that was being done here. Artificial impregnation was much more common these days than natural conception, and eric recombination was as normal a procedure as making breakfast . But Eric was so shy of anything and everything to do with females, he was in an agony of embarrassment. Strange, Russell thought, that a man who was so sexy in the domain of male to male erotica should be so painfully shy where women were concerned. Virginity was an odd state of mind, hardly a state of body at all. One day, Russell must devote some study time to its impact on a man's thought processes, rather than his body.

The boat cruised in beside the fish farm's enormous orange floaters, which marked the tops of the nets where the bluefin and yellowfin lived and fed and grew. Travers did not tie up, but lifted the gunmetal grey cylinder of the cold flask out of the well of his vessel and handed it deliberately into Russell's care. "There you go, buddy," he said in self-satisfied tones as the container left his hands. "Just got to get you to autograph the paperwork, and I'm out of here."

"Want to stay for a coffee?" Russell gestured at the lab behind him with one elbow and scrawled his signature on the clipboard held at a convenient angle for him.

"Love to, but I can't." Travers dropped the clipboard into the footwell and as he spoke was already spinning over the wheel, which jockeyed the rudder. "Got to pick up a passenger from West Quay and take him out to the *Atlantis*. They're turning me into a bloody damn taxi service!"

Russell chuckled and stood back as he started the engines. "Then, I guess I'll see you later," he shouted over the din as the jets throttled up. Travers gave him a wave of farewell.

The boat accelerated away, leaving commotion in the fish pens. Russell watched the bluefin churn up the water for a moment, but the Wilsons were nowhere in sight. In the shed at the edge of their property, the *Poseidon* lay in her cradle, a familiar sight. She had been John's pride and joy.

He had designed her, and she was built in the sub pens aboard the *Atlantis*. He used her for observing his Aquarian subjects in depth tests, where people like Eric agreed to dive to the very limit of their endurance and then perform various tasks for the cameras. But Calder and Royce were quite correct - she was a very rugged little submersible and quite adequate to the task of a commercial salvage.

For two days now, Russell had been trying to get Calder and Royce out of his mind, but they persisted like a hangover. They were the kind of men *Pacifica* did not need or want, and yet where was the law to keep them out?

And what the devil was their salvage, what cargo could be so valuable, so secret, that they would refuse to disclose the very information that might have convinced Russell to charter out the submersible?

He was still deep in thought as he stepped back into the lab. Harvey swooped onto his shoulder, making him jump halfway out of his skin, and Eric was sitting at the desk behind the computer, intent on the screen. He snapped it off as Russell appeared, but not quickly enough to prevent Russell catching a glimpse of the image framed in the screen.

A woman. Specifically, Libby Weatherall. She was a plump, robust female with a Polynesian frame, bigger than Eric in every dimension, completely healthy, with big bones, big joints and a wide pelvis that was designed for bearing children. She had already produced three, though none of them was Aquarian, and she was only thirty years old, which made her a very safe bet. Complications should not happen.

"You, uh, got it?" Eric said nervously as he looked at Russell and the flask.

"Sure." Russell shooed him out of the way. "Look, why don't you just take the whole afternoon off? Scram! You don't want to be here while I do the work. And then, you know what I'm going to do to that woman."

His cheeks flamed. If his skin had been as fair as Russell's he would have been crimson. "I do, actually," he said awkwardly.

"Then, scoot," Russell told him. "I'll meet you later."

Eric hovered at the door. "Where?"

"Umm ..." Russell was already checking his equipment. "Well, suits you? You want to meet someplace for dinner? Anything you want, Eric, really. I know how much this is costing you, and I know you're only doing it for Duquesne.."

"I want to swim," Eric said softly, huskily.

That, Russell would have predicted. When Eric was troubled he went back to the sea as if he were returning to the womb. He had been born there, he had taken his first breath there, and it was only natural that he should return to source when he felt hemmed in by strife.

"Seahorse Grotto?" Russell asked gently. Affectionately.

"Yeah." Eric took a step closer to the door. "Moonrise is just after nine."

"Sounds good. Now, go," Russell exhorted. "I'll meet you there."

Eric flashed him a smile, self-mocking and at the same time filled with gratitude, and then he was gone. The door swung shut behind him and Harvey squawked on the shelf inside the window as he watched the Aquarian leave. Russell petted the macaw buts his eyes followed Eric as he simply slipped down into the calm, warm water beside the fish pens and was gone.

As always, watching that small marvel made Russell shiver, and his skin was still prickling as he turned his attention to his work. Before he began to complex business of manipulating the very building blocks of a new human life, he sent a message to Libby Weatherall, asking her to come in later in the afternoon for a hormone scan. Libby would be excited.

She was from the first batch of Aquarians, almost the same age as Eric, though bred from far different genetic material from the stock that had made him, but her foster-sister was six batches later, and Isabelle fascinated Russell. As little like Libby as it was possible to be, Isabelle was petit, slim and supple, in many ways like a female version of Eric. What Eric did not know was that he and Isabelle Weatherall were made of the same stuff - literally. Frozen genetic material, stored at the time of Eric's conception, had been used several years later. Eric and Isabelle were half-brother and sister, and it was odd that in this offbeat way, the Weatheralls and the Devlins should become even closer. Not that Russell would ever embarrass Eric by telling him any of this. Let Libby know, and she would attempt to smother Eric with possessive affection, and that was exactly what Eric did *not* want.

With a sigh, Russell set up his equipment, pulled on a pair of sterile surgical gloves, decontaminated the work area with a blast of raw ultra-violet light, turned on the microscope and uncapped the flask brought over by Mike Travers. Ahead of him were several hours of meticulous work, before Libby arrived. On thinking it over, Eric was better of out of the lab today.

The shadows were long, his back and eyes were throbbing slightly but he was very satisfied with his efforts when a call from he door announced the woman. She thrust her head in and looked through the office, into the lab.

"You there, Doctor Russ?"

He had just finished and was massaging the back of his neck while he savoured a cup of strong black coffee. "Come straight through, love. I'm ready for you!"

"I thought the day would never get here." Libby bustled through and without delay hoisted her awesome frame up onto the bench. She was a big woman with a Hawaiian look, strong, muscular, by no means classically beautiful, but when it was an easy pregnancy and a healthy baby one wanted, frequently the willow-thin, androgynous teenage beauty was the last female to choose.

"You're eager," he said shrewdly as he consulted the computer and checked the charts of Libby's cycle.

"Been waiting for this for months," she told him, and watched as he drew a tiny drop of blood. "Just tell me when, Doc Russ, and I'll be here."

The blood sample was passed into the machine for analysis, and Russell frowned at the screen. "Well, you're already pretty close ... we're almost there, honey. Down to the last few hours. Could hardly be better."

"Lucky for me," she said cheerfully. "So, when?"

"Tonight, according to your hormone scan," Russell read slowly off the screen. "Come in between eleven and midnight, and you'll be spot-on."

She hopped off the bench and performed something like a Maori wardance. "Tonight's the night!" Kisses smacked both his cheeks, and she was gone, still prancing as she left the lab.

"Sometimes," Russell said to the macaw, "I have the distinct impression I'm the last sane person left in this world." Harvey seemed to agree.

He made another coffee, fed the bird, and tackled a week's work that consumed the rest of the afternoon. He ate on the desk, still working, and the sun was a few minutes down when he shaved and changed into white lycra trunks and a baggy blue tee-shirt.

With the day's work complete and several hours before Libby was due back on the very crest of her hormone cycle, he dug out his rebreather and locked the office up behind him. Time to send a formal message to Duquesne in the morning, to the effect that the little matter of Eric Devlin's progeny was well in hand.

The night air was warm and balmy. Tropical Cyclone Alice had gone over the horizon without a trace, and the *Pacifica* night life was as raucous as usual. Russell headed away from the light and din, his sandal-shod feet pattering on the concrete as he headed down beyond the fish farm and out to East Quay. He strolled on to the very extremity of the long jetty, past the endless ranks of moored private craft, past the stalls selling shrimp and clams and strawberry beer, past the entertainments, such as the fortune teller and the video theatre and the massage parlour. The music, noise and people were all left behind as he reached the end of East Quay, and there, the only light filtered up from under the sea, gleaming like a beacon that called him home.

He sat on the very end of the kay with his feet in the water as he checked the rebreather and put it on. The mask covered his eyes and he took a breath as he slipped down and into the warm surface layers, and looked around for Eric. The lights were twenty feet below, where the beautiful artificial grottoes girdled the flotation chamber on which all of *Pacifica* rode. Blue-white and enticing, they called Russell down, and he worked his muscles hard for the first few metres under the surface, until the weight of the water above him overcame the natural buoyancy of his body.

The grottoes were like submerged Japanese gardens, and the exhaust ducts from the city's machinery up above warmed the water until it was like swimming in an enormous bath. Fish loved the conditions, and stretching away on scaffolds beneath the city was a whole reef, man-made, thriving in the warmth and lights. Tourists came from as far afield as Himalaya and the Snowy Islands to see this, but to *Pacifica* locals, it was their own back garden.

A tug at Russell's ankle alerted him to Eric's presence and he turned leisurely in the water, let himself be pulled down and around. Eric slid into his arms and hugged him. His eyes were wide open, his mouth was closed, and his chest was moving visibly as he breathed. No bubbles streamed from his nostrils ... he was not breathing air. Russell cupped his face in both hands and then gave him a thumbs-up sign.

Underwater, the one thing Eric could not do was talk, but he was very fluent in the language-of-hand called Amerslan, and Russell smiled behind the rebreather as Eric asked anxiously,

"Is it done?"

"Well and truly done," Russell told him. "Stop worrying! Libby Weatherall danced out of the lab. She's delighted. So will Duquesne be. It was easy. Libby'll come back late tonight, before midnight. You'll be an expectant father by morning. The only one who's been fretting about it's you!" He caught Eric, spun him around in the warm midwater, watched him laugh and hugged him.

"Swim with me," Eric invited. "I have to work in an hour. A plane load of Korean tourists just arrived, they want the gardens tour tonight."

"Good, it'll keep you out of the lab while I attend to the woman," Russell signed as he let Eric tug him down, deeper into the halo of the lights. "And I'll see you for breakfast."

"A late supper." Eric twisted and turned like a dolphin.

"Supper it is," Russell signed succinctly.

The Aquarian dove, caught him around the waist, nuzzled his nipples and was gone again, as agile as an otter. Just a little less nimble, and slightly envious, Russell followed him into the shifting lances of light, which seemed to him like shafts of moonlight striking up from the depths beneath the city.

A warm night was the best time to enjoy the grottoes, and if you were there with someone you loved, it was best of all. With a quickening of his pulse, Russell dove after him, caught him by one kicking ankle, and they turned over and over, wrestling like kids in the warm updrafts.

The Koreans would be enthralled by the Seahorse Gardens, and Russell spared the tourists a thought hours later as he let Libby into the lab and helped her up onto the exam bench. She was just plain lucky, and she knew it. The project was monitoring two dozen women, and the honours could have gone to almost any one of them. Only their hormone cycles made Libby and Charlotte unlikely conspirators. The luck of the draw. They did not even know each other socially.

"Okay, here we go," Russell said amusedly as he swung the stirrups into position. "Sperm by Eric Devlin, ovum by Charlotte Farleigh, funding by G Duquesne, design by R Grant -"

"Construction contract assigned to Weatherall Inc," Libby chuckled. "This is embarrassing. Get on with it and let me get my legs down. I must look hideous."

"Nothing I haven't seen before, sweets," Russell told her honestly. "I grew up in a genetics lab, remember."

He handled the artificial impregnation with what finesse and delicacy he could, and then propped up Libby's hips and covered her with a rug and told her to stay there, be still, for a while. She chattered endlessly, relentlessly, wanting to know anything, everything about Eric. Russell told her a few unspecific details as he watched the time, and in forty minutes she was at liberty to get up and go home. In that time he had tidied away his equipment, opened a new file and input all the pertinent data.

His eye was on the clock, also, as he thought of Eric. It was midnight when Libby climbed down off the bench, organised her clothes and kissed both his cheeks. She had tears in her eyes.

"Thank you, Doctor Russ."

"Thanking me?" he demanded, slightly bemused.

"I'm going to carry the first Aquarian offspring of two Aquarian parents," she said happily. "You just wrote me into history! My sister was hoping it would be her ... you know, actually in bed with Eric to do it naturally. But I told her, not Eric. Not that one. He's not the kind." She patted her round, chubby belly. "Isabelle is going to be green with envy! I've got one up on that little sprat at last."

Russell laughed out loud. "She fancies Eric?"

"Like you just wouldn't believe," Libby chortled. "And as I said, thanks, Doc."

Crazy people were everywhere, Russell thought as he changed the cover on the examination bench and checked the day's last messages before he shut the computer down and called his time his own.

Only one message was waiting for him, but it wiped the smile right off his face. It was from Graham Calder.

Doc Russell, need to see you. Must talk. Sure we can come to some mutually satisfactory agreement. Willing to pay any reasonable fee ... or unreasonable! Call me. I'm at the Marlin Hotel, room 776. Waiting to hear from you. Calder.

"You'll have a hell of a long wait," Russell said sourly to the computer, logged off and shut the machine down without bothering to save the message. If he ever saw Calder again, he would take a delight in personally breaking the Australian's nose, so it was better and safer if he and Graham Calder simply did not share the same airspace.

Chapter Six

The sounds of Tchaikovsky filtered out of the hifi ... which meant Eric was up. If there was anything Eric loved, it was Tchaikovsky and a large breakfast after sleeping late. The blinds were still pulled over the windows but even so the apartment was growing bright. Russell stirred as the music began, searched the bed and found the sheets still warm, and then took a deep breath and smelt something good.

Bacon? Now, where the devil had Eric come by bacon, and where had he hidden it? Pigs were unknown in *Pacifica*. Chickens and rabbits were raised over on the *Atlantis*, for eggs, meat, skins and to breed more "chooks" and bunnies, but larger animals were too difficult to feed where space was an a premium.

He sat up, filled his lungs with the aroma he had not smelt in over a year, and smiled at the sight in the kitchenette across the muddled flat. Eric hadn't bothered to dress, but he had put on an apron, presumably in case the wok sprinted hot fat onto something sensitive. From the rear, the view was superb.

"Where," Russell demanded as the Russian strains of the Tchaikovsky violin concerto swelled out of the hifi, "did you get the bacon?"

Eric grinned over his shoulder. "A Chinese freezer-trawler, three days ago. They traded for it. They took half a dozen wild lobsters for a whole kilo of mildly smoked pig."

"Wild lobsters?" Russell swung his legs out of bed as his bladder began to make itself felt.

"Wild," Eric called after him as he headed into the bathroom. "I just dived for half an hour in Seal Bay and culled a few big old grandaddy red-fellers, came back with a week's worth of breakfast and two litres of rice wine. I traded the rice wine for fresh fruit. You know, for a scientist, you're not the most observant guy in the world! The bacon's been in the refrigerator for two days."

"In the ice box?" Russell yawned deeply as he concentrated on the porcelain and a tidy stream of water. "Whereabouts in the ice box?"

"Behind the photographic developer bottles," Eric sang.

"You mean -" Russell paused to flush "- you hid it!"

"I didn't hide it, I just didn't deliberately display it," Eric argued as he slapped a bag of bread on the table, clattered down the crockery and teapot, and lifted the wok over with a couple of cloths.

Still yawning, at peace with the world, Russell shrugged into his yellow silk robe, pulled up a chair and turned on the tv, which stood on the back of the table, for a news broadcast. "You got any work on today?"

"Sad to say, I have," Eric said with mock gloom. "Got to go and count some wild tuna, get some pictures of a pod of transient orcas, and it's my turn to check the shark nets. Another day, another dollar. And before you say it, I know, that's about all we're getting paid!" He had constructed a large sandwich, and took a capacious bite. "When's your own grant going to be approved?"

"Search me," Russell said indifferently. "I'm starting to think they've lost the paperwork."

"You ought to go over to the *Atlantis* and shout till someone finds it again," Eric said sagely.

In fact, he was right. Bill Murchison had a point: Russell would indeed be living on "fish-'n-fritters" if not for the halfway decent money Eric earned. But then, if worst came to worst they could always take off in the *Tiger Shark* and manage happily as water gypsies. Russell sometimes had dreams of doing just that.

They would cruise between the artificial islands like Breakwater, Headland and Pelican Rock, and live mostly off the sea. Five years before, Eric had taken part in a study, to find out just how possible that was. For two months he had lived completely alone in the islands, with just a shortwave set in case of emergency. At the end of that time he was in prime health, well fed, though he was bored and frustrated. Russell spent the following week in a state of constant exhaustion.

Such daydreams amused Russell as he finished breakfast and watched his lover shower, shave, put on blue and white lycra swim trunks and a pair of cut-off denims, and check the computer for the morning's messages before he went to work. His expression darkened and Russell asked quietly, as he began to clear the table,

"Something wrong?"

"Not sure," Eric admitted. "There's no messages for me - there never are, I don't know why I keep checking! - but that son of bitch Graham Calder is still asking for you."

"What, again?" Russell demanded. "He was trying to get through to me most of yesterday. I just ignored him. Let's have a look at that."

Tucked in at the computer, he pressed against Eric's back, chin on his shoulder, and read off the brief message. "Got to meet, Doctor Russell. Things getting urgent. Not much time left. Need that sub and that Aquarian! Adds up to real money. Call me. Soon. Calder." He harrumphed into Eric's ear.

"He might have a point," Eric mused. "I mean, you could sure use the money."

"The hell with the money." Russell swatted Eric's backside to get him moving. "We can live quite happily without the risk. And, put you in jeopardy, in order to make a barracuda like Calder even richer? Think again!" He draped his arms over Eric's shoulders. "When do you have to go to work?"

"About fifteen minutes ago!" Eric kissed him, a little off centre of his mouth. "I've already missed my ride. Chances are, I'll have to swim it. Mind you, the exercise'll do me good. Too much good food and soft living, lately, that's my problem."

Not that Russell could notice him getting soft. Eric felt the same as always: beautiful. He released the Aquarian and spread his arms in a gesture of farewell. "Then, I'll see you tonight."

"Try and be good." Eric winked one green eye at him. "I'll bring you something for dinner. Crabs. Those big ones you like best."

He was gone then, leaving Russell smiling after him. Without him, the apartment was a little drab and decidedly empty. With a sigh, Russell dawdled through a few chores as he listened to the news on tv, tidied the clutter and began to gear his mind for the day's work.

The news broadcasts never stopped. The video feed from all over the world was continual, and the *Atlantis* cut it into coherent form and distributed it on something like a sixty minute delay, so that anyone with access to a tv was always absolutely up to date with global current affairs.

The vidfilm from Rhutan was horrific enough to stop Russell in his tracks. The Ronin mercenary force had been at work overnight, there had been another massacre. The people of Rhutan were making public, impassioned pleas for the world to come to their aid, but so far only the Commonwealth of Australian Island Republics was making sympathetic noises. A fleet of CAIR patrol boats was making deliberately slow headway toward Rhutan: their speed reflected the government's desire to reach a diplomatic settlement before the military arrived, so as to prevent shots being fired. At the knots they were making, the situation would be resolved, Russell thought bitterly. There would be nothing and no one left alive in Rhutan to fight for.

Deliberately, he turned off the set and swung down the stairs into the office. Harvey was preening in the sun by the window; the computer desk was a litter of nut shells. Russell scooped up the waste basket and brushed them in while the computer flickered to life, and he asked himself why Gerald Duquesne would be deaf to the pleas for help from Rhutan.

Surely, any "right thinking" man who was as powerful as Duquesne could not turn his back on such a situation. And yet the political aspect was a nightmare, and Russell admitted to himself, he was no politician.

Who knew what repercussions there could be if a task force arrived, even though it had been invited by the people. That could open the gates to similar actions all over the world, and it did not take much imagination to see the myriad flashfire wars that could spring up, as nations raced to fight for this or that population, and were countered by other nations with opposing views. A small war could involve a dozen countries, or a hundred. The strategists would doubtlessly project a whole world at war, and it could begin with terrifying simplicity. Russell shuddered and applied himself to his own work.

He was collating data when the phone rang. Harvey fluttered and squawked. He hated the sound of the phone, and would sometimes knock it off its battery cradle. Russell propped it in the angle of neck and shoulder and continued with his work as he said,

"Aquarian Lab, Doctor Russell, how can I help you?"

"Doctor Grant - at last!"

Damn. It was Calder. Russell gritted his teeth and put the data on hold. "I don't think we have much to discuss, Mr Calder. I haven't been answering your messages because I have nothing to say to you."

"I doubt that," Calder said drily. "I mean, what would you say to ten thousand, Aussie currency?"

Scalding water seemed to rush through Russell's veins, blinding him for an instant, and then his rationale cut in again, full force. He cleared his throat quietly and gave the lab a cynical look.

"I'd say," he told Calder with complete honesty, "it sounded pretty damn suspicious. To pay me that much for the charter of the *Poseidon* and the hire of Eric Devlin's time and talent for a few days ... your salvage must be worth half a million."

"Almost," Calder admitted. "And you can't tell me you're not interested. There's not a hell of a lot of men in this world who would turn down that kind of bread, supposing I asked 'em to kill someone."

They were talking in adjusted dollars here. Some time early in the century, the world-wide currency had all been stabilised, evened out, recalibrated, to get rid of the word "billions," which was beginning to sound like an disturbing echo on every news broadcast. People spoke in billions the way they had spoken in millions in the Twentieth Century, and in thousands in the Nineteenth. Ten thousand adjusted dollars, Aus currency, was one hell of a lot of money, and Calder was right. The majority of men would seize the opportunity to get their hands on that fortune, and what they had to do to get it was hardy important.

Yet so much about Graham Calder and Brady Royce bothered Russell deeply, and he asked himself, even as Calder teased him with the baited hook, would he live long enough to collect? Was it only paranoia when he heard a voice in the back of his skull whispering that he and Eric could do this job, whatever it was, and then end up as a pile of picked-clean bones at the bottom of the sea?

"I told you the other night, Mr Calder," he said quietly but firmly, "unless you give me a lot of hard data, I cannot and will not commit my equipment and my partner to your project. That still stands, even if you offered me *fifty* thousand. I won't put myself or Eric Devlin in danger. Now, if you're ready to talk in specific terms, we'll meet somewhere private, tonight."

For a long moment the silence over the line was deafening, and every second it continued convinced Russell more and more that his assessment of Calder and Royce was accurate. The voice whispering in the back of his mind was not paranoia but simple good sense.

When Calder spoke at last his voice was sharp, harsh, abrasive, every trace of pleasantness gone. "You're making a big mistake, Grant. You're throwing away a fortune, and you're annoying the wrong man."

"Really?" Russell's nerve endings tingled as if he had been exposed to a mild electrical current. "There's a most astonishing fact about telephones, Mr Calder."

"Like, what?" Calder snarled.

Russell chuckled deliberately. "You can't browbeat a person over the phone. It's too easy to do this."

He put the phone down sharply, and instantly turned it off. If any genuine person wanted to get in touch - or if Eric wanted to call home - they would just trot into the lab. Nowhere was far from anywhere in *Pacifica*, and Eric would just assume Harvey had knocked the phone off the cradle again, so the batteries were dead.

For some moments Russell sat frowning at it, as his stomach knotted into a clenched fist of tension. Animal sixth sense was a wonderful faculty, too often overlooked, much too often ignored. Calder had the look and sound, the *feel*, of an extremely dangerous man, and despite Russell's bravado on the phone, he knew he was definitely rubbing the wrong person up the wrong way here.

For a full minute he genuinely wondered if it would be simpler to just let Calder and Royce take the *Poseidon*, and then he scraped back his chair, blanked the computer screen and picked up his jacket. "Time," he told Harvey, "to take out a little insurance."

He hung the old sign on the door: "back in ten minutes." The truth was, it might be several hours before he got back, but few callers who would care, and if there was any important business they could leave a message with the Wilsons at the fish farm, next door.

Ten minutes later he was throwing the mooring line over onto the foredeck of the *Tiger Shark*, and old Clancy Blake was waving to him from the bait-'n-tackle stall on the jetty. The engines coughed into life and he reversed pitch on the prop blades. She pulled herself out of the parking place and he cruised slowly out along Aurealis Wharf before opened the throttle and let the boat pick up a little speed.

Right now, Eric would be twenty or thirty feet down, juggling a camera and playing tag with a bunch of wild tuna. The school would go through fast, but with food they could be bribed to stay around long enough for a quick scientific survey. Their numbers were just starting to increase, since the general ban on commercial fishing.

Several trawler fleets were still known to poach on wild tuna, but there was little or no market for it outside Japan, which had refused five years running to sign the agreement. The best tuna still came from the rich farms in the Australian Islands, and even on the capricious

Japanese market, domestically raised tuna fetched better prices than wild ... the meat was that much more oily than wild tuna, which was the way the Japanese liked it best.

Ahead of the *Tiger*, the ship swelled like a mountain range, and Russell was never unimpressed, no matter how often he saw her. The closer you got to the *Atlantis*, the more incredible she was. He thought it must be like this, hiking in Nepal with the Himalayan Range, and Everest, towering overhead. Nepal, Tibet and Assam were still far above sea level, but they were ruined by overpopulation now. Even Katmandu was so populous, if often seemed the people were shoulder to shoulder with nowhere to sit down, and the skyscraper complexes towered thousands of feet over the tiny, quaint, heritage-listed temples of a bygone age.

When Chen-Goldstein-4's tidal waves had subsided and the sea level began to rise as the pole simply melted off around the impact site, the bulk of the population of Asia just got up and walked to higher ground, and short of turning out the Ghurkha regiments to shoot them dead on the road, countries like Nepal could do little to keep out the swarming refugees. The most they could do was impose the strictest possible population controls in a desperate attempt to keep the numbers under control, before sitting-down space really was a thing of memory.

The massive radar, the earth station dish and the airport drew the eye upward, east and west as one approached the ship, but soon Russell was in alongside and the whole sky seemed to be made of pale grey steel hull plates. He cut speed as he approached the ferry terminal, just behind the drydocks and sub pens, amidships, and held the radio to his lips.

"*Tiger Shark* to *Atlantis* inbound traffic authority, I want to park, any chance of a space?"

The public service over here was excellent, far superior to anything *Pacifica* had to brag about, and a young man answered at once, "I can see you, *Tiger Shark*. Come right in, there's two free spaces right in front of Papa Alberti's, and you're welcome to one. Have a nice day."

"You too," Russell called, and let the mic fall.

The ferry terminal was a cavern in the side of the ship. In stormy weather the hull closed, flush and perfect, but on a calm day like this, when the water buses and taxis and private traffic like himself, were in and out of the *Atlantis* from morning till night, the hardest thing about coming over on business was finding somewhere to park. It would have been easier to wait for the bus, but Russell had a dislike of jostling in among a crowd of marauding shoppers and their children. When a man had had enough ice cream and papaya juice spilled down his shirt, he learned his lesson.

He cruised into the calm, dark water, and then he was over the threshold and into what seemed to be an immense building, open to the sea. To left and right were moored every manner of craft; overhead were gantries, cranes and massive lights, and beyond the parked craft were the arcades, the principal shopping centre that served the population of the ship as well as half the population of *Pacifica*, to whom a trip over to the *Atlantis* was a fine day's outing.

His berth was right in front of the pizza shop, and Russell checked the time as he tied up and took the keys out of the ignition. It was too early for lunch yet, but he could pick something up on the way out. Beside Alberti's was an exclusive tailor's, a ladies' hairdresser, a wine shop which sold the horrible local product and the incredibly expensive imported wines and spirits; two gift shops, a chandler's, and a sex shop tucked in the corner, its window filled with merchandise than never failed to draw a bigger crowd than the video cinema. Russell caught a glimpse of a box of toys that would have brought tears to the eyes of a grown man, and hurried by.

The lift took him up a dozen levels and deposited him in the cool sunny decks right under the superstructure. Vertically stacked in between the terminal and the administration level were the hydroponics farm, the Oceania State University, *Pacifica* Medical Centre, the chicken hatchery, the rabbit farm, and factories galore, where everything from spark plugs to jockey shorts were made from endlessly recycled materials.

"Russell! It's good to see you, sweetheart!"

Cynthia Longfellow's voice called from the reception desk, and he turned toward her with a smile. She was forty-five, plump and lovely, wearing a black and white chequered kaftan and far too much mock-Polynesian junk jewellery. She was old enough to be his mother, and yet Russell knew Eric was right: she fancied him. He could get his feet under Cynthia's table any day he wanted to, which was flattering ... but he had no desire to, which inspired many a sigh from Cynthia.

"What brings you over?" She reached for his hands, kissed his cheek. "Are you here to see Mr Duquesne? That must be it, right? We got your news a while ago, and it was just marvellous. I mean, Eric's done it at last! We all thought he never would. Him being - what did they used to call it? Gay, was it?"

The cataract of chatter made him smile. "Actually, it was done *in vitro*. He chose a girl, I had a surrogate mother on the books, and, uh, I did the rest. Give it a couple of weeks and we'll run some tests, make sure Libby Weatherall really is pregnant."

Cynthia beamed at him. "I know. Libby called me as soon as she got home. She was *ecstatic!* She's wanted to carry Eric's child for years. Any Aquarian child, but Eric's in particular. He's so delicious, isn't he?" She patted Russell's backside deliberately. "And you would know! Am I right, or what?"

"You're right, Cyn," he said resignedly. "There wouldn't be any chance of getting in to see Duquesne, would there?" It was a tremendous gamble, and in fact not his reason for coming over. If Cynthia could find him the odd ten minutes in Gerald Duquesne's busy day, it would be the frosting on the cake, but Russell could manage without it.

She winked a cornflower blue eye and withdrew to the desk were she worked. Keys tapped on the computer, and in moments she was beckoning him closer.

"You're in luck, Russell-boy! You're on his "in" list today."

"His what?" Russell echoed blankly.

She swivelled the screen toward him. "The people to whom he is in, if they call," she explained. "See? There you are, practically at the top of the list, right under the President of The Commonwealth of Australian Island Republics." She pointed him at the private lifts, behind the desk. They were not for public access; Russell had seldom ridden in them, and never since his father's death. "You go on up, sweetie, and I'll call ahead and let him know you're coming."

"Thanks." Russell leaned over and kissed her cheek. "You're a doll, Cyn."

She giggled, which had the effect of stripping thirty years off her age. "Bet you say that to all the girls. Or do I mean boys?"

"Both," Russell said with a deliberate leer, and stepped swiftly toward the lifts.

The car was decorated in pastel blues and greens, the walls adorned with photographic prints of the ships that had made Gerald Duquesne a dollar-billionaire, thirty years before Russell was born. His province had been oil exploration, and several rich strikes while he was till in his thirties laid the foundations for everything that was to come.

When almost no one in the world outside the scientific community was paying attention to the words "ozone depletion" and "global warming" and "cometary impact," Duquesne was listening. The *Atlantis* was in the water twenty years before Chen-Goldstein-4, and the inundation of London, Paris, Sydney and Auckland. She paid for herself on oil exploration, and it was a simple matter to convert her to a "bulk refugee carrier," while a marine architect from Hong Kong, a man they nicknamed Can-Do Chou, undertook the construction of the flotation tank and platform that would slowly morph into *Pacifica*.

From the lift, Russell stepped directly into the first of several inter-connected offices. Secretaries looked up and smiled; computers hummed, extractor fans whispered discreetly, keys pattered. Data was processed here, the past analysed, the present orchestrated, the future shaped. Art, science and technology rubbed shoulders and in many instances seemed to fuse.

Mel Keegan

As always, Russell was just a little overawed. Through the long observation windows he looked down on all of *Pacifica*, and beyond it, to the serene, blue-green horizon. Helijets roared by and a wing-in-ground-effect plane was coming in from the north, fetching another horde of goggle-eyed tourists. Beyond all of this, ten or fifteen kilometres away, were the construction barges where another flotation chamber was being finished, another platform built, to double the size of *Pacifica*.

Intent on the magnificent view, Russell was unaware of the city elder's quiet approach until a hand fell on his back, and with a soft chuckle Gerald Duquesne greeted the much younger man. Russell turned, heart quickening, and looked down into blue-grey eyes he had not seen in over a year.

"You look well, sir," he said, and meant it. Duquesne was one hundred and two years old, but he was healthy and strong. His spine was straight, his hips had all been replaced with artificial ball-and-socket units, which allowed him to walk freely; his heart was mechanical, which guaranteed its vitality, his blood pressure was low and his arteries were like those of a man half his age. He wore glasses and his hair had both greyed and dwindled, his skin was worn and deeply creased, but his health was fine, his mind was good and his voice was as strong as that of a much younger man.

"I don't see enough of you," he said as he beckoned Russell into his own office. He was in baggy white slacks and a short sleeved shirt over which he wore a cricket pullover. A pair of dumbbells stood on the corner of the desk; leaning against his swivel chair was a caddy of golf clubs. The carpet was turf-green, the ceiling was bright with full-frequency fluoros. Duquesne picked up a putter and dropped a ball at his feet, but he smiled warmly at Russell. "You finally managed to make that boy do the honours!"

"Well, not quite," Russell admitted, and launched into the explanation again. As he had expected, Duquesne was hardly satisfied with the bare facts, and Russell blushed to the ears as he found himself painted into a corner. A brief description of their love-life was his only escape route, and all he could do was treat the whole subject with clinical detachment.

"Then, he's a fertile, potent, virile ... homosexual young man," Duquesne mused as he putted the ball into the waiting cup.

"That would just about cover it, sir," Russell confirmed. "He's been my lover since we were children. He just doesn't, um, turn on to girls. Doesn't matter, does it? He chose an Aquarian woman to share chromosomes with, and we'll know soon if the surrogate mother is pregnant. Surely, sir, you wouldn't want to force Eric into a domestic situation where he would be, uh, miserable."

"Of course not!" Duquesne scoffed. "Is that why you came over here, to make yourself plain?"

Russell grinned sheepishly. "No, sir. Not even vaguely. I came over to use the computers and beg a few favours, if I may."

The old man straightened, dropped his putter back into the caddy and lowered himself into his chair. On the desk beside him, his own personal terminal was on and humming. "Well, I think I might owe you a favour or two. What's it about?" He adjusted his glasses and then regarded Russell over the tops of them. "Take a seat, my boy."

"Thanks." Russell sat, leaned both elbows on his knees, and steepled his fingers. "Two men, Australians, probably from the Flinders Islands, have been harassing me lately, wanting to hire my submersible and Eric, for a salvage. They won't disclose what their cargo is, they offered an incredibly high fee, which sounded like hush-money to me, and when I still declined because I won't budge without some good, solid data on the salvage job ... shall I say, the conversation turned nasty."

Duquesne's bushy brows rose. "I see. They threatened you? You were right to come to me, Russell. Now, you realise that it may be a little difficult to track down hard facts. Give me their names, or at least what names they're working under here, and let me see what I can do. As soon as I have something, I'll call you."

"Euro-Australian male, forty-five or fifty, name Calder, Graham.

Very, very rich, well educated. Also, Euro-Australian male, twenty-five or so, red hair, name, Royce, Brady. Dresses, acts and looks like a soldier." Russell hesitated. "A mercenary. Calder referred to him as his partner. They were in Bottoms Up the other night, and I believe they have their own transport. An aircraft - Calder said they flew in, but he didn't say what kind of plane. They're still in *Pacifica*, so they'll be easy to trace. They're at the Marlin."

"Well, we'll see if we can open their CAIR files, and find out how much of the material there will turn out to be a fabrication," Duquesne mused as his fingers tapped keys, carefully entering Russell's data into the computer. "This is enough to start with. I'll connect them to their aircraft registration, and use that to trace them to the Flinders Islands. It could take till tomorrow, Russell. Be patient."

"I'm grateful, sir." Russell stood, hands in his pockets, smiling at the old man. "It's been great seeing you. I wish I saw more of you."

Duquesne cocked his head at Russell, and wore a wry smile. "I think I'd better attend to that grant application of yours, before I slide right out of this chair on the soft soap and warm oil."

Genuine humour aroused a chuckle, and Russell withdrew to the door. "Again - I'd be grateful! But that wasn't what I meant. It really has been good seeing you. And now, let me go before I outstay my welcome. Good day, sir. I hope I'll see you again soon."

A feeling of warmth always suffused Russell when he was in Duquesne's presence. If he closed his eyes, he had the distinct impression that the man was so young, and yet time had caught him up with a vengeance. As fit and strong as he was, his days must be numbered. When his time came, Russell would mourn.

He rode the lift straight down to the public levels, and headed for the arcades. The best place in *Pacifica* to get ice cream was a kiosk, ingeniously located by the lobby of the primary school. He lined up with a bunch of hip-high six year olds, and savoured a cone as he ambled the length and breadth of the arcade, picking up a bargain here and there. A singlet on special offer; tiger-stripe posing pouch briefs that Eric would love; a box of blank disks for half price; and from the sex shop, a tube of strawberry lube that would arouse more than Eric's humour. He stuffed the whole unlikely treasure trove into a carry bag and headed for the pizza shop to eat.

Mid-afternoon was sticky with heavy humidity when he took the *Tiger* back across the bay and nudged into his reserved parking space. The sun was sinking into a mass of upcoming cloud, and according to the shortwave they were due a squall before evening, something to do with the last eddies from TC Alice.

With his mind resigned to work, Russell strolled down the wharf toward Waterfront, hands full of parcels, eyes on the Pacific gulls that drifted so effortlessly on the rising wind. He picked up his pace as he headed away from Waterfront toward the lab and left behind the wharfside crowds.

Where the single shot came from, he would never know, but a lick of white heat arrowed through his shoulder like a sliver of lightning, and the next he knew the sun-hot concrete was hard against his cheek, and pain exploded through his skull as his vision was blurred out to black.

Chapter Seven

"Careful, careful, go gently," Eric's voice murmured into his ear. "You're all right, you're going to be okay, Rusty."

The soft nonsense soothed him, but the shaft of bright, sharp pain in his shoulder brought his memory back, full force, and Russell cracked his eyes open as something very like panic kindled in the pit of his belly.

Home. He knew the feel of their bed, the scents of jasmine tea and magnolia flowers ... the touch of Eric's hands. "What -" he croaked, cleared his throat, fought for breath and began again. "What the hell happened to me?"

As he twisted his head around, he found himself looking up at Eric, who sat on the bed beside him, sponging his face and torso with a cool sponge. Eric was calm, but his face had that smudged look that betrayed worry. It was morning, the sun was slanting in beneath the matchstick blinds, which were rolled half way up, and at a glance he knew Eric had not slept.

"You were shot," the Aquarian said quietly, baldly.

For a moment the words did not make any impression on Russell, and then the full sense of what Eric had said impacted squarely between the eyes. "Shot?" he echoed, and tried to struggle up, only to find himself held down by Eric's flat palms while a hot, smarting pain burned his shoulder.

"Geoff and Jenny Wilson called me at work. They saw you go down, not far from our own door. They thought you'd stumbled at first, but you didn't get up again, and when Geoff came along to see if you'd knocked yourself out on the ground - which has been known to happen! He saw this little bugger, sticking in your back." Eric reached over to the night table, retrieved a long, thin, metal object, and placed it ceremoniously into Russell's trembling hand. "That, my old love, is called a *quarrel*. A crossbow bolt. You were shot, probably off the deck of a boat, and I think whoever did this was trying to kill you. The shooter was off by about three inches, and the range was extreme ... you can tell, because the bolt was almost spent when it hit you. You were just plain lucky. If he'd been dead on target it would still have killed you, spent or not. So much the better that the crossbow isn't exactly renowned for its accuracy over a long distance! It hit the bone of your shoulder blade, chewed a chunk out of it. Luckily for us both, it wasn't poisoned."

All of this echoed in Russell's head as he blinked at the silver-grey steel bolt and tried to make sense of the situation. The metal was smooth and heavy in his palm, filled with silent menace.

"So friend Geoff yelled for Jenny," Eric went on as he fluffed Russell's pillow and arranged him more comfortably on the bed. "She phoned for a Waterfront doctor, and when you were safe, stable, called me while they were working on you, and they sent someone out to get me. I was under, five kilometres north of here, when the call came in." He drew his fingers through his hair and puffed out his cheeks. "You gave me a scare."

Thought was beginning to coalesce as Russell's brain began to work properly again. He turned over a little, tried the shoulder and grunted. "Feels sore."

"It will, for another few hours. Doc Mercer immobilised you overnight to let the whole thing fast-heal, but the skin is only just closed. It'll be afternoon before you can start to forget about it. At least -" he leaned down and kissed Russell's forehead "- you had a good night's sleep! You haven't stirred since Mercer immobilised you."

Russell cracked an enormous yawn and stretched every part of his body with the exception of the injured shoulder. Ian Mercer had not used drugs, but electrosleep, so his system was clear, and so was his head. He had slept off most of the shock of the injury, and though he was aware of the hot, nagging discomfort of the wound, the rest of him felt fine.

Fast-heal was a miracle of modern technique, and Russell was lucky yet again. Three years ago this wound would have been healing for days, possible weeks. If he moved the shoulder a little he was sure he could almost feel the super-thin mat of inert artificial tissue that was placed into the wound, and he could certainly feel the residual bruising from several shots of the enzyme, DL5, that must have saturated the area of the gash. Mercer was right to immobilise him - so long as the patient stayed absolutely still, natural tissue regenerated almost while one watched, using the artificial mat as a bridge, and then Russell's own immune system would break up the artificial matt and dispose of it.

It was not magic, he allowed; a wound would still take a day to heal, and it would still be sore, but the chances of infection were minute. Right now, the gash was already starting to itch, a sure sign that it was healing. Russell was merely a little groggy after sleeping sixteen hours, and his belly rumbled with hunger. Eric heard that telltale sound and chuckled.

"Well, it seems you're going to live," he said drily. He slithered down on the bed, laid his hand on Russell's stomach and rubbed soothingly. "Could you eat something?"

Russell reached for him, would have bear-wrestled with him if he had been up to it. Instead, he settled for holding Eric's head and kissing his cheek, which was whisker-rough. "I could eat you, one leg at a time," he confessed.

"Could you?" Eric laid his fingertip on Russell's nose. "Would you settle for an herb omelette, toasted cheese bread and a strawberry tea?"

"That would hit the spot too," Russell decided as his gastric juices and saliva began to respond to the offer.

"Then, you stay put, and let me feed you." Eric slid off the bed and turned on the tv, which stood at the foot of it. "You were on the news last night, and again this morning. The *Atlantis* news office keeps calling, asking how you are. But the incident's officially being reported as an accident."

"An accident?" Russell's voice rose sharply. "A crossbow quarrel in the shoulder is not an accident!"

"I know," Eric mused as he swung open the fridge and took out a ceramic bowl of eggs. "But Duquesne's office has decided it'll be best not to cause panic in the street. And you'd sure as hell get panic if people got hold of the fact we have a killer, or killers, here."

"I ... oh." Russell subsided and glared at the tv. Eggs cracked on the side of the food processor. "I went to see the old man yesterday."

"I know." Eric turned on the machine, and its loud burr halted their conversation for several seconds.

"You do?" Russell inched up against the pillows.

"He called me last night," Eric said over his shoulder as he turned on the wok and drizzled a tiny drop of coconut oil into it. While it heated, he turned his back on it, propped his fists on his hips, which were clad in old, well worn jeans, and frowned at Russell. "He said you'd had another call from that Australian son of a bitch, Calder. A threatening call. You didn't tell me."

"Couldn't," Russell said mildly. "You'd already left, you'd have been under, playing tag with tuna, for an hour or more by the time Calder phoned. I'd just collated a ream of data, I was starting to think about taking a break."

The wok had started to sizzle, and Eric tipped in the eggs. "Calder was really threatening?"

"Told me I was annoying the wrong person, and I'd regret it," Russell said quietly.

"Then I don't think we have to lose any sleep wondering who did this to you," Eric observed as he stirred the eggs.

Russell rubbed his shoulder experimentally and felt the new skin move. It would be so delicate that the least stress would break it, and he wisely left it alone. Eric had not missed the small gesture, however.

"Hurts?" he asked as he bread into the toaster and plugged in the kettle.

"Itches," Russell corrected. "I was punished, wasn't I? Punished, for not co-operating."

"Maybe. Probably." Eric spooned tea from the Chinese red enamel caddy into the pot. "On the other hand, they might have been simply trying to get rid of you, so that they had a clear shot at the *Poseidon*."

The suggestion made Russell wince. He propped himself against the pillow for balance and swung his feet onto the floor. He felt almost disconnected from his nerves after so long asleep. His feet were tender and tingling as they touched the floorboards, and his balance reeled drunkenly for a moment.

Eric was there at once, steadying him as he headed for the bathroom. Eric continued to hold him by the arms while he indulged his bladder's need for relief, and then tried to guide him back to bed. Russell diverted to the table, parked his bare backside on a chair and closed his eyes while he caught his breath.

"Shall I get the doctor back here?" Eric asked worriedly as he turned off the eggs and rescued the toast.

But Russell made negative noises. "Just let me get my mind and body back in the same dimension. Feels like I'm operating my hands and feet by remote control. Been asleep too long, and you know what that does to me. I wake up grouchy."

"You do, at that," Eric agreed, relaxing once more. "How about some fresh air?"

"I'm happy right where I am," Russell grumbled.

The water splashed into the teapot and Eric scorched his fingers on the toast. Crockery clattered onto the table, and as he hunted down a missing salt shaker he heard a familiar spiel on the tv. "Ah, here it is, listen to this!" He turned the sound up and twisted the set to face Russell. File pictures accompanied the pleasant, chat-like read over:

"- in an accident last afternoon on the Aurealis Wharf. Doctor Grant is best known for his work with the Aquarian Project which has produced some of the most outstanding examples of *Pacificans*, including Eric Devlin, the first Aquarian of all, designed by Mr Duquesne and by Doctor John Grant, the late father of the current project director. Investigators have decided that a person, or persons, their identity unknown, are responsible for an accident, which resulted in the firing of a steel projectile, similar to an arrow. The piece of metal lodged in Dr Grant's back, but little damage was done, and Mr Eric Devlin, Grant's partner, reports that the doctor is progressing well. Meanwhile, born to the Skye terrier of Violet Simpson - eight healthy puppies! The litter was born under licence, sired by a terrier in the Zealand Archipelago. If you are interested in acquiring a pup, contact Miss Simpson care of the *Atlantis* office, but hurry! These little charmers will soon be gone! Congratulations to Dave Lynch, who won the gold medal at last night's chess tournament, where disorderly behaviour -"

"Domestic news," Russell grumbled, and turned his back on the set.

"Cynic." Eric turned down the sound and scraped the omelette onto two plates. "I thought it was a pretty nice little story."

"You're easily amused," Russell observed tartly.

Eric sighed. "Okay, you're in a snit. I'll shut up till you're capable of addressing me as if I'm a human being."

Silence descended like a sodden blanket. Silverwear clattered, tea poured, and Russell stewed in his own juices for several minutes before he huffed a noisy sigh and reached over the table for Eric's hand.

"I'm a bastard," he confessed. "I'm sorry."

"No need to apologise," Eric said mildly. "You're still a bit shocky. And you're right, when you oversleep you always wake up like a bear with a sore head. Remember the Christmas after you were twenty-five?"

The mere mention of that Christmas made Russell cringe. They had drunk far too much, done an inspired pub crawl from The Barnacle to Bottoms Up, down to The Captain's Table and back up to The Beach Bum, all between six in the evening and midnight. Russell was comatose till three the following afternoon, and when he woke at last he could only beg someone to be merciful enough shoot him.

"What about ..." he waved a hand vaguely at the windows. "Those men are still out there. If they wanted to kill me, they could try again."

But Eric shook his head as he poured a second cup of tea. "Duquesne doesn't think so. They've shown their hand now. The safest thing for them to do would be to drag their nasty asses right out of *Pacifica* and not come back."

"Is Security going to pick them up?" Russell was only just beginning to see the ramifications of this situation.

Once again, Eric made negative gestures. "There's no point. What evidence have they got? A wound in your shoulder, the crossbow bolt that Doc Mercer took out of it, and a single threatening phonecall that's only he-say. You've got no proof that the call ever took place, it'd be just your word against Calder's. And if Calder is every bit as rich and powerful as he looked, that night at Bottoms Up. We could start a diplomatic incident over this." He pursed his lips and regarded Russell soberly. "Duquesne won't start an incident. We need the Aus Islands. Trade, population shifting, defence. What the hell is *Pacifica*? We're like a cockle-shell bobbing around on top of a buoyancy tank, smack in the middle of the ocean! Do you ever even think about it, Russell?"

"Think about what?" Russell stretched and yawned. It felt good to force air right to the bottom of his lungs.

With one expressive hand, Eric pointed at the floor. "That ain't dry land. Down there is a flotation tank the size of the Sydney Opera House. And under that ... it's down, and down, almost two kilometres before you reach the bottom. The nearest seamount is 44687. We built Breakwater on top of it. But right underneath us, there's nothing at all."

Put like that, it was enough to arouse a shiver. Russell cleared his throat and shifted in his chair as the shoulder began to trouble him again. "None of that would bother you," he said quietly. "I sometimes think, you could just slide into the water, right outside the door there, and just ... go."

"I could." Eric reached over the table with both hands, and caught Russell's forearms. "But you couldn't, and I never, never forget that." He smiled faintly. "You let Duquesne do what's best for *Pacifica*. Right now, you're pretty safe. After they've thoroughly botched one attempt on you, they're not going to have another go. God knows, you're probably the safest man in *Pacifica* just now."

Russell was shifting around with growing discomfort, and was not surprised when Eric sighed gustily, came around the table and gently peeled off the dressing. He ouched as a couple of hairs pulled, but then sighed as the pads of Eric's finger tips delicately massaged the pink new skin.

"Oh, that good," he confessed sheepishly. "What's it look like?"

"Pink little disk, the size of a bottle cap, scarlet in the middle, smooth and shiny as a carbuncle, paling out around the edges, no ridges or lumps. You're not going to scar, beautiful. Don't worry."

The feather-light rub eased the itching and created waves of calm that reduced Russell to bonelessness. He tipped back his head, leaned against Eric's chest and breathed a deep sigh. "I'll be okay by this afternoon. Promise."

"You will be - or I'll be yelling for Mercer!" Eric kissed the crown of his head. "Want to sleep some more?"

"I just slept sixteen straight hours! Don't you have to go to work?" Russell could have snapped or snarled, but the words were more of a plaintive whimper.

"Not today. I told the boss I was staying home to take care of you, and since you've been on the tv about a dozen times, he wasn't surprised. Then, how about a bath?"

"Oh, a bath," Russell groaned.

"I'll take that as a yes!" Eric tousled his hair and stepped away toward the bathroom. "Sea salts and spruce oil, I think. Make a new man of you." He thrust his head out of the tiny, tiled cubicle. "Not that there's anything much wrong with the old one."

Five minutes later, Russell was waist-deep in the fragrant hot water, and much more at peace with humanity. He soaked till the water was tepid, ran some out and hotted it up again, and was watching his fingers turn into prunes when Eric brought him a cup of coffee.

The phone buzzed just as he took the first sip, but Eric answered it before he could speak. Russell closed his eyes, rested back against the pearl tinted porcelain and listened as Eric said,

"Oh, hello, Cynthia! No, no problem, love. He's fine. He's healing as fast as ... no, no scars. No, he can't come to the phone just now ... no! Because he's shoulder-deep in the bath!" He paused to chuckle, and listen. "Well, put him through to me, here. I'll put this on the speaker. Unless fast-heal makes you go spontaneously deaf, Rusty'll hear perfectly well. Okay?" As he paused to wait once more he looked into the bathroom. "Duquesne calling. Something about some data you wanted. It just came through the satellite. Can you hear this?"

"Should be able to," Russell said shrewdly. "Turn up the volume."

Eric adjusted the phone's volume, and a moment later a voice Russell knew so very well said, "Eric?"

"Right here, sir," Eric responded. "Russell's soaking in the bath, but he can hear you. Cynthia mentioned some data."

"Correct," Duquesne said briskly. When he was represented only by his voice, he seemed like a man of sixty, perhaps seventy years at the most. The truth was astonishing. "Assuming you can hear me, Russell -"

"He can, sir," Eric chuckled.

"Very good." Duquesne echoed his good humour. "Then, you'll be interested to know that I managed to trace your men, Graham Calder and Brady Royce, to the Republic of The Flinders Islands. They own several aircraft, including the wing-in-ground-effect plane, Australian registration code RMT275. The plane is parked at our own Kowloon Marina. Oddly enough, with binoculars, I can *see* the damned thing from here! I would say it's about fifty thousand dollars' worth of high-tech tomfoolery. Just Calder's style."

Russell and Eric shared a raised brow, and Eric asked, "You seem to know a little about Calder."

Mel Keegan

"More than a little," Duquesne agreed, "and a good deal more than I want to. Graham Richard Alexander Calder, age fifty-two, was born on Lofty Island, which of course was the highest point in the state of South Australia. Served in the CAIR Navy in his youth, jumped ship in the Solomons and chased down his original fortune, running drugs, guns, bullion and slaves to any and all markets. He's among the wealthiest Australians, but not one dollar of that money can be declared for taxation purposes, since not one cent was legally acquired. God knows where he came by most of it ... I shudder to imagine.

"Sean Patrick Brady Royce, age twenty-six, was born in the Flinders Islands, and his parents are still there, one Zealander, one American. No record of service with the CAIR military, but he seems to have been recruited by Calder at the age of twenty, and sent to Moresby for training." He paused. "Moresby has been rife with mercenaries and terrorists for half a century, and from the information I have here, Royce was trained with a crack Ronin squad who call themselves White Dragon Tong."

Something about that name stirred Russell's memory, but he was still too foggy to put his finger on it quickly. Duquesne fell silent, waiting for one of them to bite, and a moment later it was Eric who said, "Hang on a second, sir. Aren't they currently fighting in Rhutan? I'm sure I just saw them on tv inside the last few days."

"You did, and they are," Duquesne confirmed. "And my intuition is that there is some connection between their presence here, their urgent desire to charter the *Poseidon*, Russell's injury ... and the White Dragon Tong's appearance in Rhutan." He paused. "I am about to send an officer from the Customs Bureau to search Calder's aircraft from nose to tail. Calder will be furious. So furious, I hope, that he and Royce simple check out of their hotel and leave! We don't want them in *Pacifica*, and although there is actually no law I can bring to bear to move them along, I can still garrotte them with several kilometres of red tape." He chuckled. "It seems that we have received an anonymous e-mail tip-off that a large quantity of cocaine is hidden aboard that airplane."

Eric laughed out loud. "Thank you, sir. We appreciate it."

"My pleasure, Eric," Duquesne assured him. "And I must also thank you for your participation, however reluctant and evasive, in the Aquarian project."

A gorgeous blush stained Eric's bronze cheeks. "Well, it's not quite a pleasure, sir," he said awkwardly, "but we managed it. You see, I'm just ..."

"The word is, or at least was, *gay*," Duquesne said simply, and with a lot of compassion that Russell might not have expected. "It's a lovely, old fashioned term, from another era altogether more civilized than our own. I shan't bother you again, unless the surrogate pregnancy fails and we must try once more. But if we score first time - and we should - then, I'll be quite satisfied."

"Good," Eric breathed expressively. "Thanks for calling, sir. It was kind of you."

The line closed down, and as the bathwater had begun to grow tepid for the third time, Russell pulled the plug. Eric helped him stand and supported him as he clambered carefully out of the tub. He stood still as Eric towelled him down and at last, when the Aquarian was kneeling at his feet to dry his legs, he slid his hands into Eric's soft hair and cradled his skull gently. Blue-green eyes looked up at him, wide and smoke-dark, and with a rueful smile Russell felt a surge of affection, though his body was reluctant to respond.

"You *are* getting better," Eric said ruefully. "Give yourself a chance, just rest up and let yourself bounce back. You ought to be resting right now, according to Ian Mercer."

"I'll be a good boy, I promise," Russell swore, and pushed his arms into the light cotton robe Eric held for him. Then he caught Eric in as firm a hug as he could manage for a moment. "Thanks. I owe you. And I love you. You're too good for me, I know that."

"You think so? Eric leaned back and arched a brow at him. "Well, you're the expect on Aquarians, you would know."

"Expert?" Russell pondered the suggestion. "Genetically, maybe. But

I've never been - ah, shall we say, intimate with any one of them," Russell reminded him, "except you."

Eric's face creased pleasantly with a smile. "What, never?"

"You know better than to ask that." Russell cupped his lover's face between both large, strong palms. "I only ever betrayed you once, when I was nineteen."

"That wasn't a betrayal." Eric argued, and carefully embraced him. "That was an experiment. You're a scientist. It's in your nature." He licked his lips thoughtfully. "Mind, you scared crap out of me! Thought you might not come back to me."

"Which was dumb, and you're supposed to be more intelligent than that, the brains were programmed into you before cellular division began." Russell's flat hands spanked smartly, both buttocks, making Eric yelp and laugh. "You're all I need. Now, if you want to go to work, I'll be fine. This is just itching furiously now. It doesn't even smart too much."

Eric straightened the yellow cotton robe for him, and tied off the belt. "The boss gave me the whole day free, and I'll take it. Trying to get rid of me?"

"Never." Russell stretched carefully and grimaced. Eric still wore that worried look, and Russell added emphatically, "It itches! What, you think it's going to heal without itching?" He kissed Eric's throat, where the adam's apple bobbed as he swallowed. "Stop worrying and get me a cup of coffee."

The Aquarian swiped up his jeans and thrust one leg into them. "What malady did your last slave expire of?"

Chapter Eight

The growl of twin V8s reached Russell's ears as he screwed the heavy lid down onto the nitrogen tank, and he quickly set the thermostat. He knew that engine sound. He knew the "voice" of almost every boat that plied the waters around Aurealis Wharf, and that one, he would have known anywhere.

It was mid-afternoon. His shoulder still felt a little bruised and stiff but the itch had dwindled away to a mild discomfort and he was back at work after a day's rest and a night's sleep. Difficult to think that not many years ago a wound like that would have knocked him off his feet for days, perhaps even a week. Still, he had been lucky. If that arrow had been poisoned, he could have died, and he never lost sight of that.

He peeled off the surgical gloves and washed his hands as the engines drew closer. He was working with Merino ram sperms from a stud in CAIR, and the ova of a kind of hardy ewe from the Greek Highlands. The Americans had high hopes of coming up with a breed of sheep which would be able to withstand the hot, arid conditions in the California Archipelago - the crests of mountains that were all that remained of the western United States. Their problem was that the acid rain had ruined the ground long before the sea rose, and now, though the Californian highlands remained above water, the soil and vegetation were so poor, few animals could survive there. Cattle and horses died; goats, donkeys and camels did better, but perhaps the cross breed of an Australian ram and a Greek ewe would come up with an animal which would actually thrive, eat almost anything and produce wool, milk and meat for a hungry population. Almost a million people still managed to scrape a living from the island chains between the Denali Archipelago - all that remained of Alaska - and the Mexican Islands. That population made Russell's mind reel. He could hardly imagine it.

He was still drying his hands as he strode out into the afternoon sun and waved. With sure movements of one hand and a practised eye, Eric jockeyed the wheel to bring his jetskiff in alongside the ramp where the *Poseidon* was sometimes hauled out of the water for service and overhaul. Geoff and Jenny Wilson were engrossed in their work, and a bureaucrat from the Hydrographic Office had come over. A motor ketch was anchored, well out beyond the fish farm's nets. She was the *Iwo Jima*, belonging to a Japanese entrepreneur who was bargaining for a cargo of bluefin for the Tokyo market. A busy day on Aurealis Wharf.

The jetskiff nudged the concrete and Eric hopped ashore with a quick kiss, offcenter of Russell's mouth. "I thought you were working," Russell said with a gesture at the smart little yellow hull that had belonged to Eric since he was a teenager.

"I am. I'm between jobs." Eric stretched and worked his neck to and fro. "Just got finished with a mob of tourist loonies. Not my favourite occupation. I have to go over to Surfside and pick up a rack of high pressure tanks, deliver 'em to Frazer Marine. I just wondered if you'd like to come along for the ride." He waggled his brows at Russell suggestively.

Russell groaned. "Don't I wish. But I've got this bunch of impatient Californian Islanders breathing down my neck, I'm right on top of the delivery deadline, and the Americans are going to pay cash, up front. Your actual US dollars, so long as I deliver on time We need the money."

"Right. Just thought I'd ask, since I was passing." Eric hesitated and laid his hand on Russell's shoulder, over the injury. "Also, I stopped by to see how you're holding up."

"I'm fine," Russell assured him, though he appreciated the genuine concern. "It's just stiff. Feels like a bruise."

"Sure?" Eric insisted, "You're not conning me?"

In answer, Russell caught him, swung him around and hugged him. "What's that feel like?"

"Like you're fine," Eric chuckled. He swatted Russell's rump and released him. "Listen, I'll be back for dinner - and don't you dare start cooking anything. There's a shop in Surfside that does the greasiest, most lethal, artery-plugging, fantastic fritters. Pineapple, banana, coconut, mango. I'll bring back a whole heap, and some lobsters and crabs. If you can scare up some green salad and a bottle of something crisp and white and bubbly, we're in business."

"You got yourself a deal," Russell agreed at once. "See you at six?"

"Or half past, at the latest," Eric promised. He cupped his hands and called loudly, across the boat ramp. "Yey, Geoff! I'm going over the Surfside, mate! Is there anything you want me to bring back?"

But Geoff Wilson made negative gestures. "Nothing I can think of, Eric - thanks for the offer! You take care, now."

"I will, if you will," Eric shouted, before he turned back to Russell. "And you mind how you go. Take a lie down -"

"Eric, there's nothing wrong with me!"

"- and think of me, if you get my drift," Eric finished with an impish, teasing grin.

Infuriatingly, Russell felt a flush of heat around his cheekbones. "I might just do that."

Agile as a monkey, Eric hopped back over onto the skiff, which he had long ago called *Sunsprite*, and restarted the motors. Russell stood back from the water's edge as the jets began to spit, and shaded his eyes with his hands to watch the signal-flare yellow hull arc away, around the nets and off into the south.

Surfside was another artificial island, little more than a clump of rocks in the middle of the ocean. But several dozen people had staked a claim on it and were steadily expanding it, every time they could afford to bring in a cargo of boulders and gravel. It was their firm belief that the seas had stopped rising, and that if they constructed a square kilometre of dry land today, it would still be more or less dry in ten years' time. Their heraldic emblem was a god of the ancient world, Marduk, who was said to have made the land masses by piling dirt upon a mat which floated on the surface of the ocean. Russell wished them luck.

With a fond smile, he turned back to work as the Japanese businessman began to haggle with Geoff and Jenny over the market value of the bluefin. He said he could get a cheaper price in the CAIR ... they invited him to go to Aus if he wanted to, because the *Pacifica* fish were better, even if their price was higher.

Such was the business, and Russell left them to it with a wince. His father had understood economics, and Duquesne had a fine grasp of them. To Russell, it was so much boredom.

His own work engrossed him that afternoon, and as usual when he was deeply committed to a project, time rushed by. The shadows were long and the lab's daylight fluoros had come on automatically as the luxometer registered the dimness, when he realised how late it was getting. He stretched out his back, scratched absently at the healed wound, and backed up the file he was completing.

A glance at the clock showed that it was already half after five. Eric would be on his way back over from Surfside, which gave Russell just enough time to shower and shave, lay table and open the wine to breathe. *Pacifica*'s wine was pretty bad, but a few minutes' breathing time often improved it.

He turned on the hifi as he stepped into the shower. The sound of Handel and Vivaldi entertained him as he enjoyed the hot water, and then tucked a towel around his middle and dried off in the air while he attended to the table. The wine was a four year old Moselle. As the cork came out he smelt the acidity of it and made a face. Pure vinegar and sugar. Eric was right - these wines smelt as if they were brewed from socks and seaweed. You could certainly pickle cucumbers in them.

At ten past six he turned the tv on for the news, and "dressed" in the blue silk robe, a hand-me-down from an uncle who had served on freighters out of Shanghai. The robe was almost decadently luxurious, besides which, it was easy to get out of when Eric pounced. He smiled as that old shiver inched up his spine and quickened his heart.

The news amused him while he shaved ... stories of local colour and interest, from the fire at Mary Dodds's Fish Café over on Tonga Wharf, to the sighting of Pacific Right whales on the horizon ... stories of international importance, from an election in the Alaskan Islands to a top-level meeting between the Australian President and the Prime Minister of Nepal. The subject was Rhutan, and he pricked up his ears.

White Dragon Tong were getting bold, taking liberties. A Malay pirate vessel had been seen, taking on a human cargo. Women, children, young men. That meant slaves, and Russell's flesh crawled unpleasantly at the thought. Most of those people would never be heard of again. They would vanish into the air, onto private ships, the homes of men whose families had been rich before the inundation, and who continued to do business from vessels the size of ocean liners.

The Australian President, Catherine Bowman, had been formally petitioned by the people of Rhutan and neighbouring Bal, for aid, military intervention, but CAIR would not commit ships and troops without support. The Americans and Zealanders said they had too many problems at home to send aid, and before closing the file on Rhutan, President Bowman had turned to Nepal, the Solomon Islands and *Pacifica*.

She would be flying into Gerald Duquesne's sovereign territory in two days, aboard the wing-in-ground-effect Australian Airforce One, and if she could convince Duquesne that the joint effort was worth the involvement of *Pacifica*'s obviously limited resources, the "show" would be on. Russell's flesh crawled again, and he found it was an unpleasant sensation.

It would be the first time *Pacifica* had sent troops into any war zone. The first time in its fifty year history that it had stood up as a nation, and really been respected as one. Not so very long in the past, Duquesne had been dismissed by the public, the government and the scientific community alike as a crackpot doomsayer, a catastrophist ... then the climate warmed through two degrees in ten years, and Chen-Goldstein-4 hurtled in from space at the termination of a thousand-year orbit that had rendered her invisible and unpredictable until the last few months before she arrived. And everything changed.

Those were days Russell could scarcely imagine. All at once, the seas rose, armies of refugees took to the roads, food prices were absurd, and "fresh water" was a contradiction in terms. Looting tore the community apart, and the sky was grey with smoke as people fought for what was left. Murder for a bag of rice was common; prostitution was survival, and the price of sex was most often a meal. In five years, the immune disease that was the plague of the late Twentieth Century ran wild, unchecked.

Like any two horsemen of the Apocalypse, famine and plague rampaged through the population, scythed through every nation like the grimmest of reapers. Times were, Russell had read, when the hardest task facing people was the disposal of the dead. As land area diminished people crowded together in the uplands. All low-lying ground was gone, crops were destroyed, there was nowhere to bury the dead, and nothing burnable to cremate them with. And still men and women continued to procreate without thought, though their offspring were filled with congential disease.

They were on a treadmill to disaster, and they could not get off it. Most historical analysts agreed that "the road to ruin" began in the Nineteenth Century, and could be traced to one single invention of Man, which changed the face of the world and, ultimately, destroyed it. The steam powered locomotive. The day the first locomotive went into commercial service, the atmospheric saturation of greenhouse gasses began, the systematic destruction of forests vastly accelerated, and in the following century, riverboats and railroads made possible the large-scale human colonisation of areas that would otherwise be impossible. The global population boomed - which only added up to more railroads and logging, mines and factories. More atmospheric pollutants. The runaway cycle had begun, and in many parts of the world the treadmill was still turning.

As the pictures from Rhutan appeared Russell sat down to watch. The Rhutanese were fighting back, and they were getting weapons. Russia and Tibet were supplying them, via Nepal, and they were giving good account of themselves, but they were not professional soldiers. For every offensive they won, they lost another two. Hunger and the lack of medical care were taking a cruel toll, but not as cruel as the contaminated drinking water and the constant Ronin bombing. Helijets beat in from offshore carriers every few hours, and the billows of gasoline yellow were dreadful to behold. Napalm, fuel-air explosives..

The face of the newsreader betrayed the feeling in *Pacifica*. She was hardened, seasoned, but even she was hushed as the story wound up, and switched swiftly to the weather report. As it came on, Russell became aware of the time once more. It was past six-thirty, where the hell was Eric?

He stood at the window for ten minutes, watching the sea and listening for the sound of the engines that would announce the *Sunsprite*, but by six-fifty there was still no sign of him, and with a sigh Russell made himself a snack. He filled a crusty roll with garlic butter and bean sprouts, and shoved the cork back into the wine to save it.

By seven-fifteen he was really starting to worry. The jetskiff could have broken down. Eric could have gone to the assistance of some other vessel in distress. He could have taken ill over on Surfside.

Or someone could have taken a pot-shot at him, just as they had shot at Russell, and come damned close.

Palms sweating, he swung downstairs to the office, tuned the shortwave and called, "Aurealis Base to *Sunsprite* Mobile. Come on, Eric, where the hell are you? Project Aquarian Office calling Eric Devlin. Eric Devlin, please respond."

Nothing. He called repeatedly over the space of ten minutes, and by the end of that time his heart was thudding painfully. Licking his lips, he picked up the phone, and for a moment fought his wayward mind, which blanked out when he needed it most. What the hell was the name of that place over on Surfside that made greasiest, most delicious fruit fritters in *Pacifica*? Damn!

Hit The Spot - that was it. He turned up the monitor and patched into the phone list. 06-144. Right. He punched numbers with fingers which felt oddly thick, and leaned impatiently against the side of the bench until a man's voice at the other end said, "Hit The Spot, d'you want pick-up or delivery?"

"Neither," Russell said quickly. "My name's Russell Grant, I'm trying to find Eric Devlin. Do you know him? He should have been in your shop about an hour ago."

A pause, and then the man responded in some kind of Aus or Zealand accent, "Uh, yeah, I know Eric. But I didn't serve him. Hang on a sec." The phone clicked, and his voice yelled at someone far off, "Oi, Mario! D'you know a bloke called Eric Devlin?"

In the distance Russell heard a bass voice say, "If you mean the Aquarian kid, yeah, I know him. What about him?"

"Has he been in today?"

"Not today. What's the problem?"

"Dunno. I've got Doc Russell on the blower here, trying to find him." The phone clicked and crackled again, and Russell was groaning as his informant said, "You there, Doc? You struck out. Mario's been in the shop since noon. If Devlin'd been in, he'd remember."

"Thanks," Russell said quietly. He hung up and stood staring at the phone for a moment while his belly clenched like a fist.

He broadcast over the shortwave for ten more minutes, but Eric was either deliberately not answering - which was ridiculous - or unable to answer. He might be too busy, the shortwave on the boat might be on the fritz, he might he out of earshot of it. Russell might be panicking for nothing.

Maybe.

He took the stairs two at a time and dressed quickly in jeans, deck shoes, a cotton shirt. On his way out, just to cover all bases, he tried the radio again, was rewarded by nothing but a burst of static, and then he called the *Atlantis*, the traffic office.

The voice answering belonged to a kid, probably someone just out of school, getting experience in the boredom of minding the office and watching the monitors. "Can you raise the *Sunsprite*?" he asked breathlessly as he shrugged into his jacket. "I'm trying to call Eric Devlin, he's not answering and he's overdue at home."

"One moment, sir," she sang, and he held the line while the kid used the much more powerful transmission gear on the ship. Maybe Eric was so far away that he was out of range of Russell's shortwave. But, why in the world would he go so far? Could he be helping someone in distress?

Then: "No answer, sir. Do you wish me to institute a search for the missing vessel?"

A full scale search involved helijets, powerboats, fifty or a hundred men and women headed to every point of the compass. The cost was appalling, and Russell cringed physically. "Not yet," he said carefully, "but you could put out an APB, ask any other vessels in the vicinity of Surfside to keep an eye out for a yellow jetskiff, registration 68549D. I'll go over to Surfside myself, right now, ask around, see if he made it there. If he didn't ... well, that was where he was going, in a straight line, when he left Aurealis Wharf, so if there's no sign of him we know where to start looking."

"Very good, sir," the girl agreed. "I'll log it in, just as you gave it to me, and I'll be waiting for your call. If you do find him, call anyway, and I'll broadcast to all vessels that the *Sunsprite* has turned up, and if you don't call, I'll jumpstart the Rescue Response squad."

"Thanks, I appreciate it. Out," Russell said breathlessly.

He snatched up his wallet and keys and was out of the building while Harvey was still screeching from the top of the filing cabinet. His shoulder was forgotten as he jogged to the marina by Waterfront, where the *Tiger Shark* was parked. It was late now; the sun was down, the ocean was silvery, the sky a deep mauve, and overhead the stars of summer were bright. *Crux Australis* was medium-low in the south, Orion was at mid-sky in the north. Moonrise tonight would be nine-twenty, and the evening tide had just begun to fall as he took the powerboat out of *Pacifica*'s inshore waters.

The lights and music, laughter and gaiety of the Waterfront community fell away behind, and Russell held rarely felt so alone as he spun the wheel over, checked the chart for a heading and opened the throttles. He kicked in the floodlights and watched the sea, visually scanning the wave crests for a drifting boat ... a drifting body. If the *Sunsprite* had struck something and gone down, Eric could be unconscious. Not that he could possibly drown, but he could be concussed, and it was a damned long swim home, even for one as strong as Eric. And predators were hardly unknown in these waters. Eric might decide to rest on the surface, just float there where his natural buoyancy would let him get some sleep, as if he was in a feather bed. His Aquarian skin would protect him from the cold and water saturation of his tissues, and he could lie face-down and breathe the warm surface water if that was more comfortable. The only problem was that he was outside the range of the shark repellers, and as much at risk as any other living thing. The bronze whalers, grey nurses and white pointers regularly came ravaging and scavenging, and Russell could not allow himself to consider the consequences.

Twenty minutes after he put *Pacifica* behind him, he saw the bright lights of Surfside and cut speed. He let the *Tiger* idle along while he used the shortwave, calling repeatedly, both Eric's name and the radio callsign of the skiff. Still, nothing. With a dry mouth he changed channels and called again.

"*Tiger Shark* to Surfside harbour office."

"Surfside, go ahead."

At least someone was monitoring the radio, which was a relief. Some of the outlying "reef daddies" were known to be far less than efficient. They could be stoned and totally oblivious to a tsunami bearing down on them. Russell held down the transmit button and lifted the mic to his lips. "I'm looking for a man called Eric Devlin. He was heading for Surfside this afternoon in yellow jetskiff called *Sunsprite*. He didn't make it home. Have you seen him?"

"One moment, *Tiger Shark*, I'll check the sightings and radio log. Someone might have seen him."

While he was talking, Russell had taken the powerboat close inshore, and as he waited for the officer to run his check, he nudged the *Tiger* in alongside the concrete jetty and tied on to a heavy plastic ring. "Harbour office, are you there?"

"Yeah, hold your water, *Tiger*, we're looking!"

"Then, *you* hang on. I've just tied up, I'll come into the office," Russell snapped, and threw down the mic.

He vaulted over onto the jetty and reminded himself that this was genuine dry land beneath his feet. Surfside was the top of Seamount 66978, an extinct volcano which, if it had been above the surface, would have been twice the height of Everest.

The smell of frying onions made his nose prickle as he jogged along toward the harbour captain's office. Yellow light spilled out through the half-blinded windows and the open door, and as he knocked and thrust his head inside he saw a muddled shed, a bank of flickering screens and two harassed young people in charge of the machines.

The boy was tall, lanky, and bearded, as if he hoped the whiskers gave him a little more authority. The girl was twenty, skinny as a broomshank, with large bare feet, an ebony tan and white blond hair. Both were dressed in slacks and tee shirts that carried the gaudy Surfside emblem.

"Any joy?" Russell asked as he slipped inside and closed the door, which shut out the restless sound of the sea.

"Not so far," the boy told him. "He certainly didn't log in by radio with this office."

"Then again, why would he?" Russell mused. "He was only coming over here to pick up a rack of tanks and something for dinner."

The girl blinked at him. "Have you tried the place where he was going to pick up the tanks?"

"Couldn't." Russell shoved his hands into his pockets. "He didn't tell me where they were, and I'm not familiar enough with Surfside to guess. Any ideas?"

The boy brightened. His name, Matt Bryant, was stencilled on his shoulder patch. "That's going to be one of two places. There's only Fast Eddy's, which is the service station, and Dive Deeper, which is the dive store on the boulevard."

Russell cast a glance at the clock. "They'll be closed."

"The dive shop will be, but Fast Eddy's is open all night," the blond girl told him. "It's on the east side."

"Okay." Russell rubbed his hands together. "Gives me one chance in two of tracking him down. Look, I'll trot over there and see if anyone did business with him. You keep looking at your records. Good God, someone must have seen him - that skiff is the colour of a bloody emergency flare!"

The night air was warm as soup but the wind was starting to get up. The sea sounded uneasy as Russell turned out of the harbour office. His rubber-soled feet were quiet on the concrete as he followed his ears and his nose in the direction of people.

The population of Surfside was officially eighty-five, but you could always double that with visitors. A couple of boats were in, a Chinese fishing junk, a ketch from Zealand, and an Australian pleasurecraft, the sort of rich man's toy which bummed around the islands, probably smuggling drugs. It was difficult to keep track of them and impossible to stop them, and most authorities found it easier to turn a blind eye unless a "bad batch" showed up, or violence broke out.

The tavern, Ma Bailey's, was doing a decent trade. Surfside brewed its own beer, and popular lore was that it was better than the "swill" made over in *Pacifica*. Russell might have stopped for a schooner, but even though his mouth was dry his sense of urgency would not let him pause.

The boulevard was the small town's single main street, stretching from one side of the islet to the other. The trees were starting to grow in, the buildings had a lived-in look, and in another ten or twenty years Surfside might be a nice place to live. He saw Hit The Spot, just back from the beachfront, smelt the aromas of frying onions, fish and fritters. Two blocks along was Dive Deeper: the lights were off, the shop was deserted for the night.

He licked his lips and picked up his pace as he crossed over into the shade of the coconut palms and mango trees. Fast Eddy's lay right on the beach, flanked by boathouses and ramps, and the dredge was anchored nearby. Eddy had to keep a decent channel cut out to let the fuel tankers dock. His bowsers were just inside the open workshop door, and from within Russell heard the *rapraprap* of power tools.

Fluoros made Eddy's skin look like purple sausage. He was fifty but looked much older, and his body seemed to have sagged southwards in recent years. His head was balding, his belly swelling, but despite all this he was the best mechanic Russell knew, and a decent man. He was in oil-stained overalls, rope sandals and leather gloves, intent on an oxy-welding set that seemed to be giving trouble. To one side was an enormous compressor and a rack of tanks of all shapes and sizes. At the sight of them Russell took a breath and crossed his fingers.

"Hey, Eddy!" he called. "How's things?"

The mechanic dropped his gear with a grunt of disgust, wiped his hands on the seat of his overalls and turned toward Russell with a grin of welcome. "Long time since I seen you, Rusty," he said in that broad Magnetic Island accent. "And I don't think I never saw both of yous in the same day!"

Jackpot. Russell's heart skipped and fresh sweat prickled his sides. "What time was Eric here?"

Eddy's brow creased like corrugated iron, and he scratched his balding dome. "Musta been about three or four this arvo. Whassa problem?"

"He didn't make it back home," Russell said tersely.

"Oh, yeah?" Eddy's face cracked in a ribald grin. "Ah, stop worrying. He probably met a pretty little mermaid."

"You mean, he was swimming?" Russell gestured at the sea, which broke just below the boat ramps, not forty feet away.

"Sure was." Eddy shrugged. "S'what Eric's all about, I didn't think nothing of it. Said he was just gunna cool off while I filled his tanks. Was godawful hot. Always is round here. This place don't get no wind, see."

"Then he must have tied up the skiff, so you could put the tanks aboard," Russell said hopefully.

"Course." Eddy cocked his head at him. "You're really worried, Rusty?"

"Spitless," Russell confessed. "I tried the harbour office, but he didn't call in. I also tried Hit The Spot, where he was going to pick us up some dinner, but he never made it there. That means he either changed his mind about dinner after he picked up the tanks, and shot straight out of Surfside, or ..." he paused and shook his head. "What time did he pick up the tanks?"

"I reckon it must'a been about fourish," Eddy guessed. "I asked him to shift the skiff cuz I had a tanker coming to gimme a fill of high-test, and I needed all the space I could get. Last I saw o' your Eric, he'd anchored just yonder, under the point, to lash down his tank rack while the oiler pulled in. There was another boat, come up alongside. Big, blue schooner, gorgeous thing. Couple of blokes started talking to him, but I didn't hear nothing they said, s'too far off."

A nerve in the pit of Russell's stomach came alive, like a jolt of electricity. "Did you see them? The men on the schooner?"

"Sure did." Eddy chewed his lip. "Never seen em round Surfside before, but. Total strangers to me. Then again, so's half of *Pacifica*."

"Did you get the name of the vessel?"

"Nah. The transom was seaward, all I seen was the bow, and, uh, truth is, my eyes aren't what they were."

Russell choked off a groan. "Okay, then can you describe the men ... or couldn't you see them well enough, either?"

Eddy pouted as he thought back. "I don't see details, over a distance, like, I couldn't read no name on a transom. But I do see colours. One bloke was dressed in light blue, and he was blond. Long, long, blond hair. I thought it was a sheila at first, till he moved about. Wore his hair in a pony tail. The other bloke was dressed in black, and he had the brightest carrot-red hair I ever seen." He paused. "Rusty, you look like you just seen a ghost."

In fact, Russell's pulse was racing. "Jesus Christ," he whispered. "Okay, Eddy, what happened then?"

"Not a lot," Eddy muttered as he grew concerned. "Eric shoved off, that way." He jerked his thumb in the direction of the boulevard. "I figured he'd probably tie up and get a pie and beer before he left. S'the last I seen of him."

A cold, creeping intuition congealed Russell's bone marrow. He touched Eddy's shoulder and without a word stepped out of the workshop. Eddy called after him, but he did not hear the words as he picked up his pace, first to a brisk walk and then to a flat-out run.

Lights glittered along the marina, where twenty boats of all descriptions were tied up. At the end, aboard a motor yawl, a party was in progress. Russell heard roars of laughter, the bellow of a hifi, the sound of breaking glass. At the root of the jetty he paused to catch his breath and scanned every boat individually.

And there, forlorn, abandoned without even its running lights turned on, was the bright yellow jetskiff, *Sunsprite*. Heart in his mouth, Russell ran once more, and just short of the boat he called Eric's name. But not for a moment did he expect Eric to answer. The skiff was well tied up, expertly secured, and as he stepped over into the well the first thing Russell checked was the ignition.

The keys were still in it. And that was something Eric would never do. If you left the keys in the ignition, the next time you looked there would be a large empty space where your boat should be. Kids made off with fast, powerful boats all the time. There was not much fun or wildness to be had in *Pacifica*, and joyriding in someone else's boat was a unique thrill. You didn't have to worry about wrecking the motors or stripping the keel.

Deliberately, Russell slipped out the keys, pocketed them, and cast about for any sign of Eric. The lights from the boat party cast a pale blue-grey illumination that augmented the moonlight, and it was enough to see by, since his eyes had accustomed themselves to the darkness.

Down in the footwell was a square of dark-on-dark, and before he picked it up he knew what it was. Eric's wallet. He opened it, by touch found a handful of dollars in *Pacifica* scrip, plus Eric's ID card, his boat licence, registration and insurance, his licence to handle high pressure tanks, his certification to babysit amateur divers with helium and argon breathing mixes, and his ATM card, which he never used anyway, because he was always paid in cash.

Russell sank down onto the side of the boat and wiped both hands over his sweating face. A big, blue schooner. A man with long, blond hair, another man with bright red hair. Eric tied up here minutes later ... and vanished.

"Oh, Jesus, Jesus, no," he whispered to himself, over and over, as a feeling of impotence curdled his belly.

He was so trussed up in painful thoughts, he did not hear the soft patter of bare feet on the jetty, and the boy's voice took him by surprise. "You okay, mister?"

He spun, halfway to his feet in a moment of blind panic, and found himself looking at a skinny nine year old in swim trunks and a too-short tee-shirt that displayed his concave little belly. "You live around here?" Russell asked hoarsely.

The little boy pointed at the shrimp trawler on the other side of the jetty. "I just live there. What's wrong, mister? D'you want me to go fetch my Mom?"

"I'm ... looking for my friend," Russell said dully. "I can't find him, and I'm very worried. He didn't come home this evening, and I think something bad's happened to him."

The little boy whistled. "Nothing like that ever happens in Surfie. You sure he was here?"

Russell patted the side of the skiff. "This is his boat. He came over to get some tanks. See that rack? There they are. Fast Eddy filled them up for him. And now he's gone."

"A guy with wavy, shiny hair, looks like an Aquarian?" the boy asked shrewdly.

"You saw him?" Now Russell could barely speak. He stepped over onto the jetty and knelt on one knee beside the kid, took the thin shoulders between his hands and tried not to grip. "When did you see him?"

"When he tied her up. There was another boat, too," the boy said, puzzled. "Your friends was having a big argument with these other two guys. I thought they were going to start fighting! Never seen a real fight. Only on tv. Anyway, one of them took something out of his pocket, I didn't see what, but the Aquarian one just shut up, real quick."

Gun. Russell swallowed his heart. "Can you describe the men from the other boat?"

"Blond one with a pony tail, and the other had his hair like a red brush on top." The boy patted his skull. "Looked real weird. Cool. Mom'd kill me if I got my hair cut like that."

"And what about their boat? You saw that too?" Russell was only going through the motions now.

"Ah' she's a beauty," the boy said wistfully. "Schooner. Blue, like an electric flash. What's wrong, mister?"

"Tell me what happened next, after the man took something out of his pocket and my friend shut up," Russell whispered.

The boy's face puckered and he shrugged his skinny shoulders. "They all got on the schooner and she upped anchor and shoved off, on her motors, cuz there was no wind."

That was the last thing Russell had wanted to hear, the words he had been most afraid of. He straightened and touched the kid's cheek. "Thanks. I owe you one." He drew a few notes out of his back pocket and pressed them into the boy's hand. "You shoot off and buy yourself some ice cream or a vidgame. You've earned it."

Teeth shone in the moonlight. "Hey, cool!"

The last Russell saw of him was an impish little figure darting away toward the boulevard. He closed his eyes for a moment, summoning his wits, and then double checked the skiff's mooring lines and fell into a fast, steady lope, back toward the harbour office where he had left the *Tiger Shark*. In this game he was probably due one break, and he had just had it. The rest, he knew already, would be down to sweat and blood.

Chapter Nine

The schooner *Queen Katherine* was making good time on a heading almost due north from *Pacifica*.

His natural sense of direction, his feeling for the run of the tides and the weather, his ability to read the way clouds massed on the horizon and the weather surged around various seamounts, told Eric Devlin almost exactly where he was, though he had not been permitted to see either a map or the navigation deck. He did not need to see them. He knew to the last kilometre where the schooner was situated, and he had a fair idea of where she was going. The only thing he did not know was, why.

The sight of a gun in Brady Royce's hand would have quelled anyone. The man's eyes were hard and sharp as gimlets, and not for a second did Eric doubt he would use the weapon. The conversation had begun as a perfectly reasonably business offer, while he was stacking the tanks, lashing them down for safety before he got the *Sunsprite* underway. The first he knew of the schooner's presence was the disturbance in the water as she came alongside, but even then it was pleasant. Graham Calder had worn an enormous smile and lobbed a can of beer across to him.

It was Fosters, real beer, not the stuff *Pacifica* had the nerve to call beer. Eric was pleased to accept it, but in so doing he invited Calder to strike up a conversation. According to Calder, Russell Grant was being an idiot, 'passing up the chance of a lifetime.' Was Eric aware how much money he had been offered? And since Russell was terminally insane, what would the Aquarian say to five grand in CAIR dollars?

"So tell me what the salvage is," Eric challenged. And Calder clammed up tight. With more patience than the man was actually due, Eric explained in considerable detail the dangers of a salvage dive. The Aquarian did not have to worry about depths and pressures and breathing mixes, it was true. While 'normal' divers would have to start planning to breathe heliox, argon and neon mixes as they progressed to greater and greater depth, the Aquarian breathed water itself. It filled his lungs and his body enjoyed ambient pressures.

He never had to worry about nitrogen being compressed in his blood, requiring decompression staging on the way back to the surface. He swam to great depths, just the way Orcas, dolphins and any marine mammal swam, and came up just as quickly. But Eric was different from the dolphins in one key area: his lungs were filled with water, he *breathed* water, while whales and dolphins breathed air.

Yet Eric was not without his own problems at those depths. When he left the warm surface waters, the fine layer of fat he wore between skin and muscle was insufficient to keep him warm for very long. In the intense cold, more than thirty metres down, he suffered hypothermia like any human, who did not have a marine mammal's body mass to hold in heat. Also, when the light levels fell he was blind in the darkness, and those were the depths where any salvage proposition got dangerous. Numb and clumsy with cold, night-blind in the deeps, he could be even more prone to accident than a regular, professional commercial diver, who was much warmer in a wet- or drysuit, and equipped with lights and machinery.

"Hey, kid," Calder promised with a vast, beatific smile, "trust me!"

Trust him? Eric would as soon trust a spitting cobra, and as he tossed back the empty Fosters can, he said so. He would not dive without a whole dossier filled with every detail about the job. It was his life that was at stake, not just a cargo. Calder's mouth compressed, and a moment later Eric started his motors and pulled the *Sunsprite* out fast. On his mind was a snack at Hit The Spot while he waited for the food to cook; then he would drop the fruit fritters into a thermos box and head fast for home. A quick stop at the Frazer Marine shed to leave the tanks, and then back to Aurealis Wharf, no further delays.

Best laid plans. He jockeyed the jetskiff over and tied up at the jetty, just across from the end of the boulevard, and when he looked up again, there was the *Queen Katherine*. Calder was determined, and from the look on Brady Royce's face, the Flinders Islander was in a mood as bitter as an Antarctic winter.

Eric glanced around, noted with some satisfaction that he had plenty of witnesses, and in a loud voice that would carry clear across the water from the boat party to the prawn trawler, he told Calder and Royce to shove off and stay well away from him, or he'd call *Atlantis* Security and let them thrash it out.

Looking into the muzzle of a gun was the last thing he had imagined, and he kicked himself hard, because he knew he should have expected it. Still, it took him by surprise and the words died on his tongue as Royce produced the old Webley automatic. Ten minutes later, he was in the schooner's opulent forward lounge, and her diesels were growling like the voice of a big animal, taking her out on a northerly heading.

He had one ace up his sleeve, which Calder and Royce knew nothing about. Russell was expecting him by six or six-thirty, and when he did not show up, Eric would be posted as missing inside of an hour. That was the straw to which he clung as he was hustled into the lounge and thrust down onto the deeply padded couch under the side windows.

Calder held the gun on him every moment while the schooner got underway, and a Malaysian girl brought coffee, brandy, biscuits and croissants. She was a pretty little thing, about twelve years old, almond eyed, honey skinned. And she was a slave. They had dyed her hair blond, tattooed her neck and shoulders with dragons and eagles, and she wore a lot of silver body-jewellery in piercings that seemed to have been well done. But all these were signs of ownership, and despite the girl's attractiveness and obvious good health, she was just as obviously this boat's slave. Eric felt a surge of pity for her as she served him coffee and a brandy, and then she knelt at Calder's feet to wait for further orders.

Dusk was falling fast, and twilight thickened into night proper while the schooner put *Pacifica* over the horizon behind her and kept going. Calder helped himself to coffee and brandy and sat in the chair opposite. He crossed his long legs, balanced the gun on one knee and regarded Eric soberly.

"You're a fool," he said flatly.

"I'm starting to wake up to that," Eric said quietly. "And I expect to die for it."

Calder's brows arched. "Do you, now?"

"You'll kill me when I've finished the salvage," Eric whispered.

But Calder shook his head slowly. "I have no intentions of killing you. You're very nearly as valuable to me as the goods you're going to retrieve. I have a market for you too, Devlin, a very lucrative one."

"Like her?" Eric gestured at the girl.

But once more, Calder made negative gestures. "You're quite pretty enough for that kind of sale, but no. I've offered you to a laboratory in the Californian Islands. They've been reading about Aquarians for decades, and have longed to get their hands on one. There's a geneticist in the Republic of Catalina who placed a standing order with me for the first Aquarian I could get."

"All they had to do was ask, they'd have been given the data," Eric said tersely. "We share data with labs right around the world."

"But it's not data they want." Calder smiled. "Nor is it sperm and ova, or a set of genetic samples, so that they can breed their own Aquarian, who won't be a man for twenty years. They want a *fully grown* test subject right now. And I do mean *test*, if you take my meaning."

"Oh, I take your meaning," Eric said sourly. "They want to run a breeding program on one side, and on the other, have an adult subject to destruction-test. Like a machine."

The Australian shrugged unconcernedly. "We're all of us machines, Devlin. It's just that we lubricate our circuits with blood, not three-in-one oil."

The observation took Eric by surprise. "That's an interesting philosophy. You really think of living creatures, and human beings as machines?"

"Biological mechanisms." Calder threaded the fingers of his left hand into the thick, black hair of the girl at his feet. "Oh yes, I do. And can I take it you'll be co-operative?"

"Give me a single reason why I should?" Eric demanded. "Why should I help you, since the only reward I've got waiting for me is a vivisection lab! Go to hell, Calder!"

In answer, as if he had been expecting Eric's response, Calder adjusted the angle of the gun and drew a new aim, on the girl's frail little body. "Like most men, I imagine you fancy yourself a knight in shining armour. As you can see, this little *mechanism* is no more than a child. No one in the world would miss her if she were dead, because no one off this boat even knows she's alive. Her family were all killed by the Malay pirate crew that overran their fishing boat, she was the sole survivor.

"But *you* know she's live, Devlin. And you'll know that if you don't give this salvage your fullest co-operation, I'm going to put a bullet in this little darlin', somewhere very painful, though not fatal. If you screw me around longer than another hour, I'll put another bullet in her. And then another. You'd be surprised, Devlin, how much punishment a person can take. And if she suffers, and how much she suffers, is all down to you. Every pang she feels is your responsibility." He smiled broadly, an expression filled with raw challenge. Eric had not seen the hunting jaguar in Calder before this moment, but the fangs were bare now. Calder's nostrils were flared with the hunt, and he was loving it. "Now, tell me, Devlin. What do you say?"

Eric could think of any number of things to say, most of them unrepeatable in polite company. He looked down into the face of the child.

Either she did not speak English or she was merely resigned. Her eyes were vast, solemn, seeming very old in so young a face. Eric sat back, closed his own eyes and said nothing at all.

Dinner was served at eight, and absurdly he was invited to the table to dine with his hosts. Not that he was treated quite like an honoured guest: an armed guard, a big Chinese with a build like a heavyweight wrestler, stood right behind his chair. Eric thought the man could have wishboned him with one hand, and not even know he had done it.

Across the table, Calder and Royce savoured buffalo steak and vegetables in a light, spicy sauce while music Eric did not recognise played discreetly. Calder watched him like a hawk, and when the dessert of almond rice was served he said,

"The water is one hundred and fifty metres deep. Problem?"

"Maybe." Eric patted his lips. "I'm an Aquarian, not a seal. It's bloody cold that far down. If I can go down and then come straight up, I can manage it. I've done it before. The longer I have to stay down, the worse it's going to be for me. I weigh about seventy kilos, and past a certain point, I'll just freeze to death, same as you would, waltzing around in your Y-fronts in a blizzard."

"Point taken," Calder agreed. "We can supply you with a wetsuit."

"I need a drysuit," Eric snapped. "Something like the new Nord-25."

"No can do," Calder said promptly. "The wetsuit, we got aboard. It's that or nothing. We couldn't get a dry-suit sent out here under four, five days, and that's too long."

"Then, I'll take the wetsuit," Eric said bitterly. "I assume it's a vessel which sank or a plane that crashed?"

The ghost of a smile crossed Calder's face. "You assume correctly. It's a helijet. A Takahashi-Bell SeaRanger Special. You know the model?"

"Not in any great detail. One or two of them work out of *Pacifica* but I've never been close to one. Never been aboard." He rubbed his palms together. "You know where this chopper is? I mean *exactly* where it is?"

Calder and Royce exchanged a speculative glance, and Calder nodded minutely. The time for keeping secrets was over. Royce disappeared for less than a minute and returned with a laptop. On the screen was a chart of the ocean bottom, mapped by sonar. One blunt fingertip indicated a marker on the side of the Seamount 65882.

"We pinpointed it on instruments," Calder told him. "Big chunk of metal, sitting in the open. It wasn't difficult to find it. It's just too deep for us to get to it. But you can."

"Oh, sure I can," Eric whispered. "But a hundred and fifty metres is deep, Calder, and very dark, and very bloody cold."

"That," Royce said indifferently, "is why we attempted to charter your lunatic friend's submersible. But since Doctor Russell Grant was determined to be such a son of a bitch, you'll have to do the job for him, won't you? " He angled a glance at the silent, watchful Malay girl.

With a hiss through his teeth of anger and frustration, Eric rubbed his eyes, and then leaned over to examine the screen in greater detail. "Current pattern?" At the touch of a key, the water direction came up, indicated with small red arrows, and he gave Calder a hard look. "You know it's going to be like working in a storm-force gale?"

"We know." Calder sat back and cradled a brandy balloon. "Two men, both professional salvage divers, died on the job before we tried to hire Russell. Their tethers broke and they were swept away. We assume you, being an Aquarian, are either stronger or know a few tricks of your lifetime's trade. Or else you're just better adapted to the conditions."

"Maybe," Eric admitted, "but I'm not a possum. It's going to be almost black as tar. Lights?"

"We have a battery of halogen searchlights. We'll drop them down the anchor cable," Calder offered. "They'll do?"

"Probably." Eric sat back and frowned at the screen. "The big problem, anyway you look at this, is going to be the cold. I assume I'll have to get into the plane and fetch something out. How long's it been down there?"

"Three weeks," Royce volunteered.

"It crashed?"

"Of course it did." Calder sipped a little brandy.

Eric pursed his lips. "Aircraft don't just fall out of the air. What was the cause of the incident?"

The Australians looked sidelong at one another and Royce said, "You don't need to know that, Devlin."

"I do," Eric snapped. "I need to know if that wreck is dangerous. Are the windshields punched in? Was she pressurised for high altitude flight? Was she carrying weapons? Are the weapons still aboard? Is there reason to suspect that the warheads may be unstable? Were her cannons loaded with depleted uranium ammunition? Because if they were, she'll be hot as hell." He glared at Calder. "Correct me if I'm wrong, but she was heading out of Rhutan airspace like a bat with its tail on fire."

For the first time Calder chuckled, and it was a genuine sound of laughter. "You're right, of course, and again, I take your point. All right, Devlin, you know your job, I'll give you credit for that. She was hit by the debris from the auto-destruct of a heat seeking missile. The missile itself did not hit her, but the shrapnel did. The damage was in the aft section, under the tail assembly. The pilots were alive when she hit the water, they got out in the dinghy. She was not pressurised, and if you stay away from the tail you'll be clear of the jags of bare metal. No hot ammunition, no unstable warload that we're aware of, and if those toys were aboard, we would surely know."

"Thank you." Eric licked his lips. "Now, I'm no air cargo specialist, but I do know that the maximum dead weight any helijet of this size can get off with is something in the order of about two tonnes, and most of that would have been the airframe, the fuel and the pilots' combined body weight. That doesn't leave a lot for cargo. Maybe half a tonne. Five hundred kilos." He regarded Calder and Royce with a speculative frown. "If she was heading *out* of Rhutan, not in, so it's a safe bet that she wasn't loaded with weapons."

For a moment that dangerous look was back full force in Royce's face, and Eric shot a glance at Calder. He knew he was safe for the moment: whatever the cargo was, they were desperate to get their hands on it, and he was the only viable tool they had.

He cleared his throat, steepled his fingers on the edge of the table and said reasonably, "If you want me to get into the plane and get that cargo out, I have to know if I need to use tools, equipment, and what resources you have. Can I lift it with my own two hands? Will I need cutting gear to get it out? Once it's out, what's the dead-weight? I can only lift a certain mass on my own muscle power. If it's a big object, don't forget the speed of the current, which is running like a gale down there. Manhandling a large item could be like holding a sail to the wind, I could be swept away, or I could loose your precious damn cargo! How do you know that the two men who've already died didn't take that express route to hell?"

The breath hissed over Calder's teeth, and he gave Royce a hard look. "The kid's worth his weight in solid platinum, Brady. You know what I'm thinking? It might be worth keeping him on afterwards. The price offered for him by that rat-lab in the Catalina is pretty attractive, but it's starting to look much more attractive to keep him. He knows his stuff."

Royce's brow was deeply creased. "Where d'you learn this, Devlin?"

Wary, watchful, Eric chose every syllable with care. "Working around *Pacifica*. Since I was a kid I've worked right alongside the divers and engineers. I keep meaning to enroll in courses aboard the *Atlantis*, get the formal certificate, because I've always been around the engineers -I know their job, inside and out. And I'm a quick study." He tapped his skull. "The fact my lungs can cycle seawater doesn't prevent me from having a brain."

"Your point," Calder said with what could have been graciousness. He leaned closer, over the table, and held his hands about a metre apart. "The object is a metal case, so big. Metre long, third of a metre high and wide. Locked. You get into the helijet through the side hatch. Later, before we anchor on the seamount, I'll get you a set of schematics for the SeaRanger, so you'll be able to find your way around.

"You'll have the floodlights. The box will be in the body of the chopper, just behind the cockpit. Drag it out. We'll send down a basket on the end of a cable. Put the case in the basket, we'll bring it up. Then you're at liberty to come up just as fast as your little webbed feet can propel you."

The job seemed acceptable, but Eric remained wary. "Contents of the case?"

"None," Royce said harshly, "of your damned business."

Eric's teeth bared. "Toxic? Nerve gas? Radioactive? Come on, man!" He glared at Calder again. "What kind of a fool do you think I am? At least tell me what I'm dealing with, let me take the necessary precautions!"

"You know, Brady," Calder mused, "this little frog is looking more and more attractive all the time. I think he'd be an asset to our operation. Think of the run-around we'd have been saved if he'd been on the staff since the beginning of this."

"Think," Eric snarled, "of how simple it would have been if you'd just come across with this information that night in Bottoms Up! Russell was hooked, he needed the money, all he wanted was some data. But — ah," he hesitated. "Let me guess. The cargo is illegal."

"Suffice to say, it isn't toxic, in any way," Calder said evasively.

"Which means the contents of that box would get you locked up in any legit nation," Eric concluded.

Calder swivelled out his chair and stood. "That's all you need to know for now, Devlin. I suggest you go and sit down somewhere where Mister Ho can keep an eye on you. Watch a video. Relax. You can study the schematics of the SeaRanger in the morning. We'll be rendezvousing with our aircraft, which was piloted out of *Pacifica* ..." he looked at his watch. "About an hour ago. You'll do the job before noon tomorrow, and then we'll think about what to do with you."

He poured another inch of brandy into the balloon. "Don't misunderstand me. You can go directly to that lab in the California Islands, without passing 'Go' or collecting two hundred units of anyone's currency. Or you can stay alive, albeit as a prisoner on this vessel, living in comparative luxury. Food, drink, a soft bed, elegance, entertainment. The girl, if you want her." He gestured with the brandy. "Think about it. If it were me in your position, there'd be no choice." He smiled ruefully. "Of course, you'll have to be kept either under guard or manacled. You could dive over the side and vanish into the blue, couldn't you? It's a marathon swim back to *Pacifica,* but I daresay you could make it."

Grumbling silently, containing a fury so vast it seemed to leak out of his ears, Eric allowed the heavyweight wrestler, Ho, to escort him back to the lounge. There, he hunched down in a chair, propped his bare feet on the table and gave his guard a look that would have withered a sequoia.

Just one thought was in his mind: where in hell was Russell?

Chapter Ten

At that moment, Russell was looking at a digital clock on the wall behind the desk belonging to Derek Cooper. It was one in the morning, and Cooper was still wearing a disgusted expression, though Russell had long since convinced him of the necessity of being dragged out of his bed at this hour.

The office was companionably dim, with only half the lights turned on. Outside, a warm night wind wafted against the windows, and the smell of fresh coffee tantalised the nostrils. Russell had not eaten since his snack at six-thirty, and despite his tension he knew he must put something in his stomach. Coffee and a toasted sandwich seemed to be Cooper's natural diet, and Russell had accepted the offer of a crisp tuna roll with limp hydroponic lettuce and biting-hot mayo.

Two storeys above the Cachalot Wharf on the west side of *Pacifica* the office was small, overcrowded and humming with machinery. Computers, radar, sonar, tracking, scanning ... this was Cooper's livelihood. And it was Russell's best bet, if he wanted to find Eric fast. He had cruised back to Aurealis Wharf at ten-thirty, and for the third time placed a call direct to Gerald Duquesne. The answer was the same as the first and second calls: *your message has been recorded, Mr Duquesne is not available at this time, but you have been placed on hold. Please wait for an operator.*

Russell waited till midnight, when he could tolerate the delay no longer. He knew exactly where Duquesne was, and the chances of getting through to the old man before noon were something in the order of nil. The Nepalese president had arrived in the evening, and

Duquesne was playing elder-statesman, trying to come to some arrangement in the matter of Rhutan.

So much for pulling strings, Russell thought sourly. As usual when the chips were down, he discovered that he was on his own, and it was just damned fortunate that he had friends who owed him a few favours. One of those friends was Derek Cooper.

Yawning, eyes closed, Cooper was pounding at the keyboard as he entered the complex strings of access codes, cyphered bypasses, recognition passwords. He only opened his eyes when he must consult with the chart on the wall and enter the actual linker codes - the uplinks to the satellites on which he bought time. Those satellites quartered the Pacific a square kilometre at a time, and neither cloud cover nor darkness mattered, since they used synthetic aperture radar.

The blue schooner was under diesel power as she left Surfside, but she was going to make a maximum of about twelve knots. That meant that she could, right now, be no more than one hundred and fifty kilometres away, and less than that if she was running against tide or wind or both. Still, it was a big, big ocean, and finding a single vessel in the wilderness of the Pacific would be like looking for a needle in a haystack ... save that if you had a thousand people with a thousand magnets, they would find your needle soon enough. Derek Cooper had the equivalent of an army brandishing magnets.

Satisfied, he hit the 'send' key and sat back. "Done?" Russell asked shrewdly. "Now, what do we do?"

"We wait," Cooper yawned. "We have a late-late supper. We watch that screen, and when SkyEye 19 spots something that looks like a ship or a large boat, it'll give us a beep, and you can decide if the fruit of its labours looks like your schooner, a trawler, a junk, a liner, or whatever."

"Whatever?" Russell arched a brow at him.

"A floating whorehouse filled with hustlers in pink garters," Cooper quipped as he reached for the coffee pot.

Russell slid into the chair he had just vacated. "How long does this usually take?"

"SkyEye scans pretty fast. I can ask for quickscan, but you lose integrity. Hold your horses, Rusty, old son. You're looking at a circular area with Surfside at the middle, maybe two hundred kilometres in radius. Give the poor wee beastie a chance."

So Russell helped himself to coffee, pulled up a chair and forced down a little food. One eye remained on the clock, and every ten minutes or so, as if on cue, the machine would beep for attention. A Chinese fishing junk; a Japanese trawler; an Australian pleasurecraft. Each time, Russell hit the 'cancel' key and the machine went back into search mode.

Frustration had begun to grasp Russell like a fist and the clock showed four a.m. when at last he saw what he had been longing to see. Cooper crowed and punched for a triangulation on those scanner traces. The schooner was heading due north and she was now just short of two hundred kilometres away. Cooper printed out the whole set of statistics and thrust the slip of paper into Russell's hand.

"That's the best I can do, Rusty, but I'll leave the scan on. Keep in radio contact with it, and it'll give you updates any time you yell." He paused. "So what's your next move? You should call Duquesne."

"I did," Russell said bleakly. "Can't get through. Politics." He studied the paper, kissed it passionately, and clasped Cooper's shoulder. "I'm on my own. What a surprise. But I've got half an idea of how to get around this, Derek. Thanks for your help, mate. I needed it."

He was out of the office while Cooper was still yawning, and jogging back around the periphery of the quays and wharves. He had left the *Tiger Shark* anchored at home, rather than parking her over here. She was on a long mooring cable, just outside the fish farm's nets, and that was the best position for her.

At four-fifteen he jogged along Aurealis Wharf, where he had been shot just days before. He plucked his keys from his pocket, searched out the right one, and sent up the shed door. The well of darkness within defeated him, and he fumbled for the lights. Flickering mauve fluoros shrivelled his eyes for a moment, and then he focused properly on the submersible.

"Well, well," he whispered to it, as if it might be sentient, dormant but listening. "So we're going to be launching you after all." He stroked the smooth, grey hull, with its shimmering, holographic *Poseidon* decal, and then dragged the boarding ladder closer and clambered swiftly up, with a chiming sound of feet on metal rungs.

The pressure-seal split with a hissing noise, the hatch went up and he lowered himself through into the lock-in/lock-out chamber, which allowed a diver to depart the sub or re-enter it, while it was submerged. An inner hatch opened, and a moment later he was groping for the switch to the red emergency lights.

Two seats, a battery of machinery, screens, gauges, gear ... with the ease of long familiarity, Russell settled himself in the right hand seat and flicked three switches. Power; computer; communications. As soon as the power was on the computers came to life, and he patched directly into Cooper's satellite channel. A schematic appeared on the monitor at his elbow, and he grunted in satisfaction as he saw that he was remote-tracking that schooner. So far, so good.

Though it had not been turned on in a week or more, the computer booted up without a hitch and he engaged the robot pilot. It would launch itself, send its aquadynamic cradle down the ramp and into the water, and it would then submerge to a depth of just one metre and extend the tow coupler. All this was completely automatic, and as soon as he had checked the power levels and activated the system, Russell lifted himself out through the hatches and sealed them up behind him.

He ducked into the apartment for a moment to grab an armful of dry clothes and big, gaudy beach towels, and the he was out again in time to watch the submersible quietly and efficiently launch itself into the dark, calm waters beside the nets. The cradle was shaped much like a boat hull, with a sharp bow that cut like a knife through the water. As soon as she was coupled up behind the *Tiger Shark* he was in business.

He hit the winch, which pulled the powerboat back in to the boatramp, and stepped over. The dry clothes and towels, he stored under the seat as he watched the submersible blow one of her ballast tanks and sink gently under the surface. In seconds more, only the tow coupler was above the water, and Russell started the motors with a snarling V8 roar.

He would wake the neighbours and frighten the tuna ... tough. The *Tiger* arced across the bay before he throttled down, reversed pitch and brought her back, and back again, until the tow coupler was within easy reach. She tethered on with a loop of bowden-cable as thick as his arm - the same brand of coupling cable used by the ocean tugs that stood by the *Atlantis*. As soon as the *Poseidon* was secure, Russell fell back into his seat and flicked switched on the panel at his elbow.

The computer tied into the machine aboard the submersible with a single hiccup, and he took another fix on the schooner. She was still heading north, making ten knots, never wavering from that course. The heading, Russell knew, was sure to be a bee-line for Graham Calder's salvage. The question was, how far away had the target boat or plane gone down? He bit his lip as he saw, on the very edge of the chart display, the tiny island freestate of Rhutan.

With the kind of language that would have earned him boxed ears in years gone by, he put the wheel over and opened the throttles. The *Tiger* answered sluggishly, since she was pulling such an immense dead weight, but she commanded four times the speed of a schooner on diesels. Still, Russell had a long haul before him, and he settled himself for one hell of a night.

For the moment he was optimistic. Calder and Royce would treat Eric with velvet gloves until the salvage was performed. If needed him badly enough to abduct him, be was valuable. But as soon as that precious, unknown cargo was aboard their vessel, Eric was in jeopardy. And on that score, Russell's very bone marrow could ice over.

Chapter Eleven

The weather report from *Pacifica* was for clear skies at least till mid-afternoon, and then the usual squall, with a two metre chop and rain from the east. Calder and Royce were satisfied with the conditions, and if he told the truth, Eric would have admitted that what was happening on the surface didn't really matter a damn four metres down. The worst cyclone of the decade could be blowing up top, and as soon as he was underwater the world became calm and serene. Bad conditions, as far as Eric was concerned, mostly involved murky water. To him, it was like breathing smoggy air, and his lungs became as irritated as those of a man compelled to breathe thick woodsmoke.

"You'll do it now," Calder told him briskly as Ho fetched the prisoner up on deck after a mildly uncomfortable night spent in one of the private cabins, forward of the lounge. The bed had been as soft as feathers, but he was chained to it by one ankle and Eric was unaccustomed to confinement of any description. Still, Calder was absolutely right. If Eric had had the chance, he would have koshed Ho with one of the numerous, grotesque Polynesian *objects d'art,* or a wine bottle, and slipped silently over the side of the schooner.

His only problems in the water between here and home were fatigue, which was unavoidable, and sharks, which to some extent he could hope to evade. The trick was to go down, hide behind a rock and stay still, the same as you would do in the hills if you spotted a tiger. Sharks had poor eyesight, and so long as you stayed put they would probably swim right past you and never even know you were there.

Luckily, the current here was running almost due south, and all he had to do was let it carry him home. Now and then he would swim to keep warm, but still, thirst, hunger and fatigue were deadly enemies, and not even an Aquarian would make that marathon swim easily.

He had calculated, roughly, that it was a three-day drift to get to Breakwater Island. It would rain every afternoon, and he could drink a little if he floated on the surface; he could catch fish, if he did not mind eating them raw. Still, he would be tired, hungry and dehydrated before he saw any of the outlying artificial islands, and he did not relish the prospect.

Then again, anything would have to be better than looking down the business end of Brady Royce's gun.

"I said," Calder repeated, louder, as Eric frowned at the Webley, "you'll do the job now, Devlin. It's just after nine a.m., there's no reason to delay. As soon as you've brought up the cargo we'll be underway."

"To where?" Eric asked sourly as he watched his new boss lift a scarlet neoprene wetsuit out of a locker.

"Home," Calder told him.

"CAIR, The Flinders Islands?" Eric caught the pieces of the wetsuit as they were tossed to him. "Not my home, Calder."

Calder smiled, a lopsided smirk. "No," he said, and would not elaborate beyond, "we're not headed back to CAIR."

Before he could speak again they heard a deep, bass roar from the south-west, and Eric turned, putting his back to the morning sun, to watch Calder's plane on approach. The wing-in-ground-effect aircraft was sleek, white hulled, and very, very expensive. The pilot cut speed, and as the flight cushion dwindled it settled onto the water and began to manoeuvre like a boat. On the nose was stencilled its name: *Rainbird*.

"I see Morse had no trouble getting the plane out of *Pacifica*." Calder waved, beckoning his pilot closer, and as Eric watched bleakly she cruised toward the schooner and let go anchors, port and starboard of the nose. A hatch opened in the side, and a smooth skinned black face appeared. "Peter!" Calder shouted. "Any problems?"

"Not a one," Morse called with hands cupped to his mouth. "Didn't see anyone on the marina when I left, didn't see anyone following. You're clear, man."

"Just what I wanted to hear." Calder swung back toward Eric and gestured at the wetsuit. "You've studied the schematics of the SeaRanger. We're breaking out the floodlights, you've seen the soundings of the bottom, the chart showing the position of the helijet, and you've got a wetsuit. What are you waiting for, Devlin?"

"Nothing," Eric muttered, and began to feed himself into the lower half of the suit. He was struggling the neoprene pieces onto his hips when he saw Ho, fetching the girl up on deck, and as she appeared Royce shifted aim. Ho shoved her against the mast in the shade of the deckhouse, and without a word cuffed her hands to one of the main lines. Royce took aim on the child's legs and looked into Eric's face with deceptive, dangerous blandness. "I said," Eric muttered, "I'm going. Let the poor kid alone."

He was sitting on the side when two crewmen fetched out two powerful floodlights and a heavy wire basket. All three were attached to a winch chain, and without ceremony Calder shoved the assembly over the side. He swung on Eric just as he was zipping the wet suit up to his neck.

"I'm going," Eric snapped. "I'll do the best I can, but it may take several dives. If it's difficult to get into the plane, I can get very cold very fast down that deep. I may have to come up and get warm, and then go back and finish the job."

Without waiting for answer, he dropped off the pitching side of the schooner and entered the water with a small, welcome splash. The buoyancy of the neoprene made it unaccustomedly hard work to go down, yet he could not afford to wear a weight belt, which would have made it too hard to come up again from a depth of a hundred and fifty metres.

He turned upside down, kicked and sculled hard, and was ten metres under the keel when he spun slowly in the water to get his bearings. He took a deep breath, scented the current and the tide like a deer scenting the breeze, and looked up at the shifting, dappled sky. The schooner hung above him like the body of a whale; fish were schooling in the north, the ocean was like a great blue orb at the centre of which was himself.

How easy it would have been to just turn southward and leave. The current was strong, fast, and it was going his way, like catching a local bus. Yet before his mind's eye was the haunted, haunting face of the Malay child, and he could not leave. With a sense of impotent anger, he grasped the lights and basket, tugged sharply on the chain, a signal to the men above to give him all the slack they had, and went down fast.

No Aquarian was constrained by the physical laws that governed a normal diver. Eric could go down as fast as he wanted to, stay as long as he needed and come up as fast as he went down. With his lungs water-filled, his whole body was at ambient pressure - this was 'saturation diving,' like the natural magic with which the orcas and dolphins were born. Yet even they could not breathe water and must rise to the surface occasionally, while Eric simply took another deep breath as he went down.

Already he could smell that damned SeaRanger. It was leaking fuel or lubricants, mildly contaminating the area, but in a way that was lucky. His nose would lead him directly to it without the need to search for it. Perhaps he did not have to surface to breathe, but he could already feel the encroaching cold, insidious, nibbling at his extremities like a feeding fish. As the water became dark, and then darker, as indigo as the night sky, he passed through a thermocline and the temperature went down fast, like a stone.

He felt the first shiver reflex, and if he had been able to speak he would have cursed lividly. It was much colder even than he had expected. A safe guess was that Tropical Cyclone Alice had dredged up a lot of bottom water - nutrient-rich but incredibly cold, from the deep, deep layers, the world of the nightmare fish and giant squid of the abyss. Those bottom waters enriched the warm surface zone, and where they flowed life would flourish. But swimming in them was a dread come true.

Kicking harder, he turned on the floodlights, and as the stench of leaked fuel and lubricants started to prickle his senses he panned the brilliant halogen lights to and fro and began to look for the wreck.

***

It was just after eight when Russell caught sight of the schooner *Queen Katherine* on his surface search radar, and shut back the throttles. According to instruments, the boat was not underway: she had two anchor lines set and her diesels were idle, not on station-keeping. So this was the site of Calder's salvage, Russell thought, and he felt a prickle of fascination.

He called up the bottom charts and whistled softly through his teeth. The sea bed in these parts was a hundred and fifty metres down, and the north-sound current was hard and fast, like a sharp, driving and sleet-cold wind. Eric could work in conditions like that, but not for long.

The question was, had he been able to make Calder understand that?

Three switches flicked over, putting the *Tiger Shark* onto robot pilot, and Russell did not bother to set his anchors. Keys tapped, and obediently the sled surfaced just astern of the powerboat. The *Poseidon* popped her top hatch, and Russell grinned mirthlessly as he released the tow couplers. He clambered over onto the contoured, soft/hard hull of the submersible.

He had closed up, checked his hatch seals and settled in his seat when he heard the solid ringing sound through the hull which meant that the *Poseidon* had automatically disengaged from the aquadynamic cradle. He test-fired each of his four electric motors, checked the battery charge and consulted his monitors for global orientation.

The schooner was a kilometre and a half in the north, just on the very edge of unaided visual sighting, and he could only assume that she had dropped anchor directly above the site of the salvage. According to the *Tiger*'s instruments, her diesels were still hot, so she had not been here long.

His worst fear was not that Eric would bungle the job and incur Calder's wrath, but rather, that he would be too efficient, get through the work too fast, hurrying because of rhe intense cold. Then, Calder would be delighted to up-anchor and go, which could very well be the last Russell saw of Eric.

He was on the point of submerging when the *Poseidon*'s surface search radar indicated another vessel coming in, and Russell delayed his descent for several minutes, though he was already closing the distance toward himself and the schooner at a steady eight knots. In moments the computer had identified the new vessel, and Russell swore aloud.

It was a wing-in-ground-effect plane, and it could only be the aircraft that had been moored within sight of Duquese's office aboard the *Atlantis*. That plane had the potential to be anywhere in the world in a matter of hours. She could be in Catalina, the Californian Islands this time tomorrow, or in CAIR by evening, or Zealand by the following dawn.

Hart beating hard and fast, imbued with a sense of desperate urgency, Russell adjusted his down-angle to thirty degrees and overran the motors for speed.

***

The cold was insidious. After a while his fingers and toes became so numb that he hardly even felt the chill, but Eric Devlin was experienced enough to know the signs. In his head was a clock, counting down the amount of time he could hope to spend at this depth before he had to go up or enter serious hypothermia.

The SeaRanger had come to rest canted at a shallow angle, sitting on the shoulder of the seamount. Below the wreck, the surface sloped down and away like a rolling hillside that vanished into the night. The pilots had left the side hatch open - they would have had a major struggle, Eric guessed, trying to extract the inflatable raft before she went under. She would have sunk by the tail as she flooded, heeled over to one side and vanished in a matter of seconds. The current had carried her a little way, but she was heavy enough to go down like a brick.

And here she was, in reasonably good condition, sitting in the waving sea grasses where a big, old potato cod, a manta ray and several octopuses had already begun to settle in and call it home. In twenty years she would be a new deep, cold-water reef. The halogen lights cast brilliant shafts through the growing murk, and as his feet touched the boulders and grasses Eric let go the chain. At once he began to fight the millrace of the water.

He swam the last few metres hard and forced deep breaths to the bottom of his lungs. If he had been a normal human, he would have been consuming air so fast, he would probably need one or more tanks lowered over the side to keep him alive until he could decompress in several stages. Also, a man used a lot more oxygen in this striking cold ... and more again when he was called upon to work.

Eric caught the side of the SeaRanger's door and hauled himself in. From here on he was working in his own shadow, which was a nuisance. Most of the light would not find its way into the body of the helijet. But on the plus side, he was out of the current and could relax for a moment, get his bearings.

He clamped his legs together and held his arms tight around his chest to conserve his body heat, which was dwindling fast. Where the hell was this case, this box they had described? He saw a selection of tool boxes in brackets on the walls; spare parts for unknown machinery; four seats, plus baggage nets, and an assortment of bags and boxes still in the nets. But nothing he could see at once answered the description of the case Calder wanted.

Mel Keegan

Just behind the cockpit, Calder had said, he would find it. Eric turned around, startling an octopus, which shot out through the open hatch. Weak illumination came in through the forward windshield, and as his eyes grew accustomed to the thick dimness he began to feel his way along the wall of the compartment.

His joints were aching in the cold. Toes, ankles and knees, fingers and wrists were the worst, but soon his whole body would begin to freeze up. The pain was nothing to do with narcosis. Aquarians never gave that normal human syndrome a thought. But they were as vulnerable to freezing conditions as the next man, and down here it was as cold as a blizzard. Eric's thin layer of dense, insulating fat, plus the wetsuit, were keeping him mobile and working far longer than an ordinary human could have managed, yet the numbness was creeping swiftly up his arms and legs as he felt along the compartment wall.

And there it was. Steel, a metre long. It was not fastened to the deck, and in the impact as the SeaRanger hit the water it must have slithered forward and hit the wall, slid into the corner and wedged there, in a pool of darkness.

Taking a deep breath, he searched for a handle or handhold, found none and instead grasped it by the corners. He tugged, heaved, and grunted as he felt the weight of it. It felt as heavy as solid lead, and even he was panting as he wrestled it across the deck toward the hatch.

He paused there to catch his breath, and visually measured the distance between the SeaRanger and the wire basket. He could tug the case out of the plane and then drag it through the grasses, across the boulders, but lifting it into the basket would be a problem. On impulse, he swam out into the gale-like current, caught the chain and tugged.

Up top, someone paid out a little slack, and he struggled back through the whirl of the current, fetching the basket with him. It was fastened to the winch chain by means of a standard hook, the same kind of assembly that linked up to the SeaRanger's cargo couplers. So long as he did not swing the basket too far out it would stay on the

– 148 –

hook, but he could not manage to get it onto the deck of the SeaRanger, so he was down to raw muscle.

Swearing lividly in the back of his throat, since he could not speak aloud, he shoved, pushed, wrestled the case over until it was half on, half off the deck, then tugged the net as close as he could get it, held it in the crook of his knee, and took the case in his arms.

The weight and the physical effort knocked the breath out of him and he thought he saw stars for a second as he moved it through space, that vital metre or two, and let it drop. As it fell into the net he sagged back against the side of the plane, numb with fatigue and cold, head spinning. At first he thought he was suffering some kind of visual aberration. Perhaps he was starting to become disorientated with the pressure, the bitter cold and physical hard work.

But no, there *was* light come toward him out of the murk, where the seamount sloped away into the indigo distance. Eric backed up against the SeaRanger, letting the force of the current plaster him to the hull, and watched the corona of the lights. Slowly, deliberately, they came into focus, and as he realised it was a submersible his heart began to race.

Calder and Royce had no access to a submersible. If they had, they wouldn't have needed an Aquarian, nor the hire of the *Poseidon*, and Eric was making wagers with himself, long before the backwash of the lights, reflecting off the SeaRanger, allowed him to pick out the shape of the craft.

Then, he could have laughed. The lights flicked on and off like Aldiss lamps, in old fashioned, standard Morse code: *Can see you Eric. Get inside. Got to leave fast.*

Russell! Bloody hell. Russell.

Eric kicked off from the SeaRanger and covered the distance to the front observation port of the *Poseidon*. He peered in through the thick glass, saw Russell's face and gave him a swift raised thumb. But instead of immediately entering through the top airlocked hatch, he beckoned Russell to follow him, and rapped smartly on one of the two handling arms.

Obediently, the robot claws came to life, and with deft, expert touches Russell nudged the *Poseidon* after him, a bare metre at a time. Just short of the cargo net, Eric twisted in the water and indicated the case. He angled the net to make it simple for Russell to take a remote-control grip on it, and then gave him all the space he needed to work.

The handling arms were very, very sensitive, and exceptionally strong. They plucked the case out of the cargo net like a careful hand shelling eggs, and tucked it neatly into the cargo niche just under the chin of the sub, beneath the forward observation ports.

The cold had struck to his very bones now, and Eric's hip joints and shoulders were aching fiercely, but before he kicked toward the *Poseidon* he deliberately took the net from the hook, and attached that hook to the SeaRanger's cargo couplers. There, let Calder and Royce excite their brain cells trying to figure that one out. They had no divers, their winch couldn't hope to lift the mass of the helijet, and the only thing they could do was cut loose the chain, or they were permanently anchored here.

His limbs were barely functional as he struggled toward the *Poseidon*. The hatch was already open and he forced himself down into the airlock, not even feeling the metal surfaces under his hands as he closed it, locked it up and hit the 'purge' mechanism.

The lock emptied fast, pumped out by powerful repellers, and when water level fell below his shoulders Eric hugged his chest tight and exhaled as hard as he could. His lungs emptied and he took two deep breaths of air. A moment of dreadful, suffocating discomfort, several coughs, a few swallows, and he had made the transition. It was like this every time, as he came back into the world of solid ground and air. Easier by far to enter the water.

Shudders assaulted his body as he waited for the inner hatch to open, and when it did he fell through into Russell's embrace, and a blanket. The heating was on high, the coffee was hot, he could smell the whiskey in it, and all Eric had to do now was stand in front of a fan blowing hot air and let Russell zip him out of the wetsuit, rub him down with an enormous towel and wrap him in a plaid rug.

With his hands about a mug and a mouthful of the Irish coffee inside of him, he could talk again. He was hoarse, as he always was when he had recently been water-breathing, but he said clearly,

"Christ, am I glad to see you. How the hell did you - ?" Even his voice was trembling.

"I went over to Surfside. A little kid saw you get on that boat, so I shot back to *Pacifica* and called in some favours. Derek Cooper's owed me a few for years. The surveillance satellite found the schooner, so I put the *Poseidon* in the water and followed." He peered into Eric's face with a worried expression. "Are you hurt?"

"No, just frozen to the bone. It's cold as a snow storm out there, and you'd have to be just plain crazy to go paddling around in a wetsuit." Eric took a slurping mouthful of coffee.

"That was the salvage?" Russell pressed him into the chair beside the radio console. "We've got it?"

"We've got it," Eric said smugly. "Whatever it is."

"Then let's get the hell out," Russell muttered as he slid back into his own seat and started the motors.

"Wait ... Rusty, they're holding a hostage on the boat," Eric told him. "To make me do the work and come back, instead of vanishing. A little Malay girl."

Russell twisted in his seat, eyes very large, wide and dark in the dim cabin lighting. "We can't take them on. We're not armed. You can bet your life, they are."

"They are," Eric admitted.

"Then there's not much we can do for the hostage." Russell's tone was icy calm. "Best bet we, and she, have is to notify the *Atlantis* and get the authorities out here, fast. We're a long way from home but they can have a helijet here in a couple of hours." He reached out, resting both hands on Eric's blanket wrapped shoulders. "Eric, if we go up against those bastards, we haven't got a chance."

"I know." Eric closed his eyes, seeing the Malay girl's face again, and sighed heavily.

Would they shoot her? What would be the point, when they had become aware that Eric was not returning? Threatening to shoot her was the best security they had, so long as the *Queen Katherine* was alone in the midst of a million square kilometres of ocean. The random factor on which Calder and Royce could never have calculated was Russell.

As soon as Russell entered the picture, every variable changed, and shooting the girl became a pointless gesture. Royce might do it out of spite and anger, but Eric doubted it. The girl was a possession, either a tool or a toy, and only a crass idiot wilfully damaged his tools or toys. Royce and Calder were rich and vicious, but they were neither stupid nor mad.

"Go," he said hoarsely. "You in touch with home?"

"Soon as we break surface I can call it in," Russell said as he set the up-angle and opened the throttles for a long, shallow ascent that would put as much distance between them and the site of the salvage as possible before they reached the surface. He twisted in his seat and frowned deeply at Eric. "You sure you're okay? You're white as a sheet."

"The word," Eric said drily, "is *bloodless*. An Aquarian isn't a fish, but some people can't seem to grasp that." He hesitated, wondering how much he should say, and then decided that Russell had the right to know it all. "After the salvage, those bastards were going to keep me."

"Keep?" Russell's brows rose. "Like the hostage girl?"

"Something like that. A tame Aquarian to do their diving for them." Eric finished his coffee and helped himself to a refill from the thermos.

"They're slime," Russell said bitterly.

"Hey." Eric stood behind the pilot's seat and draped his arm around Russell's shoulder. "Thanks."

"For what?" Russell kissed the stubbled side of his neck. "Christ, you're cold as ice."

"Give me a chance to get warm. And, thanks for being here." Eric hugged the blanket around himself and squeezed in at the forward console to look at the flickering monitor screens.

They were then twenty metres down, cruising at ten knots, on an up-angle of two degrees. They would breach the surface just short of the position where the radar showed the *Tiger Shark*, and a kilometre and a half from the schooner and Calder's aircraft. Good enough. Eric tousled Russell's hair with fingers which had begun to prickle as life returned to them.

"I owe you one. In fact, I owe you a dozen after this."

"Rubbish," Russell muttered. "You just drink that and get warm. So, what's the salvage? What's in the case?"

"I have no idea, they wouldn't say." Eric sipped the hot liquid and wrapped both hands around the mug. "They just assured me that the contents were not radioactive or otherwise toxic, like nerve gas or some kind of area-weapon."

"You believe them?" Russell asked, regarding Eric with a shrewd look.

"Yeah, I do. I didn't see any Geiger counters, no handling gear, no NBC suits, no hot-boxes, nothing, aboard that schooner. If they were expecting to take delivery of something that was dangerous, they might jeopardise my life to bring it up, but they'd never risk their own. They'd have been ready to handle it. And the only thing I saw on the deck of that boat was a crow bar and an oxy-welding torch."

"Okay, I'll buy that," Russell agreed. "I was, uh, worried."

"Makes two of us," Eric said tartly. "It's too small to be a weapons system, and besides, they were heading *away* from the war zone, not into it. You take missiles *to* a shooting party, you don't bring them home again. And that's where the cargo was coming from. Rhutan."

Russell grunted in acknowledgment. "I managed to work that one out all by myself. Do you know how close to Rhutan we are?"

"Yeah - much too close." Eric finished his second coffee, set the mug aside and held his still frozen feet to the hot air, which was blasting out of the ducts at deck level. "I imagine you informed Duquesne before you took off after me."

Mel Keegan

"Not quite." Russell gave him a wry look. "I called his office till I just couldn't wait any longer. Couldn't get through to him. Eventually I left a message and decided to fall back on my own resources." He lifted a brow at his partner. "You've forgotten - so did I. Politics. Duquesne's in conference with the presidents from Nepal and CAIR, they got into *Pacifica* last evening. God knows what they're talking about."

"Perhaps," Eric said thoughtfully, "it could be a question of who is going to foot the bill for the military intervention, if they commit to it. You know *Pacifica* isn't rich. And Australia's been as good as bankrupt since the 1980s! Nepal ... well, I wouldn't start looking at them to pay for a massive military intervention in Rhutan."

"Money," Russell said disgustedly. "Only politicians could sit there, talking for hours, worrying about money when people are being wiped out as if they never existed.." He paused to consult his instruments, flicked on the surface search radar, extended the radio masts and gave Eric a grin devoid of humour. "Hold tight now, honey, we're going up."

Chapter Twelve

Russell's first priority was to call home. Of necessity, all radio signals were scrambled, since receivers aboard both the *Queen Katherine* and Calder's plane would surely be able to intercept the transmission.

The fact that Calder and Royce would not understand a word that was said did little to comfort Russell. As soon as he began to transmit, it was like waving a red flag, handing out a free locator fix on his own position. Yet they desperately needed to get a signal through to the *Atlantis*, and as the *Poseidon* broke surface the same thought was on Eric's mind.

Tolerably warm now, Eric snatched up the binoculars, opened the top hatches and propped himself in the sun while Russell turned the submersible's blunt bow toward its transportation sled.

"Can you see them?" Russell's voice yelled up through the hatch. The robot pilot took over the docking procedure, and he joined Eric in the hatch.

The Aquarian pointed. "We've been drifting apart. There's about two kilometres of water between us, and the chop's up to about a metre and a half. Chances are, they'll never pick us up visually, but their instruments will, and as soon as they do, you have to know they'll be after us." He gave Russell a tense look. "Ideas?"

"The schooner is anchored - well and truly," Russell mused, bracing himself as the robot pilot managed the docking and powerful clamps took hold of the submersible's hull. "They try to weigh anchor, and they're in for a very big, very nasty surprise. Beside, she's too slow. She'll make a maximum of about twelve knots on diesels, we can leave her as if she was standing still. What worries me -"

"Is that damned seamonster," Eric finished, referring to the wing-in-ground-effect plane. In the 1990s it had been nicknamed the 'Caspian Seamonster,' since the design hailed from the late, not-so-great days of the doomed Soviet Union. "And that piece of hardware," he went on, "will outrun *us* as if we're the ones standing still."

Russell took a deep breath of the salt sea wind. "Then we'd better get a head start on those bastards, before we alert them to our presence ... and then get a message out to the *Atlantis* and raise some help."

The docking sled was flush with the stern of the *Tiger Shark* now, and Russell hopped over fast. Eric was right behind him, his agility returning as he grew warm. "What about the sub?" he asked. "She's going to slow us down."

"Cut her loose," Russell said grimly. "The *Poseidon* knows where she is. She'll take herself home in a day or so, a hundred metres down, where it's safe."

"But Calder's cargo is on her!" Eric protested.

"So?" Russell cast a glance at the horizon. "You want to hang around here and unload it?" He quirked a brow at Eric. "Our lives could be the price, and I don't care what's in that case - nothing's worth your life. Or mine, for that matter."

"Right." Eric rubbed his face hard and slid into the seat behind the powerboat's instruments.

A screen came alive and with swift, sharp stabs be linked into the submersible's robot pilot and began to relay Russell's instructions. A green blip from the *Poseidon* assured him that the computer understood, and already the sub was going down.

"Done," he told Russell. "Hit it!"

Russell had already primed the motors, and now started them with a roar of gargling V8s. He took a quick squint at the compass, spun the wheel over to correct their drift, and opened the throttles wide. "If my sums are right, we ought to be home in three hours," he yelled over the engine noise. "I made it out here, towing the *Poseidon*, in about five; we'll make better speed without that dead weight behind us."

"Three hours," Eric echoed, twisting in his seat to look back into the north. The *Tiger Shark* was riding bow-high now, only a few square metres of her in contact with the water, thrashing props driving her hard. "How's your fuel?"

Without even needing to consult the gauges, Russell told him, "We'll be sucking fumes by the time we get home, but we've got enough to do it so long as the weather stays fair. And besides -" he tapped the shortwave. "As soon as we've put some distance between us and them I'm going to scream for help. The *Atlantis* ought to send us some support, and if somebody meets us halfway they can refuel us or take us aboard."

The southern Pacific was calm, living up to its halcyon name, but every afternoon a squall gathered. The amount of water in the ecosystem since Chen-Goldstein 4, when the polar icecaps melted off, was much higher than it had been in - said some scientists - sixty or seventy million years. The last time the climate of the earth was this even-tempered over the whole globe, the dinosaurs were at their zenith.

If the squall held off, Russell was sure they should sight *Pacifica* about two hours after noon, and if they managed to punch a signal through to the *Atlantis* they could expect to rendezvous with a friendly vessel much earlier. He twisted to look back, and as he focused on the blue-green horizon he saw what Eric had seen a second earlier.

"She's underway," Eric said over the roar of the engines. "That means they've picked us up on surface search scanning. Can you get any more speed out of this thing?"

"Not without compromising our fuel situation." Russell peered critically at the gauges. Speed was just a question of fuel consumption, and if they blew off too much too soon, they would not get home at all.

But Eric was gesturing agitatedly astern. "It's all going to be academic if that whale overtakes us! There's no point trying to hide anymore, Rusty - they know we're here. Hit it!" And he swivelled his seat toward the shortwave as Russell adjusted the fuel mix and opened the throttles to maximum.

The V8s redlined and still the wing-in-ground-effect plane was far, far faster. To begin with, it was a jet, and the old Pratt & Whitney powerplants, two to each wing, had the range and produced the speed to cover the Pacific. But the trade-off for the plane's bulk and high speed was a lack of manoeuvrability at any speed, and as he watched the 'seamonster' come up astern Russell was thinking back to those old physics lessons he had endured when he was a boy.

The only science that had ever interested him was biology. He had never been able to make much sense of math or geometry, and physics was largely incomprehensible. But he did manage to absorb one set of values, because they related directly to real objects, such as moving boats. The more energy that was invested in moving a mass on a linear vector, the more energy must be invested from a transverse direction to convince the mass to change course. There was an equation that set out and explained all this. Russell had never really grasped it when he was fourteen, and couldn't remember it at all now.

But he knew what it meant. The plane was heavy, she could handle the acceleration of big engines, but when it came to turning sharply on a coin or stopping dead in the water, she would struggle, subjected to torque and other dynamics for which she had never been designed. And such as it was, this was all they had to work with.

"She's coming," Eric said grimly as he adjusted the shortwave. "Five hundred metres."

Russell could hear the scream of jets now, even over their own angry V8s. He cast a glance back and swore as he saw the size of the plane, seeming so close at hand. She was a monster in every sense of the word, riding on a wave of air that was compressed by her own speed and bulk, never far above the wave crests - never properly leaving the surface, but in no danger of losing "lift," so long as she maintained her speed. Wing-in-ground-effect had once been tipped to supersede both conventional air traffic and shipping, and if Chen-Golstein 4 had not rewritten history in a moment, perhaps the new technology would have proved.

Aquamarine

The shortwave scramblers cut in, and Eric pulled on headphones. "*Tiger Shark* to *Atlantis*, priority message. *Tiger Shark* to *Atlantis*, priority message. This is Eric Devlin. Are you receiving?"

When a scrambled signal came in, the radio shack aboard the mother ship kicked into high gear. The use of scramblers meant some special kind of trouble, and lives were invariably in jeopardy. Eric repeated his message only once more before the ship answered, and Russell licked his lips as his partner continued,

"Can you track us, locate on this signal?"

"Can do, *Tiger Shark*. What is your problem?"

"We need help - and fast!" Eric yelled. "We're heading for home, quick as this boat will run, but there's a wing-in-ground-effect plane after us, Australian registration code, RMT275. She belongs to the mercenaries, Calder and Royce. Access Mr Duquesne's files - he traced them. These are the bastards who shot Russell Grant last week. They abducted me for an illegal salvage at these co-ordinates. Russell came after me, and now they're right behind us. Can you get us a rendezvous?"

For a moment only silence answered, and then the man in the mother ship's radio shack was back at full volume: "Hold tight, *Tiger Shark*. We'll launch the chopper patrol squad, they'll key on your signal. Leave your shortwave open, broadcast carrier wave, until we can get a surface scan lock on you."

"How long?" Devlin shouted over the growing din, the combined noise of their own V8s and the encroaching jets.

Russell was looking at the chart displayed in the screen at his elbow. On it, the position of the wreck was marked, and the *Poseidon*, which was obediently heading for him at a steady four knots. To the northwest, right on the edge of the chart was Rhutan, and to the south, also right on the edge of the map, was *Pacifica*.

If they kept up this pace, the *Tiger Shark* would have them home in well under three hours ... save for the fact she would be out of fuel in just under two. The penalty for speed was vastly increased fuel consumption.

"Chopper squad will rendezvous with you in one hour," the *Atlantis* promised. "That's the best we can do. Can you hold them off?"

"I don't know," Eric said bleakly. "For godsakes monitor us. We'll do the best we can. *Tiger Shark* out."

He set down the mic but left the radio open, and twisted in his seat to look back. No wonder the howl of jets was so deafening. The plane was almost on top of them. Even through a veil of terror, it was a magnificent sight.

She was thirty metres from sharp nose to T-tail, with high wings and four Pratt & Whitney jets. The glitter of the sun off her glass as she rode a cushion of air six or seven metres above the wave crests left the eyes dazzled and protesting with green after-images. When she cut speed, she would sink back onto the surface and handle like a boat, but if she settled-to-waterborne the *Tiger Shark* would literally run rings around her. She could not fly - not true flight - since she was much closer to boat than aircraft, embracing the best of both worlds. But she was enormously fast, enormously powerful.

"Russell! She's on top of us!" Eric bellowed over the din.

But Russell was as aware of the monster's proximity, and even as Eric shouted he had taken a grip on the wheel. This was the moment he had been waiting for, and he took a breath to bellow, "Grab a hold of something!"

As Eric buckled his seat harness and took a white-knuckled grip on the straps, Russell spun the wheel over and the powerboat slewed through a tight arc. If she had been on the race course, she would have gone around the marker buoy with a hand's span to spare. The plane overshot and raced away at eighty degrees, and then Russell simply put the wheel over and reversed the slew he had made to bring the *Tiger Shark* in right alongside the plane's turbulent wake. Already, Calder's pride and joy was a kilometre ahead of them, and her pilot must be wondering where in hell his quarry had gone. His blind-spot was dead astern.

Russell glanced sidelong at Eric. "At this rate, well follow her all the way to *Pacifica*."

"You might hope," Eric said drily. "They're smarter than that. She's braking. Coming around. See?"

"Oh, I see." Russell checked his fuel. "But she'll take about a kilometre to slow down and another one to turn, and then she has to catch us all over again." His teeth bared, not an expression of humour. "We can do that little manoeuvre until Calder and Royce get sick and tired of watching us. Time to rendezvous?"

Eric leaned over to see the clock in the centre of the control panel. "I make it about fifty-five minutes. Fuel?"

"We'll be out in sixty, maybe sixty-five if we get lucky," Russell told him.

"We're cutting it close," Eric observed grimly, and reached for the radio mic. "*Tiger Shark* to *Atlantis*. How are we doing?"

"*Atlantis* receiving. Your chopper squad launched two minutes ago. They'll make best speed, but we have also alerted all shipping in your area to keep a lookout for you. How is your fuel situation?"

"Critical," Eric told the man. "At the speed we need to stay in front of that plane, we can't make it home."

"Then, can you come right to 0880, and enable your surface search radar. At your current speed, you should sight the tanker *Regina Maris* in about fifteen minutes, and she is armed. I repeat, the tanker is armed."

"Armed with what?" Russell bellowed over the engine noise.

"She's carrying missiles, *Tiger Shark*. She's a fresh water tanker," the radio man reported, "and every pirate between here and Rhutan is in the market for twenty million litres - that's worth a fortune in anybody's currency. She's your best shot. *Tiger Shark*, respond."

"We'll give it a go," Eric shouted, and hooked up the mic. "Come right, 0880, the man said."

"I heard." Russell was intent on the plane, which was now rendered tiny by distance and still turning through an enormous arc, manoeuvring as fast as Calder's pilot knew how. "If we don't connect with this tanker, we're in trouble. This little detour will put us seventy, maybe

Mel Keegan

seventy-five minutes from home, and we're guzzling juice so fast, I'm starting to wonder if this bucket's sprung a leak somewhere."

"Damn." Eric hung on the straps as the powerboat began to bounce on the uneven chop. "Then, this tanker really is the best shot we've got." He reached over and turned on the surface search radar. The screen lit, black and green, messy with numbers. At once he saw the plane, and as he extended the range of the sweep he picked up several other vessels in the area. Only one of them was on a heading of zero-eight-eight, and he tapped the screen with one long forefinger. "There she is ... and, bless them, it looks like they're cutting speed."

"They're doing what?" Russell nudged the wheel over and the power-boat bucked and heaved over the turbulence of the plane's wake. No part of the wing-in-ground-effect aircraft touched the water when she was in flight mode, but the vacuum effect of her air displacement literally sucked up the water behind her in a great white plume. On the screen, Russell had pinpointed the water tanker, and he gave a small whoop. "You're right, they're coming about. They're turning to meet us!"

The shortwave shrilled for attention and Eric scooped up the mic as the *Atlantis* radio man called, "*Tiger Shark, Tiger Shark*, I have informed the *Regina Maris*, they are waiting for you. The chopper squad will rendezvous in forty minutes. Can you see the tanker?"

"Got her on instruments," Eric shouted. "Calder's plane is coming about. Warn the tanker, the bastards not going to just let us go."

"Will do," the *Atlantis* responded. "Call the tanker direct. I've given them your frequency, they ought to be jacked in and receiving this by now."

As the powerboat picked up speed and rocketed into the west, Russell gazed south, after the plane. She was almost on an even keel once more, and she was coming back on an intercept course. His mouth dried and he caught Eric's arm to drawn his attention. "They're going to try to run us down. Eric!"

"I see them." Eric licked his lips. "Turn toward them. Go on, Russell - turn right into them!"

"Play chicken?" Russell's hands tightened on the wheel. "Risky."

"Very," Eric agreed. "I'm listening for alternatives." His eyes were ice green, sharp as chipped flint. "The tanker's still too far off to stand by us."

Russell's teeth worried his lip as he watched the plane begin to pick up speed. A dozen scenarios rushed through his mind and he dismissed every one. As Eric clicked off the scrambler and began to shout into the mic, he put the wheel over again and aimed the bow of the *Tiger Shark* directly into the nose of the oncoming plane.

There would be no actual collision, of course: the plane was riding an air cushion, six metres deep. But the compression storm of the air directly under her would pick up the powerboat, fling it up into a hurricane of turbulence, slam it down again, smash it like a toy. Turning into the plane's path provided no threat whatever to the pilot, but once again it made physics work for the smaller, slower and more manoeuvrable craft.

"*Tiger Shark* to *Regina Maris*," Eric was shouting as once again the noise of V8s and jets began to accumulate to ear-splitting level. "Can you see us on radar?"

The radio crackled, a blast of white noise, Eric turned up the gain as high as he could manage, but they could hardly make out the voice. Russell leaned toward the speaker, down behind the low windshield, and caught a word here, a word there.

"We can see you, and we can see the plane. You're doing good, *Tiger Shark*, but come right, zero-eight-eight, you're not on a rendezvous heading."

"Not yet," Eric bellowed. "Just steer toward us. We'll adjust course when we ... oh, my God." His eyes widened as he looked up from the radio.

The plane loomed like an express locomotive, almost right on top of them, and at the last possible second Russell spun the wheel over and sent the powerboat careening through a wide arc. The plume of spray from the plane's wake was like a deluge of rain, and the nictitating membranes automatically closed over Eric's eyes as he clutched his seat straps and hung on for his life.

The *Tiger Shark* danced on the very last thread of control, and Russell had the presence of mind to let go the wheel. She righted, but as she came to rest the engines stalled out, leaving her dead in the water, and Eric muttered the kind of language that would never have been permitted around the lab in John Grant's day.

Russell's thumb hit the ignition once, twice, and the V8s coughed asthmatically. "Christ," he groaned, "the carbs have taken a gulp. They're flooded out."

"Kick it again." Eric twisted to look back, after the plane. "We've got a few minutes. They have to turn it around yet." He plucked up the radio mic. "*Atlantis*, are you listening to this?"

"Getting every word," the man assured him. "Your chopper squad is on stripped-chassis, engine overrun, they're thirty-five minutes from you. The *Regina Maris* is making best speed. You're stationery, but she'll be with you in ten minutes."

"If we've got ten minutes," Eric said bleakly. "Calder's trying to run us down. It's not impossible that his plane might be armed. Check with the *Pacifica* Customs and harbour records, will you? They were supposed to search her, what did they find?"

"Hold on, I'll be back," the man called, and the line went dead.

"Like, where are we going to go?" Russell thumbed the ignition again and the engines coughed, spluttered, died. "They're drying out. Slowly." He looked up at Eric, and then both of them looked aft.

Far astern, the plane was leaning over on a tight angle, almost touching a wingtip to the water in the pilot's haste to turn her. He must have picked up the tanker on his own instruments, and although he would not have understood a word of the scrambled radio traffic between the powerboat and the *Atlantis*, all transmissions between the mother ship and the *Regina Maris* had, of necessity, been sent 'in clear.'

"Rusty," Eric said tersely. "Try it again, for godsakes."

"Let the carbs dry," Russell muttered. "All I'm doing here is flattening the batteries. Give 'em a chance."

"We haven't got a chance!"

"We've got a minute or so. That monster can't turn tight enough to get back any faster. And in any case, you can go over the side and straight down. They can't touch you."

"But you can't!" Eric exploded.

"I can," Russell argued. "Just because I've got ordinary, garden variety human lungs doesn't mean I can't hold my damn breath! It'll still take three minutes to drown me. And besides," he added, cheeks flushed with fury, "I expect you'll save me."

For a moment Eric's mouth flapped like a goldfish, and then he closed it and gave Russell a look of rueful exasperation.

The plane was still moving so fast, her turning arc was vast. She seemed to be cutting a circular course around the power-boat, and Russell had pinpointed a spot on that circle, the crucial moment at which the V8s must either start, or they would have to get into the sea, dive under, deep as Russell could manage, until the plane had gone by, and then just tread water and wait for the tanker.

Eric was intent the aircraft when Russell's thumb hovered over the ignition. He held his breath and hit the button hard. The twin V8s coughed, barked as if they were spitting water out of the exhausts, and then they settled into a steady growl. Sweat prickled his ribs and palms, and he throttled forward just as the plane turned directly into them.

This time he kept his own speed down. Eric was shouting at him to turn a second earlier, and he thought to himself - an absurd notion - *practice makes perfect*. As if he expected to be doing this again some time. God forbid.

The wing-in-ground-effect monster towered like a mountain over them. The scream of the jets battered painfully at the ears, and Russell's hands were light as feathers on the wheel.

"Now! Turn it!" Eric bellowed into the solid wall of noise.

Was it possible for two nervous systems to react as one? Was it worth researching that idea? Could he get a research grant to pursue telepathy under duress? Russell's hands were already moving when Eric shouted, and the *Tiger Shark* swung sideways, at thirty degrees from the course of the plane.

But this time Calder was expecting the manoeuvre, and out of the corner of his eye Russell glimpsed the dark place in the side of the aircraft - the wound of an open hatch.

He never heard the rattle of full automatic fire, but a dozen rounds of ammunition raked the side of the boat and several more skimmed the plexiglass windshield. That glass was bulletproof, designed so deliberately, in the event that the boat hit debris in the water at high speed. The rounds created star shaped impact scars, and Russell's heart leapt into his throat.

"Christ, they're armed," he muttered, far too softly to be heard as he wrestled the boat around. Then he lifted his voice over the engine roar. "Hold on! We're going to cross its wake!"

They went across suicidally fast with a bone-wrenching battering through the hull, while the plane raced away and her pilot cut speed and tried to bring her about again. But Russell pushed the throttles wide open to overspeed, and as soon as the powerboat was across the turbulence of the wake water she leapt away like a startled hare.

On the screen, the blip marking the position of the tanker was now big and bright, and Eric was sitting up, stretching his neck, trying to catch a glimpse of her over the wave crests. The radio chose that moment to shrill:

"*Tiger Shark*, watch yourselves! Customs say they found several automatic weapons aboard, all permit-legal, they weren't confiscated. The aircraft itself is not armed, but there are plenty of weapons aboard."

Eric had the mic in his hand. "Thanks, but we found that out for ourselves about a minute ago."

"You're under fire?" The man's voice was sharp.

"We were. We're safe, so far," Eric shouted. "And I think ... I can see the tanker! I have it! *Shark* to *Regina Maris*, can you see us? I have you in visual contact!"

She was a big one. In the last century she would have roved the world, carrying the very crude oil that helped to destroy the planet's delicate climatic mechanism, but now she was a saviour. Her load was twenty million litres of fresh water, and she spelled Life to hundreds of thousands of people on the atolls, the island republics of the Pacific.

"We can see you," a woman's voice called, hearteningly near at hand. "Steer right into our lee. We're cutting speed now, but we can't stop her on a nickel. Put us between you and that monster and let us see if we can knock him out of the air. Just tuck in at our waterline and stay out of the way, if you can. How's your fuel situation?"

"Russell?" Eric held the mic over.

"We've got twenty minutes' worth, max," Russell reported. "We've been burning it off pretty fast. Don't worry about us right now."

"Copy that, *Tiger Shark*. Just stay out of our firing line."

The tanker was like a vast grey whale, idling along on the surface. Eric fished around in the foot well, broke out the binoculars and scanned the deck as Russell jockeyed the powerboat closer and closer. As he made out the armament he whistled.

"If Calder has the brains of a budgie, he'll get that plane of his out of here. Damnit, Rusty, she's carrying light artillery." He passed over the binoculars.

Russell held them to his eyes, and at once saw the guns Eric had spotted. "Ex-World War ... something vintage," he chuckled. "Where the hell did they get those?"

"Recycled," Eric guessed. "Can't afford to throw anything away. No more where they came from." He recovered the field glasses, dropped them into the footwell, and tipped his head back, and back again, to see the superstructure of the tanker as Russell cut speed, arced the powerboat around and tucked neatly in at the big ship's waterline, like a calf beside a mother grey whale.

It was like running beside the *Atlantis*, and the feeling of security was warmer than being wrapped in a blanket. The analogy reminded

Russell that Eric was still naked, and he reached back for a towel. This, he handed to his partner with a grin.

"Put something on, will you? You're gorgeous, but ... in fact, I just don't want you on display. You're mine, if you take my meaning."

"Jealous?" Eric accused, but he wore a wide smile as he released his straps, braced himself between the seats and tied the towel about him, islander-fashion, so that it looked less like a towel than a sarong. "Good enough

Russell smacked his lips.

"Sometimes I worry about you." Eric grasped the back of his seat and looked up ahead. "Here she comes."

As if that were the cue, the deck guns in the bow opened up, and for the first time in his life, in the flesh, Russell heard the shrieking howl of artillery shells ploughing through the air. Just short of the nose of the wing-in-ground-effect plane, plume after plume of water erupted from the sea.

The pilot's reaction was an instantaneous reflex. Pure survival instinct. The plane dipped a wing, turned so steeply that the two port side jets stalled, and angled away from the tanker. Russell craned his neck to look up at the deck and saw the blunt muzzles of guns amidships.

This ship, this crew, were ready for pirates - they had probably got their experience in a multitude of actions fought ought against Malay fleets that prowled in search of just such rich pickings as a this. Water was sometimes more valuable than oil.

He turned back seaward, watching with slitted eyes as the plane disappeared into the blue-green distance, and with a groan Eric sagged back into his seat. Russell took his hand, held it tightly, and their fingers meshed.

"We," Eric said tersely, "and about the two luckiest bastards on the planet."

"Understatement," Russell said as he cut speed to match the rapidly slowing tanker. The radio mic cupped against his mouth and he called, "*Atlantis, Atlantis*, you have them on radar?"

"We have a surface search fix," their man assured. "Hooking into the satellite right now ... we won't lose them, *Tiger Shark*, if that's what you're thinking."

"You read my mind," Russell said acidly. "Inform Duquesne. He's going to want to know. He has a vested interest in this ... their target in Pacifica was Eric Devlin, and for that the old man is going to want blood."

He dropped the mic, and only now, as the engine noise dwindled and the power boat began to bob like a dinghy in the calm, oily lee of the tanker, did he permit himself to feel the knot of his belly, the trembling of his limbs. When Eric offered an embrace he was pleased to accept, grateful for the press of another human body against his own, a celebration of survival, until a voice called down from the deck of the tanker, with the aid of a loud hailer,

"Hey, you love birds down there, you wanna come aboard? Skipper says you're invited for lunch!"

They parted reluctantly, and Russell squinted up to see a face, and an out-swung crane. The *Regina Maris* was still under braking thrusters and almost at a stop, while the *Tiger Shark* was on minimum revs, idling along beside her. Russell waved. "Pick us up! And thanks, we appreciate it."

"I'll just bet you do!" The American chuckled over his megaphone, and then redirected it at the foredeck, where the crane driver was waiting. "Lower it away, Jodie!"

Big electromagnets grabbed on and whisked the powerboat out of the water as if it was no more than a feather. A few moments' dizzying ride up through space, and the derrick swung them inboard once more, with a howling of winches and the reek of machine oil and ferrous oxide, before the crane deposited the *Tiger* more or less neatly in the empty cradle where a lifeboat should have been.

Not surprised to find his legs trembling under him with a mix of relief and fatigue, Russell lifted himself over the side and turned to meet the skipper and officers. Eric perched on the edge of the power-boat as the captain offered a hand in greeting.

"You headed our way?" Russell asked ruefully.

The woman grasped his hand readily. She was small, silver haired, broad in the hips, with powerful the arms. Short sleeves and a low neck line displayed muscles many a man would have envied. Her accent was Californian, probably Catalina, and her manner was candid and engaging.

"We diverted, soon as we got a call from *Pacifica*. You'd be Doctor Grant, I presume?" Her blue-grey eyes flickered to Eric. "And Eric Devlin, the, uh, Aquarian?"

"Please to meet you." Eric offered his hand. "We owe you."

"Maybe." She smiled broadly. "I'm Captain Quinn. Joyce Quinn. And like I said, we just got a call from a Mr Gerald Duquesne. We're diverting to *Pacifica*, his request ... and his expense, not that we'd have requested a fee." She looked bitterly in the wake of Calder's plane.

Something in that look made Russell's ears prick. "You know that aircraft?"

Quinn's brow creased. Her face was darkly tanned, a little weather beaten, and she was probably not as old as she looked. "Oh, we know those slimes. That's Calder. We've known Graham Calder for more years than either he or I care to recall. He ripped us off for a cargo ten years ago. Last time I saw him, he was anchored within sight of Rhutan. That crew is filth, and right at home in Rhutan."

"And there," Eric said quietly, "is the connection we've been waiting for." He looked down into Quinn's face. "I think Mr Duquesne would like to talk to you, skipper. He'll be in conference with the Australian president about now. Rhutan's been begging for military intervention, but it's all a question of politics and money. Too much of one, not enough of the other."

"I heard." Quinn stepped back as Eric swung down off the side of the boat, and cocked her head at him. "Pardon me for noticing, but that's a towel you're ... almost wearing."

He hitched it up more firmly about his hips and produced a disarming grin. "I started out with clothes this morning. Your friend Calder didn't leave me a whole lot to work with."

She curled his lip after the departed plane. "Jodie's about the same size as you. Hey, Jode! Show these gentlemen to a spare cabin, and get Mr Devlin something to wear." She graced them with a smile. "Lunch in twenty minutes. I hope you're hungry for rabbit casserole and strawberry pie. We grow them aboard, you know."

"The rabbits or the strawberries?" Russell speculated.

"Both." Quinn stepped aside and gestured toward the nearest door in the grey metal deck house. A tall, lanky man with short-cropped hair and a straggly moustache appeared from the back rank of the crew.

The spare cabin afforded a view of the foredeck, guns and all. It boasted two bunks, but they would not need them, since the *Regina Maris'* estimated time of arrival at *Pacifica* was 20:00. A tiny bathroom cubicle offered toilet and shower, and while they waited for Eric's promised clothes, Russell took the opportunity to strip to the skin and share the water with him.

The young man called Jodie looked in while they were bathing, and dumped an armful of jeans, tee shirts and underwear on one of the bunks. "There you go. Hope they fit. Give a yell if you got a problem."

The door closed smartly, and in the precious privacy Russell caught Eric by the hips, pressed him back against the wall and kissed him soundly. Eric's arms circled his shoulders and the kiss was nearer bite than kiss until they were content. Then Russell sighed heavily and heaved a yawn.

"I didn't sleep last night," he confessed.

"Makes two of us." Eric turned off the water, stretched is spine and picked up the towel he had been wearing. "I was too busy worrying about the dive. Calder told me the specifics last night, but I couldn't prise any info about the contents of that case out of him with a crow bar."

"Interesting." Russell consulted his watch and his brow creased as he made a few rapid mental calculations. "The *Poseidon* won't be home for about two days. We could go out and meet her. Tow her back."

"Oh, no." Eric shook his head emphatically. "Don't even think it. Not while Calder and Royce are out there. Unless I miss my guess, they'll be just waiting for us to do exactly that ... and you can bet your life, Russell, we won't be so lucky a second time."

"Bet my life," Russell echoed. "Fascinating choice of words."

"You know what I mean," Eric said tersely as he began to dress in a decent pair of jeans and a white tee shirt that was just a little too large. He gave Russell a look that began stern and softened into affection. "Thanks."

"For what?" Russell picked up the damp towel and began to pat sketchily at his legs.

"Coming after me." Eric took the towel from him and rubbed his back. His lips feathered over the pink place, the little scar left over from the shooting. "If you hadn't, I'd have had one hell of a long swim to get home. And the seas around here are full of predators. Big ones."

Russell turned quickly, caught him in both arms and hugged him. "Reckon you owe me one?"

"I reckon I owe you three," Eric admitted. "Want to collect?"

"Oh, yeah." Russell rubbed noses. "At home. In bed. Safe and dry, warm and secure, where the only predator you have to worry about is me." He kissed Eric fleetingly and then released him. "I've been feeling my mortality a little."

"Only a little?" Eric mocked himself with a chuckle and held out his hand, pretending the shakes.

"Aquarian or not, you're only human." Russell hugged him, one-armed. "And before you say anything, fear is healthy. It keeps us alive."

"Any excuse for having the jitters," Eric argued, but his eyes sparkled with promise as he led the way from the cabin, and followed his nose to the crew's mess hall. "I want to call the *Atlantis*. I want to know where that goddamned plane has gone.

"Relax, Calder's being tracked by satellite, he's not going to disappear." Russell paused. "Not that he'll be running, Eric. You realize that."

Wide eyed in the dimness of the passageway just outside the officers' mess, Eric looked up at him, and with one thumb gestured back, and down. "He's going to know I salvaged that case. He may have seen the *Poseidon*. And whatever the salvage was, he'll want it back."

"So he won't be leaving *Pacifica's* waters," Russell agreed, "and if I were him I'd get back to the schooner. As the *Queen Katherine*'s been cut free of the wreckage on the seamount, Calder will probably be using every sonar probe he's got, pattern-searching for our sub." He arched both brows at Eric. "The chances of him finding it before it gets home - one tiny needle in a big, big haystack - are about a thousand to one. He'll run out of time before he tracks it down."

Unspoken misgivings hung in the air like summer thunder, and Eric's expressive mouth compressed. "He'll be back, looking for his cargo."

"I know." Russell looked away, through the mess hall's doors, where the tanker's crew were celebrating what they believed to be a victory.

"And we're not safe," Eric added very quietly. "Russell, there's no place on *Pacifica* that we'll be safe, and we don't have anywhere left to run. To the south, the CAIR, and the Zealand islands, and they're Calder's and Royce's home turf. To the north, Rhutan, and Calder seems to do so much business there, that's probably another of his hunting grounds." He took a breath, held it, let it out slowly. "I'm open to suggestions, Rusty."

"How in the hell did we walk into this?" Russell pulled both hands across his face, trying to force himself to think.

"We didn't. We were dragged. Because of me." Eric laid both hands flat on the planes of his chest, over those Aquarian lungs. "They came looking for a sub for charter, and an Aquarian pilot."

"And I wish to Christ I'd just hired them the sub," Russell growled. "All right, se we're in it, Eric, up to the eyeballs." He dropped his voice as a tiny, blonde crewgirl walked by, into the mess hall. "Duquesne's got to be interested in this. Give him the ball, let him run with it. Whatever the salvage is, legally - under any maritime law you want to claim! - it's ours. So, whatever it is, we trade it to Duquesne."

"In exchange," Eric mused, "for security." He made a face. "It'll be like being a prisoner in custody."

"And I'd rather a live prisoner for as long as it takes than be fish food," Russell said darkly. "We'll be shark bait, Eric, without Duquesne. So, we trade?"

"Oh, we trade." Eric's face and voice hardened. "I want that bastard, Russell. I want to chew a chunk right out of his ass. There's a kid, a little Malay girl, on that schooner ... and like the skipper of this tub says, Calder and Royce are filth. Odds on, Duquesene'll want to know what Calder's doing in Rhutan."

"He's not the only one," Russell added. "We're safe for the moment. This ship's headed for *Pacifica*, and Calder's vicious, not crazy, he won't go up against artillery."

"So I'll call the *Atlantis*," Eric said tersely. "Make sure they have that damn plane on surveillance, and then we trade." He thrust out his hand. "Deal."

"Deal," Russell agreed, and shook. "And now, will you come and eat? Maybe you dined well as Calder's table guest yesterday, but I didn't."

"And maybe," Eric said through teeth that seemed to be clenched, "every bite I ate at his table almost choked me." He went ahead into the mess, leaving Russell to frown after him. Russell had never before seen that hint of vengeful fury in Eric. The Aquarian's temperament was so even, it was too easy to forget that he could be dangerous. Russell had never seen this side of him before, and while one part of him was chilled he also felt a lick of fascination in his belly.

Without a word, he followed his partner into the mess and ignored the crew's victory celebrations, for they were far too premature.

Chapter Thirteen

Monstrous diesel engines cast a faint shudder through the frame of the tanker as the *Regina Maris*'s side thrusters brought her onto station-keeping, not quite a kilometre from the *Atlantis*. Even Joyce Quinn's vessel was a mere pup beside *Pacifica*'s mother ship, and Russell gave the immense bulk of the *Atlantis* a glance of simple gratitude. She embodied security in a world that had not been certain since long before Russell was born.

At 20:00, the sun was a few minutes down and the sky was an ocean of blood. The tanker had gone onto station-keeping to westward of Duquesne's vessel, and the sunset painted the grey hull of the *Atlantis* every lurid shade from dark gold to purple. Those colours could appear regal, but tonight Russell found them oppressive. They were the banner colours of the Rhutani Emir, Potan Kap, and on the aft landing deck of the *Atlantis*, outlined against the sky, Eric had already glimpsed, and pointed out, the shapes of the CAIR Air Force One and the Nepalese President's Flight.

"They're still in conference," Eric said softly.

"They're still aboard," Russell corrected, "but even politicians couldn't talk this long and not reach an agreement."

"Fifty says they can," Eric said acerbically. Russell frowned sidelong at him. They were standing by the rail, waiting for Jodie Chard to pilot the crane, put the *Tiger Shark* back in the water. Quinn was a few paces forward, one hand clamped over her ear, the other holding a cell phone to her head. Arranging to top off her diesel tanks, Russell guessed, since the detour to *Pacifica* had put her several hundred kilometres and a day's hard running behind schedule.

"You're cynical," he observed mildly as Eric turned toward him.

"It's hard not to be." Eric was gazing out into the growing murk of the ocean twilight. "I'm thinking about that kid. That little girl on the *Queen Katherine*. She was just cargo, Rusty."

"As you would have been, soon as you'd outlived your usefulness," Russell said pointedly. "You heard what Quinn said, every word, we both did."

Over a very good dinner Quinn had rambled, alternately angry and sour as she recalled several encounters with Calder and Royce this crew had barely survived. The *Regina* made the run from Nepal through the islands to Zealand in the south, and then north again, to her home ports in the California Islands. She was registered in Catalina, but her crew was equal parts Maori, Malay, Australian, a few Pacificans, Americans ... and several war-scarred, battle-shocked escapees from Rhutan.

The crane ground into life, bass and thundering, and Jodie Chard picked up the powerboat with the dexterity of a decade's experience. Quinn glared up at him in the crane pilot's cab, and cupped her hand over the phone, bawling to make herself heard. She was in blue jeans, black leather jacket, a ball cap carrying the insignia of this ship. And as the night wind began to buffet and she leaned against the rail, Russell saw her favouring that right leg.

Four rounds of surgery, and it still wasn't repaired. And with every spasm of pain, every revolt from nerves and tendons that no longer functioned properly, she would curse a man called Calder. Three years ago the *Regina* had been bound for Nepal with a deck cargo of Lynx warheads and a prince's ransom in synthetic drugs in the deep-freeze, along with an in-tank cargo of two million litres of fresh Zealand highlands water. Fifteen White Dragon Tong thugs boarded under cover of darkness, and Graham Calder and Brady Royce were right behind them. The battle to take back the tanker was vicious; four men were killed, three more badly wounded. Quinn's surgeon informed her that she would never walk properly again, after several 9mm rounds were taken out of a smashed pelvis.

Quinn walked again, and commanded this ship; but her hair was iron grey now, and the *Regina Maris*, whose symbol was an angel blessing the ocean, was armoured so heavily, she could have done service as a warship.

Yes, Eric was cynical. And it was difficult not to be. Russell leaned both forearms on the rail and leaned over to watch the *Tiger* settle into the water. Her autopilot tucked her right in beside the tanker's calm waterline, and with a whir the electromagnetic clamps shut down. Jodi fetched up the derrick, swung the arm inboard, and as he shut off the machinery Russell rubbed his protesting ears.

It was a moment before he realized Quinn was speaking to them, and Eric had turned toward her before Russell could make sense of what the captain was saying.

"We're wanted." Quinn jerked her thumb over her shoulder in the direction of the *Atlantis*. "Gerald Duquesne requests the pleasure of our company."

"Requests?" Eric echoed with a lopsided grin.

Quinn snorted. "The kind of request you don't turn down. Not that he'd send his goons over here and frog-march you over, you understand."

But Security would certainly show up - with a smile, with a limousine, with the old man's 'invitation' to come over to the *Atlantis*. And Security would not leave without their passengers.

"Ride with us," Russell suggested. "The *Tiger's* in the water, she's the quickest ride over, or back."

"Glad to." Quinn stuffed her hands into the jacket pockets. "What you guys been up to? It sure as hell ain't me Duquesne wants to see."

"We just butted heads with the man whose neck you'd most like to wring," Eric said acidly. "I guess that'd be enough to raise Duquesne's interest. Though why he's concerned with you, Captain, I couldn't guess." He stepped aside and gestured at the service elevator that accessed the waterline hatches. "Shall we?"

The elevator bottomed out on the engine deck, and the hatch

growled open. Through this port in the side of the ship would be manoeuvred spare machine parts or cargo, and it was an escape hatch in time of emergency. Russell dug through his hip pocket for the autopilot's remote caller, aimed it at the *Tiger Shark*'s high, sharp bow, and thumbed it. The boat nudged toward the open hatch, engines barely idling. Her big fuel tanks were almost dry, she was riding high, and it was easy for Eric to catch her stern line and hop over into the well.   He took her on manual, brought her in until her smooth glass-fibre hull grazed the barnacle-coarse side of the tanker, and Russell offered Quinn his hands to help her over. She did not glare, but deliberately brushed him aside and pulled herself onto the powerboat with less grace than determination. That hip, Russell saw, was only half functional. Artificial? If his own research proved out, the day would come when Joyce Quinn could hope to regenerate her own bone and tissue. But not yet, and Quinn knew it. Securely aboard the bobbing *Tiger*, she gave Russell a look that might have been defiance.

He answered with a grin. "Okay, so the age of chivalry is dead."

"And buried," Quinn agreed as he hopped over, and Eric brought the power boat about toward the *Atlantis.*

The starboard side watermark docking bays were all floodlit, and Quinn directed them to Bay 14, which was aft, under the superstructure. The baymaster was waiting for them, and Eric gave Russell a curious glance as they saw, right behind the man, two security agents in Duquesne's livery.

"Something," Eric said softly, "is cooking."

"Something to do with you two," Quinn guessed. "You're either going to be decorated or court-martialled."

"We're not military, very few on *Pacifica* are." Russell held on as the *Tiger* rode across the wake of an outbound vessel and nosed into the docking bay.

The baymaster beckoned to Eric, who was piloting, and Duquesne's security stepped up to the mooring clamps. Rich, dark blue uniform jackets looked purple in the fluorescent lights, but gold was still gold.

The clamps took hold with a soft shush of compressed air and at once the powerboat was a stable platform. Russell looked up into the carefully bland faces of the agents - one, a man of thirty, the other a woman ten years older. They were trained in the CAIR, and he had never seen any one of them display a twitch of emotion or even thought. No use asking them what this was about. Russell thought he could see a muscle grinding in Eric's jaw, but he also was silent as they stepped over onto the Atlantis and followed the agents to the executive elevator.

It was guarded. Two soldiers - CAIR troopers, both armed - came to attention as the security agents approached. IDs were checked, a tiresome routine, and then the mirror-walled elevator was rising swiftly, with only a slight vibration.

Not to deck level. Russell's brows twitched as the car continued upward, and Eric made a small sound as he saw the numbers flick over into the superstructure. The conference rooms were at deck level, the executive accommodations a level higher, but the car did not stop until it was high in the superstructure, and before the doors opened Russell knew exactly where they were.

Gerald Duquesne's suite of offices never shut down for a moment. All of *Pacifica* lived and breathed from this knot of nerve fibres, where super computers and ancient "folk magic" combined to produce some alchemy that would, Russell was sure, reshape the future. But he was still surprised to see the old man here at this hour, even now on his feet, toying with a putter, though the half dozen golf balls seemed to be forgotten by the desk. Straight-backed and bright eyed, Duquesne turned to greet them, but his creased face was sombre, which made him look every year of his age. He was dressed formally, still. The cut of his suit would have flattered a Catalina freight baron, yet nothing could disguise tiredness, some deep sadness, and the burden of untold years.

"Russell, Eric, it was good of you to come right here. Captain Quinn." He gave the tanker's skipper a nod, and the wraith of a smile touched his lips.

"You gave us the option?" Quinn thrust out her hand and grasped

Duquesne's strong wrist. "Not that I'd have turned you down, Gerry, we don't see enough of each other these days. But I could have wished for more pleasant circumstances ... that's a bleak look on your face."

Gerry? Russell and Eric shared a glance. Few people indeed - and no one of Russell's generation or acquaintance - was familiar enough with Duquesne to call him by a diminutive of his first name. Which could only mean that Duquesne and Quinn had done considerable business elsewhere, and for long enough that they had established that bond of trust.

He was old enough to be her biological grandfather, but he clasped her hand, pecked her cheek with a kiss, and gestured all three of his guests to the black leather chairs that surrounded the desk. Four chairs remained empty, but Russell saw the telltale signs that they had recently been occupied. Cup-rings on the polished table surface; cookie crumbs; the filter from a cigarette overlooked on the turf green carpet.

With a grunt that betrayed old bones and stiff joints, Duquesne sank into the chair at the desk's head and swivelled the computer's deepdisplay monitor around. "You know that there's been a conference here while you were gallivanting halfway across the Pacific?"

"Gallivanting?" Eric almost bridled. "I was abducted - I was damn-near killed!"

"I know." Duquesne's eyes sparkled for a moment of rare humour. "I had the whole report from Security while the *Regina Maris* made her way here. It may put your minds at ease to know that the submersible is 105 metres down, currently circumnavigating Seamount 58874, and on its way home. The schooner *Queen Katherine* is sixty kilometres behind, raking the entire ocean with sonar, looking for it, so whatever the salvage cargo you recovered, Eric, Graham Calder and Brady Royce want it badly. Their plane turned south when Joyce opened fire on it. We picked it up on SkyEye 17, watched it rendezvous briefly with the schooner, and then we tracked it into CAIR airspace. We're assuming that Calder and Royce transferred over to the schooner since everything that interests them at this juncture is headed for *Pacifica* at 4.7

knots, riding the tail-current around that seamount."

"Damn," Eric breathed, and rubbed his palms together slowly, deliberately. Russell could almost hear his partner's brain working and Duquesne waited until the Aquarian went on, "We figured they'd come for us, or for the salvage. We figured there's no place we can run or hide, not from them."

"Not quite true," Duquesne said affably, "but I'm glad you scampered home after your adventure." He spoke as if they were children, filled with mischief, certain to get into one scrape or another. In his eyes, they were so young, even Russell felt like a boy again. "The salvage dive, Eric?"

"Was deep and cold," Eric told him, "with a wicked current running. No problem I couldn't handle, and then Rusty showed up and you know the rest." He paused, wetted his lips and flicked a glance at Russell, who nodded.

"We want to trade, sir," Russell ventured.

Straggling silver brows rose, and Duquesne resettled his glasses on the bridge of his nose. "Trade what - for what?"

"The salvage," Russell said tersely. "For our own security. I can't guess what's in the case Eric brought off the chopper wreck, but if Calder and Royce want it that bad, sir, it has to be valuable. Under maritime law, it's ours." He spread his hands. "Take it. You just get those bastards off our backs, and you can have it."

For a moment Duquesne was silent, and then he and Quinn shared a cackle of laughter. "What I envy most about youth," Duquesne said to the woman, "is its blissful, myopic audacity."

"Blissful? Maybe," Quinn said wryly. "Audacious? Certainly. Myopic? I don't know, Gerry. Are they being near-sighted? Right now I don't know a damn thing more than they do ... and what I don't know is starting to scare shit out of me."

The old man sobered and nodded. "All right. A trade, Russell. Not that it was necessary, given the circumstances, but we'll call it a trade and flatter the honour of youth."

"You lost me," Russell said honestly. He had begun to feel that floundering sensation, when the water was a hand's span over his head and his human lungs had begun to burn. Beside him, Eric was just as fuddled. And tired, Russell noticed. Probably hungry too, all of which was conspiring to shorten the Aquarian's temper.

Did Duquesne see Eric's lips compress? If he did, he respected the younger man's need to know, for he spun the tracker ball over and poked a long finger at several keys, and the deepdisplay monitor displayed a open file. Three head-up displays shimmered in its fluorescing depths; Russell inclined his head this way, then that way to view text, images and video, and swore beneath his breath.

Framed in the left of the screen were Ranjit Narayan and Catherine Bowman, both faces all too easily recognizable after the last week's vidcasts. Narayan had been elected president of the Republic of Nepal three years before. Bowman was in her second term as the CAIR president, and these were arguably the most powerful political figures in the southern and eastern hemispheres. And right below their images was the head file picture of another document.

Who would not recognize Potan Kap? Like anyone on *Pacifica*, Russell had been following the Emir's progress for too long. But what Potan Kap had to do with himself and Eric was another question, and his skin crawled. Across the desk, Joyce Quinn swore luridly. Her rings tapped rhythmically on the table and her upper body swayed with reined-back fury. Brown eyes glittered with anger as she looked from the screen to Duquesne and back again. Russell and Eric merely waited.

"Bowman and Narayan are bathing, getting a meal, conferring with their advisers," Duquesne began. "We were in conference for eighteen hours, and I dare say they are as exhausted as am I." He toggled a key and the file pictures fell into the background while the foreground displayed a regional map. Zealand and CAIR to the south and east, *Pacifica*, Rhutan just eight hundred kilometres away, and the Republic of Nepal far to the northwest. But not far enough. Duquesne frowned at each of his guests in turn. "What do you know about Potan Kap?"

"Too much." Quinn's sun-worn face was a bleak mask. "I've had every story from the kids I lifted out of that pest hole of his. What do you want to hear, Gerry? That ten year olds, girls and boys alike, go work in the bordellos for food? That two out of three babies are born diseased, one in twelve women will die birthing, one kid in five doesn't live long enough to get work in the bordello? You want to hear about the drug abuse, the illiteracy, or maybe the seven hundred political prisoners in that cesspit?"

"Political prisoners," Russell went on, "who had the courage, or the stupidity, to speak out against a regime that's been suffocating those islands for years."

Shrewd eyes, grey now but once as blue as Russell's own, studied the screen. Duquesne was too old, had seen too much to be appalled by any evil, yet how could he not be touched by human distress?

"Rhutan," he said softly, almost to himself. "An island state, supposedly a republic, but the government - I'll dignify it with the word! - is one man. A republic? Potan Kap may call it that, but to you and I Rhutan is a feudality. Decaying. Rotted from the inside, like a tree that's stood a hundred years too long."

"But it could stand another hundred years." Quinn leaned closer, on the table, and Russell physically felt her anger as she studied the columns of data marching through the display. "It's a mass of petty warlords, but so long as they answer to one central core command - Potan Kap himself - the system will hold itself up. Like the Caribbean pirates."

"Until something," Eric suggested, "or someone comes along to challenge it, overturn it." His brows arched at the screen, where the faces of so many political prisoners were displayed, one after another, given a single second each. The slide show was endless." And I'm guessing something or someone just happened."

A bark of laugher, not a sound of humour, issued from Duquesne's chest. "There, Joyce, you see? Aquarians are not all gills and fins. The boy has a brain."

Was he talking about Aquarians in general, or Eric in particular? Russell felt that odd little shiver that always troubled him when a man he thought of as his lover became, however briefly, a specimen. Duquesne meant nothing by it, certainly no insult, and yet Russell felt Eric bristle for a moment, heard him sigh before he turned his eyes down and simply waited for Duquesne to go on.

"A feudal state," the old man mused. "Potan Kap is Cambodian, or Laotian, or both. His clan were royalty before the inundation, with holdings and estates scattered from the Persian Gulf to Vietnam. After Chen-Goldstein 4, it seems Rhutan was their last province to keep its head above water, and it was natural that the family would relocate there, while they had scorned even to notice the island before.

"But today's Rhutan is a sovereign territory of Kap's own making. He gave *himself* the title of Emir ... he was nominally Muslim in his youth. Certainly he was educated as a Muslim, with a degree from Bahrain University. His father died weeks after the degree was conferred, and before the young man could return to Rhutan, a republican coup took place on the island. Royalty was unwelcome there - anyone's royalty. Potan Kap was quite literally unthroned before his coronation. And by all accounts, he was broke. His bank accounts in Bahrain and Paris were emptied, and he maxed-out every credit card he possessed.

"Perhaps not so surprisingly, he disappeared for eight years, and no security service in the world knows what became of him, where he was. But he eventually showed his face again in the Zealand islands, and his misadventures in whatever forbidden zones had changed him."

The display popped up two images now, renditions of the same face, changed by time. On the left, the student, darkly handsome, saturnine but pleasant - highly intelligent, if Russell was any judge, and no more than twenty years old. On the right was a man of thirty, his hairline marched back, the lines either of suffering or excess etched into his face; and his eyes blazed.

"Sweet Jesus," Eric breathed, "what happened to him?"

"As I said," Duquesne went on, "no security service in the world can answer that. But he reappeared in Zealand, and from there made his way to the Flinders Islands. About the time you were born, Russell, Potan Kap rallied an army of equally mad-eyed mercenaries from the atolls and islands between *Pacifica* and the Burmese highlands, which were even then part of the Republic of Nepal, and they seized Rhutan in a moment when the island was vulnerable. Tropical Cyclone Arthur did most of the work for them. All Kap had to do was pick up the pieces, shoot the dissenters and award himself the title of Emir."

"And then," Eric said quietly, "it was his pleasure to punish the people for the coup, for the eight years he spent in some kind of limbo."

"Fast forward thirty more years," Quinn said sourly, "and Rhutan is what you see today. Sick, impoverished. Desperate." She shifted in her chair, easing the hip that seemed to have been jury-rigged to get her walking again. "Did you watch the show, when the Bal Islands moved a fleet of missile carriers into Tagamaya Lagoon?"

The whole world had watched that "show." The Rhutanis had believed that their dream of freedom was about to be realized. The Bal Archipelago was much larger, and surely the threat of missile cruisers just over the horizon would send Potan Kap scurrying for his very life. For almost a week, it seemed that a new commonwealth would be formed, and the socialist order of the Bal Islands would help to heal Rhutan's poverty and sickness. Even *Pacifica* held its breath.

And then Potan Kap answered with another mercenary army, its ranks fleshed out with thugs who did not even attempt to conceal their White Dragon Tong affiliations. The Rhutani uprising was crushed in three days of bloodshed, the missile carriers withdrew from Tagamaya Lagoon, and all vidcasts out of Rhutan stopped.

"And now?" Russell's belly had tightened with foreboding. "Sir, Eric was taken out of *Pacifica* to salvage a helijet that was on its way out of Rhutan. Calder and Royce are dealing with Potan Kap, they have to be."

Duquesne seemed to age before their eyes. The lines in his face were etched more deeply than ever, the hollows around his eyes seemed darker, and for a bare moment Russell caught a glimpse of the skull beneath thin human skin and flesh. He might have been imagining it, but Quinn saw it too, and it was the woman who said, "Gerry, what's wrong? Something's happened."

The moment of frailty was gone and Duquesne's voice was strong, with a knife's edge of determination that could have sounded ruthless, even cruel, in another man. "Calder and Royce have been dealing with the government of Rhutan ... with Potan Kap ... for years. President Bowman's security services have been trying to nail down one solid piece of evidence that would imprison or execute them, but Graham Calder was never so stupid as to leave tracks, and there is a downside to a judicial system that pledges justice for all. A man is innocent until proven guilty, and a system like that in *Pacifica*, the CAIR and Nepal, allows no margins in which to scribble. No area where damning evidence can be manufactured. So Calder and Royce are free to do business between Zealand, Rhutan and Moresby."

"Moresby?" Quinn echoed. Her face scrunched in a frown. "It's nothing but one big boot camp for ronin right across Oceania. White Dragon Tong train there."

"And launch surveillance pop-satellites from a facility in the mountains," Duquesne added, "and trade in every kind of armament. *Every* kind."

The deepdisplay flickered, a three-level file opened and stabilized. Russell tilted his head to see the text data streamer and then lifted his chin, changed the angle to see the video. "This is from the CAIR. President Bowman's feed?"

"She brought it in on disk," Duquesne said tersely. "The risks of transmitting this data ... no. And President Narayan had heard the same from his own sources, though he had nothing concrete to confirm the intelligence until the CAIR security service provided this."

Satellite imaging; footage from a high altitude "popeye" that had cruised over Rhutan, no larger than a pelican, no more suspicious than a little weather probe. Perhaps the Rhutani tracking system had not even picked it up at all.

But displayed in the fluorescing monitor were enhanced images that made Russell's blood chill. Eric shifted closer, his leg lay along Russell's; perhaps he needed that small human contact, for the data on the screen was appalling.

"Missile silos," Duquesne said unnecessarily. "Almost complete. Built back into the bedrock of that extinct volcano, right behind Potan Kap's fortress. I do believe an air strike would winkle them out of there, but we know from intelligence provided by President Narayan that long before an air strike could approach Rhutan, those aircraft would be knocked down by surface to air missiles provided and installed by White Dragon Tong armorers."

"Shit," Quinn swore quietly. She cleared her throat and looked sidelong at Russell and Eric before fixing Duquesne with gimlet eyes. "Gerry, why are you telling this to us? This is intelligence, for chrissakes. Nothing to do with civilians."

The old man's head shook slowly. "In a month, perhaps less, it'll be public knowledge, and what I'm about to tell you will be the business of every soul within a radius of six thousand kilometres of Rhutan."

"Missile range." Eric's fists clenched on the desk.

"There's more." Duquesne rolled the tracker ball over and the display changed to text only. "This was intercepted by CAIR spies in Moresby. And they died for it. White Dragon Tong executed them publicly twelve hours after this transmission was made."

Russell had already read the text, but it was as if his brain refused the information. He read it again, and a third time before simple words began to make sense. His palms were wet, his skin crawling, and beside him Eric said, "Mother of God, this can't be right."

"It can." Duquesne sat back, the chair squealed quietly under his weight as he closed his eyes, took off his glasses and rubbed his eyeballs with thumb and forefinger. "The missiles are old Chinese vehicles, fully refurbished, ready to fly. The warheads are French, American, whatever, salvaged from a site in Mongolia and rebuilt by ronin technicians with connections right back to Kure, Japan. And the weapons grade plutonium is Australian, mined out of the interior fifty, sixty years ago, before Roxby Downs was capped. President Bowman is trying to back-track, find out where it's been hiding for six decades, but it's all acade-mic.We know exactly where it is today."

"Sitting in a bunch of French warheads, rebuilt by Japanese techni-cians, on top of Chinese missiles, in Rhutan," Russell whispered.

"Not yet." Duquesne leaned forward again, elbows on the desk. "Our own scientists inform me that it will take three, possible four weeks to arm the warheads. We have that much margin. And then not even the CAIR will be safe."

The silence was heavy as a sodden blanket. Russell was cold to the fingertips, and Eric's face was pale as old wax. So this was what brought Bowman and Narayan to *Pacifica*. Rhutan was about to reinvent itself as the regional superpower, and every freestate from Nepal to Zealand was breathless with fear. Potan Kap would dominate the whole area for decades.

And *Pacifica* itself was just 800 kilometres from Rhutani waters. Russell blinked his eyes clear and saw Eric's troubled face. Quinn seemed to have put on a leather mask that was a poor approximation of her features. And Gerald Duquesne was very old indeed.

The comm at his elbow chirped discreetly. "Mr Duquesne, Madam Bowman and Sri Narayan have returned."

"Admit them," Duquesne invited. "And send in coffee." He hesitat-ed, one brow arched at his quests. "Have you eaten?"

He could send for supper, and in fact Russell and Eric had not eaten since lunch, but Russell's belly was so knotted, even the thought of food sickened him. "Coffee will be fine. Eric?"

"Yeah." Eric pressed his face into his hands for a moment and then addressed Duquesne directly. "There's no way the CAIR, and *Pacifica* and the rest of them are going to sit back and watch it happen. All right, we can't touch Calder and Royce with the law, but -"

"But this time they have so far overstepped the law, they have entered the realm of the political, the military, and the day has come when they are answerable to the same forces as Potan Kap himself."

The voice was deep, strong, and Russell knew it from scores of vidcasts. Catherine Bowman was sixty, still red haired, tall, wirey-thin, with sharp blue eyes and a gait like a marine on the parade ground. A burgundy brocade caftan moulded around her, her makeup was flawless, but if Russell cared to notice, wisps of wet hair clung to her neck. Behind her were four men; one was obviously her secretary, for he was juggling the briefcase and the laptop, and a second was also probably a parliamentary representative from the CAIR. President Ranjit Narayan of Nepal was as immediately recognizable as Bowman, and the young man in his wake could only be a secretary. No bodyguards were needed in Duquesne's sanctuary, but Russell recalled the armed guards on the elevator, and his belly squeezed again.

"Madam President." Duquesne came to his feet. "Sri Narayan."

Taking their cue from Duquesne, Russell and Eric stood, and Bowman looked them over curiously. "Doctor Russell Grant, ma'am." Russell offered his hand.

She took it lightly. "Of course. It was your submersible Calder wanted to charter. And Mr Devlin, I presume?"

She did not say, 'the Aquarian,' nor did she peer at him, and Russell could see that Eric was either relieved or flattered, possibly both. "Eric Devlin, ma'am. Your countrymen snatched me out of Pacifica to dive an airplane wreck for them."

"Yes, we know." Bowman's eyes crinkled as she smiled. "And I assume Mr. Duquesne has made you privy to our intelligence?"

"He has." Quinn leaned over and thrust out her own hand. "Captain A J Quinn, commanding the armed merchant vessel *Regina Maris*."

"Captain." Bowman clasped Quinn's hand lightly and gestured her to a chair. "Has Mr Duquesne given you any inkling as to what you're doing here?"

"Not a word," Quinn said acidly. "Then again, Gerry always did play his cards pretty close to his chest."

A flicker of surprise crossed Bowman's face now. "You're acquaint-ed?"

"Since they airlifted me to *Pacifica* for emergency surgery." Quinn slapped the hip that seemed to trouble her constantly. "A task force out of *Pacifica* answered our distress call, or we'd have lost the *Regina*."

"The tanker?" Bowman's eyes flickerd to Duquesne.

"They were boarded, three - or is four? - years ago." Duquesne sat back, fingers steepled on his middle. "Calder and Royce are not above a little piracy on the high seas, when the stakes are rich enough. Captain Quinn was left for dead, dumped on the engine deck."

"Not quite as dead as they assumed," Quinn said sourly. "And right now getting impatient as well as tired and hungry. You want to share the rest of the intelligence, Gerry, that's fine. If not, my fuel tanks will be topped off by now and I could use a few hours' sleep."

Duquesne lifted both hands. "Patience, Joyce. "There's a little more before I put a ... a proposition to you." His eyes strayed along the table. "And to you, Russell, Eric."

A small voice in the back of Russell's mind bade him keep quiet, keep still, and he hunched down in the chair, aware of Eric's leg lying along his thigh, of the Aquarian's deep disquiet, of the electricity that had begun to snap in this room as Ranjit Narayan's secretary opened a briefcase and passed a sheathed DVD down the desk to Duquesne."

"Dr Grant, Mr Devlin." Bowman's voice distracted Russell as Duquesne slipped the DVD into the drive. "You're most extraordinary men. In fact, you're quite unique."

"Flattery?" Eric wondered, eyes shrewd, tone guarded.

"Fact." Bowman frowned at her palms. "Do you know how many years we have been trying to apprehend Calder and Royce? We won't do it by any legal means. This much soon became clear! We know everything, we can prove nothing. Calder is far too thorough to leave loose ends."

"Loose ends?" Eric echoed.

"She means, survivors," Russell elaborated. "You'd have been dead, just to guarantee your silence, as soon as you outlived your usefulness."

"But we survived." Eric stirred, restless and ill at ease in this company. "I guess that makes us unique enough to make Calder want us both dead."

"It does." Bowman leaned back a little and beckoned to the second young man who had accompanied her. "I'd like you to met Detective James Heron. Graham Calder, and more recently Sean Patrick Brady Royce, have been the focus of his career. And I think he may be closer to an arrest tonight than he has been in more than a decade."

The man was forty, bronze skinned, brown eyed, with a self-mocking smile that was engaging, and dark hair tied at his nape in a thick pony tail. "Jim Heron, Flinders Islands CIB." I was assigned to Madam Bowman's party when Calder and Royce were reported in this area."

"They still are in the area," Eric said bleakly. "They'll be on the schooner, trying to pick up our submersible before it can find its way home."

"We know." Heron gestured at Duquesne. "He was good enough to share data, and he's as eager to see Calder and Royce nailed as we are. Calder won't yet be aware of the gravity of the situation. Talks between political leaders in the islands don't even raise a mention on vidcast outside of the host island. So the only thing on his mind will be -"

"To recover his salvage, and bury us," Russell finished. Eric's face was taut, but his cheeks were faintly flushed with anger now, and that was healthy. The same anger knotted Russell's insides. "You're going to make an arrest, Detective?"

"Perhaps." Heron dropped his voice as the deepdisplay came alive with President Narayan's data. "You're the closest thing I've ever had to witnesses, Dr Grant. And the only way you're going to be safe is to get the albatross off your back."

"You can do that?" Eric's voice was a piercing whisper.

But Duquesne's terminal had begun to display and conversation hushed around the desk. A few minutes of poor quality video; a dozen images, and a digitized phonecall. Men in grey and blue uniform coats, strutting on a wharf as if they owned it. Automatic weapons slung carelessly from shoulders. A scene of atrocity in a market square, where produce was seized and a protesting old man was gutted like a fish. And on the wharf, and in the market, the backs of the uniform coats were turned, showing the insignia, embroidered high on the left shoulder.

"White Dragon Tong," Ranjit Narayan said in a soft, deceptively mild voice. He had folded his hands into the wide cuffs of a rich brown jacket and could have been an antique dealer, an art teacher, a beloved grandfather. One struggled to remember that this was the man who signed death warrants and sent young people to war. "You see, Potan Kap has strengthened the ranks of his Tiger Regiment with these men. They are ronin. Assassins and thugs, vicious and without principle. I believe, even the CAIR must be anxious about their presence in Rhutan."

Bowman leaned closer on both elbows. "It won't be easy to get into Rhutan. First, the air- and surface-search surveillance system makes an undetected approach by air or sea impossible, and you may believe me, gentlemen, the last thing on our agenda should be to fly into the teeth of these - thugs, as Sri Narayan has called them. White Dragon Tong are not an army, they have no discipline, they answer to no one save Potan Kap himself. They are not even a guild of assassins, who could be expected to obey some code of honour. They are what you see on this video. Thugs who have been trained by the best mercenary instructors in Moresby, and armed with the best weapons systems in this whole theatre."

"Damn," Russell whispered. "But you're going to put a task force into Rhutan, aren't you? Get that crap out of the madman's hands, sabotage the missiles."

"A special task force," Duquesne added blandly. "Confiscate the plutonium, salvage or destroy the missiles *and* silos, destabilize the Emir's power base so thoroughly that White Dragon Tong simply leaves. They don't back a losing horse! And without them, Potan Kap is no more than a warlord, long past an era when his kind were welcome in the world."

"Amen to that," Eric breathed. The deepdisplay lit his face in bizarre shades and shadows as he looked along at Duquesne. "And you still haven't told us why we're here, why we're being given this intelligence weeks before it'll be public knowledge. Or what you want from us," he added. His throat bobbed as he swallowed. "But I know what I'm guessing."

As did Russell, but it was Quinn who snorted, "He's recruiting. Am I wrong, Gerry? Why don't you come right out and say what you want? You know I won't turn you down, unless the crew jumps ship right out from under me - and they won't. I've got kids on that tanker who took months to heal after we brought them out of Rhutan, and they've only been living for a chance to get back in there and - shall I say, settle a score."

For the first time a genuine smile tugged Duquesne's mouth. "You're not obligated, Joyce. Understand that."

"But I've got the only missile-armed, capital-size ship in this part of Oceania," Quinn added shrewdly. "I'm reading smoke signals out your ears, Gerry. What do you want? You're going into Rhutan with the Australians, aren't you?"

"And a task force from Nepal," Sri Narayan added, smooth as silk over broken glass. "You see, Potan Kap's Rhutan is too close to our eastlands." He shrugged expressively. "In my grandfather's day, Nepal was a tiny country, dwarfed by India, by Bangladesh and Burma. And then - ah! A piece of a comet, and they tell me, only a small piece, is coming like a falling star into the Antarctic, and Bangladesh is gone, Thailand and Vietnam and all the flatlands by the sea. Madras and Calcutta and New Delhi, all are going underwater, and an army is marching. Refugees, you see, walking for their lives, upwards, always upwards, toward the roof of the world."

"And you promptly allied yourselves with Bhutan and a bunch of other fly-specks on the map, dew a line on the ground and shot whoever stepped over it," Quinn said with brutal honesty.

How could Narayan deny the truth? "A mater of survival," he said with the same placid self-possession. "We would have been overrun. It was our ground, Captain Quinn, and so the ground rules were ours to make. The refugees looted and stole every kilometre of their flight. They left barren wasteland behind them, and before them, in the foothills of our mountains, was the last agricultural land left in which to be growing the crops to feed these same refugees who would have ravaged those farms also." He smiled indulgently. "In the end, Captain, it was we who protected those farms by whatever means, even the gun. It was we who fed the survivors through the years when India became a salt-water swamp and a billion souls perished."

"Please, please, Sri Narayan, Captain Quinn." Duquesne was playing referee here. Quinn had assumed the role of devil's advocate. "Doubtlessly, your predecessors took the only humanitarian and logical course they could see, and history proved them to be be correct, insofar as the end *has* justified the means. Nepal is one of the three most powerful states in our world. The Commonwealth of Australian Island Republics, in alliance with the Zealand Islands, and the California Islands, are your neighbours and allies. No one at this conference would contest your vote, nor your sovereign claim to surviving land east and south of the original state of Nepal."

Not, Russell thought darkly, that it would have mattered who had objected, or how, to the fact that Nepal had taken control of the highlands as far east as Cambodia. Oh yes, their eastern borders fell well within Potan Kap's missile range - and Narayan was right. The most fertile lands, where the majority of the region's agriculture took place, were in those highlands, now island chains, and vulnerable. Calder and Royce were not the only pirates in these waters, nor even the most feared.

"So you want the *Regina*," Quinn said with fat satisfaction. "And...?"

"And the support of a combined fleet from the CAIR, Zealand, Bal, Nepal," Duquesne said, shrewd as an old, lame wolf. "But they won't assault Rhutan." he gestured at the deepdisplay. "We're all well aware of the futility of sending air- or sea-strikes against an island fortress with high-tech surveillance and a short-range missile arsenal that would be envied by Catalina."

For a moment the assembly was so silent, Russell could hear himself breathe. Duquesne seemed to be waiting, and Russell gave a start as he realized, the old man was looking directly at Eric. Wary, cautious, Eric wetted his lips, canted his head this way and that as he reviewed the multi-level displays, and said evenly, "You can't approach Rhutan by air or surface, so you've got one option left, and you damn well know they'll be sonar scanning for big subs. All you've got left is stealth, isn't it? Small submersibles like the *Poseidon* ... and Aquarians." He hesitated. "Like me. That's what's on your mind, isn't it? That's what Rusty and I are doing here, rubbing shoulders with presidents and diplomatic secretaries, when we'd usually be watching these guys on tv and wondering what kind of crap they were getting us into now."

Duquesne took off his glasses, produced a yellow cloth from his inside pocket and absently polished the lenses. "Captain Quinn is right, Eric, I'm recruiting ... and you're far too intelligent to miss your guess regarding the assault on Rhutan. But all we have at this time are the bare bones of a plan. The computers will run through the night, and by morning we'll be better able to tell you what you're inviting yourself into, if you choose to be recruited."

"We have the choice?" Russell asked pointedly.

"You're civilians, you're no one's to order." Duquesne slid the spectacles back onto his nose. "But I would ask you to consider the stakes we're playing for, as well as the odds of our success."

"The freedom of our world," Catherine Bowman said, low, husky with emotion.

"And the odds?" Eric prompted.

"Are good. We'll know better by morning." Duquesne nodded into the fluorescing depths of the deepdisplay. "For now, I'd like to adjourn this conference, pending data analysis and the reports on various strategic computer models that have only begun to run since the *Regina Maris* set sea anchors. Ladies and gentlemen ... you have the hospitality of this vessel and of *Pacifica*, but should you choose to go ashore, please do so only in the company of armed guards." He stood, stiff, more than a little stooped tonight, and his face was grave. "Until morning."

"Mr Duquesne." Bowman was always gracious. Narayan accorded Duquesne a formal bow, and the secretaries began to repack.

Feeling very much like a fifth wheel, Russell pushed back his chair and found his own spine tight, tense. Eric remained seated, watching the deceptively mild Nepalese leave, and did not stir until the CAIR detective called him by name.

"You and Doctor Grant are to stay aboard the *Atlantis* tonight," Heron was saying. "You're aware, obviously, that Calder and Royce will return to *Pacifica* to recover their cargo -"

"To attempt to recover it," Eric corrected. "And they can think again. I worked too damn hard on that wreck to let them just take it."

"Excellent." Heron chuckled richly. "They you won't mind ... assisting the police with their inquiries."

"Do what?" Russell demanded. "You're Flinders CIB, you're the hell out of jurisdiction here."

"Mr Duquesne has been kind enough to recognize my credentials." Jim Heron mocked himself with a grimace. "It's not a question of protocol. I just don't believe he wants custody of Calder and his apprentice - they're too bloody dangerous to lock up, and the state of *Pacifica* doesn't euthanase after conviction. You want White Dragon Tong goons here, and a prison break? Fine, turn the key on Calder."

"Whereas you'll put him down?" Eric perched on the edge of the desk, arms folded, intent on the detective.

"In the Flinders Islands, Mr Devlin," Heron said without a trace of banter, "his feet won't touch the floor. You want to read about the man's execution?"

For a moment Eric's eyes shuttered, and Russell knew where his mind was. He was back aboard the schooner, with a child, a little Malay girl. "Yeah," Eric said at last. "Maybe I do at that."

"Then let me set it up," Heron said quietly. "A baited trap, something Calder and Royce could never resist."

"Their salvage," Russell said bleakly.

"And us," Eric added. "It's got to be a matter of pride for that bastard. "We're the first to slip through his fingers. What did the lady say? Loose ends."

"All right." Russell's teeth worried at his lip as he checked the time. "The *Poseidon* is making its own way home, but it'll be twenty-eight, maybe thirty hours before she docks."

"Convenient." Heron stood aside and gestured them toward the executive elevators. "You'll be in secure quarters tonight, and under surveillance every moment, I promise you, until the show is over."

The show? Russell was less inclined to glibness, but he sealed his lips until the policeman had seen duty done. The quarters assigned to them were at deck level, in the same section as Bowman's and Narayan's own, and he could never remember being accommodated with such elegance. These suites were several strata above even the best rooms at the *Acropora*, over on *Pacifica*, and the hotel had earned four stars in the latest travel guides from the CAIR.

Yet the frown on Eric's forehead remained just as deep after he had prowled the suite, and his shoulder muscles were hard with tension when Russell pressed against his back, a full-body embrace. They were at the long starboard viewports. The night was indigo at sea level, brightening to aquamarine in the west, with a scatter of jewel-bright stars. The green standing lights of scores of vessels punctuated the oceanic night; taxis zipped to and fro between the *Atlantis* and *Pacifica*, which lay on the mother ship's port flank, and a helijet was coming in on a vector that would have brought it up from the Australian islands.

"You're wound up." Russell swept aside Eric's hair and dropped a kiss on the back of his neck. "Heron will look after Calder and Royce, the *Poseidon* will make her own way back, and Duquesne's computers are going to chew through every gambit before they commit us to action. Relax."

"I wish I could," Eric admitted. "It's been a long - and fairly crappy - day, Russell." He turned into Russell's arms and slid his own arms around the larger man's torso. "And spare me the lecture! You're coiled tighter than I am." He tilted his head at Russell, studied him from beneath lowered lashes, and before Russell could speak the Aquarian's hand had tucked into his groin and discovered the truth there.

Fear and pounding anxiety made the hormones race. Adrenalin flooded the system, but the fight-or-flight reflex was never optioned. The blood continued to pump, sweat prickled a man's skin, but systems in the human body that had been designed to cope with the flight from the cave bear and the hunt for the mastodon usually went unassuaged. Most people took a pill, cracked open a bottle, hit the gym and vented their hormones on the heavy bag.

Eric took Russell by the hips, walked him backward a measured five paces and dumped him unceremoniously onto the bed. Russell took a breath as Eric's weight settled on him, knees spread his legs wide, almost arrogantly, fingers bruised his shoulders, yet Eric's mouth was so gentle against Russell's, any complaint was banished.

It was going to be rough tonight, Russell knew at once. And he knew what Eric wanted. The anger - resentment at being abducted and used - had been simmering in his belly a whole day, and though he would sublimate it into a ritual of sensuality, the act itself would still be rough enough to leave Russell finger-bruised, a little sore, rueful.

Not that he felt the bruises at the time. As Eric stripped him naked, went down on him without preamble and sucked him fiercely, Russell could barely think, let alone hold any awareness of the thumbs clamped about his pelvis, the knee that held down his thigh as he whimpered and tried to buck his hips up into the Aquarian's mouth. His cock was white hot, his balls surging, and when Eric plastered a ravenous kiss against his mouth he tasted himself there and growled, chest-deep with wanting.

Very rarely was it like this, and some part of Russell's mind that was still functional savoured the sensation, even the surrender, as Eric rolled him over, slid an arm under him and pulled him up onto his knees. He caught a glimpse of his lover's shaft - slick and gleaming in the amber lights. His belly flip-flopped and his buttocks clenched once, twice, before the centre of him relaxed.

Was there a gene, expressed somewhere in Eric's complex design, that brought alive the wild creature in him, when he was threatened? Russell wondered, somehow filed the thought for future research. Then all he could do was howl as Eric plunged into him like a seal diving into the ocean, and at once began that plunging rhythm, so near to the swim cycle of the dolphin and Orca that humans were entranced, captivated, even aroused by the marine mammals without ever realizing why. The sensual roots of the human mind saw that swim cycle and responded. Some men felt a hot kick of arousal, many women would be wet as they watched the power and supple grace of that surging rhythm, so like the flex and beat of human mating.

He heard his own voice crying out, sharp and high, as Eric ploughed him and the day's stress, anger, came together in one bright ball of energy in his gut. Eric's sweat was slick and clammy on his back and sides, Eric's teeth were clenched into his shoulder, and coming was close, hovering in Russell's nerve endings, shimmering there, needing just a little more as Eric drove him hard.

As if he knew , Eric reached down into the hot, sweated nest, high between Russell's legs, and closed his hand about the root of him, pulled, demanding rather than coaxing, until Russell bucked his cock into the Aquarian's grip, working for his own release while his body was besieged.

Very rarely did colours dance behind his eyelids as he came, but tonight it seemed an aurora burst in the frontal lobes of his brain. He was shouting, he felt the rawness of his throat, but as he spent himself all he was aware of was the last volley of thrusts, each deeper and harder than the last, until Eric stilled for a split second and came with a cry that seemed more wild than human.

Exhausted, sore, purged of the overload of stress, Russell flopped down on the bed. His heart valves and arteries would doubtlessly be grateful for the release. Nothing was more dangerous than that kind of aggravation bottled up, suppressed with a pill, or by sheer willpower. He sucked air to the bottom of his lungs, turned his face on the cool, skin-smooth surface of the quilt, and gave Eric a mocking look.

Heavy eyed, flushed, panting just a little as even he used every molecule of oxygen he could find, Eric drew out of him and went down on his back. He pulled both hands over his face. "Christ, Rusty, I'm sorry."

"I'm not." Russell turned onto his side and pulled up his knees to ease his back. "I needed that."

And Eric indulged himself in a fleeting smugness. "I know." He yawned deeply and stretched until Russell heard his joints crackle. "Share the shower with me, then we'll see what they're dishing up for dinner on the executive level. Then get some sleep. Let Jim Heron do his job."

"Sounds like a plan," Russell agreed, and as his head began to clear he let Eric catch him by the wrists, pull him up and urge him into the bathroom.

Chapter Fourteen

The volcanic mountain had been dormant for more than two thousand years, and seismologists dismissed it as long dead. Few tremors shook the highlands of Rhutan, where the land mass had once been the shoulders of a crater over five kilometres across. The last great of eruption of the monster called El Dumagat - for which Potan Kap's fortress was named - had turned the earth's insides outward, smothered the island in a beetle-black casing of basalt and obsidian that defied nature's attempts at colonization for centuries, and left the heart of the volcano cold and dead.

In 1539 Spanish ships established a port on the south side, where rain-fed cachments provided an abundant supply of fresh water, and goats were imported, freed to roam as a food source. Mules were landed just before construction of the fortress was begun, on the high ground, the very brow of the dead mountain above the blown-out crater that had become a lagoon and storm-safe anchorage.

Five centuries later, the fortress still stood, but the Spanish architects who laid its foundations might never have recognized their own work. The ramparts were crowned with ground station antennae, radar, laser inferometers, and a network of high tension pylons that shimmered wickedly in the tropic heat.

Short duration, low orbit SkyEyes had imaged Rhutan many times, and Potan Kap must be aware of them. Once, his fortress towered over the Pacific but now it lay not far above the shore of the lagoon. And that lagoon was so deep, it was the Achilles' heel that was impossible to defend.

Early afternoon was heavily overcast, the sky thick with clouds, and the weather service was predicting a storm. Russell stood with folded arms, still drowsy after sleeping late, eating a self-indulgent breakfast and luxuriating in a bath that was several degrees too hot. Today Duquesne was holding court in the *Atlantis's* cartographic and meteorological facility, where the view ports were vast and the room filled with industry. At one of the ports, Russell watched the clouds billow up out of the north and listened to the ongoing, endless discussion without comment.

The CAIR, Nepal, Zealand, Bal - all had promised ships. A ragtag but large fleet would be standing off, ready to make its move on Rhutan, but first that fortress must be opened like the shell of a coconut, its defenses neutralized. All this had been confirmed by night's computer simulations, and Duquesne would not diverge from the findings of those VR war games. The same machines modelled the weather, the tides, the ebb and flow of climatic change, and the slow, steady rise of the sea.

As Calder and Royce had already discovered days earlier, the only small submersible in the region was Russell's own *Poseidon*, and and without reservation, Russell had signed her over to Duquesne for the duration of the conflict. He had no qualms about the 'charter,' for Duquesne would simply replace her if she was lost, and the replacement vessel would be technological generations later than the *Poseidon*.

But Gerald Duquesne was recruiting, as Quinn had said, and Russell's belly churned every time he looked across the half-lit navigation table. Eric was there, and with him, deep in conference, five other Aquarians.

Tom Romano, taller than Russell, broader, raven-dark and brown-eyed, like his Guatemalan gene-father, just twenty-four years old, and a champion athlete. Russell liked him, even though Romano could be an arrogant son of a bitch. His sense of humour was sharp enough to slice razor blades, and he had inherited every particle of his American gene-mother's fierce intelligence.

By contrast, Phil Neal was as socially dull as an Aquarian could possibly be. At twenty-eight he was already plump, because he hated to work out, and since his PhD had been conferred he was more likely to be found in the radar dome of an AWSP. Four Airborne Weather Surveillance Platforms flew out of Nepal and could make it as far as Zealand, if some crazy *Pacifican* pilot did not mind making the last hundred kilometres as an unpowered sailplane. Phil Neal did not have a death wish, Russell was sure, but his work so consumed him that he saw little else, and certainly not his own mortality.

Zoe Bader was too young to be in this company. Russell bridled at the presence of a kid not yet twenty years old, yet Zoe was an Aquarian, and the most brilliant student of her graduation class. Her subject was electronics, her specialty, communications, and she *was* old enough to serve legally in the armed forces of the Flinders Islands, or Bal, or Catalina. She was a pretty kid, Russell thought absently, with red-blonde hair and the big shoulders, powerful legs, of a swim racer. Aquarian.

Eric was sitting between Zoe and Tom, and across the chart desk from them were Phil and the final two Aquarians who had been recruited this morning. And when he glanced in their direction, Russell's heart turned over.

Isabelle Weatherall was Eric's sister in every sense of the word. They were of the same generation, the same 'brood,' and John Grant would have smiled when he called them siblings. She had Eric's colouring, his hair, even his eyes. And Eric knew it. He accepted beautiful Isabelle as a friend and colleague, while he was so leery of Libby Weatherall, Russell wondered how he would find a way to work in concert with her.

Libby was the last of the Aquarians who had answered Duquesne's call to arms. She sat with Isabelle, bigger, stronger, as broad as a man, as loud, and yet so female that she often overpowered so-called straight men. She overwhelmed Eric today, but not for that reason, and Russell's brow creased in a deep frown as he considered the cause of Eric's disquiet.

An Aquarian embryo had taken root in the woman's womb. The first child to be born of two Aquarian parents, un-engineered, save that the embryo was transferred to the womb of a surrogate - Aquarian - other. In fact, Libby was carrying Eric's child, and just the thought of it must stand Eric's hair on end, while Libby herself was glowing with measureless self-satisfaction. Their presence here had taken Russell unawares, but his protests died unvoiced when Duquesne called the group together and addressed them over the navigation table. The half-lit 3D table displayed the entire ocean "roads" between Pacifica and Rhutan, and as they saw it, both Isabelle and Libby swore.

"Yes, you know those seaways well," Duquesne had said, silencing Russell without even knowing he had done it. "Forgive me ... I don't spy on my Aquarian children! I hope you know me better than to believe that I do. But I certainly keep track of you, all of you ... with the dedication of a good father."

Did Libby and Isabelle know that they were monitored? For that matter, did Eric? From the wry look on his face, he did, but the women were nonplused. They lived on the other side of *Pacifica*, close to the Kowloon Wharf where seaplanes and large vessels berthed, and their business was freight. Russell had always known that they owned and operated three vessels, the *Mary Ann*, the *Lord Jim*, and the dive boat *Scorpio*. But what Russell had never known was that they had run cargo in and out of Rhutan for years, before the Tagamaya Lagoon incident, when the seaways were suddenly swarming with Rhutani patrol boats, and no one was safe.

"Yes, you know why you're here." Duquesne was the grandfather this morning, the patriarch of an enormous and still growing clan. "You known Rhutan, the people, the language, better than anyone else in *Pacifica*. Especially you, Isabelle."

At first she was shocked that he knew; but then, what good father would not? On the chart table's monitor appeared the face of a woman, and Russell was just waiting now, knowing that Duquesne had already broken this trail.

"Genevieve Farace," the old man said gently. "Your lover, Isabelle."

"Once, before the missile carriers in the lagoon." Isabelle knuckled her eyes and her shoulders lifted in a scrunch that barely classified as a shrug. "You must know that her father was imprisoned a year ago. They said he was a dissident, charged him with seditious writings on the Internet ... God knows, maybe it was true. Jacques is ... was brilliant. I don't even know if he's still alive, neither does Genevieve."

"You keep in touch?" Eric asked quietly.

His sister even had his voice, his inflection. "Email. Not even Potan Kap can find a way to shut down the Internet. I haven't seen Genevieve in ten months." Her eyes were haunted as she looked along the table at Duquesne. "For a year, only the work she's done for the Emir has kept her father alive, you know that?"

"We know." Duquesne beckoned for coffee as a steward passed by.

"She's an engineer," Isabelle went on distractedly. "Like Zoe, I suppose. The last I heard, she was working on the Emir's communications systems."

"Was she?" Duquesne rolled the tracker ball, and the SkyEye image of the fortress appeared in the monitor. "The communications systems were finished months ago, Isabelle. Rhutan went on-line with more power that any other state in the region save *Pacifica*, and has monopolized our bandwidth with propaganda ever since ... yet Miss Farace is still working for Potan Kap?" Isabelle nodded unhappily. "In the old Spanish fortress?" Duquesne pressed gently.

Isabelle's throat bobbed as she swallowed, and she raked back her hair with hands like claws. "I know what you're saying. She's probably working in the silos. She has the tech to do that work. Missiles."

"We think so." Duquesne took a mug from the steward. "Tell me, Isabelle, does Miss Farace speak of being harassed by the Emir's people?"

"She's a woman under seventy. Of course she's harassed!" Isabelle said bitterly.

"I appreciate your concern," the old man soothed, "but you misunderstood my question. Is she harassed in a *professional* sense?"

The Aquarian's eyes cleared and her brows rose. "Quite the opposite. In fact they trust her, probably further than they should. She's toed their line since they took Jacques away. It's been a year, they're sure by now that when they say 'jump,' Genevieve will jump, through whatever damn hoop they hold up. She e-mailed a few days ago, in fact. She has clearance to come and go from the fortress at any hour, her ID will get her through. It's necessary, I think, because she can be called to the project at any hour, any day."

The unvoiced implications rang like a bell. Libby swore beneath her breath, Eric cleared his throat, and Russell felt a heavy thud in his chest, in the elastic moment before Duquesne asked the obvious.

Would Genevieve Farace take the risk, for the sake of her father if nothing else? Would she want a hand on the knife at Potan Kap's throat? Would she use her security clearance to take CAIR and *Pacifican* agents into the fortress?

Appalled by the suggestion, mesmerized by it, Isabelle knew Farace would run this gauntlet. No question. Who in all of Oceania would decline an opportunity to be rid of Potan Kap and the White Dragon Tong thugs who buttressed him?

Russell's eyes were unfocused on the billowing storm clouds, but the first flecks of rain on the glass a hand's span before his face returned him to the present. His shoulders were stiff, his legs throbbing. Stress was more exhausting - and a lot less healthy - than running a marathon.

Behind him, Eric was talking and he forced himself to listen. "Narayan's information is that the fortress is full of ronin goons, and they're dangerous. Rusty and I saw them in Moresby a couple of years ago. Understand what you're getting into. One mistake, and we're dead, all of us. Farace can get us in, but it's not a game." He was looking at Libby Weatherall as he said, "Feel free to bug out of this one. Mr Duquesne has the right to ask, not to order."

"We weren't ordered," Libby said darkly. "And I'm not bugging out, kid. You know what he wants of me, and it's a risk I'm prepared to take.

If I can't pilot our old *Lord Jim* to Rhutan, tie her up in the lagoon and sit on my ass for six or eight hours, there's something seriously wrong with me."

She was making too light of it, but no on contradicted her. It was two days' voyage to Rhutan, two days home, aboard the century-old lugger, even under diesels. The *Jim* had recently been refitted, her engines were probably more sound than her hull. She could make the voyage easily, and she was perfect for the job. Who would notice another old boat creaking into Rhutan lagoon?

"In fact," Libby said bluffly into the silence following her emphatic denial of Eric's invitation to quit, "I'm going to get over to the wharf and check her over, get her ready for sea. I don't know when the boss wants us to shove off, but we better not drag our heels when the word comes down. Isabelle?"

"I'll be right behind you," Isabelle promised, though she did not stir from her place at the chart table.

The comm at Duquesne's elbow chirped, and he set aside his coffee. "Go ahead." The line was too soft and Russell was too far away to pick up the voice, but the old man frowned at the Aquarians he had recruited, and Russell held his breath. "Major Powell's group is waiting for you now, on the service deck."

A twist of something very like dread coiled through Russell's belly. He stuffed his hands into the back pockets of his jeans as he watched Eric and the others scrape back their chairs and gather an assortment of photocopies. According to the handouts, Major R J Powell was with CAIR Overseas Special Assignment. He was an instructor, not a soldier - lame, deaf and partially blind after a mission gone wrong. Malay pirates cut him so badly, he barely survived. Survival, or the teaching of it, was now his vocation.

Eric's face was pale, his eyes wary as he passed by Russell. They clasped hands for a moment, and Russell whispered, "You watch yourself."

"I will," Eric promised. And then he was gone.

It was necessary, Russell told himself over and over. None of the Aquarians was a soldier, and yet very soon they might be required do things, see things, for which professional soldiers trained for months, years. This group, five special human beings of a new order of Mankind, would have a matter of days to train, and Russell was filled with misgivings.

"Isabelle?" Duquesne's voice was very quiet, filled with compassion, calling her back from the group of Aquarians before she could leave the cartographic room. She turned toward him; he beckoned with a smile like a doting grandfather and she went to him, but flanking Duquesne were two techs Russell recognised by face, if not by name. The big blonde woman was a logistics and systems analyst. Better than any simulations machine, she would find the safest way into and out of Potan Kap's fortress on the shoulder of El Dumagat. Russell trusted the human mind far further than he could ever trust a computer.

At Duquesne's right was a thick-set man with sparse red hair, crew-cut about a head that looked unfortunately like a pudding. His name was Marius, Russell remembered. His field was virtual imaging, and he was toying absently with a DVD case. Doubtlessly, the disk was pre-loaded with every iota Narayan's and Bowman's agents had been able to provide.

They would be modelling the fortress, Russell guessed, and his heart squeezed. A sudden rush of heat dizzied him, and he stepped out of the cartographic facility, the better to breathe.

The air was fresh, cool, wet. He turned his face to the rain, let it soak his clothes, wash away the fuddle-headed aftermath of too much anxiety, too much caffeine. Big jets were running up, someone was on takeoff procedures, and he looked aft along the horizon-like deck of the massive ship, toward the landing pads on the stern.

In a haze of shimmering heat and partially-burned jet fuel, CAIR Air Force One lifted skyward, turned its blunt nose southeast and folded its lift rotors into backswept delta wings. Canards extended, the tail jets screamed up, banshee-like in the heavy pre-storm air, and Russell watched until she was no more than a speck in the southern sky. Bowman would even then be committing ships of the CAIR and Zealand naval forces to the fleet, and the thought took Russell's eyes seaward, to the leviathan mass of Joyce Quinn's armed tanker.

Owned in California, registered in Catalina, crewed by Australians, Pacificans, Malays, Rhutani - where did the *Regina Maris* belong? Russell leaned his weight on his palms, on the rail, lost in the dark whirl of his thoughts until a young man's voice said, close by,

"Doctor Grant?" He was a freckle-nosed kid who should have been in school, Russell thought. Disturbingly pretty, and at an age when kids were best kept under quarantine with others of their own kind and age. "Doctor Grant, Mr Duquesne requires your presence at a vessel commander's briefing this evening at 19:00, in the Argonaut Auditorium."

He was about to ask what in hell the kid was talking about, when he recalled the *Poseidon*. A vessel commander? Was he? Insofar as the small submersible could be classified as a vessel. And by inference, when he received the call to the briefing, he knew already that Duquesne wanted him to take the sub into Rhutan lagoon. It made sense. No one knew the *Poseidon* better than he did.

"I'll be there," he promised, automatically checking his chrono. It was just before three. Eric would be deep into a preliminary briefing, and if Russell was any judge, trying to make head or tail of the military mind. *Pacifica* had no actual armed forces; their nearest claim to a military was the security service, sometimes angrily referred to as "Duquesne's goons," but they were civilian specialists, almost all of them serving with security for a time before they returned to their own careers or businesses.

With four hours to call his own, Russell deliberately shook himself awake. He pulled the clean, cool ocean air into his lungs, picked up his mandatory escort from Jim Heron's contingent, and took the service elevator back to the docking bay where the *Tiger Shark* had been refuelled.

The detective's name was Curtis. He was young and good looking, but Russell had seldom dealt with so unpleasant a character. Tall, wide shouldered, dressed in casual clothes that would not draw attention to him in any company, Curtis was studiedly silent and even his gestures seemed designed to avoid attracting notice. Russell's attempts at small talk were smartly rebuffed, and he turned his back on the man. Australians were not usually so deliberately unpleasant, and he could only assume that Curtis was under orders not to get familiar.

The rain was heavier but the storm had not yet broken over *Pacifica* as he jockeyed through the traffic, brought the powerboat up to her own slipway, and fumbled for his keys. Curtis clambered awkwardly out , took stock of the boat ramps, and without a word positioned himself at the corner of the *Tiger's* shed, where - now Russell took the trouble to notice it - there was almost all-round visibility.

The lab and office were semi-shut down; the apartment was quiet, but the lights were on. Harvey squawked as Russell let the door close behind him, but the macaw's perch was surrounded with waste corn and nut shells, and Russell saw at a glance that his water was brimming. Who the hell was in here?

Then, the sound of snoring from the apartment. Russell made a face at his reflection in the mirror by the door. Bill Murchison was here, and he was crashed out, asleep. What a surprise. Use the bathroom, empty out the refrigerator, raid the first aid cabinet for whatever he could find to treat the current hangover, and then fall face down on the nearest bed and sleep ten hours. The perfect way to hold onto his student grant. At least he had fed and watered Harvey, and for that alone Russell let Murchison be. The odds were, Bill had no idea what was happening. It could be days since he had seen tv, looked at a monitor or read a news handout.

Russell swung open the fridge, helped himself to leftover pizza and soda, and turned on the screen by the lab's east-facing window. The *Poseidon's* routines called up in exchange for his password, and he swivelled a chair to face the display.

The sub was still ten hours out from home, but she had not been interfered with. Her battery power was good, her motors running at temperature, her brains were in good shape. She would bring herself home, dock herself in the sled on the slipway right outside, at something like 2:00 a.m.

This information, Russell phoned over to Duquesne's office, but Cynthia answered with a slightly sheepish chuckle. "We jumped your system, Russell. Sorry."

"You did what?" Russell swallowed on a bite of unchewed food.

"We overrode your monitoring system," Cynthia elaborated. "We're actually monitoring the sub. It's safest that way. Calder's schooner is only thirty kilometres behind her, and if they spot her, we'll nail the whole crew while they're trying to bring her up."

Because the *Poseidon* would take evasive manoeuvres, she would not be easy to seize. None of this troubled Russell; the fact that his systems could be overridden, his protocols "jumped," did. But then, every computer system in this lab - and on *Pacifica* - had been designed and built about the *Atlantis*. So Duquesne, or the goons, had built in a back door, so that they could assume control in a critical situation? The first impulse was to bridle, but before Russell could voice his annoyance he saw the sense of it and just chugged the soda to the bottom to recover his calm.

"Well, you're doing a great job, kid," he told Cynthia, with a sharp edge of cynicism. "I've got an idea. Why don't you call me, tell me, when my sub gets home?"

She either failed to hear the cynicism or was unmoved by it. "We'll do that, Russell. There's three hundred, forty-seven messages in your mail cache, honey. You want the computer to take care of them?"

"Yes," Russell said tersely. "Dump the spam, categorize everything else, sort by sender. If anybody's trying to sell me anything, trash it. File my work and social messages by time-stamp, I'll get to them later."

Later. When all this was over. If, Russell thought bleakly as he put down the phone, he and Eric made it back to *Pacifica* alive. The possibility that they would not had only just begun to take shape in his mind, and of a sudden he wished he had not eaten the pizza.

The storm broke over the *Atlantis* and the *Regina Maris* with the force of a bomb, and yet was gone in an hour. The sea still churned, whitecaps still raced on the horizon, but as the weather front went by, southwesterly, the sun broke through and by six *Pacifica*'s waters were oily-smooth.

With thirty minutes to spare, Russell showered, changed, picked up a disk copy of all his data that might be considered pertinent, collected his unpleasantly anonymous security service agent, and undocked the power boat from the submersible's sled. The traffic lanes were hectic on the way over to the *Atlantis*, but a berth was being held for him in bay 22, and the Argonaut Auditorium was right above.

Burgundy red carpets and drapes, a stage large enough for a pocket-size Shakespearean production, a decent sound system, two hundred seats, arranged stadium-style, ranked so steeply from the stage that some students swore their noses bled when they sat at the back. Russell hesitated in the entrance way, looking for faces he knew.

And there was Eric, seated front and centre, right by the podium, beckoning to him. A sheaf of printout lay on a vacant chair beside him, and Russell slid gratefully into it. Eric gripped his hand for a moment, and Russell whispered, "So how was your day?"

"Interesting," Eric said softly, under the muted noise of two hundred other quiet voices. "They seem to be teaching a crash course in short-term survivability."

"Like?" Russell prompted, fascinated in spite of himself.

"How to use your eyes as a survival tool ... look around, analyze what you see. Where are snipers likely to be? Where are you likely to put your foot on a mine? What kind of mines you can disarm with a candy-wrapper, which ones you should radio-tag and leave alone. How to load and unload and unjam an assault rifle, or tell one end of a 9mm automatic from the other. How to find cover, get into it, stay in it till you're safe ... how to recognize explosives by their chemical smell, and set detonators."

"Christ," Russell muttered, "what is it they want of you?"

Eric's eyes were very dark. "The plan is, Isabelle makes contact with her lover. Farace uses her ID and good conduct points to get a handful of us into El Dumagat. We let Farace lead us to the communications complex, and when we're inside, we kill it. Air- and surface-search radars, lasers, and bottom-search sonar have to go out. It's possible we may have to use some kind of diversion, and if we get the chance, one or more of us will try to get into the silos, wreak some havoc there. But even if we can't, killing the surveillance system will do." He swallowed. "The instructors are promising a task force right behind us, in international waters. We do our job, get our heads down and stay put. The task force?"

"Ask the skipper." Russell gestured toward the hall's small, elegant entrance, where Joyce Quinn had just appeared, looking ridiculously out of place here, in denim and leather. "If she's here, Eric, that means the *Regina Maris* will be sailing, and Quinn wouldn't commit the tanker without a task force in her wake."

"All right." Eric rubbed his palms together, a small, anxious gesture.

"You can do it?" Russell asked very quietly.

"The job?" Eric took a breath, held it, let it out. "Oh, we can all do it. A trained monkey could do it, we'll breeze through ... if a whole bunch of White Dragon Tong bastards will just stay the hell out of our way and let us! We're not soldiers, Rusty. Understand this. They're not going to *make* soldiers of us in a few days."

"Duquesne knows that." Russell laid a hand on his arm. "Hear him out, trust him ... and like you said to the others, don't hesitate to bug out."

"Believe me," Eric said beneath his breath, "I won't."

Would not hesitate, or would not pull the plug? Russell would have asked which he meant, but before he could speak the sound system came alive. On the stage, framed by triple spots, were Duquesne, Major Powell, and a face from the computer modelling lab to which Russell wished he could put a name. It was too many years since he had dealt with the woman. R J Powell was short, large-bellied, thick-armed; one idea of his face was coarse with the orange-peel skin of old, poorly healed burns, and if one cared to noticed, his left eye gazed sightlessly ten or twenty degrees away from the direction of the sighted eye. He wore audio-aids in both ears, and as soon as he had made his way onto the stage, supported by two canes, he lowered himself into the nearest chair, and Russell realized with a faint start, both of his legs were artificial.

The auditorium darkened and the screen illuminated with a regional map. To the southeast, the fragmentary islands of what had once been tropical northern Australia. To the north-west, the eastern Nepalese highlands, once known as Cambodia, long before Russell was born. And strung between the two, *Pacifica*, Rhutan, Bal, a dozen other island states under Potan Kap's shroud of influence, every one of them frightened enough to have sent representatives to this briefing.

If he twisted in his seat, in the auditorium's half-light Russell could see Malay faces, Indonesian, Chinese, Polynesian, as well as the civil and military advisers from the CAIR and Zealand. A pulse sped in his throat and temple, and as Duquesne began to speak he turned back to the stage.

"Ladies and gentleman, thank you for being here at such short notice. We regret that time does not permit more latitude in preparation and scheduling, but I know everyone here is aware of the situation. Stealth and speed are critical, but our engineers have completed various virtual reality models of the action that is about to take place, and Major Powell's training programme is well underway.

"We're going to show you the models first, and then I'll throw the floor open to question and discussion. Feel free to ask anything, debate everything, no matter how seemingly trivial, with me, or my associates here, Major Raymond J Powell of the CAIR, and Doctor Lydia C Wyman, whom many of you know as the *Atlantis*'s Chief of Computer Sciences. Michael ...?"

One of his numerous secretaries thumbed a remote, and before Russell had properly digested the old man's opening gambit the model was already playing.

Virtual reality was uncanny; the latest generation of computer graphics gave the mock-wargame a curious, disturbing reality. Russell felt the crawling sensation in the pit of his belly and could not take his eyes from the screen, no matter that he might have preferred to get out and run, and keep running.

Rhutan had been constructed from SkyEye images, and video captured by Narayan's agents. The extinct volcano shimmered in the late afternoon heat; El Dumagat was white walled, ancient, spined like a porcupine with the ten-metre quills of hundreds of aerials. Sunset flooded over the lagoon in accelerated time, indicated by the time-index at lower right, and then as darkness fell, aquamarine and indigo, and the stars rose, the counter reverted to 'real time.'   S c o r p i o was up. The moon was a white crescent above the silhouette shapes of fortress guards patrolling the ramparts high above the lagoon. The water was calm as a pond; in the top right s muted inset screen displayed the projected weather forecasting for the night. Every aspect of what appeared on this screen was very, very much closer to reality than not.

The surface water parted and four shapes emerged, dolphin-slick, graceful. Four Aquarians. Russell's breath snagged in his throat as he recognized Eric. The computer had predicted that he and the athlete, Tom Romano, would be first into the light and air of Rhutan. Eric was a professional diver, Romano, a champion swimmer whose whole reason for existing seemed to be his physical abilities. Once, Russell might have envied him. Behind them were Zoe - frighteningly young - and Phil Neal, just as plump and out of shape in the VR model as he was in reality.

They crossed the waterline on a stretch of beach where fishing boats had been hauled out, nets strung for repairs. A figure stirred in the shadows above coral sand that glared in the moonlight. Four chairs to Russell's right, Isabelle leaned forward as she recognized the model of her lover.

So this was Genevieve Farace: tall, wide shouldered, long legged, with dark, cropped hair. Something about her hinted just slightly of the masculine, but she was the kind of androgynous creature that could touch men and women alike. She was not beautiful. Russell saw her face as she came down the beach to meet the Aquarians; her face was too wide, her jaw too heavy for her to be called classically or traditionally beautiful, but she was striking, unforgettable.

She beckoned the Aquarians into the shadows, and now the mobile eye of the unseen observer took to the air. Russell found himself with an owl's eye view of a night-dark village marketplace. A tavern was busy beyond the deserted stalls; a dog picked through the refuse of the day's trading. Somewhere, children fought, and a helicopter beat in over the sea from the north side of the island.

The fortress lay that way. The camera eye turned and zoomed, following the chopper, and Russell saw the white walls of El Dumagat. Guards patrolled there; lights flickered along the ramparts, real enough to raise Russell's hackles.

Now Farace had changed clothes: she was in black slacks and blouse, sandals, a white lab coat, and clipped to the pocket of the coat, her photo ID and the smartcard that would get them into the fortress. The camera panned over the Aquarians now, and Russell gave a start.

They were dressed in shabby clothing, two out of four were barefoot, and around their necks each wore a chain to which was clipped an ID card. At the screen's top right, a brief text file was inset, and Russell took his eyes away from Eric for long enough to learn that the fortress routinely used manual labour, "day labour." Otherwise unemployed young people from the fishing towns strung out down the coast would come in and work for food vouchers. Or just work to stay out of the cells. Russell had heard every story of Rhutan.

The images now were surreal. Bowed-headed, the Aquarians dragged their feet up to a checkpoint. The guards were surly - some Malay, some White Dragon - and treated the day-labour with contempt. The IDs were scanned, and since the machine was happy the guards took no further interest in hopeless human beings who had most probably been shanghaied to do hard, dirty or dangerous work in return simply for their liberty.

A lot of the fine detail dropped out when Farace swiped the smart-card through the lock and took the labourers inside, but there was, Russell saw, no doubt whatever about the layout of El Dumagat. The mass of work that had been invested in the simulation was dizzying. The mainframes aboard the *Atlantis* must have run in concert, all of the night and most of the following day, but despite the animated perfection of the images and action, once again Russell's hackles were on end.

What if, what if ?

A million variables lay behind every frame of the movie. The result they were viewing was a consensus between four tactical computers, a best-guess from the thinking machines that predicted the weather, second guessed *El Nino*, tracked the paths of near-Earth asteroids and comets, forecast the boom-bust cycle of crops, animal populations and governments.

The machines were probably right. The inset data flow in the top left of the screen promised an error factor less than one half of one percent, and no single factor had been overlooked.

When the simulation ended and the auditorium's light came up, the body of the chamber was almost silent. Duquesne, Major Powell and Doctor Wymark waited for questions, ready to field any argument, but Russell's only input would have been anxious protest. What about the danger? These people are not soldiers, they're athletes, divers, technicians, scientists - what are the odds that they'll come back alive? How can this be asked of them?

The odds were already displayed in the screen's inset. The simulation admitted an error factor of one half of one percent. *One* of the Aquarians was sure to be injured; who it was, was another matter. And although these people were not soldiers, they were young, strong, each one a specialist in his or her field, highly intelligent, vastly motivated, ready and even eager for Powell to teach them in a matter of days what ditchwater-dull conscripts would take months to learn.

No need to take people like these and make them fit, educate them in basic technology, teach them how to think in the field, rely on themselves. Russell swallowed hard as he looked up into Gerald Duquesne's seamed, lined old face. The brains, the self-sufficiency, the genes for strength and courage and cunning had all been designed into these people. And every one of them could be said to be the child of Duquesne's brain and soul, if not his body. Aquarians.

Questions dribbled in, most coming from government representatives who were less trusting of technology, more inclined to believe that they had just been shown a movie, less ready to accept that an extraordinary job must be done before the liberty of the hemisphere expired. Like a diplomat, Duquesne took every question. He was tired, by now running on pills, Russell guessed, a melange of stimulants and painkillers that kept that old body functioning long after people half his age would have quit.

Some of the misgivings came from statesmen from the islands. Did the CAIR and others like them guarantee the task force? Would it be in place in time? Was the modelling of the interior of the Emir's fortress reliable? Who was this agent in Rhutan, the woman, Farace? Could she be trusted?

There, Duquesne paused and looked down thoughtfully into Isabelle's face. "That, ladies and gentlemen, is the pivot point of this whole ... crusade. And your concerns are well noted. We all share them. But the mission won't launch without the complete cooperation of Engineer Farace, and to this end, Isabelle Weatherall will be making a covert visit to Rhutan. Her vessel is due to leave *Pacifica*'s Kowloon Wharf at dawn tomorrow. Now, as all vessel commanders will know, this is a four day return voyage, and CAIR's Major Powell has scheduled a six day program of intensive instruction for the individuals who will be undertaking the penetration of El Dumagat."

It was the representative from Bal who raised his hand. The man was little more than half Duquesne's age, but old enough to have missed the salient details. "I understand, Mr Duquesne, that we cannot launch air strikes directly against Rhutan." His accent was so thick, the words were indistinct. "But why should you recruit civilians to this intensely dangerous mission? On behalf of the Bal Confederacy, I offer you the services of the most skilled diving engineers, every one a professional in ocean floor oil exploration, salvage or ground-line maintenance."

For just a moment Russell glimpsed the exasperation Duquesne was keeping leashed and masked, and then the elder patriarch's smile was back and he turned aside. "Major Powell, would you care to elaborate?"

On a semi-visible prompter at Powell's elbow, the Bal representative's name had appeared and Powell was able to begin, "Mr Ambassador, we appreciate the gravity of your query, and on behalf of the nation states allied in this endeavour, I would like to profess our gratitude for your offer. If it were possible to use professional divers, be assured that we would option that most generous proposal at once."

No need to add that the most skilled divers in the hemisphere lived and worked under Duquesne's umbrella, right here in *Pacifica*. Russell held his patience with an effort so visible, Eric nudged him.

"However," Powell went on, "Potan Kap is very well aware that Rhutan's lagoon is his one weakness. His Achilles' heel, if you will. Naturally, there is considerable surveillance in the lagoon, and the waters approaching it. The shortest swim in from a craft - surface or submersible - offshore is three kilometres, and this must be completed underwater ... without benefit of artificial breathing apparatus, Mr Ambassador. Rhutan's surveillance systems have been programmed to scan for the very metals and plastics of which such gear are made ... and I'm afraid your diving engineers would be seen, captured, and eventually killed, before they could achieve our objective."

He paused, letting the sense of what he had said sink into that part of the assembly that had, like the Bal representative, missed the details. "Only a creature that can swim three kilometres underwater can make the approach and, as it were, fool Rhutan's surveillance mechanisms.

The computers will ignore fish and marine mammals ... and I think Mr Duquesne would agree with me if I said that the Aquarian subspecies of Mankind is in fact a marine mammal, and the most significant step in human evolution since our ancestors stood upright. Ladies and gentlemen, rest assured that the only *operatives* who can literally trick their was through Potan Kap's surveillance net are Mr Duquesne's grandchildren. The Aquarians."

A sigh, perhaps a groan, rippled through the assembly, and then a hush. Russell waited, but there was no more from the audience. Doctor Wyman talked them through the logistics, threw in enough statistics to thoroughly confuse them, and Russell stopped listening. All he needed was the ocean floor charts, loaded into the *Poseidon*'s computer, and a set of coordinates, giving him the drop-point. The place the strategists had determined as the safest, shortest route into Rhutan for four marine mammals who just happened to also be human.

The briefing broke up shortly after Wyman's address, and every vessel commander was given a loaded DVD. Russell slipped it into his pocket without even looking at it, since he knew what it was. He had turned to follow Eric out of the auditorium when a secretary called his name.

"Doctor Grant, would you meet Mr Duquesne in his office in ten minutes?"

"Only if there's coffee and donuts," Russell said, not quite pleasantly. He caught Eric's elbow. "Come with me to Duquesne's."

"I didn't hear my name on the guest list," Eric said drily, though he let Russell draw him closer as the auditorium emptied.

"You got a class tonight?" Russell guessed.

"Yep. And another in the early hours." Eric knuckled his eyes. "Nobody said this was going to be easy."

"So come with me to Duquesne's," Russell repeated. "Remind the bastards that you're an individual, not some damn cog in their machine."

For a moment Eric blinked at him, and then laughed. "Point. That's what I'm starting to feel like."

"Go here, go there, do this, study that." Russell took a deep breath.

"All right - this one time, and for the right reason. But don't let them think they own you."

"Coffee and donuts," Eric said drily.

They were in Duquesne's outer office with a minute to spare, and waited fifteen before a secretary invited them in. Duquesne was in the big, black leather recliner by the windows, looking out at the lights of *Pacifica*, a carnival in the ocean.   For some time he said nothing, and Russell had begun to wonder if he was due a rebuke, when the old man said tiredly, "There'll be blood, Russell. People will die. Innocents. No matter which way we ran the simulations, we saw deaths. Does that mean that history will call this scene a war?"

It was Eric who said, "A small war, sir. Barely a hiccup by comparison with the great war that was fought from the beginning to the end of the Twentieth Century, without pause. And someone said ... I don't know who ... the alternative to war is often not peace, but slavery."

The big leather chair swivelled away from the windows and Duquesne frowned at the two young men. "Not always true, but yes, often. And in this instance, I believe that generations would pay for our sloth or disinterest. I'm close to the end of my life now, or at least to the useful part of it. I wouldn't live to see the future Potan Kap forged out of the wreckage of everything that has been built here."

"Everything you built," Russell said quietly. He was looking at *Pacifica* then, and painfully aware of Eric at his side.

"Perhaps." Duquesne thumbed the chair's adjustor to tilt his spine and head, and Russell realized, that old body was fatigued and aching. "Russell, I want you to go to Rhutan with the Weatheralls." Duquesne frowned at Eric. "You'll be under instruction, Eric. Let Powell teach you everything you have it in your power to learn in six days. It won't make you a soldier, but you'll know what you must do to accomplish what you saw in the computer model."

"I'm not knocking it, sir," Eric said bluffly. "It's just so far from anything I ever intended for myself, it'll take a day or so to settle down, get used to the idea."

"So be it." Duquesne's face creased in a faint smile. "Aquarians were designed to be adaptable. Forty years ago, when the preliminary work was done, we had no way of knowing if the sea would continue to rise until the whole Earth was inundated. John Grant and I conceived of a glorious creature to whom such a world would be natural. We dreamed of a future where every born human would inherit the ocean as their heritage. The dream sustained us through darker times than you can imagine! But never, Eric, never once did John and I imagine that our children would become the soldiers who fought for the liberty of us all."

"I don't think anyone ever thinks of his child becoming a soldier," Russell said slowly. "But when the time arrives, not many of us would show you our flukes and run." He looked sidelong at Eric; the Aquarian answered with a minute nod, and Russell went on, "You want me to ride with Libby and Isabelle?"

"I want you to see Rhutan with your own eyes before you take the *Poseidon* into those waters." Duquesne settled back. "Go aboard the *Lord Jim* in the morning. Elizabeth has been briefed. She'll pilot the lugger through Hildebrand Passage on diesels - I know she's done it under sail also. Isabelle will make contact with Doctor Farace, and you, Russell, will run fresh scans of the ocean floor between the tidal zone and ten kilometres seaward ... the data is on your DVD. Then, turn off the machines, boy, and use the eyes and the brains Mother Nature gave you. *See* Rhutan, the seaways, the lagoon, the people." He smiled tiredly and worked his shoulders into the embrace of the chair. "Then come back and brief *me*, my boy."

"I'll do that," Russell promised. "Five days, sir."

"By which time," Eric added, "this half-assed diploma course of Powell's should be almost through."

"And," Duquesne added, though he appeared to be asleep, "Graham Calder and his apprentice should be in custody. The *Poseidon* will enter our territorial waters in four hours, Russell. We're not going to wait for her to dock. The salvage tug *Amadeus* will rendezvous with her, pick her up, bring her directly to the *Atlantis*. Be here at 01:00, both of you, and we'll see what was so valuable that Calder and Royce jeopardized their lives and liberty to make the salvage."

It was a gentle dismissal, and they stepped out. In the executive elevator, Russell leaned over, set his lips against Eric's ear and whispered, "Can you get an hour, come to bed?"

"Don't I wish." Eric dragged his hands across his face. "I've got twenty minutes or less, and Powell wants me to do something passably intelligent with a detonator."

"Explosives?" Russell drew back and frowned at him. "You know what you're doing with that crap?"

"No," Eric admitted. "But I will." He leaned over, kissed Russell noisily, and stepped out of the elevator. "01:00, at the tug dock, Rusty. Be there."

"I will," Russell promised, and as Eric disappeared into the crowd waiting for the service elevators he looked around for his shadow. Curtis had been waiting right by the executive car. "You want a drink?" Russell offered. "Unwind, let your hair down, tell me your life's story?" No response. "Hot chocolate, shoulder to cry on, talk shop?" Russell choked back a chuckle. "White dust up the nose, the old two hustler trick, back room of The Beachbum?" Even this elicited no response, and the silence now made Russell snort with laughter. "In that case, you get to watch another door, sunshine, because I'm going to wade through a week's worth of overdue data processing. Don't get lost now."

Without even glancing back, he headed for the docking bay.

Chapter Fifteen

The ocean salvage tug *Amadeus* was a big, ugly brute of ship. Between them, she and her two sisters, the *Gustav* and the *Ludwig* had the combined power to manoeuvre even the *Atlantis*, and when a Pacific storm greater than Force 8 was forecast, they stood by the mother ship. The *Ludwig* was currently on contract in Zealand waters, pulling a Chinese trawler off the notorious fangs of Wanganui Reef; the *Gustav* was docked, undergoing a major engine refit, and the *Amadeus* had been riding at anchor by the construction yard where *Pacifica's* new platform was being built.

The tug dock was in the very stern of the *Atlantis*, under the flight deck, a mass of gantries, cranes, cradles, robots that chugged autonomously about their business, oblivious to the furor as the *Amadeus* brought in its precious cargo.

In the clamps on the tug's aft deck, the *Poseidon* seemed so small, and yet a monstrous winch screamed and ran hot enough to stink as the submersible was lifted up and the derrick swung her over, settled her in the docking cradle right before Duquesne's people, and the party from the Flinders Islands CIB.

Of them all, the predator was Detective Jim Heron. His eyes were raven-bright, gimlet-sharp, as a crew of engineers clambered up onto the cradle. The salvage for which Graham Calder and Brady Royce were going to pay with their lives lay snugly in the cargo niche in the chin of the submersible, with the big handling claws folded, mantis fashion, around it. Russell was reminded of an Emperor penguin guarding its single egg.

He came up on tiptoe to see over the lip of the cradle and gave a grunt as he recognized the case. A metre long, a half metre wide, a quarter metre thick, steel, heavy enough to punish Eric as he struggled to get it out of the wrecked SeaRanger and into the *Queen Katherine*'s salvage nets.

Two engineers laboured under its weight, lifted it out of the *Poseidon*'s grasp and over onto the ringing steel deck at Duquesne's feet. Russell and Eric moved closer under the blue-white floodlights to watch, as a kid in bright red coveralls struck a torch, pulled the mask over his face and cut through the locking bolts.

Technically, the salvage belonged to Russell and Eric, but they had gladly ceded their claim to it, and Russell was merely curious as the young tech turned off the cutting torch and used a pair of bolt cutters to lever open the chest, which still glowed with heat.

Foil peeled aside, and then a layer of beta cloth, and Russell listened with a faint smile to the profanity from the onlookers. So the cargo was gemstones - still valuable in any nation, while bullion was of limited value and actual currency had no more value that scrip dollars. Diamonds, emeralds, rubies, sapphires, sparkled under the floodlights, each set of stones separately packaged, some of them almost recognizable in their settings. Indian, Cambodian and Russian splendour, the pillage of ages that found its way from the hands of one thief to another, and another, the haul gradually growing in size as the service for which it was traded became more heinous.

At last, the looted wealth of long-vanished nations - British India and Bengal, French Indochina and Siam - was traded for weapons grade plutonium that itself had been stolen many decades ago from an Australian mine, and ended here, in a tug dock in *Pacifica*. Russell found the process dizzying, but the final pieces of two separate puzzles had been supplied, and both Duquesne and Jim Heron were fatly satisfied. For Duquesne, he had whatever proof he had needed that Calder had done the deal with Potan Kap. This haul could mean nothing else. And for Heron, he had at last discovered the irresistible bait for his snare.

So this was the price of their liberty and security. Russell looked side-long at Eric, saw the light in his eyes, and was not surprised when Eric said quietly, "Just one of those stones would send me back to school for the degree I ducked and avoided when I was a kid. And you could write your own research ticket for the next decade."

"We traded," Russell reminded him.

"At the time it seemed more important to me to stay alive and have those bastards off our backs," Eric said ruefully.

"And now," Duquesne said, amused, perhaps mocking gently, "you're under Major Powell's tuition, and the bastard on your back, as you put it, is Potan Kap himself, so burdensome that Calder and Royce seem small by comparison."

Eric's eyes cleared, and he gave Duquesne that impish grin that had seduced men and women alike since he was a boy. "Something like that. Too late now."

"Too late for us all," Duquesne agreed. "Potan Kap will allow us little more latitude. The stakes for which we're fighting are frighteningly high." He cocked his head at Eric, and the floodlights cast a weird reflection from his glasses. "Come to me after this is finished, both of you. You wish to continue your education, Eric?"

"I've been thinking about it lately." Eric licked his lips. "And I do know that Russell is worried about his grant. You know he's still cruising on what was left of his father's research funding?"

"Yes, well, come to me when this is all finished," Duquesne invited, "but for now I'm going to pass this whole affair - and you with it - into the hands of Detective Heron, before he bursts a blood vessel in his eagerness to take command." He allowed himself a small chuckle. "Mister Heron, the matter of Calder and Royce is your business. As your president pointed out so correctly, *Pacifica* has no legislation for the euthanasia of criminals, and yet the risks involved with incarcerating Calder and Royce here are difficult to underestimate. Please, Detective, avail yourself of whatever facilities *Pacifica* can offer, and be assured that your jurisdiction is recognized here."

As the old man left the dock, Heron almost danced with glee. "We traced the plutonium to sources in Catalina, we know where it came from, we know where it went, but as for Calder and Royce, the middlemen, the brokers, we were never able to prove enough to arrest them for a parking violation."

"You're a happy man," Russell said drily. "*Atlantis* Tracking Command should still have a fix on the schooner."

"Fifteen minutes ago," Heron said with a certain vindictive pleasure, "she was forty kilometres off our northern beam. They saw the tug pick up your submersible, Doctor Grant. They know more or less where their stash is, and I'm going to tell them *exactly* where it is, with such precision, GPNS wouldn't help further."

"You're going to tell them?" Eric echoed.

"On live, public vidcast television," Heron affirmed, "Just before a suppression order unfortunately curtails the public service."

"Wave the red flag, wait for the bull to charge," Russell observed.

Heron sobered. "This bull won't charge. It'll come slithering in like a snake, trying to steal what it thinks is its property. It won't be an assault, it'll be stealth. And we'll be waiting for them."

"And us?" Eric wondered, hands in the pockets of his cutoff denims.

"You, Mr Devlin, are in excellent company. Major Powell has been briefed, that there could conceivably be an attempt on your life. You're under the protection of the CAIR armed forces. And as for Doctor Grant, you'll be leaving *Pacifica* aboard a lugger named the *Lord Jim*, on the dawn tide. Since no one outside the corps of specialists recruited to this project knows you'll be aboard, you'll be safe ... or as safe as you can be, entering Rhutani waters. I suggest you get some sleep."

"I didn't know you cared," Russell said glibly. Heron had caught him knuckling his eyes and yawning, and at 2:00a.m. his body had begun to demand sleep. The *Lord Jim* was shoving off from Kowloon Wharf at 6:45, and he could sleep when she was underway. He would rather have had a shower, a meal, Eric and a soft horizontal surface for an hour, but even then Eric was looking a his chrono. "You have to go?"

"Powell wants me. I'll sleep later," Eric promised. "His classes are running around the clock. There's six months of study to cover in six days."

Russell swore silently. "He thinks it can be done?"

"Oh, sure." Eric made dismissive gestures. "They've done it before. It happens often, Rusty, that when a special assignment comes up, soldiers just can't do it. They need a physicist, a biologist, God knows, a dress designer, whatever. They recruit the best civilians they can find and then train them up fast." He hesitated. "It's like being worked up for a prize fight. Does that make sense?"

It did, and Russell took Eric by both shoulders for a moment, held him at arm's length to look at him. "You'll be all right."

"I'm always all right," Eric said softly. "You just watch yourself, Rusty. They're sending you to Rhutan aboard an unarmed lugger built in your grandfather's day. I don't like one thing about it."

"But it's the best way to get into Rhutan, and out again. To *slither* in and out. There's times when stealth will work where a full frontal assault would be a bloodbath."

"I know that." Eric took Russell's face between his hands. "I won't see you before you leave."

So Russell kissed him now, deep and hard, and did not care who was watching. Then Eric slid out of his embrace and was lost in the chaos of technicians, security men and robots, on his way to Powell's class.

"Shit," Russell swore, silently but passionately, and headed for the elevator that would take him to the chart room. He had a mile of sea floor data for review before he took a launch over to the *Lord Jim*.

***

Dawn was violent, bloody and unlovely, and even while she was still tied up, the lugger pitched like a cork in a bathtub. She left *Pacifica*'s waters under diesels before Libby set out a full spread of sails, left the rig on auto-trim, handed her over to the computer pilot and hit the bunk.

Tired but too wound up to sleep, Russell sat up on the crazy tilt of the deck, wind breaker zipped to his chin, hands wrapped about a mug of hot chocolate, and watched the sun rise over the wasteland of the Pacific. Two days to Rhutan, through tangled seas where Malay pirates operated unchecked, afternoon storms tore through the ocean like water-demons, and the granite claws of the Hildebrand Passage could rip a steel hull to tatters. Russell buried his nose in the mug and tried to trust Libby Weatherall, reminded himself again that until the Tagamaya Lagoon incident, she had run the Hildebrand as part of her business - freight, in and out of Rhutan, six, eight times a month, aboard the *Jim* and the other two boats.

In the bow cabin Isabelle was asleep before Libby turned in, and the *Jim* was so quiet, Russell might have been ill at ease. The sun was well up before he rolled himself in a sleeping bag in the aft cabin under the helm.

Exhaustion and stress overtook even the most hardy, but Russell was still astonished to wake with the late afternoon sun streaming through the west ports and the smell of stewing meat inspiring his stomach to hunger. He heard footfalls right above, and knew Libby was on deck, for the soft singing coming from the main cabin could only be Isabelle. The timbre of her voice was so much like Eric's that Russell felt a useless pang of need.

The air was chill, and he wrapped a blanket around his shoulders, felt the rasp of his stubbled chin as he opened the narrow door and slid out between the radio set and a lashed-down crate. Isabelle gave him a wry smile and gestured at the coffee pot swaying in the sling by the table where she was working.

The laptop was analyzing streams of data, and a moment's guilt assailed Russell. His own work was waiting for him, if only he could unglue his eyelids. He helped himself to a mug of the strong black

Colombian coffee and slid into the seat across from Isabelle.

"I got an e-mail through to Genevieve," she offered.

"She'll see us?" Russell wished there was sugar. The coffee was bitter enough to shrivel his tongue.

"Of course she will." Isabelle took her hand from the keys and rubbed her arms. The cabin was not really cold, but it felt damp. "You don't know Genevieve, but you will. She's been in a kind of bond service since they picked up her father. In the early months they watched her, every moment ... we stopped seeing each other. Didn't even e-mail for months more, in case they were monitoring her. And they were. Even now the only way we dare e-mail at all is through an account at the factory where her brother works. Once a month, using fake names, nothing personal in the message."

She looked haunted, and Russell said gently, "You were in love."

"We were." Isabelle's eyes closed. "Perhaps we still are. I still dream about her, the way you would dream about him, about Eric, if you lost him."

Russell's heart twisted painfully in his chest. "Will she do it for you?"

"A year ago, I could have told you without hesitation, yes." Isabelle shook her head slowly. "People change, Doctor Grant."

"For chrissakes, call me Russell." It seemed so strange for Eric's gene-sister to be calling him 'Doctor Grant.' As if they should be family, yet could never be, at least as far as the law was concerned.

"All right." Isabelle smiled. "And don't think I haven't noticed."

"Noticed what?" Russell was still half asleep, and genuinely blank.

"This." Isabelle drew her hands across her face, her hair, traced the shape of her mouth, her nose. "Your father whipped up several of us in the same batch, didn't he, in case some of the gingerbread men didn't turn out."

Heat bloomed in Russell's face, surprising him with a surge of something close to embarrassment. "I'm afraid so. You know you're Eric's sister, don't you?"

"I sure as hell ain't Libby's!" Isabelle actually laughed. "But the same lady was surrogate mother to us both, and that made us legal kin from birth." She sighed, shrugged, spread her hands. "Stop trying to work it out, Russell. It only makes your head ache. Run with the ball instead. Thank that geneticist's god of yours that we Aquarians *exist*, just at the moment when Duquesne would lose everything he ever worked for, if we didn't. You believe in fate, destiny?"

"Yes," Russell said without hesitation. "I do. I also believe that the Fates, all three of the old bitches, help those people who are already up on they feet and trying to help themselves."

The Aquarian laughed, a rich, warm sound. So like Eric. "Then I suggest you get busy. The patch of ocean floor you're most interested in comes up in six hours. You haven't even set up your gear yet, and Libby'll be piloting us through the Hildebrand Gap before ten."

"Goddamn, is that the time?" Russell peered at his chrono.

"I thought you'd sleep the sun across the sky! Hey, Russell, it's okay, really. You've been dancing on the edge, and you're not a soldier any more than Eric is. Or me." She rubbed her arms again, but the chill came from within. "We're riding a following current. Lib says we'll make Rhutan Lagoon in the early hours. We're just an old work boat. They shouldn't even search us, but if they do ... act dumb, all right? You're a labourer or a boytoy, or both, more balls than brains." She tilted her head at him and laughed, like Eric. "Relax, honey, your virture's safe with me."

"And Libby?" Russell demanded, only half joking.

"Is pregnant with Eric's kid, and she can't see any further than that. You're safe, Lothario." With a grunt of determination, Isabelle tugged the laptop closer. "I got work to do, Russell. Unless I miss by guess, so do you."

"Slave driver," Russell muttered, but she was right.

The stewing meat tasted like buffalo and goat, cunningly disguised in a red wine stock, with onions, garlic, a selection of vegetables Russell could not even guess at, and enough noodles to fill the crock. He ate too much while he set up the bottom sounders, hooked up the analog computer, booted the software and tested its new readings against existing charts of a well known region.

Right under the *Lord Jim* was the Sea Mount 28599, also known as Mount Peregrine, for the Maxi racing yacht that had grounded out there in the first year after the island went under completely. What had been home to eight thousand people became a hazard to shipping using the fast seaways between the Pacific and Indian Oceans. After a water tanker almost followed the ocean racer, Nepal put a radio beacon on Mount Peregrine, and for decades it had served as a navigation marker.

The *Lord Jim* went over Sea Mount 28599 with four metres of water under her keel, and Russell read off the analog results, current scan against records. His equipment was in good shape, and from here it should be simple. His hardest work was to monitor the system, be ready to shut everything down if the *Jim's* passive surveillance detected a scan in progress. Like braking hard when your radar detector fired off. Russell had seen the strange old 'car chase movies,' but never really appreciated the situation. To begin with, he had never ridden in a car.

Storms, seismic activity, mining, gravity slides, dredging, many things could alter the face of the ocean bed. Nothing would impede the *Poseidon* any more than an aircraft would be inconvenienced by a new building constructed right in front of it, but safety factors could be radically affected. Duquesne needed fresh data, and Russell took the job as seriously as any engineer.

A few minutes before ten the diesels began to growl. The sails autoreefed and Libby called down by intercom: the Hildebrand Passage was three kilometres off the bow. Adrenalin raced through Russell like a shot of speed. Taking a vessel through the Gap was like flying a plane through a canyon.

When Russell was a boy, the mountain peaks to northeast and southwest were still above water, the nesting grounds of whole colonies of birds and turtles. Thy were gone now - radio marked for the safety of ships in the roads through to the Indian Ocean, but they were so close under the surface that if a Pacific easterly raised two metre seas, those mountain peaks were above water again.

Chicken and go around, and a vessel would be circumnavigating the whole of the island of Kolaka, which put a half day on the journey and, worse, took the boat into waters just as dangerous. To both east and west of submerged Kolaka were the anchorages of Malay mercenaries, and Russell was old enough to remember the vidcast when a freight skipper called Kurt Hildebrand ran "the Gap," the canyon between Kolaka's two mountains, and left a would-be pirate vessel in wreckage behind him.

Hildebrand's Passage had been well charted since then, but it was still no simple trick to get through. The submmerged landmasses, now mounts, were so full of iron ore that radar was unreliable, navigation computers hazarded guesses. But where Hildebrand ran the canyon on his wits and instincts, Libby Weatherall took the *Lord Jim* on diesels, cut headway to a few knots and kept her eyes glued to the Global Positioning Navigation System readout.

Like fangs, the mountains speared almost to the surface, and the passage through was a bare kilometre wide. Calm seas, light winds and full daylight would have made it easy; a two metre chop, twenty knots blowing out of the southeast, a thick overcast in front of a crescent moon, and Libby's work would raise a healthy sweat.

Intent on his own equipment, Russell barely noticed the Gap go by, and as soon as the *Jim* was through his ocean bottom sounders kicked into high gear.

The work was absorbing, and he was grateful for the quiet and privacy of the night watch. Libby and Isabelle turned in as soon as drowned Kolaka was safely astern; the radio was on open monitor, listening for Malay traffic that, too close at hand, might signal that they had been seen by a pirate. In that event, every computer aboard would flag the *Atlantis* for 'an assist,' and the *Jim* would overrun her diesels to buy the precious minutes until the four Strike Force helijets arrived from *Pacifica*.

Rain fell in the early hours, but the ocean was calm enough for Russell to drowse and let the automatics look after the lugger. She was an old hull, but every system aboard had been replaced, and one person could safely pilot her on sails or engines. The clouds drifted apart and sunrise was more modest, prettier, than yesterday's violent dawn. The radio forecast strong winds for *Pacifica*, but for Rhutan, clean skies, light air, good flying conditions.

As the boat butted her way steadily northwest Russell retuned the radio, and sure enough, sixteen hours out of Rhutan he picked up the only legal station on the island. The language was a variant of the mongrel tongue of the islands, Malay, Indonesian, French, Cambodian, others Russell could not even pick out. Though he could identify the source of half of what he heard, the whole was incomprehensible, and he was surprised when Isabelle's voice said from his shoulder,

"It's a political broadcast. Literal translation: 'You've never had it this good, so keep your mouths shut or you could be shot.'"

"Oh, lovely." Russell turned down the volume. "You want to monitor that?"

"Sure. You look like you could use some sleep."

"Breakfast first," Russell decided. "Are we on schedule?"

"In front of it." Isabelle stooped to check an old fashioned barometer. "We'll see the lights of Rhutan just after midnight and if we're lucky we'll slide in with the fishing boats and be tied up two hours before sunrise."

Russell cracked four eggs into a mug and whisked them with a fork. "Your ... Doctor Farace is expecting us?"

She gave him a mask-like look. "She'll be there for us, Russell."

"No insult intended," Russell said pointedly.

"None taken." Isabelle turned up the volume on the radio and booted up the laptop. "If you're going to grab some sleep, shake Libby. You feel the chop rising? I better get a new forecast."

The wind swung westerly while Libby was yawning over breakfast, but the forecast from Rhutan was still for moderating conditions toward evening. The Commonwealth of The Philippeans was battening down for a cyclone, but the tail of it would barely touch Rhutan in two days.

Tired, restless and recognizing the telltale signs of stress, Russell slathered on a lot of sunblock and wedged himself in an unused corner of the deck. He slept sporadically, saw the sun cross the sky and lose itself in tangle of cumulus low in the west. The *Lord Jim* butted doggedly into the inhospitable waters between Kolaka and the mountaintop islands that had once been upland Cambodia, Burma, Thailand, and now flew the gaudy banners of Greater Nepal.

He worked the afternoon through, collected data, ran what collations his limited equipment permitted, and in the mid-evening slept again while Libby watched the boat's systems and Isabelle listened to the radio. She was familiarizing herself with the language, Russell realized. It had been over a year since she had spoken it regularly, and soon now their lives could depend on her fluency. Disquieted, he went silently by without disturbing her, and settled to read in the aft cabin.

He would never have expected to sleep, but a large hand on his shoulder surprised him and he jumped out of the midst of a dream to find Libby peering down at him. "We just saw the lights of Rhutan," she told him bleakly. "They'll have us on surface search right now, and you'll want to be awake.

"Right, thanks." Russell struggled for orientation, dragged himself out of the bunk with an effort of will and put his flat hands on the nearest bulkhead until he had his balance. He had never liked being jerked awake, even by an alarm, and he never slept so soundly when his bed had a second occupant. There would always be that awareness of Eric beside him, of the warmth and comfort of another human being.

Uppermost in Libby's mind, he knew, was the very real possibility that they would be boarded. Their cover story was good - the *Jim* was a freight lugger, a tramp. They were looking for a cargo in Rhutan, nothing illegal about that - but when they were likely to be boarded and searched by ronin from White Dragon Tong, nothing was certain.

The least they stood to lose was their entire electronic outfit, even if the ronin let them go on. They could make their way back to *Pacifica* without electronics, even without radio, but it would not be high on Russell's list of priorities. With all this in mind, Libby had bought the lugger about and was approaching Rhutan from Antuka, better know to island fisher folk as Rainbow Reef.

The reef was so heavily fished, only dynamite would return a haul now. Lanterns bobbed here and there in the starlight, marking the positions of boats out of Rhutan, and sometimes there would be a concussion through the night air as explosives tore apart another section of the dying reef. Russell might have mourned for the tragic stupidity of destroying one of the last remaining reefs in the world for a handful of fish, but he was intent on Isabelle, who was even then monitoring the close radio traffic.

Sharp voices barked, punctuated by static white noise, and she called up to Libby, "Watch yourself. There's a cruiser a few kilometres east."

"Bothering the fishing boats?" Russell asked quietly.

But Isabelle shook her head. "No. They're just a routine patrol ... they're so used to the dynamiting on the reef, they pay it no mind." She smiled bitterly. "We might even pass for a fishing boat, Russell. No one here fishes with nets anymore. These waters are a wasteland, dead. You just blow up another piece of the reef and scoop out the dead fish with your hands. Get enough to feed your kids and raise a few scrip bucks at market tomorrow, and then head in."

"And we," Russell concluded, "are going to tuck in between them, run dark and silent until they turn for home, and go in with them."

"Bright lad." Isabelle looked up at him with Eric's face, and Russell shivered.

A plume of water rose not far off their starboard beam and Russell counted seconds until the *Lord Jim* rolled and yawed in response. As she righted and settled Libby shut down the diesels, hit the remote to take down the single sail that had been set, and Russell checked that his equipment and Isabelle's was dead.

Now they bobbed along with the fishing boats that were steadily destroying the reef, and without even running lights showing, they were as anonymous in the water as any hull out of Rhutan.

The sky was patchy with clouds. He saw Orion setting and knew it was well after midnight as he stretched out on the foredeck and tried to rest. Sleep was a long time coming, and it seemed he had just closed his eyes when he heard the throaty growl of an outboard, several hundred metres away. Then another started up, and another, and Isabelle's voice called,

"Libby, a whole bunch of them -"

"I've got ears," Libby said dryly. "The radio?"

"Nothing. We're clear. KRL4 Rhutan's just broadcasting wall to wall gamlanrock and cheap commercials. The patrol boats have passed us right by."

"Amen to that." Russell sat up and rubbed his arms in the light chill, and as he reached for his windbreaker the *Jim*'s own diesel inboards began to growl.

Luck was with them. Five assorted vessels of every size and vintage had turned for home as if they worked in convoy, and when the *Lord Jim* tucked in behind them, no one aboard the trawlers seemed to notice or care. Six kilometres off the starboard bow bobbed a single flashing light, and even Russell knew its sequence. It was called The Sentinel, or the Gateguard, for it was the light that marked the sharp headland where Rhutan's lagoon opened, gape-jawed, onto the ocean.

With the patrol boats out of the picture, they chugged in under the Gateguard at close to minimum power on the *Jim*'s engines, lights doused, not even a running light showing, like the local trawlers. They were under observation, Russell knew. Security up in the lighthouse would look them over with night vision 'scopes, but what was there to see? An old lugger piloted by a big, broad woman in a threadbare sweater over a pair of battered blue jeans. Isabelle and Russell were below, and stayed there until Libby called down in the mishmash language of these islands. Russell would never learn to speak it if his life depended on it.

"We're through," Isabelle told him. Her eyes reflected the lights of the chrono and barometer, almost luminous. "You should stay on the boat."

"Do I have to?" Russell was wary.

"You don't speak the language."

"So I'll play fat, dumb and happy, half-witted."

"You're European," she added.

He frowned deeply. "That's a problem?"

"Not necessarily," she allowed. "There's a lot of dirt poor, Euro-looking people in the islands. They get out here working this ship or that ship, and they either miss their ride or jump ship because of conditions aboard, or else shack up with a sweetie they just met and fell for. They get marooned here till they can get a ride out, and it's not easy these days, Russell, because not many ships come by that are big enough to need crew or collect strays."

"The *Regina Maris*," Russell said quietly.

"Right." Isabelle ducked to look out the nearest port. "We're getting close. I have to go ashore, but Libby'll stay with her. If you want to take a look at the island, you just watch your ass. Put on the shabbiest rags you can find on this boat, act hungry and scared, and you may have some bullshit to put up with, but you should be okay."

"Harassment?" Russell wet his lips. "From Potan Kap's people?"

She angled a wide eyed look at him. "White Dragon Tong. You just remember what the radio said last night. 'You never had it this good, keep your mouth shut, you can get shot.' Remember that."

"I will." Russell took a breath. "And I'd like to take a look ashore. Get a feel for what you and Eric will be walking into."

The lugger had cut speed, he felt her start to drift, rock with the small lagoon waves, as he threw open a drawer and began to rummage among the oddments of clothing left by crew members long departed.

A pair of shorts, a size too large for his hips and ragged at the cuffs. A tee-shirt, stained with fish blood but well washed. A pair of rope sandals that fit pretty well, if he overlooked the coarse feel of the fibres. He left his chrono carefully hidden behind the radio set, and watched, tight-lipped, as Isabelle put the laptop into its case, and the case under the bunk in the bow cabin.

Deliberately, he concealed his own equipment. The DVD of his latest data collect, he buried right at the bottom of a bin of raw oats in the galley. Isabelle chuckled. "You're a quick study, Doctor Grant."

"I'm just full of surprises," Russell said bleakly, and then took a quick breath as he felt as well as heard the *Jim* scrape her port side bumpers against a solid surface. "Where are we?"

"Fishermen's wharf." Isabelle looked at the LED chrono on the barometer. "And I'm late. Genevieve's been waiting for twenty minutes already. I didn't think we'd have so long to wait before the trawlers turned for home. The reef must be deader than we know."

He heard the tremor in her voice, and for just a moment put himself in her position. If Eric had been the engineer living and working here, if Potan Kap had taken the elder Devlin into custody .... twelve months since he had seen Eric's face, felt the press of his body, smelt that mellow, male scent of him. Isabelle's belly would be full of butterflies, and the likely presence of White Dragon ronin was only partially the cause.

Without a word, she climbed up through the hatch and hopped over onto the dock. Russell heard her feet hit solid wood. She and Libby exchanged a few words in the jumbled *lingua franca* of this place, and then her sneakers pattered away toward the shore. She was dressed in white cotton slacks, a plain white smock, and Russell guessed she hoped to pass as a local "fishwife," a nurse or one of the foreign aid workers who could still occasionally get a pass to enter Rhutan.

It was five minutes after four; sunrise was two hours away, and the time worked in their favour also. These were the island's deadest hours, when most locals and ronin alike would be asleep, or drunk, or both. And if Russell wanted to acquaint himself with Rhutan, there would be no better time.

He smelt fish and wet wood, stale bait, old engine oil, and the ozone tang of the sea, a companionable smell, perhaps because every harbour the world over smelt like it. The sky was not black but dark blue, and so clear than he saw the colours of the stars and planets, the red of Mars, the blue of Sirius. Jupiter was big and bright as a coin in the west as he padded along the shifting wooden dock, headed for the rip-rap wall above which was Rhutan's waterfront market.

Despite the hour, music crooned out of the taverns and the hustlers were still at work. Russell was thinking of Joyce Quinn as he scuttled through the shadows beside a den with a gold elephant rampant on its painted-black windows. The pungent aroma of hot peanut oil wafted out of the back, and from the front came the reek of stale, spilled beer and the unmistakable aroma of burning hemp.

Voices shouted, raucous and bantering; a girl squealed, or was it a boy? Was it pleasure or pain, encouragement or fear? Russell could not tell, and the not knowing deeply disturbed him.

He passed on up the adjacent alley, which led steeply from the waterfront. To left and right white walled houses clustered, so close that the overhang of their eaves almost met. A lamp burned here and there; flames flickered. He saw no sign of electricity in these poor people's houses, and his nostrils flared as he smelt the truth. There were no functional drains, and the the men pushing a barrow, working along an off-branching alley, were emptying latrines.

From a doorway a young face looked out; a boy was soliciting with a luscious pout and painted eyes, until he saw Russell's shabby clothes. Then the beautiful, child-like face screwed into an expression of derision, and the boy stuck out his tongue and banged shut his door. Once, Russell might have laughed, but not now.

He followed the alley on up the hillside that had once been the shoulder of the volcano, high above the sea, and as he rounded a rough brick wall and found himself in the yard of a ruined Spanish church, he checked his stride. There above him, outlined against the brightening dawn sky, was the fortress.

El Dumagat raked at the clouds with a forest of aerials, every kind of antenna Russell could imagine, the tallest carrying marker lights, since they intruded on the air lanes. Little air traffic was permitted in or out of Rhutan, but Potan Kap maintained a fleet of SeaRangers. Russell's mouth twisted into a humourless smile. One of those SeaRangers was currently wrecked on the side of a seamount, and its cargo of gemstones was aboard the *Atlantis*, the bait for a trap. Had Calder already made his move? Russell felt a thrill though the pit of his belly. It would surely happen soon.

The sky was brightening steadily, and he saw the first flush of pink in the east. The windows of the old Spanish church were glassless, blind, and from within came scuffling sounds that he assumed were rats or feral cats, until faces looked out. A child of five or six; an old woman, the gaunt face of a man not much older than Russell himself, but so ravaged by disease that he could have been of Duquesne's generation.

Again, he heard Joyce Quinn's voice. Poverty, ignorance, disease were everywhere here. He acknowledged that this was the poorest part of the island, where the peasant fishermen somehow survived, but surely, Russell thought, no community should carry a place like this, much less permit it to exist within sight of the fortress where the lion's share of the island's wealth was being squandered on missiles, plutonium, the outdated technologies of death.

As the sky showed its first blue he turned back toward that waterfront, and had not gone far before he realized his mistake. He had gone too far, stayed out too long. The streets had begun to stir, doors were open, kids and dogs had already tumbled out to play, and he heard the cries of hawkers from the wharfside market. Fish, fruit, bread, water, were offered at prices even *Pacifica's* people would have protested. Here, the poor hung back, big eyed with longing, tight lipped with resentment, while their better heeled neighbours from the west and north of Rhutan stripped the market.

From the cover of an alley mouth Russell watched, and wondered why the throngs of poor did not just surge up and take what they needed. Moments later, he saw what they had already seen, and swore lividly.

Four ronin, all too obviously White Dragon men, were prowling the market. Automatic weapons slung, sidearms in a variety of open holsters, Malay knives unsheathed and flaunted. He remembered the video smuggled out by President Narayan's agents, and pressed back against the white plastered wall as if he could become part of the shadow there.

The ronin were harassing the young people. A young man, a girl. No one came forward to help. Russell wished he could look away, but the scene had a macabre fascination, like the needing to see the casualty lists after a dreadful battle. He was not even sure it could be called rape, since the young people neither resisted nor protested, as if it were too common an incident, and certainly not worth jeopardizing one's life.

White Dragon Tong were the most hated mercenaries in Oceania, and Russell felt the seething hate from the people who jostled on the fringe of the market. No one spoke out as someone's son or brother was manhandled, someone's sister or daughter was used even more casually than the boy. And then the ronin moved on, and the crowd closed in behind them, eerily silent. When they dissipated once more, the young people were gone, swept along with them.

Angry, disturbed, Russell took his chance. He slithered from shadow to shadow, hugged any wall, any corner, where he would be unseen, and did not stir until he was sure that he could make his way to the next spot of concealment. Were these the tricks of stealth Eric was being taught? The techniques that would get the Aquarians through El Dumagat, and out again?

Heart in his throat, Russell moved from frond-shaded stall to uptipped barrow, from stack of empty crates to water barrel, and froze once more to use his eyes, on the edge of the rip-rap wall above the rotted wooden berths where the trawlers tied up. He could see the *Lord Jim*, and the impulse was to hurry on, but he also heard the bass growl of big inboard engines.

A patrol boat was cruising the harbour, and a pulse hammered in Russell's head. If they saw the *Jim*, recognized her as being 'off island,' she would be boarded. If the security men did not buy the story of her being an independent freight hauler bumming for a cargo, she could be impounded. Anyone aboard could be arrested. Had Isabelle returned yet? Libby was surely still aboard, and for a blinding moment Russell considered the very real possibility that he could be caught here alone. No papers or money, no access to radio or phone, no idea how to contact Genevieve Farace, just the paralyzing knowledge that two Aquarians were Potan Kap's prisoners, and if Russell showed his own hand in any way, he would join them.

Fear was a ruthless kind of ally, for it pressed Russell back into the shadows of a flagstaff on the breakwater, held him motionless as a jackrabbit mesmerized by a spotlight, while the sleek, white hulled patrol boat came ambling along the shabby chaos of the fishermen's wharf.

Across the lagoon, on the 'high side' where the owners and executives lived, were the marinas. By daylight, now, he could see them. Yachts and pleasure craft, even several science vessels and one big, 'new century square rigger,' bobbed gently at their moorings. The patrol boats did not cruise there.

And beyond the trawler moorings, further out even than than the shacks and slums where Rhutan's impoverished lived, he saw a tattered fleet of sampans, jostling like ants on a nest. Survival, Russell thought. These people simply clung to survival, and prayed to anyone's god that their day would come.

Was luck with them? By whatever fortune, the patrol boat growled on by and did not cut speed until it was alongside the sampans. A loud hailer bawled across the rag-tag congestion of tiny boats, and Russell's heart began to beat again.

The fishing boats were deserted, but he did not run along the shifting planked walkways to the *Lord Jim*. Hands in pockets, he shuffled, looking depressed, even despairing, as a man might look when he had been trying to find a way out of this place for weeks and had actually given up hope. Short of the lugger's bow he stopped, used his eyes, but no one saw him and he stepped over onto the *Jim*, felt her rock beneath his weight - saw Libby Weatherall's face at the half open hatch.

She was angry, but she waited until Russell was below before she demanded, "What in chrissakes happened to you?" Russell gestured at the ramshackle town.

"I went ashore. I wanted to take a look for myself. Something wrong with that?"

"You've been gone hours," Libby snarled. "You don't speak a word of the language, and you stick out like a sore thumb."

"In these rags?" Russell looked down at himself, in the tattered clothing.

She made a face. "You're too well fed, too fit, too healthy, and that's a barber salon haircut. Where's a dead broke ship-jumper going to get money for that?"

"Whoring?" Russell hazarded without a suggestion of humour.

Brown eyes narrowed on him. "So you went ashore, took a turn around the town, and saw the rough end of beautiful Rhutan. Satisfied?"

"Satisfied," Russell said bitterly. "So long as Isabelle is safe and we just get out of this hole alive. Where is she? She not back yet?"

"She'll be back before the tide tonight." Libby returned to the antique sextant she had been polishing. "The fishermen go out to blast some more of the reef just after sundown, and we'll sneak right out with them." She looked him up and down critically. "You look like hell.

"Thanks." Russell helped himself to a tall glass of water from the refrigerator and drank it to the bottom. Fear made a man's mouth dry as dust. "Anything you want me to do around the boat before we shove off?"

But Libby made negative noises. "Just park yourself somewhere and stay put. We shouldn't be boarded, not now. Four patrols have been by, but the *Jim*'s old enough and battered enough to look like just another island hopper." Her eyes glittered as she looked at him across the sextant. "That was the plan."

So Russell forced down some food, drank in the vain hopes of assuaging the thirst of fear, and sat by the radio, listening to the local public station. Libby spoke enough of the language to translate occasionally, and between propaganda broadcasts the gamlanrock was curious enough to distract him, primitive and raw as an open wound.

The heat of afternoon was oppressive, and against the odds Russell slept. The voice of an Imam stirred him, the last sound he might have expected to hear, and he forced himself awake. The sun was slanting in through the west ports, and he heard a telltale metallic clatter - Libby was tinkering with the engines. He swallowed a moment of nausea as he forced his feet under him, and dragged his forearm across his sweated face.

The rock and sway of the deck under his feet banished every trace of the nausea: someone had just stepped aboard. Russell back off toward the bow cabin, and did not relax until he saw Isabelle's face in the hatch.

Drawn and tired, she let herself down into the close, humid cabin, and Russell handed her the water bottle he had just fetched for himself. She drank with a thirst he knew, and as she drained the bottle Libby appeared, oil smudged and anxious.

Isabelle's voice was croaky, as if her throat were filled with dust. "Genevieve's with us. She's scared," she said without preamble. "Scared spitless, but she'll do it." And from a pocket in her slacks Isabelle produced a DVD case. "If I'd been stopped, searched, with that on me ..." She shuddered animatedly. "I have never been so frightened in my entire life."

"Goddamn," Libby swore, and took her sister in a big-armed embrace. "So Genny's all right?"

"She's surviving, like anyone here," Isabelle said, muffled against Libby's shoulder. "They leave her alone, because they've still got her father ... or, they *say* Jacques is still alive. If I were Genevieve, I wouldn't know whether to believe it or not."

"But you wouldn't dare take the risk that they were telling the truth," Russell said softly. "If it were my father, I'd be a good boy for them."

With an effort, Isabelle dragged herself out of Libby's embrace and tore the sweat-soaked smock shirt off over her head. Beneath it, she was naked and as perfect as any Aquarian, but Russell was too preoccupied even to notice.

"Genevieve's been a good girl so long, the bastards let her alone," Isabelle was saying. "And she knows what she's seen, Russell." She dragged the smock over her midriff, trying to dry off while the cabin was so humid, fresh sweat sprang from every pore. Her eyes were dark, haunted. "We don't have much time. A tanker plane, a big LoadLifter seaplane, came in two days ago, about the same time we were shipping out of *Pacifica*."

"A tanker plane?" Russell echoed. "Oh, sweet Jesus."

"Yep." Isabelle dragged her hair back from her face. "Hydrolox, Libby. Rocket fuel. They've already got four operational missiles in the silos behind El Dumagat. The warheads will be on-line in fourteen days, maybe less."

"So soon?" Russell was shocked. "Ah, why not? It's not as if they're redesigning the bomb here, or even redeveloping warhead technology. This is old news, ancient technology. Piecemeal. Connect A to B, plug it into C and push button D. There's nothing experimental about it."

"Right. And we," Isabelle said bleakly, "are almost out of time. Genevieve is scared out of her wits, but she's with us, just like Duquesne's damn computer model knew she would be."

Neither of them had noticed the gentle rock of the hull, but Libby had. "If either of you is interested, the tide's turning. The fools will be putting out to dynamite the reef in a couple of hours, and we're out of here with them."

"Two days to *Pacifica*," Russell breathed. "Home."

"For so long as Potan Kap lets us keep it," Isabelle whispered.

Russell searched uselessly for some word of comfort.

Chapter Sixteen

The Jarvis Marine Clipper had touched down an hour after dawn, refuelled at the tug dock in the stern of the *Atlantis*, and her side cargo hatches were open now, to let the hydraulic handling arms put the submersible aboard. Eric clamped his hands over his ears as he stood in the tug dock to watch. A dozen motors were running, the public address blared over the bay, and the techs were running up one of the *Atlantis's* side thrusters on static test. The noise was indescribable.

Slung in a transport sled, the *Poseidon* was rigged for the flight, and Eric had spent half the night aboard her, checking every system, ever failsafe. The Clipper would take her into the radar dead-zone in the lee of an uninhabited atoll called Keppel, and there the *Poseidon* would be released into the sea.

As the submersible settled into its cradle the hydraulics shut down, and Eric took his hands from his ears. He looked quickly at his chrono, and was surprised. According to Duquesne's surface search tracking, the *Lord Jim* was due back at any moment, and they were reserving a berth for her aboard the *Atlantis*. For the time being *Pacifica* was not judged safe for either Eric or Russell, and the reason inspired Eric to a wolfish smile.

A cruiser registered in Catalina put in last night, but the *Samantha* was not the property of an American called Reilley; she was Graham Calder's boat, *Gretchen*, swiftly renamed and re-registered, but not swiftly enough. SkyEye 49 had imaged her rendezvousing with the *Queen Katherine*, and both Calder and Royce were aboard the cruiser, tied up in the marina right outside the Acropora Hotel. Their only question was how to get aboard the *Atlantis*, and take their salvage from the strongroom where an apparently over-zealous, live vidcast had reported it stored.

The puzzle would keep them busy for a time, and Jim Heron was in no hurry to pick them up. So long as they were separated from the *Gretchen*, parted from the outrageous cache of perfectly legal weapons stored aboard, the shooting party could be confined, casualties controlled. Not that blood would not be spilled, but Heron was not prepared to sacrifice his men to set some kind of arrest record. Eric approved.

The submersible was safely settled in her sled, powerful electromagnetic clamps holding her in place, and he jogged along to the technicians' 'bullpen' area, where three phones were nestled in a soundshield. The code for *Atlantis* Traffic was 544. He punched it in, waited, and when a human voice replaced the recorded information he asked,

"Has the *Lord Jim* put in yet?"

"She's in docking bay 12, port bow," the young voice informed him, "but it's swarming with security. You won't get through."

"Thanks, I'll take my chances." Eric hung up. Swarming with security? That was a good sign. It meant Russell had hit the money, and Eric's belly flip-flopped with an unpleasantly queasy sense of anticipation.

His hands wore several new calluses, his brain was filled with so much that would have been alien just a week before. Eric might have wished it still was, and yet he knew that his survival, and the survival of others, depended on the jarring new knowledge.

The kid from Traffic was right, bay 12 was full of uniforms and stony faces, but for five days now Eric had worn clipped to his lapel an ID smartcard that would have passed him right into Gerald Duquesne's private apartments at two in the morning. He flourished the card, it was scanned just once, and the security men let him through.

The lugger was comfortably battered, a little threadbare in places. Eric liked her. He stepped aboard just as Libby Weatherall stuck her head out of the hatch, and as usual her face brought Eric up short with a kind of dread fascination. Inside that woman's body was a new Aquarian life. Blood of Eric's own blood. Although he knew the science it was still somehow incomprehensible to him, and yet again he filed it for future reference. He would come to terms with the situation in four months, or five, when the evidence was growing before him and - he mocked himself - he could no longer run away from it.

The woman favoured him with a grin, but her first words disarmed Eric. "He's in the bow cabin, getting the data together."

"Thanks." He felt a flush on his cheeks, but a moment later he was below, out of the glare of the spotlights and the intrusive cameras that must record this whole show for some ghastly archive.

Russell was tanned, several shades more bronze than he had been when the lugger put out; he was windblown, unshaven, the lines etched a little more deeply into his face, and to Eric's biased eyes, he looked good enough to eat alive. Russell was intent on a laptop, but some sixth sense made him turn, and Eric pulled him into an embrace that was more grab than hug.

Since they were boys, seldom had they been separated for more than a few days, and Eric had not realized how much he was going to miss Russell, as if Rusty were part of him, and Eric was not a functional whole when a key component was missing. Russell gave a gasp as his ribs crushed, and then his hands came up, cradled Eric's face, and a peck of welcome became a celebration. Rusty's tongue, warm and alive in his mouth, was sheer pleasure, and Eric did not end the kiss until a barrage of noise from the docking bay announced the departure of the video crew.

"I guess you missed me." Russell's hands slid down Eric's back and cupped his buttocks.

Eric bucked his hips against the bigger, broader body. "Whatever gave you that idea? Seriously, this isn't the place. But I do want you, and I've done enough horse trading to get us a suite tonight, and six hours of uninterrupted sleep. Not that we'll use it for sleeping, you understand."

"Horse trading?" Russell pulled them together and held on. "Why the fuss?"

"Because you were supposed to spend the whole night debriefing," Eric told him, dropping any attempt at levity. He traced the shape of Russell's mouth and nose. "Then grab some rest and a handful of wake-up pills before showtime." He paused. "It's on for tomorrow."

He felt the jolt race through Russell's body. "So soon?"

"The sub's already on a Jarvis Marine heavy lifter," Eric told him quietly. "We go aboard at 17:00. You're piloting the *Poseidon*, no one's more qualified than you for the job. You've got five Aquarians with you. Me, Tom and Phil, Isabelle and Zoe."

"Like the simulation. The computer model," Russell said slowly.

"Unless you found something between Keppel and El Dumagat to change Duquesne's plans." Eric cocked his head at Russell. "Anything unexpected?"

"No." Russell let the Aquarian slide out of his arms, turned back to the laptop and gathered a series of DVDs. They slid into a slim grey case, and this he slipped into the breast pocket of his shirt. "The ocean floor scans popped up the same data we've been navigating on for the past several years, and there's nothing about Rhutan that Isabelle or I saw with our own eyes, that contradicts Duquesne's intelligence."

"Which is what the old man wants to hear." Eric leaned his shoulder against the bulkhead and studied Russell closely. "You okay?"

"Sure." Russell rubbed his eyes as if they were gritty. "I just saw a little more of Rhutan than I wanted to, and it's tough to file it away and then lose the file."

"So don't forget it," Eric suggested, "keep it in mind at least long enough to know what you're fighting for. Tomorrow."

The other man's blue eyes closed. "Four flight-ready missiles in the silos. A tanker load of hydrolox. Maybe ten days before the warheads are on-line, a fortress full of anti-aircraft and anti-shipping weapons, and against all this, a bunch of half trained civilians, one of whom should still be in school, a sweaty-palmed biologist piloting a science survey submersible, and a shit-scared engineer who's been puppet-on-a-chain for a year or more, since her father was picked up. Christ, Eric, what are we doing? None of us should be involved in this."

A rush of adrenalin coursed through Eric, leaving him prickling and hot. "Ask Duquesne. Ours not to reason why, Rusty. Because if I personally start reasoning my way through, the last you'll see of me will be flukes as I get out of here."

At last Russell discovered a faint but genuine smile, and he patted the shirt pocket, the DVD case. "Then let me give the data collect to Duquesne, and let's go somewhere and unwind. We have thirty-two hours before showtime?"

"We do," Eric affirmed as they went up on deck, "but Libby Weatherall is due an unpleasant surprise. See those techs, the hoses? They're refuelling the *Lord Jim* already. She's going to turn around on a dime, Libby's going to get this bucket out of here and back to Rhutan, be there just about the time we - the word they use is *deploy*. It's her job to be our fallback way out of there, in the event the mission gets screwed and we can't get out on the *Poseidon*. You don't want to be trapped there, especially not if the Emir's secret police know you're someplace on the island. I'll be very glad to know the *Lord Jim* is there, but I don't like to think about the risks Libby's taking."

"It was her decision to be involved," Russell observed, "same as it was ours. Let me get rid of the data collect, and I can promise you my undivided attention until I can't keep my eyelids apart."

"Deal," Eric agreed.

Their suite was just above water level, inboard, no windows, just standard executive accommodation. But the bed was wide and just firm enough, and the shower stall was big enough for two. After showering on the lugger for the best part of a week, Russell surely felt less than clean. Eric knew how tiny the boat's head was, and water aboard was always rationed. For so fastidious a man as Russell, it was an aggravating inconvenience, and Eric was not surprised when Russell luxuriated in the hot water, washed his hair, let a heavy stream pummel him, and then pulled his lover into his arms and began to hump slowly, deliberately.

The water would never run cold here, and minutes later Eric slipped an arm around him, turned off the faucets and reached for towels from the dryer cabinet. Still damp, they hit the mattress, rolled over, and over again, until Eric was comfortably trapped under Russell's greater weight. He let Russell catch his hands and fasten them above his head, and Russell grazed across his chest, sucked and then bit into each of his nipples, raising a stream of white heat that plunged into Eric's belly, and on into his balls.

This ravenous hunger for Russell was something new. They had never been separated for long enough to suffer it; nor had they been manoeuvred into any situation where one of them, or both, might soon be injured. Eric refused to let himself even think about the more bleak scenarios. It had not been levity, that if he permitted himself the latitude of logic, rationale, he could easily be out and running before he came to his senses.

He gave Russell every particle of his attention, and Russell took it. Eric was unaware of the passage of time, absorbed by his own body, the sensuality that consumed him when Russell spread his legs and lay between them. For this brief time, Eric's whole universe spun about the throat that had swallowed him, the fingers that had found his prostate and were kneading him in slow, steady circles that inspired a delicious ache.

He knew what Russell wanted, and when Rusty took his legs over his shoulders Eric heard himself whimper. Was that his voice, sharp and high, sounding curiously like a wild thing as he waited to be pierced. Russell was gel-slick, big and hard tonight, as if waiting a week had doubled his need to possess, and Eric's palms, pressed flat against Russell's chest, felt the fast, heavy beat of his heart. Russell was not going to last long, and Eric knew it. Too excited, too hungry, and far too desperate for release.

It was months since Eric had heard the actual words, but Russell whispered them tonight, hot and moist against the Aquarian's brow. Eric did not need to hear them; the love they shared was a given. An unchanging constant. He cradled Russell's head between his hands and took a quick breath as Russell poised, found the right angle, and let his weight carry him into Eric's body.

The sensations always overwhelmed Eric, as surely as the emotions Russell aroused in him. Time was gone again. It could have been a minute or an hour, that Russell drove into him, rode him like a wild porpoise, and came in him. Eric had only to reach down between them, grasp his own taut cock in a tugging grip, and coming seemed to be snatched from him, stolen out of him. That was his voice again, high and keening, and then Russell released him, grabbed for the towel to mop sketchily at them, and enfolded the Aquarian in a possessive embrace.

Time restarted, and Eric was not surprised to look at the clock and see that an hour had passed since they showered. He sprawled flat, rubbed his eyes and dragged in a yawn. "You're due to debrief in four hours, honey. You better sleep."

In fact, Russell was already succumbing. He had the energy to fetch a washcloth, perform that small service for himself and Eric, and then he was asleep. Eric lay awake for some time, and watched as Russell dreamed.

He was disturbed, Eric realized. He twitched and murmured in his sleep; what had he seen, or done? Eric's teeth worried at his lip. He might never know - he would certainly never ask. When and if Russell wanted to say it, he would share whatever bitter images troubled him without Eric's need to dig for them.

With a sigh that might have been resignation, Eric closed his eyes and courted the sleep he also needed. It was a long time coming.

***

Whether Russell hated the military or just distrusted them, Eric was not sure. He had been fully briefed for the mission, and was on stand-by, just waiting for 'showtime,' but he was welcome at the session where Russell debriefed, in the early hours of the morning. The *Lord Jim* had already been turned around; while Russell treated the CAIR, Zealand and Nepalese officers in Duquesne's private suite as if they were fish that had been left lying in the sun several hours too long, Eric had no more to do than stand back, listen to a confirmation of what he already knew, and take pleasure in watching his lover.

Did Russell know how beautiful he was? If Eric was any judge, he had no slightest idea, which was fortunate, for Russell could have become very vain. In the small hours of the morning he looked fatigued, yet at the same time Eric saw about him that certain glow which only appears around a man who has been well bedded, and knows he is loved. Eric approved.

Since Libby Weatherall was gone already and Isabelle had debriefed hours earlier, Russell was fielding the interrogation alone. During the last break he had said it was a lot like defending his thesis, and several of the officers could make a perfectly normal man seriously consider homicide. Levity? But then Russell's face would darken, and Eric knew he was remembering what he had seen, or done, in Rhutan. He held his silence, kept his patience, and after three excruciating hours, the debriefing was over.

Dawn had begun to break; the sky was clear, the stars still bright, in what Eric had begun to think of as 'the last perfect day.' The final few hours before *Pacifica* lost a kind of virginity. She was going to war. By midnight the war may even be over, but never again would Gerald Duquesne's sea-girdled citystate be able to claim pure, political neutrality, unsullied pacifism, untainted diplomacy.

In a way it was sad, but Eric was also aware of the inevitability. Narayan and Bowman had attempted diplomacy many, many times. Potan Kap was uninterested. They had even threatened; the Emir was amused.

Four flight-ready missiles. A tanker load of hydrolox. Weapons grade plutonium supplied by Oceania's most notorious terrorists. Obsolete military technology, fifty year old plans for a clean, efficient, devastatingly effective bomb that could have been built as a grade school lab project. Eric's marrow seemed to curdle.

The pager on his belt chirped and he lifted it to read the message in the faint illumination from the *Atlantis*'s bridge, which loomed like a skyscraper right behind him and Russell. They had come out to watch the dawn rise, thinking themselves safe from intrusion, but even here the project code named Aquamarine followed them.

"What is it?" Russell was leaning on the rail, one arm slung around Eric's shoulders, as if he were trying to make believe they were tourists.

"It's Internal Security calling," Eric read off the pager.

"Not Powell's squad, or Duquesne's office?"

"No. It's somebody from the *Atlantis*'s own Security Bureau - Duquesne's goons."

"And they want ...?"

"Me to call them, right now. Shit." Eric worked his neck and shoulders around. "What in the name of God do they want?"

"Maybe somebody straightened out all their paper clips," Russell said drowsily. "So call them. Maybe it's nothing. Routine check-in."

"All right. Stay where you are," Eric insisted. "I'll be right back."

"I'm not going anywhere," Russell promised.

The nearest phone was in a deck master's office, not twenty metres away. Eric picked up, punched 388, and waited till a human answered, after the routine recorded drivel. "It's Devlin, you asked me to check in."

"Putting you through to Agent Heron's desk," the young man told him, "please hold."

Agent Heron? That was a new one on Eric. Unless Duquesne and Bowman had struck some kind of reciprocal deal, where CAIR police officers would be recognized in *Pacifica*, and *Pacifica*'s security services would be awarded automatic jurisdiction in the Australian islands.

It made sense, Eric decided. Operation Aquamarine made them

allies in war. And if Duquesne had decided to make that concession, Eric was gratified. In the last week he had come to know the detective well enough to respect and trust him. *Pacifica* could have used a few like him.

A moment later the man's voice said, "This is Detective Jim Heron, how can I help you?" The noncommittal public face of the police.

"It's Eric Devlin. You paged me," he said tersely.

"So I did." Heron's tone changed to one of smugness, even glee. "You could ... help the Flinders Islands CIB with our inquiries."

"Do what?" Eric demanded. "Come on, Jim, get on with it. Do you know what time it is?"

"About the right time for a pair of bastard mercenaries to take a crack at what they *think* is their property," Heron guessed. "Under the CAIR judicial code, I need three independent eyewitness, not in my employ nor in any way connected with my department - unquote - to make the identification prior to charges being formally laid." He paused. "You want Calder and Royce on a transport, headed for maximum security in the CAIR, a three day trial without the option of appeal, and termination by lethal injection within seven days?"

"I could live with that," Eric said tersely. "What about the *Queen Katherine*? Don't tell me you've lost her. I don't want to hear that."

Heron chuckled. "They're trying to hide, using the Triton Islands as a radar blind - they're heavy in iron ore, you know? But we've had the schooner on SkyEye surveillance all along. She's not going to slip through our fingers."

The Tritons were only fifty kilometres away, and Eric's pulse quickened. "Pull her in, Jim."

"I don't have the jurisdiction," Heron said doubtfully.

"The Tritons are just inside of *Pacifica*'s oceanic territorial claim." Eric paused to let the import of what he was saying sink home. "Some dumb-ass kid just called you 'Agent' Heron, so *Pacifica*'s got to be recognizing you."

"I was seconded to your security services this morning," Heron told him with a certain satisfaction. "But I'd still need a reason to pull in the *Queen Katherine*. I can't just commit a patrol boat and three SeaRangers without a good reason. Duquesene would have my balls."

"Your reason," Eric said darkly, "stands about shoulder high, she's maybe twelve years old, and she's that boat's common property. Point one, she's underage for the crap they're dealing out. Point two, she's being held against her will and forced to comply. Point three, slavery is against the law in every sovereign territory I know about. You got so many charges you could lay on 'em, Jim, you could throw darts at a list."

For a moment the line was quiet and then Heron was back. "This I can do. And meanwhile, why don't you get your butt down here and identify these bastards?"

"Calder and Royce - they're aboard the *Atlantis* right now?" Eric was surprised.

"They came over on a day-hire boat, ostensibly to do the tourist thing, forged papers. Good ones. They don't - yet - know they're under surveillance. They're on deck 9, skulking around the service elevator. They know damn well that they can get into the secure area if they hotwire their way around a couple of smartcard locks. In fact, we'll make it easy for them to get in. The box they're looking for is right where the vidcast said it would be ... of course it's ballasted with gravel."

"And of course," Eric added, "once they've committed to the major crime, they're in a restricted area, you'll change the lock codes and they can't get out of the strongroom without re-hotwiring their way around the same three, four security doors, which takes another half hour."

"Closer to an hour, even if you know what you're doing, if you don't want to trip every alarm on the ship. So come on down, drink some very good Carpentaria coffee, watch the show, give me a testimony," Heron invited. "I'll send you the vid from Australia, when closing arguments have been made."

Eric felt a deep sense of satisfaction. "Russell and I will be there in ten minutes. We've got that long?"

A pause, while Heron consulted his monitors. "Brady Royce just started on the first smartlock. And I'm about to send a patrol boat and two SeaRangers after the *Queen Katherine*."

An episode was closing, another was opening. Eric was wide awake, beginning to feel hyper, as he returned to Russell and relayed the news. It was full daylight now; the Pacific sky was that rich blue that promised a hot day, fine weather in the morning, and the clouds low on the horizon pledged a storm for the mid-afternoon. Russell's eyes widened as he heard the report of the detective's project. For Heron, it was the culmination of half a lifetime's work.

"Will you come with me, identify the bastards who shot you?" Eric's brows arched. "You were abused, I was just used. I'd say we both have an axe to grind."

"I wouldn't miss this for all the hustlers at Bottoms Up." Russell was already moving. "Calder and Royce are doing the job themselves? Isn't that unusual?"

"Not when Brady Royce is the best in the business with smartlocks," Eric said thoughtfully, "and Graham Calder likes to call himself the finest strategist and planner working today. They're up against the Mount Everest of thefts - put yourself in their position. It wouldn't do your reputation a mite of harm if you could tell tomorrow's clients that you, personally, were the guy who beat Gerald Duquesne."

There were other reasons for Calder and Royce to do the job themselves. The whole operation was very *ad hoc*, they could not bring anyone in fast enough from Moresby or the CAIR without drawing attention to themselves, and their window of opportunity was narrow. It was move now, or lose the chance forever. And finally, Eric wondered, if it was himself, would he trust the payoff for the biggest transaction of his career to a third party?

Jim Heron was working in his own office. The lights were dim, four screens flickering, sound tuned out. With Heron were four others; a civilian observer from the CAIR, his counterpart from *Pacifica*, and a tech in charge of the machines, and Eric was surprised to see Joyce

Quinn sitting in the darkest corner of the office, drinking coffee with one hand, flicking a cigarette lighter with the other. She was right beside the extractors, and though the end of the cigarette glowed orange Eric's sensitive nose smelt no trace of smoke.

"Good morning." She gestured at the coffee. "Make yourselves comfortable. This will take a while. And I'm going to enjoy every minute of it."

"You could have identified them," Russell said sharply, "there was no need to bring us down here."

"Under CAIR law, as I told you," Heron corrected, "it takes three independent witnesses to make an ID leading to the automatic award of the death penalty. There can't be any room for error. The combacks can fish-gut a government."

"So that's the skipper, and either one of us," Russell mused, "and the third -?"

"Gerald Duqusene." Heron gestured upward and forward. "The vid-feeds are being relayed to his private apartments. Doctor's orders, the old man is getting bed rest today, whether he wants it or not. God knows, he must be a hundred years old -"

"Older," Eric said ruefully. "And he's been running on uppers for days, if I'm any judge, which isn't too bright when you're that age."

"But necessary." Russell handed him a coffee mug with the *Pacifica - Go Orcas!* team logo. They were a lousy basketball team, but filled with enthusiasm. "If I were Duquesne, I'd use anything I had to, to keep going till this is over. They could take me out and bury me, just as soon as I knew everything I'd worked and lived for was safe."

"Tomorrow." Eric supped the coffee, which was scalding, right off the hotplate, and yet shivered. "By dawn, Rusty, it's over, one way or another."

Operation Aquamarine. The words were seared into Eric's brain cells.

The mission crest was a genderless human figure, swimming on an aquamarine background, rainbow sunrays plunging past him or her into an indigo abyss. An image filled with optimism and motivation.

Eric cast a glance at another team logo, the basketball squad crest, and smothered a deeper shiver. The Orcas went into every game determined to be giant killers, and came out of it as fish bait.

On the monitors, Brady Royce punched keys into a palmtop, ran the leads into the door at the smartcard override jack, and the door obediently opened.

"Did he do that, or did you make it easy for him?" Quinn wanted to know.

"A little of both," Heron admitted. "He hotwired the door, but we'd already disabled the alarm system for him, so he'd be through, first time. He's got enough ego to be convinced he did the whole thing. Two doors to go, and now he's got the opening sequence he only has to trick his way around the subsets ... ten minutes per lock, maybe. Then he's into the strongroom. You realize, he used a laptop to hack your mainframes - we were aware of it, we let him do it under controlled conditions. He thinks he's rerouted all the video monitors on this deck. The mainframe gave him confirmation. Actually, he hacked a subroutine that had been set up to play a virtual reality game with him. It was ... quite clever."

Something in Heron's tone made Eric ask, "You wrote the routine?"

The detective mocked himself with a grin. "I was fishing for compliments. Sorry."

"Consider yourself complimented," Eric said dryly. "So they believe they're unobserved, you've already disabled the alarm system, they hotwire the doors right into the strongroom, and you seal the tomb right behind them." He leaned on Russell's shoulder to watch the screen. Russell had pulled up a chair and was dividing his attention between the monitor and the laptop Heron had slid across the desk toward him.

On its screen was a formal Flinders Islands CIB document, and he was systematically filling out the blank fields. Name, address, phone and e-mail contact, his own ID number, and a report in his own words of where, and how, and why, he had become acquainted with Graham Calder and Brady Royce. Eric watched him key in a few lines and stifled a chuckle. Russell had a way with words; it would read like a novel.

However much help Royce had, the second door yielded in eight minutes. The phone at Heron's elbow chirped discreetly and he picked it up. Eric listened without real interest. "Oh, good morning, Mr Duquesne ... yes, they're both here ... yes, sir, I'll do that ... no problem, sir."

"What?" Eric prompted as the phone clicked back into its recharge cradle.

"You're wanted at Operations," Heron relayed. "New data just came in from Nepal. Grandfather Duquesne wanted to be sure I was getting the ID on these bastards."

As if on cue, Russell pushed away the laptop. "Done and done. We'll just wait and see the payoff, and then go show our faces where we're wanted."

"A few minutes," Heron promised. "He'll be through the last door faster than the second. I've re-armed the whole security system behind them, and there's eight big, strong detectives from Lofty Island waiting right outside. With guns"

Russell made a snicking sound with his tongue. "The trap springs. You've waited a long time for this, Jim."

Heron shrugged philosophically. "I've made a career of them, but I had to wait until *they*, Calder and Royce themselves, were so desperate, they'd play the percentages and run a risk. You know their problem? They've been so successful for so long, they think they can't be beat. They were so *sure* they could trick the security systems here, they took the punt. Played the hand."

"Look at the stakes," Eric added. "In their position, wouldn't you?"

"There was enough in that chest," Quinn said acidly, "to buy their own country, be kings or emperors. God knows, I'd take a crack at it, to get it back before it was broken up and landed in fifty places across Oceania."

The detective angled a glance at her. "Very few people in this world wouldn't take that crack. And egotistic buggers like Calder - well, he just knew he couldn't fail."

As Heron spoke the third, final door slid open. Russell sat up straight, Eric held his breath. The tech in charge of the machines looked at Heron for his cue, and Jim held up one hand, signalling *wait*.

The strong room was half lit; shelves were laden with document cases, bullion, terminal storage drums, specimen containers, hotboxes, quarantine containers, none of which were of the slightest interest to Calder and Royce. And there on a low shelf to the right of the door, was the chest they were looking for.

They stepped into the strong room. Behind them trundled an autotrolley, the same kind of smartcart that followed engineers on the flight deck like doting puppies, and would carry up to a hundred kilos. The cart rolled in on its big, soft wheels, and as its tail cleared the strongroom door, Heron pointed at his tech.

The sound came up on the surveillance monitor just as the armoured door closed. They heard the whine of big servomotors and the gunshot sound of a dozen finger-thick deadbolts firing home. Framed in the screen, Calder and Royce spun toward the door, but rage dwindled into impotent shock while Eric watched. He saw the denial phase skitter across their faces, the inability to believe that it was over; and then a kind of grim determination.

Eric turned his back on the screen. "White Dragon Tong will be after them. Wherever you put them, you take your eyes off them, and you lose them."

"Oh, we know. That's why Duquesne didn't want them in his halcyon *Pacifica*." Heron reached out, keyed the audio pickup. "Good morning, Mr Calder, Mr Royce. You may recognize my voice, but in the event that you don't, I'm Detective Inspector James Heron of the Flinders Islands CIB. And you," he added with incalculable satisfaction, "are under arrest. Be aware of your privilege of silence. If you forego this privilege, subsequent statements made by you, or upon your behalf by any legitimate party, will be deemed admissible testimony under the CAIR Judicial Code, Article 489. Legal representation will be provided for you at once, and you will hear the charges immediately upon your acceptance of formal arrest, at which time your legal representative has the right to appeal. If you should refuse to accept these conditions of arrest, be aware that armed officers of the Flinders Islands Police Special Task Force are on standby, and will not hesitate to use whatever force necessary, up to and including incapacity and termination. Be advised to surrender. Please acknowledge your understanding of this Miranda."

The prerequisite legal jargon elicited the response Eric would have predicted. "Go fuck yourself," Graham Calder said to the camera looking down into his face.

The detective turned off the pickup and beckoned his tech. "Repeat the Miranda until they're ready to accept the terms.'

"You uh, often repeat it a few times?" Russell hazarded. "Forgive me, I just never heard all that legal eagle patter."

"It can be repeated scores of times by the machine." Heron reached for a half spent coffee cup. "In the end, it's almost a passive weapon. Just words, offering all the fair deal men like these are going to get. But eventually the repetition would drive a saint to drink. It works." He lifted the coffee cup in salute. "I'll be here for a day or two yet. After Aquamarine, why don't we get together, have a few drinks, celebrate."

The shiver in his bone marrow was back. *After Aquamarine.* Eric forced a smile, thrust out his hand and clasped Heron's wrist. "Tomorrow, Jim. We ought to be back on the Jarvis Marine lifter. I'll buy you a B&F, you can tell us how you tracked these bastards across ten years."

"I'll take you up on that." Heron's eyes lost their glitter of self-congratulation as he clasped Eric's hand, and he was bleakly sober as he added, "After Aquamarine."

"Yeah." Russell laid a hand on Eric's shoulder to draw him out of the cramped, dark little office. "We'll see you then, Jim. That was a hell of a job."

Without a word, Eric followed.

Chapter Seventeen

The ocean was a deceptive place. From an altitude of five thousand metres it seemed serene and unchanging, but as the Jarvis Marine heavy lifter began to descend on a long, slow glidepath with the atoll called Keppel as its threshold, the chop became more evident, and soon Eric could pick out the wash and ebb of the wave patterns against and around the vanished island. Keppel was just a nub of rock, iron-heavy, barren, windy, but beneath the surface it was a mountain as vast and forbidding as Everest.

Eric's world was strangely divided. To him, the sea was often more real than Russell's environment, and he had often thought of renouncing the land and air, retiring to one of the habitat colonies that had begun to spring up on the new 'sunny shelves,' where the sea was a mere ten metres deep, and warm, over lands that had once been strewn with villages, livestock, forests.

Forty years of tropical storms had washed away almost every trace of human habitation. New reefs were growing up as the rise of sea level slowed and salinity levels stabilized. Farms and mines were beginning to abound, where air-breathing humans had come to terms with the lock-in, lock-out environment of their new homes.

The Clipper bucked and heaved like a live thing, riding turbulent air at one hundred metres. The chop was a metre and a half, and the pilot was swearing. At two metres he would abort the landing, and with the current running at opposition to the wind this was as difficult a touchdown as Eric was ever likely to see. Behind him in the massive hold, Russell was already in the *Poseidon*, powering her systems up, and the other Aquarians were messing psychotically with the submersible's gear, as if fiddling with it would improve its performance.

And each of the Aquarians had his or her own gear. A passive 'bug' that would allow the submersible to monitor each of them and yet was, hypothetically, undetectable. A tiny package of wire and chemicals and electronics, almost too small to be seen yet, enough to make marshmallow of a delicate mechanism such as a computer. Sudden death to the eyes, ears and brains of Rhutan, installed and operated by techs from White Dragon Tong.

The ronin were the worst of Eric's fears. Without them, Potan Kap was an aging man with questionable sanity. A despot, vindictive, either careless or deliberately cruel. Eric had spent days studying the Emir's personal file, a scrapbook of trivia, the flotsam of a wasted lifetime, cobbled together by Neplese and Australian agencies and presented as information or indictment. Eric could not decide which.

Coddled as a child, brilliant at university, Potan Kap had been the darling of enormous family. A marriage was arranged for him when he was eight years old; his bride was an oil sheik's daughter from the Emirates on the Persian Gulf. But Princess Carmel was killed before she was sixteen, when a company jet went down over the Red Sea. Potan Kap was in his final year of university, in Bahrain, and his family had just acquired millions of hectares of Burma and Thailand. Their sovereign territory was growing, and surely their favourite son must believe that he wore some special cloak of invincibility.

And then - blank. An almost empty page in the middle of the dossier. The young man walked off the campus in Bahrain, and where he went, what became of him, neither Bowman's nor Narayan's agents could discover. The years before he reappeared were disastrous for his house. Massive storms washed away most of the family's territory; assassins shot dead two of his brothers, a car bombing killed outright three of his sisters, shattered a fourth. His mother died of drug overdose after the bombing, his father had already died after suffered a series of strokes. Chaos gutted the clan, its holdings were either submerged, salt-poisoned or storm-ravaged. The common people of Rhutan seized control of what remained of their island, and the incredible wealth that had once set Potan Kap's family so far above their people that they must have seemed almost like gods, was gone.

Somewhere, somewhen, in those years, the young man almost certainly found his way to Moresby. He had a daughter there, so Bowman's agents swore, a woman now in her mid-thirties, born to a White Dragon prince. Like all the White Dragon women, and the boy children, Juliette Yuan was so shielded from the bloody business of the tong, she probably believed her family was disgustingly wealthy from trade. Her existence put Potan Kap in Moresby in the 'lost years,' and it was a safe bet that he trained with the ronin. And met Graham Calder there.

The three houses behind White Dragon were Yuan, Fujioka and Tran. Ancient history lived on in an absurd world that Eric could scarcely even imagine, but if Bowman's information was correct, White Dragon had a long term goal that was well served by Potan Kap's ambitions. The elders of those houses dreamed of empire, and the fantasy was more possible now than ever. Chen-Goldstein 4 had toppled the great nations; predators squabbled like hungry cats over the ruins, and within the first few crucial decades the new pecking-order was sure to be established.

The ground rule: tigers eat first.

"On final approach," the pilot called over the comm. "Touchdown in twenty. Nineteen. Eighteen."

Eric threaded his arms through the handholds behind the cockpit and ahead of the cargo hold, and watched the ocean race up. The Clipper was just skimming the wave crests now. One would touch her, her keel would butt through it, the smack of the impact would shake every part of the airframe, and somewhere someone was praying. Eric gritted his teeth and held on.

"Three. Two. One." The pilot was off by four seconds, but the final impact brought the heavy lifter down and all at once she was bobbing and rolling like a boat. The engine pitch changed, the handling characteristics made the pilot swear again, and through the vast forward glass Eric saw the east side of Keppel.

Ugly, barren cliffs, great rust-red patches, the white mounds of guano, marking the place where sea birds had tried to establish colonies only to abandon them. The Clipper cut speed, came about, pointed her nose at the open sea, and Eric stirred as he heard the grind of the winch in the hold. They were taking up the slack on the cables that would lift the *Poseidon*, and the Aquarians were already going aboard.

They were a mixed bunch, and Eric wished he was more certain of them. Tom Romano could be trouble. He had more arrogance than was healthy, and at twenty-four he was at least as interested in seducing anything that moved as in just getting his job done and getting out alive. He was in love with himself, Eric was sure; the strutting and displaying had less to do with courtship than personal aggrandisement. He was aboard because he was a champion swimmer, and Duquesne felt that this special group needed physical prowess to counterpoint its brains. He was probably right, Eric allowed.

Exactly the opposite was Phil Neal. Four years older than Romano, he was the living proof that even Aquarian genes were no guarantee against getting right out of shape. Yet Phil was so smart, the brains were leaking out of his ears, and his specialty was tracking. Physically plump, socially dull, intellectually brilliant and as unhealthy as an Aquarian could be. Perhaps Romano was along to provide the counterbalance.

Or perhaps the athlete's weight was on the team to counterbalance Zoe Bader. Rarely did Eric disagree with a decision of Duquesne's, but no matter how brilliant Zoe was, no matter that she had done more ground-breaking work before she was twenty than most specialists ever did in their lives, a young girl of nineteen years belonged in the classroom, studying, or getting laid in the back seat of somebody's jetskiff. Tell that to the CAIR, or Bal, or Nepal, where age and gender equality had put men in the kitchen and nursery, and women into the cockpits of the new spaceplanes that were on test, launching from Narayan's highlands, close to the equator.

Eric sighed, and sealed his lips. Doubtless, Duquesne knew exactly what he was doing. He felt the grim determination clench the muscles of his face as he checked his own gear once, and climbed aboard the *Poseidon*.

The passive monitor was bean-sized, and adhered to his skull, right behind his left ear. It was coloured to match his skin, and to even a close examination it would appear as no more than a small pimple. Its microchip was almost too small to be seen with the unaided eye, its power source was lithium, and little larger. Eric was not even aware that it was in place, but he checked its output signal with a palm-sized receiver that reported an audio track, his skin temperature, his pulse, the level of battery power, and used the signal for a GPNS location.

The electronics and explosives pack was very little larger. The surface area of his thumb, the thickness of his small finger, it was adhered to the base of his skull, where the hair was thickest. A small part of his scalp was shaved there, the package attached, and its sheath sprouted a healthy growth of hair so similar to his own, Even Eric could not actually *see* it , when he checked with a mirror. But he could feel it with his fingertips.

The surface of the sub was cold on his hands and knees. His feet were shod in cheap black canvas shoes, he wore ragged cutoff denims and a grey tee-shirt a size too large. No chrono on his wrist, no jewellery. Nothing to set him apart from Rhutan's legions of impoverished, hungry and desperate people.

The top hatch slammed into place with that metallic ring. He reached up, cranked the seal closed, and fed himself forward in the cramped space to the pilot's position. Romano seemed to refuse to take his big feet out of the aisle, so Eric simply climbed over him, stood on him more or less unintentionally, and ignored the growl of protest. Isabelle and Zoe were talking in whispers - Isabelle seemed to be trying to reassure the kid - and Phil was running some abstruse calculation on a palmtop that struggled with the near-gibberish maths. Experimental mathematics was not among Eric's interests, and he passed by with only a cursory glance at the tiny screen.

The pilotal instruments were alive, and Russell's face was lit in weird green patterns. The screens cast shadows that hollowed his face, made him look five days dead. Eric touched his shoulder, and Rusty took his hand tightly for a moment, looked up into his eyes, haunted, anxious, before he marshalled his thoughts and said,

"There's the *Regina Maris*. She's right on station.

And aboard her, eight SeaRangers from *Pacifica*, each one missile armed. Her guns were loaded, she had taken on a heavy ballasting of seawater so that she rode low and stable in the water, and her common rooms had been turned over to hospital facilities. Most of *Pacifica*'s medics were aboard; the mess hall was now an OR, and Joyce Quinn was, in essence, in command of a warship.

Behind her straggled an unlikely fleet. Two patrol boats, a floatplane tender, an armed cruiser from *Pacifica*; from Nepal, two helo-carriers, the missile cruiser *Tamarind*, and an engineer's tender. From Bal, three missile cruisers, each carrying four fully armed Seadragon jumpjets. From the CAIR, four patrol boats, the frigates *Townsville* and *Adelaide*, the helicopter carrier *Farraday*, and an armed, armoured tanker; from Zealand, the carrier *Auckland*, two patrol boats and an engineer's tender on which had been mounted forward missiles and an aft landing deck, and two wing-in-ground-effect planes the size of the Clipper, both armed with rotary cannon.

Other ships followed, smaller, lighter, from island republics as far as Moresby, and Eric was in no doubt but that Potan Kap knew they were there. He could access just a few short-duration satellites, but just after noon a launch had been made from an uninhabited daughter island, five kilometres off the north tip of Rhutan. If a SkyEye had not been popped into low orbit, Eric could not imagine the reason for the launch. The satellite may have a lifespan of twenty orbits - a little more than a day. It was long enough.

A whisper from Russell captured Eric's attention. "Just got the signal from the fleet ," he said softly. "They're standing by. *Pacifica* just launched two surveillance satellites ." He looked up into Eric's face. "Showtime."

"Showtime," Eric echoed, and an icewater sweat broke from his pores.

Keppel was a radar blind spot so perfect, Duquesne could have pur- pose- designed it. The Clipper heaved in the comparatively gentle lee- ward swell, and Eric held on, waiting for solid thud, like a blow in the spine, as the sub hit the water. He rode it on his feet, braced on the back of Russell's seat, and through the half-globe of the forward viewport he watched the waves wash up, and over, as Russell angled the nose down six degrees and throttled up the fans.

The descent angle was deceptively shallow. In minutes the surface was twenty metres above, evening sunlight had given way to blue- mauve twilight, and Russell went onto instruments. At this time of day the sun was too far from its zenith to strike far into the ocean. And the *Poseidon* was still diving. Eric watched the gauge, sharing Russell's patience as they made their approach depth.

Two hundred metres down, they were far outside of Potan Kap's sur- veillance, and still outside the lagoon, and inside the incredibly deep volcanic crater, the Emir did not bother to scan, as if he believed the walls of the extinct volcano were impenetrable ramparts. The *Poseidon* levelled out and Russell checked his position.

"Get some rest, honey," he said very softly to Eric. "It's going to be a long two hours."

Eric squeezed his shoulder, and then took his advice. Fruit juice, a seat in the back where the amber lights were low. He closed his eyes and set the part of his mind that seemed to be mostly recording machine on playback. Against his eyelids the VR mission rolled like a movie. The computer model was so real, he almost seemed to have memories of events that had not yet happened. He knew the lie of Rhutan's land, knew a few words of the barbarous, hybrid language, the routines of the guards on El Dumagat's approaches, the floorplan of the fortress itself.

The other Aquarians talked in undertones, and only Romano sounded gung ho. Zoe was scared, Isabelle preoccupied and anxious, Phil Neal just so caught up in whatever mathematical phantasm was going through his brain that he could barely be civil. What he was doing, Eric had no idea. Nor could he even attempt to do Zoe's job. Isabelle was along to monitor both Potan Kap's radio and the passive bugs, and Eric realized with a small start that he was along in the same capacity as Romano. To supply the brawn of a professional diver, while the others supplied the brains.

So maybe he should go back to school, chase the damn degree that he had thrown away as a predictably dumb twenty year old. In those days he would rather be in the sea, cavorting with the dolphins that lived around *Pacifica*, where the warm exhaust vents encouraged fish - easy food for cetaceans, who could be equally as lazy as humans. He would rather be out on the *Tiger Shark*, bumming around, earning a few dollars here and there as a charter skipper or a dive guide. Rather be tangled in the sheets and watching the dawn sun on the *shoji* blinds cast oriental patterns on the wall by the bed, and on Russell's pale skin. Eric sighed, but Duquesne had said - come see me, when all this is over.

Just one of those gems would turn Eric's life around, and would guarantee Russell whatever funding he wanted, halfway to retirement.

After *Aquamarine*.

The unspoken inference was loud in Eric's ears. First, they survived.

Some trance-like state possessed him, and the two hours passed without his conscious notice. The first he knew of their position, or the mission elapsed time, was the gradual tilt of the deck under his feet, the apparent weight on his back against the seat. Russell was taking them up, and as the tranced state lifted Eric pushed out of the seat and made his way forward.

Russell glanced up at him, and tapped the instrument surfaces. "We're in. Under the fence, though the tunnel, whatever you want to call it. They didn't pick us up. I'd have registered it."

"We're in the lagoon," Eric whispered. "Damn."

"Coming up fast, and dead on time," Russell affirmed. "It's 19:07, and you guys better get your act together. And Eric?"

He paused, in the act of turning to speak to the others who would be leaving the submersible. "I'll be careful," he promised.

"You do that." Russell's eyes were wide, dark, troubled. His voice was a rasp as he added, "We're out of time."

The deck was already levelling out, and Eric flicked a glance at the depth gauge. The *Poseidon* was riding at fifty metres, and she would hold there. Russell set the computer pilot and twisted in his seat to watch as the Aquarians went into the airlock, two by two. Romano and Zoe first. Phil next, and Eric right behind him, while Isabelle took the seat beside Russell's and checked her monitors. The last Eric saw of him, Russell wore a face like a mask, and then the airlock sealed and began to flood.

The first breath was always the hardest. After days of air breathing, Eric's brain would try to make him hold his breath when the water reached his chin, but the thinking mind sent his head under the surface, took that first breath. A stream of bubbles left his nostrils as he pulled up with his diaphragm, emptied his lungs of every molecule of air, and then dragged in the first "wet breath." Cold, heavy, even a little strange - like the first lungful of smoke. And then his Aquarian's reflexes took over, he was running on automatic again, with no more thought of breathing than a child running in the sun.

The outer hatch popped and he saw Romano and Zoe, hanging in the twilight world of fifty metres, waiting for them. Phil stuck his head out, shivered in the chill of the outside water, and Eric was sure he would have ducked back inside if it was an option. But Romano was eager to be moving, and Eric hustled Phil out of the airlock with both hands on his back.

They were out then, in freefall, and Eric turned in the water to wave at the glass bubble where Russell sat. He saw nothing from within, but both Russell and Isabelle would be monitoring them, and Eric's mind was on *time*. They were on schedule, and Genevieve Farace would be waiting.

The submersible swung in the water and the searchlights flicked on, low-beam, yellow light that shafted through the blue twilight, pointing out the heading on which they would swim. Romano was off first, flaunting the athleticism that had won him trophies while Zoe and Phil were in the laboratory, and while Eric and Isabelle were earning a living.

Follow the *Poseidon*'s lights. It was as simple as that. Satellite imaging and computer modelling had already recreated this whole place in the VR world of circuit and interface. Eric knew exactly what they would see when they broke surface.

A tumbledown jetty, dense forest, a tiny cove of white coral sand, washed in the last crimson hues of late sunset, swiftly turning to mauve. It was 20:47 when four Aquarian heads bobbed up above the surface waters of the lagoon. The sky was peacock blue in the east, Scorpio was up, the moon was almost half full, the sky was lightly cloud covered, the air was warm. Eric held the last water breath as he got his bearings, took stock of the place, and then expelled it with that characteristic hacking cough that had made some waterfront comedians liken Duquesne's "children" to cats hacking up hairballs.

Above the forest glittered the lights of other villages strung out across the slopes, and above the whole cauldron of the flooded crater were the bright, piercing lights of the fortress. El Dumagat sat up there like an idol, forbidding, sullen, pagan.

Romano was already making for the beach, and Eric kicked off after him. Even if the lagoon had been covered by surveillance, they would have looked like porpoises in the deeper water, and as they approached the shore, like a bunch of kids skinny dipping in the sunset.

A figure waved briefly, and then the movement was gone. Eric picked up the signal first time and called softly to the others. Zoe came to him as they pulled themselves though the small, restless surf, and Eric dragged back his hair, plastered it flat to his skull, as he waited for his muscles, brain and inner ear to grow reaccustomed to gravity.

He still felt heavy as the figure waved a second time. He waved back, and the shape moved against the confused shadows of the trees. A woman, tall, broad shouldered, with short cropped hair and the ubiquitous black slacks, white shirt of the clerk, any country, any vessel.

He knew her from the computer model, and as she came to meet them, Eric offered his hand. "Doctor Farace. I'm Eric Devlin. You're expecting us."

She was not a beautiful woman, and the stress of the last year had etched lines of pain into her face. Worry could age a person, and if Eric was any judge, Farace was surviving at the cost of her youth and health. Was she forty? He guessed, younger, while she looked older.

"I know you, Mr Devlin, from your image. Isabelle supplied the photos for the ID smartcards. I have them here, you must wear them at all times." The accent was thick, even barbarous, part French, part Malay, a hint of the islands.

The ID cards were well done. The size of a credit card, each carried a number, a barcode, a photograph, and was clipped to a cord that went around the neck. Eric put on his own and frowned at the woman. "What happens if these are scanned?"

"They'll come up in the computer as 'itinerant day labour,' no address, no papers, no permits. Trash labour jumps ship on every island, even *Pacifica*, and before long is begging for a day's work, because if you steal food to eat in this place, they beat you the first time and shoot you the second."

"I had to ask," Eric muttered, peering at his own ID. "So where did you get these?"

Farace looked at him, long and blankly. "From people who no longer need them."

"From ..." Zoe's voice was naturally pitched high, and she was shrill tonight. "From people who got a ride out of Rhutan?"

"From the dead bodies," Romano said patronisingly, "of guys who just couldn't survive here. Doctor?

"They died," Farace said blandly. "There was sickness in the shacks a few months ago. Sometimes we find a body hidden away, a ruin, a basement ... the dogs and rats have already done the gravedigger's job for him, but sometimes the card is found. They can be very useful, indispensable, to the living."

"Jesus Christ," Phil said bitterly. "All right, let's get this over and get the hell out. Which way? Move, lady!"

Despite his rudeness, he was right. Eric glared at him, but Farace made no comment. Behind her was a path, lost in the deep shadows of evening, and as they stepped into the trees she fetched a torch from the string purse on her left shoulder. The beam was poor, but enough to pick out the guide-wires of the night's new webs, which were being strung across the path in many places. Spiders came to the island as stowaways in cargo, escaped from the market and throve in the forest. Eric ducked the webs, fascinated by the tiny, crab-like creatures. They were unknown in the more or less sterile environment of *Pacifica*. To his grim amusement, Romano sweated and swore in horror at the arachnids. Not quite macho behaviour - and after the jibes he had borne, Phil would make sure that all of *Pacifica* knew about it by week's end.

Wet, clammy clothes dried as they walked, and then became sweat damp. The night was humid, the path wound up, and up again, climbing the slope above a tea garden, a vineyard, a village of shacks where pigs and chickens rooted in the undergrowth and children stared, blank eyed, from windows where lamplight had begun to flicker.

Eric's clothes were dry when Farace brought them around a hairpin bend in the trail and held up her hand to stop them. A hundred metres on was a guard post set back against a crumbling white wall. The ruins of a Spanish lookout post lay to Eric's right, and to the left was a low wall protecting a sheer drop, a slope that had been scoured away by landslides until only a cliff remained.

From her purse, Farace produced her own ID and clipped it to her lapel as she turned and fixed the Aquarians with a glare. "Keep your mouths shut. This may be a hard task for the elite of a rich sovereign state, but here you are cheap day labour, understand? They look at you, you keep your eyes down, they speak to you, you are deaf, yes? They harass you for sexual relations, you learn how to flirt, all a big joke, everybody has a good laugh. Do this and you will pass by like common labour. I bring workers into the facility often, I work nights, just as often. Nothing is strange today, no one will question my presence her, nor yours - unless you show them your teeth."

"We understand," Phil Neal said bitterly. "You may not believe this, but brains were designed into us when they drew the genetic blueprint."

"Too bad muscles weren't," Romano muttered, another jibe at Neal for which he would pay soon enough.

"Even muscle-bound chowder-heads like Romano here have the brains designed in," Phil said calmly, "they just never wake up and use them."

A pace behind Romano, Zoe Bader was shivering. Eric stepped closer and dropped his voice. "You okay, kid?"

"Yeah. I - that is, she said, if they harass us for sex." Zoe swallowed hard enough for Eric to hear. "She means me, doesn't she? I'm the only girl here."

But Farace made a noise of scorn. "More likely, they opportune this one." She nodded at Romano. "Big, handsome guy. Or maybe you." She was looking at Eric now. "Pretty eyes, pretty hair. You?" She studied Zoe and shrugged. "I think the guards tonight are Choi and Ohara. You? They won't even see you."

The girl took a sharp breath, and Eric held her upper arms in his hands. "Just do the job you came for, Zoe. This was in the computer model, remember?"

That part of it was scorched into Eric's brain. Based on intelligence received, the computer predicted that the guards would almost certainly harass the incoming day labour. One member of the party would by opportuned, and would submit ... which one, the model could not possibly specify, but since it was unlikely to be Phil Neal, that shortened the odds for the others to one in three.

"Just do as I say and you pass by like nameless, faceless labour," Farace hissed. "You show your fangs, you get us all killed!"

"We heard you the first time, lady," Romano said sourly.

So Farace gathered the tattered group behind her and set a smart pace to the guard post. The sea moved restlessly against the boulders at the bottom of the cliff; the tide had turned, and though the lagoon's ramparts softened the energy of the waves, still the ocean was unspeakably powerful.

Two guards lounged, smoking and talking in undertones, and as they heard approaching footsteps they ground out the cigarettes. Rifles were unslung, sidearms cleared, but the men visibly relaxed as they saw Farace. Their faces were insolent, mocking, and though the language was strange Eric heard the jeers in their voices. Had Farace herself endured the harassment predicted by the computer? If she had, she gave no sign of it tonight.

Eyes down, Eric listened intently and heard the name of Choi first. Moments later it was Asashi, and then Farace called the labourers forward for their cards to be scanned. One by one, they swiped through the machine, and a perfectly legitimate ID code number came up on the system. The image on the card had been overlaid with photos provided by Isabelle, and certainly in the poor light the forgery was impossible to pick out, especially by two half-wits who were more interested in groping the labourers than identifying them.

Their victim was Romano, and while one part of Eric was outraged, another part was relieved. Almost, Tom Romano had it coming, since he routinely flaunted his body, teasing anyone who cared to notice. Ten years' worth of strutting and teasing caught up with him tonight, and Eric looked away from the quick, ungentle coupling in the darkness behind the guard post.

It was over in minutes, and the White Dragon ronin gestured for the labourers to pass by. Eric looked Romano over, head to foot, but aside from scraped knees and a bite bruise on his neck, he was unscathed and simply furious.

"I'll live," he growled as they put dozen metres between them and the guards.

"Bruised pride," Eric guessed.

"Sore ass," Neal corrected with fat satisfaction.

Romano's eyes flayed him alive, but there was no sharp rejoinder tonight.

"Shut your mouths!" Farace's face was fierce. "They hear one word of English with that damn *Pacifica* accent of yours, and we're dead!"

The silence was stinging. Even Eric bristled, but clamped his teeth and followed her to a new glass door hung in a centuries-old frame. Indonesian script on the top panel was undecipherable, but when Farace swiped her access card through the scanner and opened it, they heard at once the whir of fans and the low hum of big, powerful equipment. Generators. A thrill of mingled dread and anticipation raced through Eric's whole body, leaving his palms damp and his scalp tingling. Showtime.

The door snicked shut and an automatic deadbolt fired home. It would take another smartcard to reopen it, and Farace fingered the deceptive little piece of plastic thoughtfully. Her eyes met Eric's and she said very quietly, "Do not get separated from me. Do not allow your colleagues to wander. This place is a labyrinth, you can be lost in minutes."

"We studied the floor plan in VR," Eric whispered.

"You will find that a computer model and reality can be distressingly different," she warned. "Stay close. Despise me if you will, but covet my access card and never be far from it.

Despise her? Eric was surprised. Was that what she thought? And then he remembered her former remark, referring to the Aquarians as the 'elite of a rich sovereign state.' Perhaps it was the Rhutani who despised *Pacifica*, the CAIR, Nepal and others, the rich freestates that hung back, did nothing to help the persecuted here, until their own homes and kids were threatened. The allied task force was not here for the sake of the Rhutani people. It was here, tonight, because Bowman, Narayan and Duquesne, the three most powerful heads of state in the hemisphere, refused to live under a nuclear threat.

And the Rhutani people? It was a question to put to Duquesne, and Eric determined that he would do it.

El Dumagat never rested. The hum of generators became louder as Farace led them deeper into the fortress. Old brickwork, new concrete; armed guards, techs and engineers in gone-grey lab coats, and everywhere, convict labour. Young people, old people - anyone who spoke out against the Emir. Or was accused, Eric reminded himself. Isabelle swore that Jacques Farace had said and done nothing to have found his way into a cell right here in the fortress, and how must his daughter blame herself for putting him there? She was an uncommonly gifted engineer, and to control her, they arrested him.

The convicts, political prisoners, wore dark blue pajamas, were barefoot, and each wore a tattooed barcode on his or her cheek. They were doing the hardest and dirtiest of jobs, Eric saw, and to the last individual they seemed resigned. They hauled rock out of newly-excavated caverns, where the fortress's lower levels were being opened up directly into the mountain. They carried water and machine parts, lubricants and solvents, to the machine shops; cleaned down the machinery, carried away waste water, and generally performed the tasks that service robots performed aboard the *Atlantis*. The technology and resources were not available here; cheap labour was.

The computer model was, despite Farace's warnings, accurate to an error factor of just a few percent, and Eric knew exactly where she was taking them. Techs from White Dragon Tong had set up the island's surveillance systems in a blockhouse adjacent to the missile complex. For Operation Aquamarine, the location could not be better, and if Eric closed his eyes and concentrated he could bring to mind the whole 3D schematic.

The missile complex had been carved out of the mountain and

opened on the seaward side, where the silos were now charged with flight-ready weapons. But the whole complex was open through to El Dumagat, making use of a natural cavern system that had been massively expanded in recent years.

The tunnels led back into solid rock, and Eric could literally feel the weight of it on him. Neal seamed unperturbed, Romano was still smarting, both psychologically and physically, but Zoe was white as candle wax, sweated, and when Eric touched her shoulder she jumped.

"It's the tunnels, the rock," she stuttered. "I never ... underground. Never."

"Claustrophobia," Eric murmured. "Breathe slowly, deeply, kiddo. Give me your hand. Come on, give me your hand."

Her fingers were like ice. Small, a girl's hand - the first Eric had ever held. So little like Russell's big, capable fingers. Eric felt that if he closed his grip he would smash the girl's fragile bones. He gave her a wink of encouragement, and wondered where Russell was. They had not heard an alarm, so the *Poseidon* could not have been picked up, and by now Russell would have followed the 'game plan,' and found some place to hide the submersible on the surface, where Isabelle could eavesdrop on local transmissions, and monitor the passive radio bugs.

How far did they walk through the mountain? Eric lost track of time and was following Farace blindly when she broke stride, inserted her card into a smartlock, and a three metre armoured door rumbled open. Eric took a quick breath as he stepped through, and Neal swore softly.

Before them, under powerful arc lamps, was the heart of the complex at which Duquesne's imaging team had been able to make only informed, inspired guesses. The heart of El Dumagat was a concrete wasteland where laser torches filled the air with ozone and sun-white sparks, and the service doors to the missile silos were open for the weapons to be monitored.

A team of fuel maintenance technicians was even then pumping a load of the hydrogen-oxygen fuel into the tanks of a Chinese missile, and Eric might have watched if Farace had permitted them the time. It seemed the worst sin of which a drone could be guilty was standing idle, for she hustled the group toward the adjacent blockhouse.

Vast shockglass windows overlooked the missile complex, and inside the facility Eric saw a mass of machinery that, a week ago, would have mystified him. A hundred hours of instruction later, he recognised the master computer, its analog, the backup mainframe and the terminal storage 'bin;' a network server and eight slaved terminals; a self-contained workstation that was probably devoted to imaging and VR modelling; and four monitors coupled to a second freestanding workstation that carried its own analog, in a glassed-off alcove right behind it. And this workstation was jacked into a major buffer set right into the rock. From the buffer ran three conduits, and Eric's pulse skipped.

A novice would not have known what to target, to hurt this system, but at a glance Phil Neal and Zoe Bader knew, and after a week's compressed classes, Eric and Romano had few doubts. For the first time Eric began to fully appreciate the concept of multiple redundancy. If Zoe had been the guards' choice, and she had fought, been injured, Romano would have been left behind to take care of her, get her back to the shore for 'extraction.' Eric and Neal would have been here with Farace, and if the unpredictable befell Neal, and Farace was picked up by suspicious ronin, Eric might be here alone.

They had been lucky so far, and they knew it. Romano had put aside his anger, Zoe was wild-eyed but was so relieved to be out of the tunnel that she was in full control. Phil's eyes glittered with something very like lust as he saw the White Dragon systems, and Eric himself felt a lick of excitement as he saw the work going on inside the surveillance facility.

One of the mainframes was laid open for service, its electronic innards strewn across the brushed concrete floor. To one side of the doors stood a trolley overloaded with three new machines, while the blockhouse was already at capacity. A pallet of concrete bricks stood alongside the outer wall, and Eric saw at once why the labourers had been brought in so readily.

The facility was expanding. A wall was being taken out, space made for new systems. Plenty of work for day labourers, people who were so desperate for a meal or a coin that they would lay bricks with their bare hands for eight hours. Tools were not allowed here. They could easily double as weapons. And Farace was obviously working the night shift anyway - on that dismembered mainframe.

A large section of the wall was already down, and if Eric stooped he saw that on its narrow end the blockhouse was open to the cavern's high rock roofing. The job for which they had been brought in was simple: take down the wall, clean the bricks off with a wire brush, under a howling extractor fan that pulled dust out of the machines' space faster than it could be generated, and then just stack the bricks for the rebuild. The wall was moving back three metres.

Armed ronin prowled, talking and laughing amongst themselves, but no on paid much attention to the day labour. They had been cleared at the guard post, they had been brought in by a trustee who was motivated by pure self-interest. They all knew Farace; they all knew that her father was in a cell somewhere in El Dumagat.

She turned toward the Aquarians with a sour look. The harsh fluorescent lighting made her face over into a relief map of the ocean floor. She was tired, even unwell, Eric saw, and certainly desperate. Genevieve Farace was closer to the end of her rope than even she knew, and - like many Rhutani? - embittered by the fact that the powerful nations around them did not come to their aid before they themselves were threatened. In fact, through his ambition Potan Kap had cut his own throat, set free his own people, and Eric saw the Rhutani point of view all too clearly. He met Farace's accusing look and nodded.

"You can see the work," she said loudly, "get on with it, and you eat tomorrow. And you girl, come with me. I need your smaller hands and dexterity." Then she dropped her voice and said very softly, "You know where to bite them to hurt?"

It was Phil Neal who said, "You get on with your job, lady, let us do ours. I *design* systems like this."

"How very interesting for you," she said acidly, turned her back and stalked away.

"Jesus God, I hate women," Neal muttered.

Eric angled a surprised glance at him. "You're straight - that is, you were living with a woman, weren't you?"

"Blame him." Neal pointed at his crotch. "He has a mind of his own. Believe me, Devlin, you got the best deal. Stick to your own kind and have a nice life."

"Thanks, I intend to." Eric dusted his palms off on the seat of the denims and sized up every aspect of the job.

The physical work was so easy, a monkey could have done it with a minimum of training. But while they carried bricks, they would watch the patrols for at least an hour, see if there was a pattern in them, timing. It would take only minutes to set the micro charges, but they would also need to be well away, 'lost' in the facility, before those charges detonated, and before the bodies of the two surveillance engineers working the late shift in this facility were discovered - or this was a suicide run. Eric wanted no part of that, and glanced covertly over his shoulder as he picked up the first brick.

There was the guard patrol: two ronin, armed and lounging negligently while they watched the fuel maintenance techs. Tonnes of hydrolox were being slowly pumped aboard the four missiles, and the ronin should not have been smoking. The sign over their heads was in one of the local scripts, but Eric would have gambled a week's pay that it said, 'no smoking.' Like handing out an invitation for the idiots to light up.

Eight bricks later, the ronin moved off, walking away from the blockhouse and into the shadows behind the fuel tanker. Eric lost sight of them and looked the other way, wondering if a second patrol was working a counterpointed route, but he saw nothing. Just the two guards then, performing one perimeter walk, right around the missile launch complex. And there were three blindspots.

The tanker itself. The massive conduit carrying power into this cavern. The cranes and hydraulic lifters that manoeuvred missiles, warheads and machinery and were currently dormant and parked at the opposite end of the complex from the tanker.

Three times on their patrol, those guards would be out of direct sight of the surveillance blockhouse. Now, get the timing.

The only chrono in the group was on Farace's wrist, but she was as aware as the others of the question of time. As the guards approached the blockhouse from the chaos of machines and cables Eric glanced sharply at her, and she nodded, lifted her left wrist to signal that she had marked the time.

Ten bricks. Twenty. Eric lost count. His lower back growled unpleasantly and he gave a thought to people who did this work all day, every day, and were paid in food. There were the ronin, strolling, careless. Behind the tanker. Behind the conduit. And then the longest blind zone, when they passed into the lee side of the big, ugly machines. Two minutes, three, in that dead zone?

Sweating, dusty, thirsty, Eric watched the ronin stroll back. They barely glanced at the labourers and then moved on. Eric turned toward Farace then, and she was looking right at him. Two starfish-finger motions of her right hand, and she mouthed silently, *ten minutes*. *Again*, Eric mouthed, just as silently, with a rotating gesture.

And she nodded. Affirm the timing on the second patrol. Be sure.

He hated bricks. He had never realized how much he hated bricks, and concrete. Dust filled his sinuses, his eyes were gritty and his palms were raw.

The ronin were back in ten minutes.

Under his breath Tom Romano swore fluently, and Eric heard Phil Neal breathe, "Thank you, Jove." But Zoe was shaking, Eric could see it from three metres away, and Farace wore a face like a thundercloud.

The ronin strolled on, laughing, as if the labourers were the punchline to some wickedly funny joke. Eric picked up another brick, held it, but as the White Dragon men went behind the tanker, so preoccupied with their conversation that they may not even have noticed the fracas behind them, Eric never had the chance to lay the brick on the growing pile. Romano was still furious, nursing a rage that had only been waiting to unleash itself on anything, anyone from White Dragon, and he had the size, the strength, for that fury to be terrible.

Eric actually heard the man's neck break as Romano stooped like a raven on the nearest tech. He was dead before he could have realized the assault was coming, and the second man died moments later, at Genevieve Farace's hands. An adjustable wrench tried to bury itself in the back of his skull, and when he pitched forward onto the work bench blood gushed from the wound.

Eric looked away, only able to guess at Farace's intense passion. Had she suffered the same situation Romano had borne? She did not have his youth, nor his beauty, and the ronin who used her must have made her well aware that they were doing it to intimidate, humiliate. She had kept her silence for the sake of her father, but the time for that was suddenly over. Her teeth were bare, lips drawn back, and if that fury were directed at him, Eric would have recoiled.

Without even waiting for the bodies to fall, Eric and Phil Neal were moving. Zoe had jumped right out of her skin at the sudden violence, the shocking red of fresh blood, but as Eric called her name quietly she groped for the electronics pack hidden among he hair. Neal grunted in discomfort as he peeled off his own pack, and Eric felt the burning smart as he pulled the irritating little packet off his own shorn scalp.

Just one pack would gave been enough to cripple the facility. Four would make so thorough a job of it, White Dragon would be months getting this complex back on line. Some of these machines would never function properly again.

Now, the computer model was less than accurate. Best guesses had been made, as to what equipment would be installed here, and where it would be. What was indispensable, what was merely useful, and what could be ignored. Without a word, Phil Neal placed his own charges: the power conduit first, the uplink terminals. Then he swiped the charges out of Romano's hands and with a dexterity Eric envied, he placed them to cripple the mainframe, and to make marshmallow out of the analog computer.

Zoe was breathing hard, as if she had run a race, as she placed her micro charges where they would disable the backup mainframe and the terminal storage tower. Eric prowled the walls, and his charges were tucked into the power jacks of the buffer boxes, the satellite relay controller, the server. In six minutes, nothing in this facility would be functional.

Six minutes. He grabbed a quick breath and took stock of the group. Farace and Romano were lifting the dead bodies back into their chairs. Zoe had gathered scattered printouts, stacked them back into what would look like order. Neal was covering the spill of bright new blood with a discarded lab coat. The tech whose neck had snapped in Romano's hands had died with his eyes open. His face looked merely surprised, and when he was wedged in his chair he seemed to be gazing intently at the monitor before him. The other man's eyes were shut. Farace let him slump back in his chair, tilted his head back, propped his palm behind his neck, so that he seemed to be on a rest break.

"Time," Eric whispered. "Farace!"

"We're out of here," she said tersely. "How long? The charges."

"Five minutes, ten seconds," Eric read off the tiny LED timer closest to him.

Her eyes widened. "We won't get out of El Dumagat in five minutes. The timers should have been set longer. You set them?"

"Six minutes was the computers' best guess," Neal told her brusquly. "Any longer than that, and some White Dragon tech is sure to just walk in here, find them and turn the buggers off."

"Then we will be in El Dumagat when they detonate," Farace whispered.

"But we can be lost in the complex. Zoe. Zoe!" Eric grabbed her by the upper arm. "Zoe, hold it together. We're on our way out of here."

"Which way?" The girl's eyes were feral. "I don't know the way out, I don't remember the tunnels."

"*She* does." Eric glared at Farace.

"Stay close to me," Farace said bleakly. "The best way out is the same way we came in. If we're challenged, keep your mouths shut. I don't know what excuse will get us through."

"Then you better think of something, lady," Romano warned. "The next time those bastards lay hands on me -"

"You let them, moron," Neal snarled. "You roll over and play dead, you salivate over them, or we're *all* screwed, and so help me, I'll see you in hell five minutes ahead of me!"

Romano's big hands clenched tight. "Your time will come, Neal."

"For Christ's sake!" Zoe's hands were clenched into her hair. "Get out of here and *then* kill each other!"

The kid was right. The house was burning down, and the lock-horned bucks would fight until it collapsed on them. "Move," Eric snapped at Farace, "or we won't have to worry about cover stories, we're going to be ground meat with the concussion in here when these charges blow."

He could head Major Powell's voice. Several times the Australian instructor had turned to his lieutenant and said, ostensibly for her ears alone, "Bloody civilians, they scare shit out of me.

They were starting to scare shit out of Eric now. Every member of this group was an individual, a soloist. Five brilliant musicians, each playing a different tune, and the result was deafening, dangerous cacophony.

The impulse was to run, and it was stupid. Farace walked back toward the armoured door that sealed off the tunnels from the missile complex. A clock ticked in Eric's head - where were the ronin? They must be close!

With a plastic snick, Farace's card inserted into the smartlock and the door growled open. Here was danger. The rumbling sound of that door would be audible right across the complex, and its opening would be visible for just as far.

When it was barely wide enough Eric shoved Zoe through; Neal was right behind him, Farace and Romano crushing through last, and Farace attacked the smartlock. The door stalled midway through its opening cycle and hesitated, while the machine processed her card.

And from the direction of the blockhouse came a shout. Then another, a second voice. Eric's heart beat heavily at his ribs, Zoe's fingers dug into his arms, and Eric had taken a breath to run when the armoured door began to close. Big, heavy, blast-proof, it took long seconds to close and lock. And then Farace took hold of the smartlock in her big hands and wrenched. The lock twisted, but it took Romano's brute strength to tear it out of its mountings. A shower of magnesium-bright sparks cascaded from a ruptured conduit, and the lock fused.

"They can still get that open?" Eric guessed.

"There's a manual override," Neal said bitterly, "you just crank it open and closed, but that takes time. Run!"

As desperately as he had tried to remember the way through the labyrinth of tunnels that seemed to honeycomb the entire mountain, Eric was lost in the first hundred metres. Signs were printed in script he could not read, dead ends abounded, where the just-begun stubs of tunnels led to nothing. Galleries had been opened up to in every direction. This one was stocked with aviation fuel, that one was a freezer, loaded with food, the next was an arsenal where belted ammunition was stored right beside colour coded drums that made Eric's blood congeal. Each colour indicated the content. Explosive, chemical, bacterial. The left-over trash of a generation gone mad, before the great leveller, Chen-Goldstein 4, plunged out of space like the hand of Shiva.

How far had they run? Did Farace even know where she was going? The clock in Eric's brain was still ticking, and his skin crawled as he waited for it.

The explosions were far too small of them to be felt through so much solid rock, but the complex's alarm system triggered within seconds and the tunnels filled with the shriek of sirens. Sweat broke from every pore and Eric's belly churned as he cast this way and that for his bearings. Zoe had clamped both hands over her ears, Romano was poised like a cornered animal with nowhere to run. Phil Neal was glaring at Farace, literally daring her to have lost her way.

As for Eric, he was so thoroughly lost, so disoriented in the maze of El Dumagat, he might have run straight into the oncoming ronin.

***

"They're in trouble, aren't they?" Russell hardly needed to ask. Isabelle's face was a study in dread, and Russell reminded himself, her lover of eight years was in the warren-like excavations at the heart of El Dumagat. He peered over Isabelle's shoulder, intent on Eric's monitor. The bean-sized transmitter adhered to the thin skin behind his ear was still sending; Eric's temperature was high and his pulse was fast as metabolism began to race with crisis energy.

The combined audio channel from all four bugs was still being fed to Isabelle's headset, but as Russell read off the monitors she touched a key and the whir of the *Poseidon*'s cooling system was overridden by the very sounds Russell had prayed not to hear.

The submersible had dug her nose into the fetid mud between the gnarled, twisted root masses of massive trees that clung to the slope at the brackish tidal zone, half a kilometre up a rainwater runoff gulley. It was a risky place to ground her, but after an hour of hunting Russell was out of options. He knew he was in no danger of being picked up by the surveillance systems: close inshore, White Dragon simply did not scan, since the coves and washaways were in the heart of Rhutan itself, and how could Potan Kap or his ronin believe that an enemy could strike this deep into their fortress? Arrogance would be their downfall.

The *Poseidon* came up to five metres depth, extruded a probe above the surface and tasted the environment, like a snake lick-tasting the air. She registered no radar, no laser. The probe would have heard them, and yet would have seemed like a bit of trash bobbing on the surface.

Satisfied, Russell began the hunt for a hiding place, and as he began to sweat and swear he realized just how wrong a computer model could be.

Rain had fallen here recently - torrential rains that caused several mudslides. The stream that he had come upon so easily in the VR projection was unnavigable, and he pulled the sub out, backed off, started over. The computer had predicted that he would find his hiding place in minutes; in reality an hour had passed when Russell ploughed the nose of the *Poseidon* into the mud between the mangroves and shut her down to recharge both her batteries and her oxygen tanks for the journey back out. Carrying six people aboard a tiny science sub on a four or five hour round trip was a delicate question of logistics.

One thought tormented him as he watched Isabelle's face clench with concentration over the monitors. If the VR model was 'off' with its calculations here, how far off would it be off when it came to an area that had been guesswork from the outset - the missile complex itself.

The audio track was such a mess of sound, Russell struggled for some moments to find a frame of reference. What was a loud sound at a distance, what was a soft sound close at hand? What was the shush of fabric, what was the whir of a machine? And then Eric's voice sent an electric jolt through him.

"Russell," he said loudly, deliberately, "Russell, you have to be listening to this, and it's too late for keeping our mouths shut and trying to slither out the way we got in. You must be hearing this! Isabelle, put it on speakers for him!"

"She already did, honey," Russell murmured. "Come on, old love, tell me what's happening."

"Russell, we're on cockpit audio record," Isabelle warned. "Anything you say will be in the archive a hundred years after you're dead and gone."

"I'm glad to know that," Russell said acidly. "Come on, Eric, talk to me!"

"Signal the fleet," Eric's voice said sharply, even as Russell urged him. "Do you hear me? Signal the fleet!" The volume doubled, and Russell guessed his partner was talking directly at one of his companions' transmitters, so as to double the pickup power of his own.

"They're blind," the was saying. "The charges went off, all of them. Their surveillance is marshmallow, half those systems are trash. We're somewhere in the tunnels, holed up, just can't make it out. No time.Signal the damn fleet!"

Without even thinking, Russell flicked the shield off the key of a special transmitter that had been rigged while the sub lay in the cradle aboard the Clipper. It only broadcast one signal, on every frequency common to the fleet. He hit the key and watched the panel before him light up, peppered with telltales. Breach of radio silence. Heavy power drain, for five seconds exactly before the transmitter shut down.

"Aquamarine is in the air," Isabelle whispered. "Dear God."

"They're in the tunnels, they'll be safe, it's got to be like a nuke shelter down there." Russell's heart squeezed painfully.

Isabelle pressed her face into her hands. "You better hope so, Russell, because the air strikes are going to level the fortress. There won't be one brick left standing on another, El Dumagat is rubble, Potan Kap is dead, and every ronin with him who isn't smart enough to pull out and run in the next thirty minutes."

According to the computer model, the tunnels were deep enough, safe enough, to withstand a moderate kilotonnage nuclear strike. But Russell felt a sliver of ice thread through his belly as he trusted not only his own life but Eric's to a machine that had already been wrong.

The audio channel was a confusion now. Gunshots, ricochets, voices shouting, screaming, in languages Russell could scarcely identify. He heard Eric once, Romano several times, nothing he could make out clearly, and the drumbeat in his chest was physically painful.

Five minutes - less now - and the lagoon would be filled with Potan Kap's security squads, while overhead the air would be bright and loud with the incoming strike force. Missiles, Zealand jumpjets, helijets, armed SeaRangers, anti-aircraft missiles, flak from El Dumagat. The ronin would be firing blind with the surveillance computers offline, but only a fool would believe White Dragon would go down without some kind of fight, even a fight they could not win. If nothing else, they would cover their own asses while they secured their escape.

Almost as if his thoughts were broadcast, a concussion rolled over the west end of the island, not far enough from the *Poseidon*, and Isabelle said, "Missile strike. It's started, Russell.

"We won't get the sub out of the lagoon now," Russell warned. "The ronin will be swarming." And the Poseidon could not dive, hide herself, without at lest five metres under her keel. The gulley where she lay hidden opened onto a mudbank that had steadily been built by years of rains and gravity slides. She would be visible to 'eyeball scanning' long before she commanded enough water to go under and disappear. Russell's fists clenched, knuckles white as bone, on the panel before him and his mind whirled.

The computer model predicted that a hiding place for the sub would be easy, and the lagoon was deep throughout, there was no mud flat, no gentle shelving, just a precipitous drop-off into the abyss. No problem getting the *Poseidon* back to fifty metres and just waiting out the battle there. The Aquarians would make their way to the shore, swim out and take shelter in the warm waters of the lagoon. If they saw Russell's spotlights they would go aboard the sub, if not, they would just wait in safety until the 'friendly fire' eased back, and then Russell would surface and pick them up.

It was not going to happen that way. Russell pulled in a breath, kneaded his eyes and marshalled his thoughts. "What did Farace tell you about the tunnel system?"

"It's a warren, deep and convoluted." Isabelle's brow creased. "They'll be safe from the airstrike, but Jesus, listen to the audio feed! Russell, the tunnels are crawling with ronin *because* it's safer down there, and - shit, they're not soldiers, and even if they were, they're not armed!

"But they did the crash-course in weapons handling," Russell added. "Zoe's just a kid. I never wanted her along. Phil - too intelligent for his own good, trip over his own shadow. Tom Romano -"

"Is a dickhead," Isabelle said curtly, "but he knows what he's doing on the rifle range. Decathlon." She arched her brows at Russell. "Eric?"

"Is fast on his feet and can think circles around Romano," Russell told her without hesitation. "Genevieve?"

"Has killed before," Isabelle said quietly. "Many times, in this last year. There has always been a resistance, but they were as impotent as you imagine." She paused as the audio peaked at a wicked level.

Voices were screaming now, just sound, not words. Pain, panic, fury. Isabelle closed her eyes, and for himself, Russell could easily have clamped his hands over his ears to shut it out, if he had not known that Eric was in the middle of that pit.

"All right, so they're not going to get out to the lagoon, and neither are we." Russell forced his brain to work. "Thank Duquesne, we have a fallback."

What genius or experience had made Duquesne contract Libby Weatherall to refuel the *Lord Jim*, turn her around and get her back to Rhutan fast? At the time Russell had considered it a ridiculous, unnecessary risk. Now, he swivelled the seat, worked his legs out from under the panel, cursing the sub's compact design.

Fallback. There was always a fallback plan, a safety net. And Eric would be thinking of that right now. Russell was so sure that without waiting for Isabelle to speak he popped open the overhead lockers and lifted down the gear that had been stowed there while the *Poseidon* was aboard the Clipper.

"You want to stay here? Keep on monitoring their audio if you want." He shoved his arms through the backpack's uncooperative straps. Goddamn it, this thing had been set up to fit a gorilla.

"You're going to Point Zephyr?" Isabelle guessed.

Stupid military code. Russell buckled the backpack at his waist and tucked the leather gloves into his belt. "It's the best shot we've got. Come with if you want, but you could stay and monitor them."

Her face was waxen in the instrument lights. "Screw that," Isabelle hissed, never more like Eric's twin than when she was furious.

Russell cracked the airlock and lifted himself out into the humid, aromatic night air of the primeval tidal zone forest.

Chapter Eighteen

The man's blood was hot and iron and sticky on Eric's hands. It was like gutting a fish, but a human face looked up at him, eyes bulging, as life was wrenched out of the body, and Eric's belly turned over with a wave of sickness.

The ronin had come around the corner with a Huo Shan machine pistol in one hand and a Malay knife in the other. How many others were behind him? For the moment Eric neither knew nor cared. This one man spelled *death*, and he was not even thinking as he snatched the plastic stock up and halfway out of the ronin's grip, and aimed the ball of his right foot into the hilt of the knife. He had not intended to kill, and he felt mostly surprise as the knife plunged in under the man's breastbone.

The whole act was that fast, less than a second, and before Eric could even take a grip on on the pistol his hands were filthy with blood. He could see that an artery was severed, not even a surgeon would save the ronin, and Eric could only watch as the young man pitched to the concrete and lay, face-down, in a spreading red puddle.

"Devlin! *Devlin!*"

It was Farace's voice, hacking like a saw through the cotton that filled his head. He turned toward her, jaws clenched on the sickness. Was it like this for everyone, the first time? The first time they took a life, and discovered how easily life was stolen, how irrevocable was the act, and how very final was death.

"I'm alright." Eric blinked his eyes clear and checked the Huo Shan. Chinese manufacture, ten or twelve years old, made in the factories in

Mel Keegan

Honan, standard issue to half the armies in the world, weapon of pref-
erence for most terrorists, since the bulk freighter *Tai Ping* went up on
a new seamount on her way to Nepal four years before; her cargo of a
quarter million of these assault pistols was never recovered.

Behind Farace, Phil was still holding Zoe, but the kid was so glassy
eyed, even Eric could see that he was wasting his time. She was not
going to make it, and she was fifty-five kilos of dead weight. Tears half
blinded Neal. For all his professed misogyny, he had liked the kid,
maybe because she *was* a kid, as brilliant a himself, young and inept
with sheer inexperience.

They were in a dead end, an unworked stub of fresh tunnel, off the
main route that would have taken them back along the way they had
come into El Dumagat, but the passages were alive with ronin, and
they were trigger happy. Fifty or more convict labourers, day labour
and dissident prisoners, had broken the leashes and run when the
explosions began. First, the wail of alarm sirens from the missile complex and then, two minutes after the surveillance systems went down,
the first deep, roll of thunder.

Missile strike. And another, another. Great shudders through the
rock as El Dumagat came down - how far above? Instinct made Eric
duck as the rock overhead seemed to tremble, and then there was
something else, something different. A slow, steady pulse, thud-thud-
thud, almost a sensual rhythm that hit him in the pelvis. He knew
what it was, recalled it from the VR classes through which he had
sweated and squirmed as a reluctant recruit.

Flak guns. Old, outmoded, low-tech. Effective. They would fill the
air with so much whirling, grapeshot trash, a two billion dollar
SeaRanger would be smashed as surely as if White Dragon were firing
cutting-edge SAM missiles.

"Sweet Jesus," Romano muttered, tilting a ear at the rock as if he
could hear the pulse, when in fact he could feel it through his bones.
"It's on."

"And they're dead on time." Farace was looking at her chrono.

"Are we safe down here? It's deep enough to be nuke-proof," Eric guessed.

"We're safe," Farace said darkly, "until some dumb-ass ronin come for us."

Romano gestured with the rifle he had taken from the soldier who killed Zoe. The girl was the first thing the man saw as he came around that corner, and in the split second after he put six rounds into her, Romano snapped his neck. He was not a White Dragon man, but one of the Emir's elite Tiger Regiment. 'Regiment' was the wrong word, another of Potan Kap's expressions of arrogance, since only one hundred Tigers stalked the fortress, and without the ronin they would be easy prey, even to the common people of Rhutan.

"Ammunition," Phil said thickly as he let Zoe's body settle gently on the concrete. He dragged his sleeve over his face. "We don't have enough ammunition to sit here and defend this hole. Do we?"

"No." Eric had already checked the clip in the weapon he had just appropriated. It was half empty, just twenty-five rounds available, and he clicked the Huo Shan over onto single-shot mode. "If we try to defend this hideaway, we're dead."

"So we get out." Romano's eyes had a wild gleam Eric did not like. He turned the glare in Farace. "Which way, lady? This is your fucking ant heap!"

"Not mine," Farace snarled. "Watch your mouth, Romano. To me, you're just excess baggage now ."

Now? Eric stepped in between them. "Quit this crap, the both of you! I don't give a shit if you gut each other, *after* we're out of here. Farace." She blinked at him. "There's a way out, isn't there? If Romano's excess baggage, you don't need him. Nor any of us. You don't need muscle power, or designer brains? Then there's a way out, lady, and you know it!"

A humourless smile quirked one side of her mouth. "Designer brains. You're smart, Devlin. Use the brains Duquesne gave you, worship at his shrine, kiss his ring tomorrow."

"You hate him," Phil observed, still capable of surprise.

"She hates us all," Romano corrected. "We sat on our asses in safety, living high, while the people here were shafted by a maniac, and we didn't come rescue them till the crazy man pointed the missiles at *us*."

"This is not the time!" Eric raised his voice, not intending to shout, and taken aback as his own noise bounced back off the close walls. "Farace, get us out, take up your crusade with Duquesne and Bowman and Narayan. The people here are not politicians, we don't make their decisions about when and where to fight, we just go where they send us, God help us, and some of us won't get back." He glanced at Zoe's still form. She was dead now. The six rounds had chewed palm-sized chunks out of her left side, and she had been barely conscious, unaware of what was happening. Eric tried to wet his lips but his tongue was like dust. "Which way out, Farace?"

Grudgingly, she drew an air-map with guttural footnotes. "Along the passage, left beside the machine shop. Behind the standby generator there is a service elevator. It goes up to a cargo pad."

"They're destroying the fortress, Farace," Phil said, as if he wondered what had happened to her intelligence in the last ten minutes. "There's nothing up there! You want to die in a service lift, halfway up a twisted shaft?"

"You're not under the fortress anymore." Farace did not even look at him. "Air cargo is brought into Rhutan at a small field -"

"About a half kilometre from the silos, on the ocean side, away from El Dumagat," Eric finished. "We all saw the computer model, we just don't know where we are in these damn tunnels. They bring air freight in on the private field since a bunch of rebels - your people, I guess - took a pot-shot with a stolen weapon at a helijet right over the Emir's private quarters."

"Burning wreckage came through the windows of his bedchamber," Phil went on, "and after that there's been a no-fly zone over the fortress." He looked probingly at Eric. "You trust her? *You* I trust, you're all instinct, Eric. Tell me?"

"I ... don't know," Eric admitted. "But I do know that Isabelle trusts her enough to be in love with her - or loves her enough to trust her. Whichever."

"And you'll go with your sister's gut instinct," Phil concluded. He nodded thoughtfully, studied Farace as if she were an odd specimen on a glass slide. "Stress and rough times mess up your head. Have Joyce Quinn tell you about a bunch of guys she pulled out of here. They were loony-tunes for months."

"She told me." Eric shifted his grip on the pistol. "Farace, the longer we wait here, the worse our chances get. If you're sure about the way out, we go right now."

She was sure. Without hesitation, she moved to the corner of their tunnel stub, peered around and stepped out into the passage. If the others followed or nor was their affair, but she was leaving. Eric swore beneath his breath, took last look at Zoe Bader's dead face, and stepped out after her.

How far to the machine shop? Did Farace know this labyrinth as well as she thought she did? Was the machine shop guarded? Misgivings coiled through Eric's brain like worms through an apple, but he was too preoccupied with the route ahead to think of the way behind. A professional soldier might have thought in all dimensions, but Eric's heart jumped into his throat as voices and shots burst out behind them.

Romano was a pace to the rear, big and broad, and Eric was sure the athlete had made a dash to get into concealment as he hurtled by. Then Eric saw the hole in his back, a deep-chewed gash, like a shark bite, wet and dark and bone-splintered. Romano had been picked up by the force of eight or ten rounds, thrown like a rag doll, and a pace ahead of Eric hit the wall and went down hard.

White light ripped through Eric's brain. If Romano had not been that pace behind, those bullets would have been in Eric's own back. It would be him lying in a jumbled heap of limbs with that look of outraged surprise on his face. Adrenalin hit him in every muscle fibre and with the next breath he was sprinting.

There was the machine shop. The lights were out, the lathes and argon tanks, lasers and hydraulic lifters loomed like petrified animals, but Farace did not stop. As if she had often been this way before, she dove through, trying to get in behind the machines.

Cover. Phil was way past panting. He was wheezing, grasping at his side, and only the fact that he had Aquarian lungs kept him going. Those lungs, designed to pull oxygen out of water, would never fail him in the air, but he was cramped and hurting, unaccustomed to the exertion. So far out of shape, a natural born human would have been dead by now.

A few paces ahead, Farace stumbled into a dim recess and Eric glimpsed her shape as she hit the control to summon the cargo elevator. The machine shop afforded cover, but when Eric turned back he found that he had full line of sight from the elevator back to the passage, and there was nowhere else to run.

A grinding rumble in the shaft above informed him that the car was on its way down. Eric's palms prickled on the pistol as he brought it up to cover himself, for he also heard the heavy footfalls in the tunnel. The ronin had stopped briefly to look at Romano, but they were coming on again.

The service elevator had no indicator panel to tell where in the shaft it was - it was straight up, straight down, no stops, no need for an indicator. But the closer it came, the deeper and louder its rumble.

It was loud indeed as the ronin dove into the machine shop. Eric counted seven rifles and pistols, all automatic. He lifted his own weapon, in that split second absurdly aware of its inadequacy.

Muzzle flares danced in the gloom, leaving blinding corneal after-images. Russell must be hearing this - he would still be on the *Poseidon*, by now safe in mid-water, and listening in.

It was a lousy way to make an end, Eric thought in a surreal moment of calm and sanity, as his finger closed on the trigger. A lousy way for them to finish what should have been a lifetime's love. And yet *Pacifica* was free even now, and generations of Aquarians would follow him, in the peace Eric had helped to earn. It was still a good deal, and if he could have found a moment to share it with Russell, Eric would have been content.

His finger closed on the trigger and squeezed down, and the pistol jolted in his hands. A ronin tossed backward under the weight of a high-impact round. Behind a massive lathe, Phil was on his knees, hands over his ears. Farace was firing one handed, shouting - the elevator was here, the cage was opening. And then her voice was torn away and somehow Eric heard the *smack* as she was thrown into the wall.

For a split second he took his eyes off the ronin, but before he could pick Farace's shape out of the murk white heat burst through his whole nervous system.

***

The guns were blind-firing from El Dumagat, and the night sky was full of wild, uncoordinated flak and flaretails. Many civilians would be killed by 'friendly fire,' Russell knew, but if there was another option, he could not see it. The sensible were in a deep hole with their arms over their heads, and yet when he turned back on the slope and looked down, across the lagoon, he was not surprised to see a hundred tiny vessels, no bigger than sampans, trying to make it out. Many were foundering; some were burning. Russell looked away.

Tiger Regiment security squads were moving, but the fortress itself was a welter of flame. The first flight of SeaRangers and VSTOL jets had laid waste, without prejudice, to million dollar satellite arrays and ancient Spanish stonework. If Potan Kap was in there - and he would have been - then he was dead. This was the computer's prediction and Russell prayed that, for once, the model would prove out.

Point Zephyr was a map reference. West of the rampart where the fortress was blazing, the crest of a ridge of bare rock afforded 360° visibility. From that perch, one could see the ocean on three horizons. It was difficult to be jumped there, it was an easy rampart to defend, and the prevailing wind would carry away the toxic smoke of burning fuel and synthetics.

The slope was punishing. Russell had not realized how out of shape he had become, but he was hurting when he reached the top, his human lungs struggling, legs trembling, thigh muscles burning. Isabelle was aching just as much, but her Aquarian lungs brought her to the top of the ridge without her even panting.

Russell rested there for some minutes, coming to know why this place was coded Zephyr. The wind was constant, welcome, cool. He turned his face to it, let it dry his skin and feed his lungs, and then he looked down on the lagoon and swore.

They must be fighting in the street. Potan Kap's Tiger Regiment would have been sent to secure the waterfront, for the marketplace where Russell himself had stood just days before was a welter of smoke, and several buildings were still ablaze. Gunshots echoed up, hollow, sounding empty with distance, but Russell was not deceived. Whose ridiculous idea was it to turn out the Tigers? Did they really believe that the waterfront could be secured? Or was the elite regiment buying time - escape time?

He had caught his breath now, and checked his chrono. How long, before he and Isabelle should conclude that the Aquarians were dead, and make their way to the lugger? He studied the woman's clenched face and said, "An hour?"

"An hour. No more." She looked down over the lagoon. If they're going to get out alive, Russell, they'll do it in that time." She patted the rock on which they sat. "This whole mountain is hollow, honeycombed, you know? Genevieve told me. And like an anthill, there are many ways in and out ... all fiercely guarded by the drones."

The analogy troubled Russell, but he kept his silence, watched the outbound flak, the occasional wildfire anti-aircraft missile, and the incoming fire laid down by Seadragon jump jets and the fleet of missile armed copters from *Pacifica.*

It was like watching a huge animal die. The creature's end seemed longer and more painful because it was so massive, and yet past a certain critical point, death was inevitable. For Potan Kap's Rhutan, brain death occurred when the surveillance systems were destroyed, and all that Russell saw below, across the lagoon, was the thrashing of uncoordinated limbs.

Time was Russell's enemy. He seemed aware of every second, and every minute brought its own dreadful certainty. He was sure that the Aquarians were gone. White Dragon Tong ronin were the most feared and hated mercenaries in Oceania; what chance did a pathetic little band of half-trained, under-equipped civilians have against terrorists trained in Moreseby and armed by the best covert arsenals in the world?

"Russell. Russell?"

He turned toward Isabelle, but she also was listening, the voice was not hers. *"Russell!"*

It was from below, on the seaward slope, east of the crest. Russell braced himself on the rock and looked down, dizzy in the gloom, aware of the drop beneath him, the distance to the surf-smashed boulders. He saw nothing at first, and then picked out movement. A flailing arm, a figure staggering along up the punishing incline.

"Russell, for godsakes!"

It was Phil Neal, Russell recognized the voice now that Phil was closer. It had been hard to distinguish, since Phil was panting as an Aquarian should never pant. Russell could barley imagine what would stress an Aquarian's lungs that way in air.

Until he clicked on the torch from the survival kit he had loaded into the backpack, and saw that Phil - overweight, unfit and happy about it - was struggling up the torture of the cliff trail with a body across his shoulders that was the equal of his own weight, possibly more.

Russell's first thought was that it was Eric, but the shape was wrong. Too small to be Romano. Too big by far to be Zoe. Where in God's name was Eric?

Then, there he was, following in Phil's wake, picking his way from boulder to boulder with a stumbling gait that sent Russell's pulse hammering. He was hurt. But he was on his feet, he was moving, and he carried two assault rifles slung over one shoulder.

"Eric? Eric, come this way, give me your hand!" Russell beckoned, angling the torch to illuminate the best way around the crest's boulders. "What happened? Ten more minutes, and we'd be out of here. You're hurt!"

Just below the boulders, Phil conceded defeat and quit, stooped under the weight of his burden. Even then, Isabelle was shinning down the rocks ahead of Russell, and before Eric could speak, Farace's weight was lifted off Phil's shoulders and set down on the only flat surface Isabelle could find.

"That," Phil gasped, "is the day's good deed that is going to have to last for the rest of my life. Damnit, Isabelle, she weighs a tonne!"

"She lifts weights," Isabelle muttered as she worked in the light of the torch, and found the wound. "Oh, Christ. Oh, no, please God."

Eric's voice was hoarse, rasping, as he set down the rifles. "One round, lodged in her lung. There's blood in her mouth ... entry wound, no exit wound. It's still in there. She needs surgery, Rusty, and fast, or she won't make it."

"Eric? Let me look at you first, while Isabelle get the wound cleaned up." Russell peered at him, half seeing him in the backwash of the torchlight. "You look like hell."

"So do you," Eric told him acidly, and then cupped his good hand around Russell's neck and pulled him closer. He winced sharply as Russell hugged him, and leaned heavily against the bigger, stronger body. "Shoulder. Flesh. Straight in, straight out, missed the bone."

Still, Eric's face was lined with pain, and Russell felt a surge of anger. "Feels like you were hit by a boat in the water," he guessed.

"Powerboat," Eric affirmed, and gave Russell a bleak, bitter look. "I'm the lucky one. Romano and Zoe didn't even get out ... Farace probably won't make it. Phil - I don't know. Maybe he has a guardian angel. He's the one I was betting *wouldn't* make it, and he's the one who picked her up and carried her out because I can barely move this arm. And he hates her guts. Go figure."

"He hates her?" Russell echoed, just beginning to calm as his pulse slowed, his heart settled. He had dragged the backpack closer, unzipped several pockets, and was juggling antiseptics, field dressings, painkillers, a water bottle.

"Later," Eric said gruffly, apparently mesmerized by the fires by the lagoon, the tracer, flak and flaretails still sporadically arcing overhead. "We better get out of here, Rusty. The ronin are on the move, and if the Tiger Regiment aren't right behind them, they ought to be. We're not safe here."

"No place on the island is safe," Phil growled. "So how far's the wharf?"

"Isabelle?" Russell invited. "You know this place better than any of us. It's why you're here, you and Libby."

She had been listening with some surreal calm as she swabbed the wound and felt gingerly around the edges of it, perhaps trying to locate the round - praying that it had lodged between Farace's ribs. "It's eight, maybe nine hundred metres, not a kilometre. Downhill from here, bottom of the cliff, go left around the lagoon, there's a shallow bay. No beach, they've built a quayside into the rock for the fish farms. Crab and lobster and octopus, for the markets in Nepal. Libby should be tied up there."

Russell squeezed shut his eyes, bringing to mind a chart of the island. From that quay the lugger would make its way around the very edge of the lagoon, slinking by right under the lighthouse, the Sentinel. The ramparts of the ancient crater would protect her from the fleet's incoming fire, and she was a small, moving target in the dark, well out of the main body of the lagoon.

Eight hundred metres. Shallow bay, quayside. The VR model was there in his memory, and he opened his eyes, blinked his vision clear. Isabelle had Farace's wound as clean as it was ever likely to be in the field, and the white patches of two dressings were stark on Eric's much darker skin. "Hold the torch," Russell said hoarsely as he delved into the backpack and fetched out a pre-loaded hypo.

The broad spectrum antibiotic would cover Farace, give her a fighting chance against the smorgasboard of bacteria that had been punched into her bloodstream when the bullet went through her clothes. More crucial was the blood loss, and the fact that her right lung was pierced. She was blue-smuged about the eyes and cold despite the night's humid warmth, and her mouth was flecked with fresh, frothy blood.

She was not going to make it. Russell was sure even while he taped a field dressing over the wound, but if they could get her as far as the *Lord Jim*, at least he could treat her in sterile conditions, get her down her flat, keep her warm, set up an IV to cushion the racing shock. He cast about for inspiration, and beckoned Phil to fetch the two rifles Eric had been carrying. He stripped off his own jacket, zipped it, turned it inside out with the sleeves trapped inside, and fed the two rifles through it. The makeshift stretcher would leave Farace's legs to drag, but he upper body could be carried more or less flat, and they would make better time down the precipitous slope.

Without being prompted, Eric grabbed the first aid kit, stuffed it into the backpack and pulled the pack over his good shoulder. A grunt of pain, and he glared at Phil. "Well, help him! You and Rusty and going to have to carry her between you - I can't lift a damn thing with this hand, and Isabelle's going to have to find the safe way down, we're blind in the dark!"

Neal looked disgusted, but he and Isabelle manhandled Farace onto the jacket, and then as the woman went ahead with the torch, he and Russell each took a stock and a barrel, and lifted. Russell swore - Neal was right, she was as heavy as any man, heavier than some. Eight hundred metres. Mostly downhill.

'Downhill' was an understatement. The cliff path was an obstacle course of boulders and sliding shale, where Russell's heart was in his throat every few seconds. The drop to the boulders below seemed an abyss, and the gradient was sheer. His human lungs strained, and Phil was panting before they reached the drifted sand and pebbles at the bottom. Russell's arms were agony, his back already felt wrenched, but Isabelle did not stop for a moment, and a pace behind him, Eric said quietly, against the noise of the surf, "Don't take a break, Rusty. It'll hurt worse then you start again."

Neurotransmitters, were what he was talking about. You worked a muscle group until the neurotransmitters that carried pain signals were exhausted. When there were simply no more chemical signals to spell 'pain,' there was no more pain. Not that the muscles were not being overworked, damaged, just that the brain didn't get to know about it. And a certain point was reached when endorphins kicked in, and then it was near-euphoria.

The human body had a lot of ways to fake it, and Russell was not fooled. He knew that the sudden absence of pain was a shortage of one kind of chemicals, and the equally sudden euphoria was the output of another kind. Whatever worked. He just plodded in Neal's wake, trying not to step on Farace's dragging legs, while Neal plodded doggedly after Isabelle, and Eric struggled with the wounded shoulder and the weight of the backpack.

Twice, Farace came close to consciousness. She spoke, but the words were gibberish to Russell. Isabelle might have understood, but she was too far ahead to hear the mumbles. Russell just kept moving, shuffling along and listening to the din of battle from across the lagoon. Artillery shells screamed in the air, jet engines howled overhead, but the missiles had stopped. At a million dollars each, one swiftly ran out of that kind of ammunition.

The air reeked of cordite, of smoke and the burning kerosene smell of hot jets, and the skyline ahead was bright with fire. That was the fisherman's wharf below the old town, Russell knew. The wharf into which the *Lord Jim* had put when Isabelle came in to make contact with Farace, and when Russell had gone ashore, a lifetime ago. Much closer was the so-called fish farm where blue crabs and rock lobsters were cultivated in the ever-moving, nutrient-rich waters, away from the areas of habitation and their effluent.

A cluster of shacks marked the farm, and a moment later Russell saw the stone quayside. No lights showed, the huts seemed to be deserted, but at least there had been no buring here, and the work boats were gone. Panting audibly, he turned his head, looking for Eric.

"Can you see it? Can you see the *Lord Jim*?"

"Watch it - Rusty, watch yourself!" Eric made a grab for him, almost overbalanced Russell, and Phil did fall. Russell only saw the pitfall as Farace fell hard between them. It was the body of a man in uniform. Isabelle had somehow missed it, but now she spun, angled the torch back, and in the off-key illumination Russell was the purple and gold colours of that uniform.

"Tiger Regiment," Isabelle said hoarsely. "The bastard did turn out the elite, and they came here looking for resistance people."

"And they died here," Eric added. "I see them now ... there's six dead that I can pick out, Isabelle. Which means there's more in the shacks, or in the water."

There had been a hand-to-hand battle here, Russell realized, but if no Tiger Regiment men remained behind, then they all had gone down, probably before a rising tide of Rhutani who had pulled out on the workboats. And Libby Weatherall?

Gasping, feeling the hurt run back into overstressed muscles, Russell peered along the wharf. He almost failed to see the masts in the tangle of debris where a shack had come down, right on the waterfront. "Eric, there she is. Go ahead, tell Libby to run up the diesels."

Eric had seen the lugger in the same moment. He let the backpack fall and hurried on down the wharf. Russell heard him calling Libby's name, over and over, but not until a light showed aboard the lugger did he begin to breathe again. She might have been dead, the *Jim* might have been so badly damaged that she would never make the run out of this cauldron.

A muted flashlight probed off the deck. Silhouetted in it, Eric waved, shouted something that Russell could not quite make out, and then the bulky shape of Libby Weatherall hopped over onto the quayside and hustled toward them.

"Isabelle! Oh, thank God," Libby was saying, babbling with some mix of excitement and dread. "You're lucky I'm still here. The Tigers came, there was a bitch of a fight -"

"We saw," Eric said tersely. "A lot of dead Tigers."

"They walked into a wall of Malay knives, and I grabbed the chance to get the *Jim* the hell out," Libby told him. "I kept her off, in the dark, till the workboats shoved off, and then brought her back in. I wasn't going to wait much longer. You may not have noticed, but it's dangerous here ... where are the others?"

She was looking out into the darkness behind them, watching for Romano and Zoe, and Russell saw her flinch as Isabelle said, "They're dead, Lib. Didn't make it out of the fortress. You want to help me with Genevieve? She's hurt real bad."

"Oh, goddamn them," Libby said softly, peering into Farace's face. The blood on her mouth, the blue around her eyes, told it own story and Libby muttered, "It's in her lung. How many?"

A streamer of tracer licked overhead; a SeaRanger beat in from the east and chain guns opened up on the location of the tracer. Russell ducked instinctively, and Phil Neal beckoned him and Libby. Between them, they manoeuvred Farace's dead weight over onto the deck, and Isabelle helped Eric over. They were still organising their gear, finding balance on the shifting deck, when Libby started the diesels, and Russell grabbed a line for support.

The bow swung around, she turned out into the dark water toward The Sentinel, and Libby opened the throttles. The lighthouse was dead, just a tumble of stone and steel; flames wreathed the stub of it, where its generators seemed to have melted down.

Under a pall of smoke, the darkness was thick. Libby was on instruments as she took the lugger around the perimeter of the old crater, often perilously close to the shore. It was the safest route, for the body of the lagoon was full of burning boat wreckage, and debris constantly fell out of the sky. As they left the fish farm's wharf a stream of sun-bright tracer slammed into an inbound helicopter, and the spontaneous detonation of its missile load made Russell's ears spasm in pain.

He and Eric stood together in the bow, waiting out the minutes as the *Lord Jim* made her way to freedom. Eric's body was feverishly hot in Russell's arms, and if Russell held him too firmly he would murmur in pain. The shoulder would be a week healing, and Aquarian or no, he would not be in the water for that time. Russell was aching, his muscles shaking both with unaccustomed abuse and emotional relief, and he pressed his lips to Eric's damp forehead.

"If I was the praying type, I'd be thanking God right now."

"For getting me out of there alive?" Eric was acid with cynicism. "Zoe's dead, Rusty. That kid's life hadn't even begun, and she's dead, and I can't put sense to that."

Because there was no sense, Russell thought bleakly, and trying to work it out could drive a man insane. He dealt Eric a light hug, and even then heard him yelp in discomfort. "We're almost out. Libby's got to be headed for the *Regina Maris*. Quinn had her close in, they were going to fly SeaRangers off the deck, and the rest of her's a hospital ... you see The Sentinel? Or what's left of it."

Stray rounds were still ripping through the air in every direction. Tracer punched into the cliff where the lighthouse had stood and a an avalanche of pulverized gravel came down, so close to the lugger that Russell's heart was hammering. On the deck behind, Isabelle yelled against the noise,

"Libby! Lib, she's not going to make it! I can barely feel a pulse."

And they read Libby Weatherall's response in the pitch of the diesels as the throttles shoved forward to overrun. If the engines had been old, they would never have tolerated the treatment, but by some blind luck the *Lord Jim* had been refitted only weeks before, and the reconditioned engines over-revved without protest. Russell's pulled his sleeve across his face, kneaded his eyes, which were gritty with cordite and full of the green splotches of after-images that mimicked the tracer. The extra speed was for Farace, but it served them all, taking them faster out of the crossfire.

The lighthouse was astern, they saw the open sea, and Russell was believing that they were out when the ocean tore up, off the starboard bow, and it seemed that the air bust apart, right overhead. More stray rounds - from the fleet or from El Dumagat, Russell did not know, and nor did it matter. The lugger pitched and yawed like a wounded whale, and the timber of the mast screamed. A moment later it was coming own, spear-like splinters pelting the deck, and both Russell and Eric dove flat, searching for cover that was not there.

Eric's voice cried out, sharp and high, and Russell twisted toward him, sure that a javelin had come down on him. But Eric was just bunched around the injured shoulder; he had fallen on it, the field dressings were dark, soaked with new blood. He lay gasping like a land-ed fish, but Russell could find no fresh wound.

"Help me. Phil, move your fat butt and help me!" Isabelle's voice was almost unrecognizable with fright.

Even Eric roused, dragged himself off the forward deck and, hugging the arm against his chest, made his way aft. The computer pilot had engaged - Russell knew this without even glancing at the instruments, for the diesels had shut back to maximum safe rpms, and the lugger was handling sluggishly.

Where the hell was Libby? And then Russell saw her, sprawled in the cockpit, propped against the side of the wheel well, where she had been tossed by the force of the impact. The splintered piece of mast timber, like a hunting javelin, had speared into her abdomen, but for the moment she did not seem to be in pain. The look on her face was more of surprise, as her hands clutched uselessly at the wood protruding like a weapon from her belly.

Reacting blindly, not even thinking, Russell grabbed for the back-pack and plunged his hand into it, searching for the case of pre-loaded hypos. Pain would begin in moments. He fitted the short needle in the backwash from the instrument light, and seconds after Libby began to grunt, and then to scream, he gave the shot. Her head lolled back, and as she surrendered to the mercy of unconsciousness, Phil Neal hooked his hands under her arms and lifted her up, out of the wheel well.

Isabelle took the helm, disengaged the computer pilot and redlined the throttles again. The *Lord Jim* surged ahead, and as she rounded The Sentinel and turned her bow to the open sea, Russell was on his knees beside Libby, cutting the tee-shirt and slacks away from the wound.

"*Regina Maris, Regina Maris*, this is *Lord Jim*," Isabelle shouted into the shortwave, over and over, until she was answered. "We're coming out, we've got wounded on board. Give me a radio fix, and standby your infirmary!"

"Copy that, *Lord Jim*." The comm officer from Joyce Quinn's armed tanker - Russell knew that voice and, absurdly, struggled to put a face to it. "Describe the nature of your casualties, and while you're at it, come starboard 330 and line up on the beacon, you should be able to pick us up visually."

There she was. Russell was never so glad to see a light in the dark-ness. It was like this when you'd been eight or ten hours, bobbing in a life raft, praying to the sea gods that someone would find you after you'd been a fool, swamped your skiff and almost drowned yourself. Russell was twelve years old, and if Eric hadn't swum for help, he would have died that night, when the grandmother of storms came in. Just four hours after John Grant pulled him out of the water, *Pacifica* took the battering of its life.

The lights tonight were high, winking, gold-red-gold: the beacon on the tanker's helipad. She was still several kilometres away, and as Isabelle picked her up visually she turned the bow into those lights and opened the throttles again.

Libby was half-conscious once more, and muttering. Russell

thought she might be talking to him or to her sister, but her hands were clasped about the mess of her abdomen and he realized that she was talking to the life that had just begun there. A natural born Aquarian life, not the product of engineering; nominally her own, and in fact Eric's child.

It was already dead, or soon would be, and Russell's eyes clouded at the tragedy. Two Aquarians had died tonight; two more were injured, and a fifth would never be born. He looked up over Libby's prone shape and found Eric's eyes on him, filled with his own pain, and with compassion.

"I'm so sorry," Russell said quietly, in some absurd way feeling that he himself was at fault, though he was not a surgeon, and even had he been, there was nothing he could do for either Libby or Genevieve Farace on this pitching deck, in the dark and salt spray.

"It's all right, Russell. There's no blame." Eric clamped his good hand over the wounded shoulder. "There's going to be an inquiry, but you'd have to be a magician to do anything for her ... or for Farace." His eyes strayed to the other woman. "She may be dead already."

A searchlight blazed out and down from the still distant tanker; another light picked them up, and when they were caught in the twin beams Russell heard the bass voice of a BigLifter. The chopper rose like a huge insect from the forward helipad, and beneath it was slung a cargo recovery cage, easily big enough to accommodate four bodies lying, eight standing, or any combination.

The lugger's diesels shut back to idling, and Isabelle let the computer pilot take her. The BigLifter was shortening the distance, and it was the swiftest, most efficient way to get the casualties up onto the tanker. The pilot's voice boomed out of the sky on the loud hailer, as if anyone aboard the *Jim* needed instructions. Over-efficient Catalina marine protocol.

In a hover over the lugger, the industrial chopper was on minimum power, and the open cage grazed the *Jim*'s deck. Farace and Libby were settled side by side. Eric sat beside them, cradling the shoulder. In the chopper's searchlights his face was grey as old wax, and Russell wanted him in the infirmary also, fast.

"I'll take the boat," Phil offered, as Isabelle continued to stand by the helm with a tormented look. "Go on, kid. That's your foster-sister, your gene-brother and your lover, and they've all been stomped. Go-with. Leave the boat to me, I'll just tuck her into the fleet, leave her on auto and get some shut-eye."

"You're a good guy, Phil," Isabelle said, as if the observation surprised her.

"I always was, people just don't notice." Phil slapped his plump belly. "My airbag deployed early, I'd rather be in the lab than on a beach, and because I'm an Aquarian that makes me weird. Move, lady, before they pull the cargo up!"

So Isabelle stepped aboard, and she and Russell, on their feet, moved this way and that to help stabilize the cage while it rose away from the deck. Phil waved up, and then Russell lost sight of him as the copter pilot turned back to the tanker.

At his feet, Libby muttered to the stillborn Aquarian life inside her; Genevieve Farace lay without a sound. Eric leaned heavily on Russell's shoulder, as if he could barely hold himself upright any longer. Russell's arm went around him, and Eric held on as the BigLifter manoeuvred its load to the deck nearest the infirmary and set the cage down there with a gentle rasp of steel on steel.

Medics from the *Atlantis* were aboard, and Russell had only to stand back and let them take over the terrible responsibility. Eric was last on the list of this small triage, but to Russell's astonishment the crew went to work furiously on Farace. If her chances were poor, they would have treated Libby first, but Libby was immobilized on a gurney, shot full of antibiotics and sedatives, an IV set up, and then the battle for Farace began.

"Either of you guys smoke?" Joyce Quinn's voice took Russell by surprise. They were at the edge of the helipad, Eric was blanket-wrapped and shaking, sitting propped against Russell's shoulder as he waited for the medics to have time to even look at his comparatively minor wounds. Quinn was flicking a lighter, and the end of a monstrous cigar had begun to glow."

"We have more sense," Russell told her.

"Yeah, it's a filthy habit, got to quit one day." Quinn took a drag, blew smoke through both nostrils and gestured at the island of Rhutan. "You might like to turn around, cast your eyes to the southwest and watch the show."

"Show?" Russell was too tired to follow her. His whole body hurt, though there was not a mark on him. He turned anyway, and frowned at the line of Rhutan's crater-like landmass

"That." Quinn pulled the smoke in deep. "Isn't that a pretty sight?"

A flock of helijets had just risen over the ramparts. Below their top-cover, two powerboats and a wing-in-ground effect plane shot out of the lagoon, and the whole company throttled up as if the devil himself were behind them.

"What is that?" Eric asked, dazed and half-aware.

"That," Quinn told him with measureless satisfaction, "is what's left of White Dragon Tong pulling out. The ronin are leaving. the Tiger Regiment was culled to just a few dozen men who're in manacles right now. The same SkyEye that imaged them saw this bunch take off a minute ago, and you can believe me, they won't get far. They've got half the ace pilots from Zealand and the CAIR right behind them, and they're a long, long way from home."

"They're going to try to make Moresby?" Russell's eyes tracked their lights while his body seemed to be on an extended shutdown cycle.

"They'll have to try, because nobody else will give them sea room," Quinn growled. She paused as the *Atlantis*'s medics stopped work on Farace long enough to get her inside, into the waiting OR, and the second triage crew turned their attention to Libby. "Every bush pilot between here and Moresby will have been watching this on vidcast. The ronin would be bounced a hundred times before they made it halfway home, even if the Zealanders weren't refuelling those damn jumpjets right now. I heard, they kept back a full warload of missiles in case Potan Kap tried to make it out. Almost seems a shame to waste 'em."

The name roused Eric from his growing stupor. "Did he show?"

But Quinn's head shook and the end of the cigar glowed brightly again. "The whole tunnel system under El Dumagat caved in. The prisoners working there opened the cells, about a thousand came streaming out - see it on the vidcasts. SkyEye 144 taped the whole thing. Then the fortress just fell in on itself. El Dumagat isn't there anymore."

"And the Emir?" Eric's heavy eyes watched the last visible lights of the fleeing aircraft.

"He sure as shit isn't with the ronin," Quinn snorted. "They lost a lot of men tonight, and you know that code of theirs. If Potan Kap thought he was going to get out with the ronin, he would find himself with his throat laid wide open and a bayonet up his royal kazoo."

"Then, it's over," Russell breathed.

"Bar the shouting," Quinn judged. "The inquests. The debriefing. The reports. Who did what, where, how much it cost, what worked, what didn't, who was killed ..." She paused and shook her head over Libby Weatherall. "Man, I'm sorry."

"For what?" Russell asked tiredly.

"Two of you are dead, and they just told me, this woman is ... was carrying an Aquarian kid."

Russell looked away. "There'll be others." He touched Eric's cheek gently, but Eric seemed to have stopped listening, and as Russell felt the first shocking tendrils of relaxation stun his own nerves into submission, Eric slithered down into an untidy heap in Russell's arms. Quinn had taken a breath to bawl for a medic but Russell stopped her. "No, he'll be okay. I pumped him full of antibiotics and painkillers. Let them work on the others."

"Your call." Quinn peered at her chrono in the harsh back lighting from the helipad. "The tanker'll be underway in an hour. We're pulling out."

"Headed...?" Russell cradled Eric against him.

"*Pacifica*." Quinn stubbed out the cigar. "We'll get you home, Doctor Grant. But you better tell the Clipper crew what you did with your sub."

"If it even exists anymore," Russell sighed.

She was on her way to the bridge, and turned back for a moment. "And if it doesn't?"

He looked up at her, and then down into Eric's pale, still face. "Then Gerald Duquesne will buy me a new one. That was the deal."

Quinn chuckled. "Gerry'll see you well taken care of. It's in his nature." She slapped her hip. "I know him. Well."

As she spoke a medic gestured her politely out of the way. "If you'd just step aside, Captain ... Doctor Grant, we'll take Mister Devlin now."

They strapped him to a gurney, wheeled him away in the direction of the Infirmary, and Russell remained where he was, sitting on the side of the helipad, looking glazedly at the deck.

Until Quinn hooked a hand under his elbow and lifted him bodily. "You look like shit, Doc, you know that?"

It didn't surprise Russell. "I don't deserve such flattery."

"Hot bath, Irish coffee, broiled chicken, eight hours' sleep, in that order," Quinn offered.

"I should be in the Infirmary," Russell began.

"Devlin'll sleep when they're done, he won't even know you're there." Quinn cocked her head at him. "We'll be halfway back to *Pacifica* when you wake, and you'll look like a human being."

Russell was too tired to argue.

***

Daylight.

For long seconds Russell lay still, struggling for a sense of place and time. Orientation swam like squid in a deep cave, where dream and reality so far overlapped that he had even lost his sense of self.

The thunder of explosions, tracer like bolts of laser in the dark, dead faces glaring, filled with accusation, the *phwap-phwap*, armour-heavy drone of heavy lift helicopters –

No.

The blades of the fan in the ceiling. A breeze of cool air on his bare skin. Sunlight filtered between the horizontal slats of the blind. The distant bass of a hifi system on a boat passing by. What had happened to noise pollution controls? Someone was going to pay a fine today. When you crowded an ever-growing population into an area as small, as finite as *Pacifica*, you had to control pollution - chemical, noise, light - or people went buggo.

The weight lying against Russell's left arm stirred, turned over, and he opened his eyes. Eric's hair was tousled against the pillow. In his sleep he frowned, as if he too were haunted by what he had seen, and done. Or perhaps the freshly healed wounds were troubling him, and with that thought Russell laid a hand on his forearm to wake him without a shock.

He mumbled, his lids cracked open, and he relaxed with a groan. "Thank God."

"For what?" Russell sat up and worked out his back.

Eric turned flat on his back and stretched his hands toward the sides of the wide bed. "For making it a dream. For letting me wake at home, and still have all my limbs and eyes." He gave Russell an apologetic look. "The Counsellor said I'd be dreaming weird crap for a while. It's natural."

"Yeah." Russell stroked the hard, beautiful contours of the Aquarian's breast. "Same here, and I didn't do the job you did."

"You did enough." Eric yawned deeply and sat up, obviously still favouring the abused shoulder. "What's the time?"

"Just before eight. Time to shower and shave and look halfway civilized, and still get over there before it starts."

"Only because we're getting reserved docking space, and we're on the podium, not down in the crowd," Eric said ruefully.

Russell kissed his throat , his neck, both nipples. "So how does it feel to be famous for fifteen minutes?"

"Be better to be rich and famous," Eric said philosophically, "and when the fifteen minutes expired we could count the money."

No edge of regret sharpened the remark, but Russell still sat up and regarded his partner with a frown. "Second thoughts?"

"About trading the salvage, sight-unseen, for our security and liberty?" Eric's brows arched. "I don't think so. Calder and Royce will be executed, we're as safe as if they never showed up here. White Dragon took the whipping of their lives, Moresby will be feeling the pain of the defeat for a decade to come. They'll leave us be." He smiled at last, which stripped years from him. "I'd say we got a good deal."

And a new submersible to replace the wreckage of the *Poseidon*, Russell thought as he lifted Eric up into a cautious embrace. And the offer to negotiate a research grant. And e-papers in the cache yesterday, without Eric even needing to file an application. His place was open at University of *Pacifica*, the vast campus, Deck 4, on the *Atlantis*. The new submersible, *Poseidon*-II, would be state of the art, pre-loaded with every system that had been a dream when John Grant launched the original. Research money guaranteed for five years, extension options. Russell smiled into Eric's soft, warm hair. And at last the wayward Aquarian - always Duquesne's favourite - would get his butt back into the classroom.

He would study open-water mariculture on the warm, sunlit shoals that had been pasture and orchard when he was born. The field was tipped to be the boom industry of the near future, and Eric might still hit the money. For himself, Russell would never grasp how money worked, and had ceased to trouble himself about it. He was content to have the lab, rent, power and groceries covered for an indefinite but long time to come, a new sub on the slip, the *Tiger Shark* back from the shop wearing new bodywork and paint that erased the damage of her altercation with Calder and Royce. And Eric, safe and smiling in their own bed, right beside him.

"Time," he said regretfully, "to move, or we're going to be late, and this is one occasion where it'd be pretty crass to show up late."

"Understatement," Eric agreed, and with an effort peeled his spine off the mattress.

Russell paused to enjoy the rear view of his lover heading for the bathroom, before he rolled to his feet and pulled the sheets off the bed.

They were five minutes early as they jostled through the inner lanes of traffic, and with the place on hold for them in docking bay 17, the *Tiger Shark* was safely berthed while other inbound traffic cruised on in an almost fruitless search for parking. The big shows, a campus event, a basketball game, always brought the crowds in from *Pacifica*, and today the crews of the allied vessels of the fleet were also aboard.

Like a carnival ground, the deck of the *Atlantis* was strung with bunting. Pavilions were set for the officers, guests of honour, those to be decorated. The survivors of Operation Aquamarine.

Like royalty, Duquesne held court in the big blue and white pavilion. It was open on both sides; the front opened onto the already crowded deck, the back, onto the side of the massive ship. Duquesne was sitting today, and Russell thought he looked frail, older. They had come through some kind of baptism of fear, if not fire, and everyone had paid a price.

To his left sat Catherine Bowman, who had flown in overnight from the CAIR. To his right was Ranjit Narayan, as calm, or simply smug, as ever. Nepal's power could not be compromised. Even Potan Kap could reach only the Eastern Realms, and it was common knowledge that Nepal's central government had very limited interest in highlands that had once been Cambodia. So long as agriculture flourished there, the eastlands were no one's concern.

Behind the figureheads were the captains and pilots who would be honoured today. Joyce Quinn was one of them; to her right, the survivors of Zealand Strike Force 4. Six pilots who had lost four comrades, when lucky hits and a wicked flak barrage knocked down two Seadragon jumpjets so fast, the pilots had no chance to punch out. Behind Quinn were the Sea Rescue crews who went into the lagoon and salvaged hundreds of civilians, from scores of swamped boats; the medics who worked around the clock aboard the *Regina Maris*; the pilots who had pursued the fleeing White Dragon craft almost a thousand kilometres, and destroyed them to the last nut and bolt.

And to Quinn's left sat six others, who would be honoured before them all. Four Aquarians, two 'natural borns,' the humans as designed by Nature, rather than by dream and desire. Phil Neal was preening. Isabelle Weatherall looked drawn with fatigue and a little dozy, as if she had taken something. Beside her, still confined to a wheelchair, Genevieve Farace was pale as a ghost. Flesh had dropped from her bones and Russell thought there was more grey in her hair than he had noticed before. But she was alive, her eyes were bright, and her surgeons swore the lung was repaired. She sat with one hand in Isabelle's, the other in Libby Weatherall's. Libby also was still physically unwell, and to Russell's critical eye, she looked less dazed than despondent. She was half healed already, but the abdominal surgery had been extensive. Aquarians in future would surely be natural born, but not from her body. That was no longer possible, and she mourned. She had a right to mourn, and the counsellors had stepped back, given her time to let grief run its course.

In the chair beside her, Russell was silently supportive. On his left was Eric, also silent, preoccupied with thoughts of those who had not returned, for the last two chairs on the rank were empty, and the reserve names on them could only remind him of that night. Zoe Bader and Tom Romano had never been his friends, but the death of any Aquarian left an empty space. Like the tiger, they were still so rare in the world that they could all be gone in a single incident.

Videodrones buzzed overhead, annoying as insects. The vidcast would be on screens around the world, and archived for access by generations of kids to whom 'the Rhutan War' would be as immaterial and mysterious as conflicts like Korea and Vietnam and Argentina.

It was long, tedious, as Russell had known it must be to pleased the politicians and the vidcasters, and his mind wandered after he and Eric, Isabelle and Libby, Genevieve Farace and Phil Neal had received their awards. A gold star on a blue ribbon that chafed the back of his neck. Two gold stars that lay on the empty chairs, posthumously awarded for the honour of gene-parents and surrogate families. Aquarians were not the same ... or, not yet. Russell looked from Eric to Libby and back. The next generation would tell.

Four priests spoke essentially the same litany, prayers for the dead. A Christian, a Muslim, a Hindu, a Buddhist, broadcast to their people scattered in many nations that had somehow come through Chen-Goldstein 4, reinvented themselves, learned the skills of survival, and had even begun to flourish in unpromising soil.

And then wreaths were throw onto the water beside of the *Atlantis*, one for each of the dead. Two Aquarian; four Zealand Strike Force fighter pilots; nine officers and ranks from the Sea Rescue Squadron, and lastly, one enormous wreath of tropical blooms that covered the spectrum, for the dead of Rhutan itself, who had risen in the night and challenged the Tiger Regiment, often with their bare hands.

The island had no government yet, but a 'people's collective' had formed, and its committee had been flown in to the *Atlantis* to represent Rhutan. They were a rebellious quartet, Russell thought. Farace was right. The great sovereign states only rode to the rescue when it was in their own interests, and the principle player in Potan Kap's downfall was his own ambition. Years would pass, Russell guessed, before old enmities were buried or forgotten. Perhaps a new generation could begin afresh.

Past noon, the official ceremonies were over at last. A seafood and chicken buffet was served for the guests of *Pacifica*, but Russell had been hoping Eric would not want to stay long. Being here, even been saluted, celebrated, only brought back the memories he wished most to discard.

The politicians had their heads together with the Rhutani representatives when Eric licked the last shrimp salad from his fingers, leaned closer to Russell and said, "You mind if we get the hell out, Rusty? This is giving me the shivers."

"Been waiting for you to say that." Russell dug out the keys to the *Tiger* and pressed them into Eric's palm. "I've got work to do anyway - it's the best therapy money can't buy."

"Work?" Eric was already shouldering his way toward the elevators.

"You didn't see the message on the machine this morning?" Russell made his way around the very large senator from Bal.

"I didn't look at the cache." Eric glanced back. "Let me guess. They sent you the bill for the bodywork on the *Tiger* instead of directing it to Duquesne's office?"

"No." Russell chuckled. They stepped into the elevator alone and he slid an arm around Eric's waist. "It was the OSL, wanting to know where the hell Bill Murchison's data is. What a surprise."

"So Murchison gets drunk or stoned or both," Eric said wryly, "and naturally the Oceanogaphic Studies Lab calls us. What are we, his keepers? He's a grown man, we're not responsible for him!"

"True," Russell mused, "but we've been backing up for him for so long, they probably figure that if they jiggle the hook the data will magically appear." He paused as the elevator opened, depositing them on the cool, humid rink, right at the waterline of the massive ship. They turned left out of the elevator, headed back toward their docking bay, and Russell added, "The lab may be right."

"They are?" Eric lifted a brow at him.

"The last I saw of Bill, he was passed out on the boatramp, sawing wood. He won't be functional in any sense of the word before tomorrow, and the lab needs that data by this evening." He slung his left arm over Eric's shoulders. "I could volunteer our services ... pack the cooler for dinner. Crab salad, fried chicken, champagne on ice. We take the jetskiff over to Breakwater, get the damn data, transmit from the boat."

"And watch the sunset," Eric finished.

"You may be too busy to even notice the sunset," Russell warned.

For the first time in so long, Eric laughed. "You got yourself a research assistant, Doctor Grant."

Russell looked him up and down, mock-critically. "Not entirely what I had in mind, but it's a place to start."

With his arm around Eric's shoulders, he steered the Aquarian around a service robot Eric had not noticed, through a vast gang of tourists who had just come over from a Japanese passenger ship, and into the docking bay.